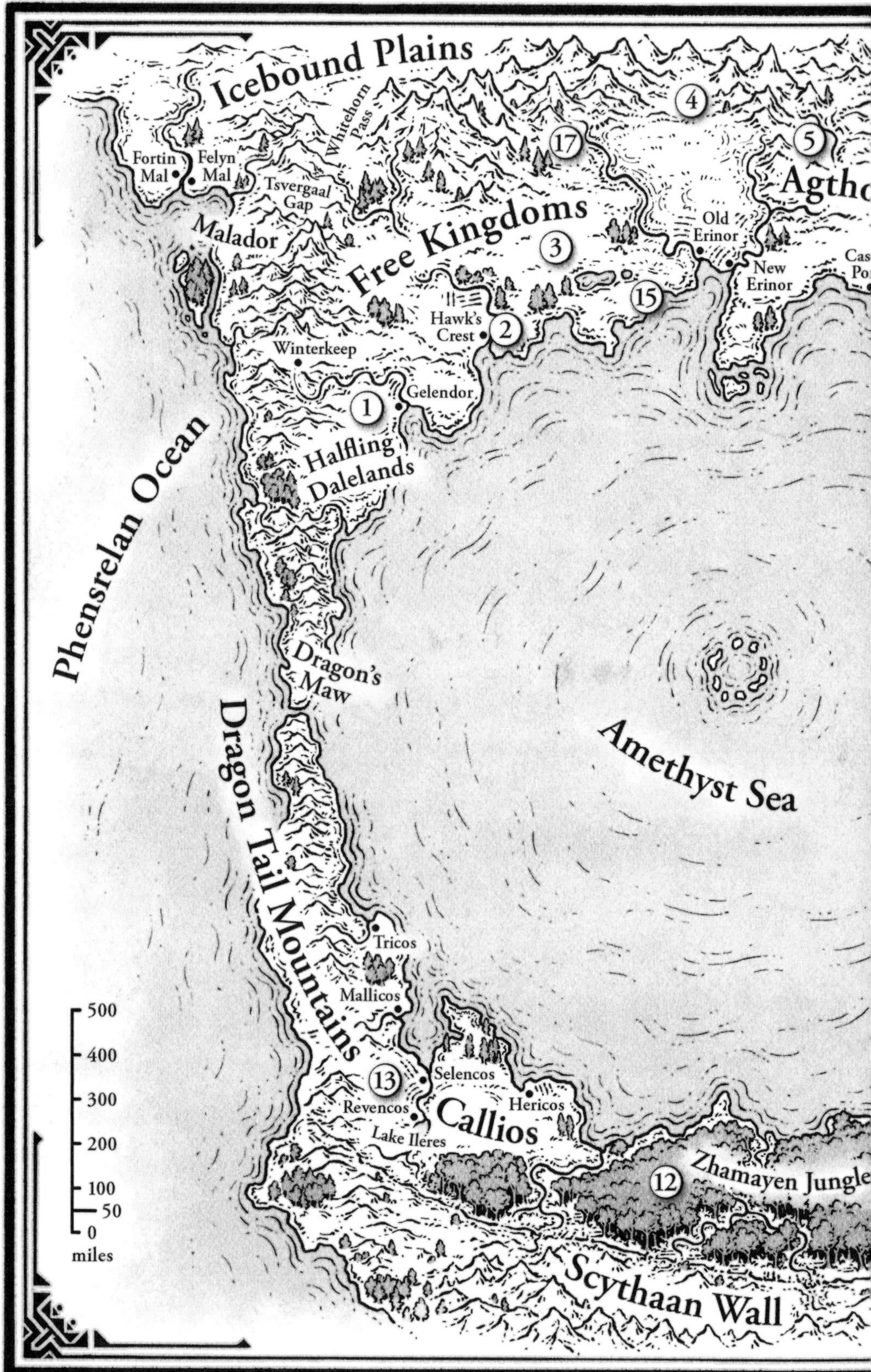

Icebound Plains
Whitehorn Pass
Fortin Mal
Felyn Mal
Tsvergaal Gap
Malador
Free Kingdoms
Old Erinor
New Erinor
Hawk's Crest
Winterkeep
Gelendor
Halfling Dalelands
Phensrelan Ocean
Dragon's Maw
Dragon Tail Mountains
Amethyst Sea
Tricos
Mallicos
Selencos
Revencos
Hericos
Callios
Lake Ileres
Zhamayen Jungle
Scythaan Wall
500
400
300
200
100
50
0
miles
1
2
3
4
5
12
13
15
17

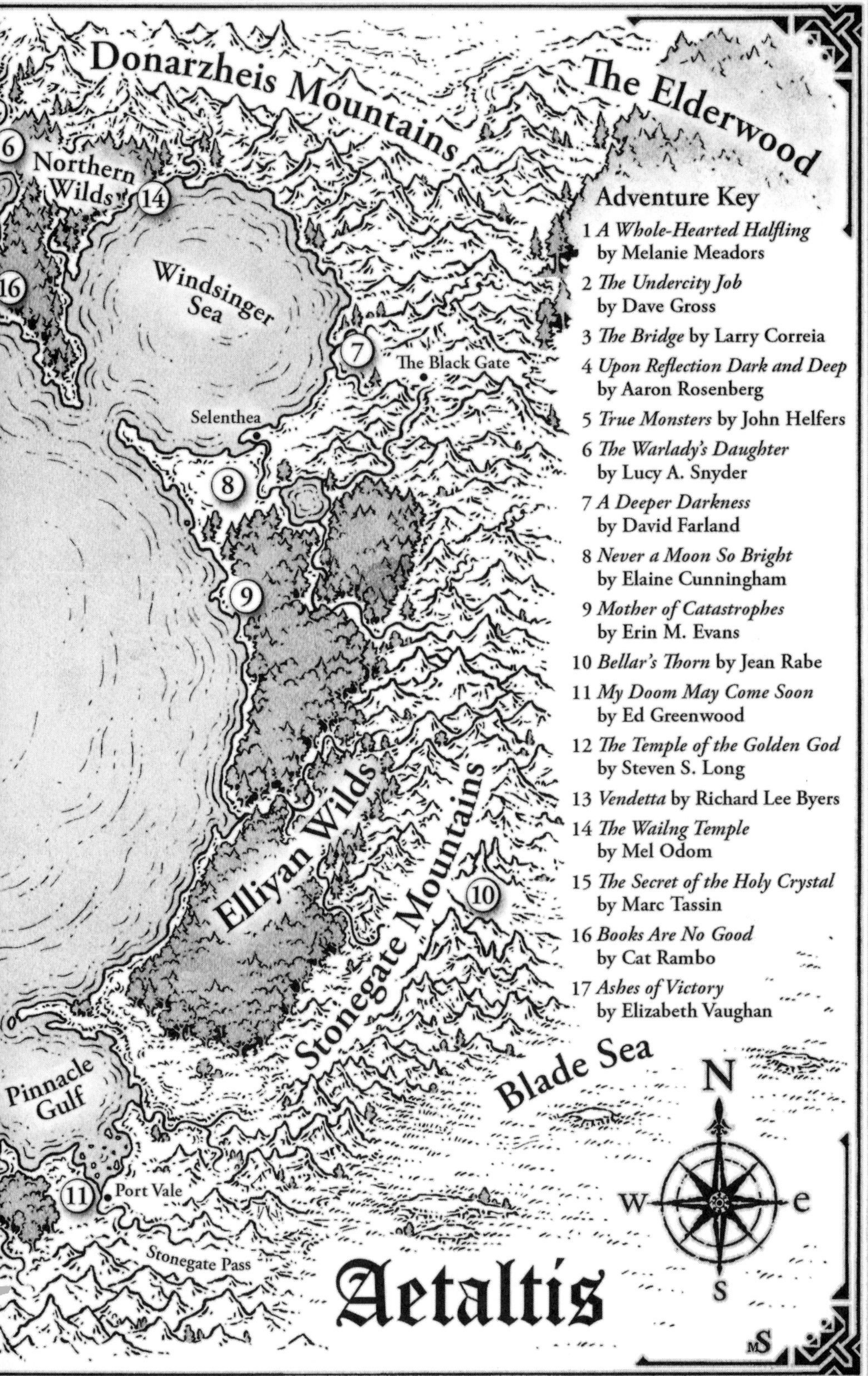
Donarzheis Mountains
The Elderwood
Northern Wilds
Windsinger Sea
The Black Gate
Selenthea
Elliyan Wilds
Stonegate Mountains
Blade Sea
Pinnacle Gulf
Port Vale
Stonegate Pass
Aetaltis
N
W
e
S
Adventure Key
1 *A Whole-Hearted Halfling* by Melanie Meadors
2 *The Undercity Job* by Dave Gross
3 *The Bridge* by Larry Correia
4 *Upon Reflection Dark and Deep* by Aaron Rosenberg
5 *True Monsters* by John Helfers
6 *The Warlady's Daughter* by Lucy A. Snyder
7 *A Deeper Darkness* by David Farland
8 *Never a Moon So Bright* by Elaine Cunningham
9 *Mother of Catastrophes* by Erin M. Evans
10 *Bellar's Thorn* by Jean Rabe
11 *My Doom May Come Soon* by Ed Greenwood
12 *The Temple of the Golden God* by Steven S. Long
13 *Vendetta* by Richard Lee Byers
14 *The Wailng Temple* by Mel Odom
15 *The Secret of the Holy Crystal* by Marc Tassin
16 *Books Are No Good* by Cat Rambo
17 *Ashes of Victory* by Elizabeth Vaughan

AETALTIS

CHAMPIONS OF AETALTIS

EDITED BY

MARC TASSIN &

JOHN HELFERS

May Droth's trials be fair!

CHAMPIONS OF AETALTIS
Mechanical Muse | www.aetaltis.com

Published by Mechanical Muse, LLC
7999 Poplar Drive
Dexter, MI 48130

ISBN-10: 0-9905296-4-9
ISBN-13: 978-0-9905296-4-4
Worldwide Rights
Created in the United States of America

Editor: Marc Tassin & John Helfers
Cover Illustration: Mitchell Malloy
Map: Mike Schley
Cover Design & Interior Layout: Shawn T. King

I'd like to extend a special thank you to all the members of the newly formed Mechanical Muse team:

Michal Cross
Matthew Eberle
Shawn King
Mitchell Malloy
Melanie Meadors

Your creativity, dedication, trust, and vision are my inspiration.

"Each of us has a different power! If we combined forces, we could be almost unbeatable!"
—Ant-Man, Avengers #1

A Time of Shadows, An Age of Heroes

More than three hundred years have passed since the fall of the Atlan Alliance, and the people of Aetaltis have finally brought order to their fractured world. Fledgling nations have grown into powerful kingdoms, thriving merchant states have re-established old trade routes, and the priests of the Enaros have rebuilt their great temples. But in this time of hope, the shadow of an ancient evil is rising once again.

Deep beneath the surface of Aetaltis lurk the armies of the fallen god Endroren. For centuries, an order of holy knights known as the Warders of Alantra maintained powerful mystic seals that held the forces of darkness at bay, but when the Alliance fell, so did many of the ancient orders—including the Warders. Now, after centuries of neglect, the wards are failing, and the dark ones have returned.

For the first time since the Age of Darkness, orcs, goblins, trolls, and a host of other fiendish monsters threaten the good people of the world. They strike with unrestrained cruelty; attacking, killing, and destroying all that lies before them. The recently reborn holy orders have combined their divine strength with the temporal power of the new kingdoms to face this growing threat, but the dark ones are many and the defenders are few.

But, there is hope!

Lord Drakewyn of New Erinor has called upon the brave men and women of his land to take up arms against their common foe. In response, a small army of independent heroes, known as adventurers, has joined the struggle. These stalwart men and women fight the battles ordinary soldiers cannot fight, go where the holy orders dare not go, and serve as beacons of hope in a world growing darker with each passing day. From hardened dwarven warriors to crafty cheebatan rogues, from fleet-footed fey scouts to mysterious Selenthean mages, these brave souls provide what ultimately may prove to be the only hope for the people of this troubled land.

CONT

ENTS

INTRODUCTION

MARC TASSIN

The world needs heroes.

We live in a time when we're surrounded by fantasies that tell us how terrible everything is going to turn out. They promise dystopian nightmares; a fight to even scrape by, and worlds where everyone you meet is in it for one person—themselves. In these worlds, hope is an illusion for fools and dreamers, and the future holds little, or no promise at all.

Aetaltis is not one of those worlds. Aetaltis is a place where, no matter how hard people get knocked down, they climb back up onto their feet and keep fighting. It's a world where a person is more likely to stand up and battle beside you than stab you in the back. And it's a world where a brighter future can be glimpsed, just over the horizon, if we can just fight on a little longer.

It's not a safe world. Not everyone will make it, and the journey is going to get rough. But there are heroes that will stand up and fight to make the world a better place.

The world needs heroes.

Our world needs heroes.

And while I may not have the power to provide the heroes our world needs, what I can do is work with some of the most amazing authors I know to deliver stories that remind us that we can build a brighter future—and that we don't have to do it alone.

So take up your sword, grab your spellbook, and mount your trusty steed. You're about to travel to the world of Aetaltis, where heroes still walk the land, and hope remains alive.

And maybe, when you close this book, you can take a little of that hope with you back into our world.

MOTHER OF CATASTROPHES

ERIN M. EVANS

BECAUSE IT WAS ONLY DAVROS IN THE CLOSED, LITTLE ROOM with her, Melloryn didn't hesitate to speak her mind. "She's shekking us," the elf said, tossing Nagheeshynarifa's missive onto the table.

Davros made a curious face, but didn't look up from the arrow he was shaping. "Who, Gheesh? I don't think she knows how." He considered the line of the arrow. "Here's a better question: does Gheesh even shek?"

Melloryn bit off a retort about newardine digestion—nothing more *gwircalayin* than talking about their employer's bodily functions. Davros was trying to distract her. "We don't need a third."

"Don't know the job, so you can't really say that."

"What can't you and I handle? What haven't we been able to do already?"

Davros chuckled, looking up at her finally. The sunlight through the grimy window lit the human's face, blazed on the sixteen gray hairs speckling his close-cropped brown hair. Melloryn stopped herself from counting again—there would only be more and more and more as her only friend's aging outpaced hers.

"You never like change," he said.

"First," Melloryn said, "every time Nagheeshynarifa adds a blade to our arsenal, it goes badly. Second, this one's an *orog*. Third, no, I don't like changes. And I think the first two prove I'm right in that."

Davros smiled, tied a charm around the head of the arrow. A modest bit of magic tickled the air. "You going to say Gheesh doesn't know what she's doing?"

"An *orog*," Melloryn repeated. "You and I and an *orog*. Picture that—just picture it. We're not skullcrushers or bonebreakers. We're not front-liners. What is the *orog* adding to the pot?"

Davros shrugged. "Ask Gheesh."

Nagheeshynarifa, the newardine spymaster folks called the Blank-Faced Widow, hired the partnership of Melloryn Ianthippe Ydrithe and Davros Trebon for quiet jobs, problems that might seem far from the filigreed courts of the Free Kingdoms, but whose fallout would shake those marbled floors nonetheless.

"Makes *me* wonder what the job is," Davros said.

"With an *orog* who might suddenly get swallowed in her own Darkness?"

"And an elf who might steal all my magic and bring the next cataclysm?" He stood and rubbed her arms in a comforting way. "Come on, Mell. Give her a chance. It sounds like it might be a lot of coin."

Melloryn relaxed even as a part of her noted—again—how *gwircalayin* her friend's offered comfort was by the rules of the fey. "And if she does turn on us?"

Now Davros scoffed. "As if you and I can't handle one wild *orog*."

Melloryn rolled her eyes, but she smiled. "Fair." Her eyes skimmed his hairline. Another one, buried in his left eyebrow, a shaft of silver she could swear hadn't been there before. Seventeen.

Her heart squeezed.

"Besides," Davros went on, "the *orog* has the mission. So we're going to have to meet her, or skip out on the coin."

That fact, more than any of the others, made Melloryn suspect that Nagheeshynarifa knew exactly what she'd done. It was easy to see how, after all, the newardin might have seen in her maddening logic that each of them brought certain isolated skills to the job, but missed the fact that an *orog* did not fit with a human and an elf—even an elf like Melloryn.

But then, Nagheeshynarifa had made sure they couldn't take the job without meeting the *orog*.

IN THE CORNER OF A DISREPUTABLE TAPROOM, THE OROG waited, a mountain of muscle and bone that seemed to have somehow suffered more than a few landslides in its time. One shoulder sat higher than the other, one arm seemed thicker. Her face drooped in a scowl that had no effort at all behind it, simply how her face fell.

Her dark eyes peered across the taproom at Melloryn, over a nose like a river rock, and it was impossible to tell whether the *orog* was thinking anything at all. Four flagons littered her table, and Melloryn caught herself making a disapproving face.

"Want to get an ale first?" Davros asked. "Make it casual?"

"Let's just get this over with."

Heads turned as Melloryn led the way across the taproom. She clenched her fists—shekking humans. For an elf, she was plain and she knew it. It was why her mother always suspected she'd gone to live among the other races—to humans, she would always be ethereal, beautiful beyond measure.

And not a lot else, Melloryn thought, allowing herself the very un-elven fantasy of punching a particularly unsubtle fellow in his stupid, bearded face.

"Afternoon," she said as she reached the corner table. "Do you mind if we join you?"

The *orog*'s beady eyes considered the two of them for what felt like an eternity. "Did the Widow send you?" she asked, her voice surprisingly soft, but not the least bit feminine.

"Are you expecting someone else?"

Davros settled into a chair. "I'm Davros. This is Mell."

"Melloryn." Old urges nibbled at her. "Melloryn Ianthippe Ydrithe," she added, her full, formal name, waiting for an offer to sit.

"Aghi." The orog shifted in her too-small seat. "Those ales been sitting there awhile, but they're for you."

Melloryn eyed the nearest one. *It's polite out here,* she reminded herself, even though it would have been nothing but rude in the Court of Ydrithe.

"Much obliged." Davros pulled one of the flagons toward himself. Melloryn sat and blew out an anxious breath. Aghi watched him drink and pulled out a folded bit of parchment. She held it out, eyes darting from Davros to Melloryn, as if she wasn't sure who to give it to.

Melloryn took the orders and left Davros to his stale ale. The flowing lines of newardine language nearly filled the page. "Did she tell you what it says?" she asked, eyes on the spymaster's esoteric script.

"Yes," Aghi said. "She didn't explain much, though. Just that you'd say—"

"Full and deeping burnt!" Melloryn crumpled the parchment and turned to Davros. "It's Tulbeth again."

"Yes, that," Aghi said. "Who is Tulbeth Again?"

"Thorn in our behinds," Davros said. "What's he done now?"

"Does it *matter?* Something stupid."

The third son of Lord Elgin D'Addarian, a nobleman of the Free Kingdoms widely renowned for the prowess of his guard and his generosity on feast days; known better, in the right quarters, for his singular ability to come out of every conflict standing on his opponent's neck. The Lady Moria D'Addarian, they said, dabbled in poisons even while she made offerings to Alantra, Mother of All, and practiced the Centering of old. The eldest son, Alaric, stood at his father's right hand, staunch defender, unequalled heir—*slippery bastard,* Melloryn thought. The second son, Jundar, led the largest force of his father's army, a capable general, a natural leader—an iron-fisted tyrant, in Melloryn's estimation.

And then there was Tulbeth. The thorn in all their behinds.

"It is a plant?" Aghi asked. "Or a person?"

"Tulbeth D'Addarian," Davros explained in quiet tones, "is what happens when a child gets all the wealth, all the love, all the opportunity, and none of the brains or skills to make it worth the effort of the Enaros to pour his destiny into him."

"He's a mediocre wizard with delusions of greatness, and a papa with deep pockets and a deeper belief that he hasn't found his true calling," Melloryn said, still skimming the page. Plenty of coin on the table at least. "You sign on with Nagheeshynarifa, you're going to wind up saving his… Oh, for blistered Modren's sake."

"What?" Davros demanded.

Melloryn felt as if her heart had crawled into her stomach. "He's gone adventuring in the Elliyan Wilds."

Davros raised an eyebrow. "Blistered Modren, indeed."

She folded the parchment and set it back on the table, mouth pursed. That's why the *orog*. That's why the need for brute force. "Why did she hire *us* for this?"

"Come on," Davros said. "You know a better tracker?"

"You *can't* use magic in the Wilds. It goes wrong. It could kill you."

"I can track fine without magic, thank you very much. And your blade works dandy inside the city or out." He smiled at Aghi. "She's very quick."

The *orog*'s drooping face managed an even deeper scowl. "I'm sorry," she said in her rumbling voice. "I don't understand. You have to explain things to me. I move faster than I think, though. I promise." She nudged one of the warm ales toward Melloryn. "You look like you need this."

Melloryn clenched her teeth, but took the ale. *You're not in Ydrithe anymore,* she reminded herself. *And you need a deeping orog to get through the Elliyan Wilds.*

WHEN THE ELVES OF YDRITHE TOLD THE STORY OF THE FALL of Ellor Nyall, they could not avoid acknowledging the folly of that court's mighty queen, the hubris that led to the near-end of the world, and the banishment of her name from every elf's tongue: *Endroren gifted us with magic and we were wise to make that power part of our very selves. But the queen of Ellor Nyall reached too far...she wished to be as powerful as the Enaros themselves, as eternal as a god...*

Even as a child, Melloryn thought the queen of Ellor Nyall made an easy figure of blame. After all, given the reality of unfettered magic, who wouldn't reach for what came next? She didn't believe, even then, that her grandmother, her aunts, her matriarch, her mother, would truly turn away from the chance to gain something greater—had the spells gone right, the elves would have had a leader who could have protected them when the Cataclysm came and the *endrori* rose out of the ground.

The queen of Ellor Nyall had gambled—an object lesson in the dangers of pride, perhaps—but Melloryn couldn't imagine being queen of a court and just sitting on her hands, waiting patiently for the next catastrophe, when the world seemed to spit them out as regularly as if they were melon seeds on a hot day.

Had the spells gone right, the queen of Ellor Nyall would have been hailed as the savior of the entire world.

Instead, she had birthed the forest that nearly swallowed the world, and became *Ir'nata Elliyan,* Mother of Catastrophes, a cautionary tale that had never quite stuck for Melloryn.

ON MAPS, THE ELLIYAN WILDS WAS A DARK BLOTCH THAT ran right up to the sea, far past where a forest would naturally grow. Melloryn had heard tales that the cursed wood reached down into the brine, so full of furious magic that not even the Amethyst Sea could stop it. No reaching branches scraped their skiff's belly as they sailed up the coast from the Wilds' southern edge, but the enormous trees blanketing every inch of the sandy shore sent a shiver through Melloryn. Like they were claiming the dead soil just to have it.

"Nobody touches anything magical," she said. "Got it? No charms, no wands, no spells."

"Why?" Aghi asked.

"Because the forest will eat it," Melloryn said. "And maybe you." Given his proclivities, Tulbeth was as likely a smear on the ferns as anything they could bring back to his father. The ever-practical Nagheeshynarifa had negotiated a fee for returning the scion's remains, at least.

They found the boat Tulbeth and his friends must have taken, turned over and already blanketed by vines, and camped nearby while unlikely maples loomed over them.

"Are you having trouble sleeping?" Aghi asked, after Melloryn had finished her watch and spent a solid half hour staring up at the purple-leaved acantirra, the thorny Melgren oaks choking out the starlight. Her pack clanked as she fished through it. "They said we might. I brought a sleeping potion."

"No, thank you."

Aghi waggled a metal flask with a blue thread around its neck. "Sure? I brought two."

"Sleeping potion means if something comes out of the wilds, there's little to no chance that I wake and have my sword in hand before some monster you haven't even conceived of eats us all. No, thank you."

Now, a half-a-day into the Elliyan Wilds, Melloryn wondered if she'd ever sleep soundly again. A thousand bits of *wrongness* pecked at her. The forest grew dense as brambles, trees crowded close as folks at the Festival of Droth, watching fighters beat each other brainless. There was no birdsong, only the pervasive sense of always being assessed by something.

A vine snaked across the ground toward Davros' ankle. Melloryn slashed it in half, so quick Davros jumped only when the blade scraped the ground.

"Problem?" he asked. But Melloryn was already wading into the thick ferns, pulling them aside with gloved hands. In their midst, a flower the size of a bucket, the color of a bruise grew, with more vines reaching out through the underbrush. Heat radiated off the plant, its stem pulsing gently. The vines twitched, many of them already cut short from another, recent blade.

"Aghi," she said. "Pull the weed."

Aghi tore out the plant, its roots raining dirt and wriggling like thin worms exposed to the light. She shoved it in the croft of a nearby tree, the vines groping at her powerful arms.

"Well," Davros said, "no greens for dinner, I guess."

Melloryn didn't smile. "You can't turn your back on anything." Even the *endrori*, thralls of utter darkness, didn't breach the Elliyan Wilds.

Just stupid rich-boy wizards, Melloryn thought as they paused along the winding path through the broadleaves. *And desperate bought-blades.*

And *Ir'nata Elliyan.* Legend said the transformed queen still lived—if one could call it living—as the dark, beating heart of the cursed forest. Melloryn's nerves itched. For once, faced with the growing eeriness of the Elliyan Wilds, she had a hard time seeing the lost queen as an unlucky victim.

Tulbeth is not making it to the middle, she told herself, scanning the trees. The path between them was only a mossy strip laid over their tangled roots.

Davros knelt beside a thornbush, hunting for signs of Tulbeth's passing. "You're sure about the magic?"

"Trust me," Melloryn said.

"You should not touch that," Aghi said. The orog hovered anxiously over Davros, thick hands clutched together. "It is poisonous."

"He knows what he's doing," Melloryn said. "It's why Nagheeshynarifa hired him."

"I'm not touching it," Davros said mildly. "Definitely poisonous." He looked up at the *orog*. "Where'd you learn about plants?"

Aghi studied the path ahead. "Just did."

"I like her," Davros said as they picked up again. "To begin with, she's well-prepared."

Aghi's shoulder bags clanked and clattered with a wide array of weapons and potions and gewgaws. Everything a merchant said they might need in the Elliyan Wilds. A waste of coin, and Melloryn found herself wishing she knew which merchant had taken advantage of the *orog*.

"When you're that big, it takes a lot to load you down," Melloryn said dryly. "You think she's prepared for what happens if the magic in the Wilds wakes the Darkness in her?"

"You worry too much," Davros said. "She's not like other *orogs*."

Ahead of them, Aghi stiffened—Melloryn would swear to it. If betting hadn't made her mother's disapproving voice echo in her head, she'd have laid down double coin, standing in the woods, watching Aghi grow uncomfortable at Davros' notice that she wasn't like the others of her blood.

"Are you all right here?" Aghi asked. "You seem tense."

"Of course I'm deeping tense," Melloryn snapped. "Do you know *anything* about the Wilds?"

Davros shot her a look. "Mell."

"A little," Aghi said. "Dangerous. Magic's all crazy, but the dark ones don't come here." She paused, looking up at the trees. "There was a battle once, they ran in here, and the dark ones didn't give chase. It's a different kind of dark, I guess."

Melloryn frowned at the half-told story and the missing facts. "You don't know about Ellor Nyall? The first catastrophe?"

Aghi shrugged in an uneven way, still looking at the trees. "Before our time. The past is past."

"Convenient maxim," Melloryn said.

Davros straightened, dusting off his breeches. "Come on. We're not getting any closer to Tulbeth standing around here."

THE ELLIYAN WILDS HAD BEEN ANCIENT BEFORE THE ATLAN Alliance had come to Aetaltis. More than three and a half thousand years had passed before the first of Davros or Aghi's ancestors had treaded the land. To the Alliance, the story of a powerful elven court might as well have been cradle-tales, the fancies of a diminished race pretending at lost greatness.

Aghi's ancestors would have hardly had a chance to hear such tales before the Horde Wars came, before sullen Endroren woke the spark of Darkness in the *orogs*, twisting them to his side. What made some easy-made puppets and others survivors?

It's a different kind of dark, I guess. Whatever the orogs had, was it different from what lay in the elves? From what was supposed to have turned the heart of Ir'nata Elliyan?

Clearly. After all, *orogs* numbered among the *endrori*, the dark weapons of the fallen god. Elves did not.

Aghi helped her clamber over a thick branch that snaked along the fern-strewn ground as if it had once held designs on being a vine, despite its heft.

"Are you all right?" Aghi asked again.

Melloryn gritted her teeth, well aware of what she looked like. Sweat shone on her pale skin, drenched her cornsilk hair. Her head ached with the effort of ignoring the constant sensation that *something* was whispering to her, just a breath too quiet to make out. The Elliyan Wilds buzzed with furious magic that jangled her nerves, shaking the magic wound around the very core of her self. Melloryn told herself she would not vomit.

She wiped her upper lip, her forehead. "This place is dangerous."

Aghi nodded. "Cursed. Broken. It feels like someone warped it."

Melloryn flinched at the word. Maybe it was true, but to say it out loud? To say it as if Ir'nata Elliyan, as if any elf would have perverted nature willingly? *Gwircalayin,* she thought. *Nothing but a slight on us all.*

Aghi gave her a smile like a rockslide and held out a waterskin. Melloryn took it. *A slight coming out of an elf's mouth,* she reminded herself. *From another's, just a word.* "Thanks."

Aghi nodded, shooting an anxious look at Davros, down on the ground again, communing with the bent ferns and crushed mosses along an ancient, crumbling stone wall. Crimson flowers shaped like ruffled flagons dripped down its length.

"It's a bad story in your home?" she asked. "The Ellor Nyall?"

Melloryn waved at the eerie trees surrounding them. "It doesn't end well."

"So, this is like climbing down into the Deeplands. You are very brave."

"It's not like the Deeplands."

Davros yelped and scrambled back from something near the wall. Melloryn hardly had to think but she was at his side, blade drawn. To her surprise, the *orog* nearly matched her speed, ready to defend Davros.

"It *bit* me." Davros clutched his hands to his chest and nodded at the flowers. "*And* creeped me up."

With her sword, Melloryn nudged one of the tapered flowers hanging down the wall. Its opening gaped like a mouth, the better to lure insects.

It wriggled against her blade. She saw the dangling legs, the useless petal-wings, the fact it *was* a mouth. The flower blinked at her, bared its tiny teeth, and she nearly failed her decision not to vomit.

"Fairies." She wiped the sword on her breeches.

"Not anymore," Davros said.

Maybe not for four thousand years—she imagined the wave of magic Ir'nata Elliyan had released, the tide of green that swallowed the land, that *warped* it, yes. Given the fairies, there was no other word on her tongue. Maybe the fairy-flowers were hundreds of generations from anything different.

Or maybe they'd been trapped here like countless others. There was no telling what came from that first catastrophe, and what the Wilds built of its own slow-growing madness.

Aghi dropped her bags, rummaged through them, and pulled

out a small healer's kit. "You're bleeding," she said. "Here."

"It's only a nip," Davros said, but he was clearly rattled.

Aghi ignored him, dripping a bright red tincture on the bite before bandaging it. "Maybe poisoned, could get infected."

Davros managed an uneasy smile. "See, Mell? It's good she's prepared."

"It's only going to get worse the deeper we go," Melloryn told him, unable to shake the sense they were being watched. "It's only going to get darker."

"Well," Davros said, eyes still on the fairy-flowers, "at least I've found a trail. Something big came through here and it left man-sized bootmarks. Little bastard's not more than a few hours off."

THE AIR GREW THICKER AS THE DAY WENT ON, AND THE path became harder and harder to pick out of the brambling undergrowth. Snapping twigs broke the quiet now and again, and the strange call of a beast Melloryn couldn't name echoed through the canopy.

"Is this normal?" Aghi asked. "Is this how you usually rescue this one?"

"Normally, he gets himself kidnapped," Melloryn said. "Follows some lead after supposedly easy magic: lost scrolls, secret caches from before the Ritual of Limitation, 'working' portals. And it turns out—shock of shocks—that he's been talking to a shekking ganglord with ties to one of his Papa's rivals."

"Used to be we'd just deliver the ransom," Davros called back. "Then Mell slipped her halter, got all *gwircalayin,* and Lord D'Addarian realized he could send a better message with a blade of Ydrithe."

"Deeping Enaros, stop trying to speak elvish. That's not

what that means."

Aghi pushed a tree branch out of the way, so the others could pass. "What does it mean? *Gwir-cal-a-yin?*"

"Elf word," Davros said. "Means you got bad manners."

"It *means*," Melloryn said, "something that's deviant. Something done out of order. Something inappropriate."

Aghi frowned. "So Tulbeth is *gwircalayin?*"

"To elves, everybody else's *gwircalayin*. Got rules about the proper way to scratch your backside."

"Davros, you know what's *gwircalayin?*" Melloryn slashed another vine, just to hit something. "You trying to speak Elvish. Shut it."

"He sounds as if he ought to be considered deviant," Aghi said. "He would be deviant if he'd been born an *orog*. No one would save him if he could not save himself."

Davros glanced over his shoulder at her. "Huh. I would have thought you'd want to keep your numbers up. I mean, the...the good numbers."

"We are fewer," Aghi said grimly. "So there is no room for weakness."

Words that came from *somewhere*—Melloryn thought of Ydrithe and her mother, and the unavoidable fact that Melloryn Ianthippe Ydrithe was *gwircalayin*, and unapologetically so.

Ignoring stupid rules, pointing out what she thought was madness, that was enough to make her not enough of an elf. But nobody in Ydrithe would have expected her death because of it. She wondered where Aghi's family was.

Melloryn cleared her throat. "If he were an *orog*, he'd have done a lot better fighting off that first batch of kidnappers."

Davros snorted. "Right! The cheebats!"

A sharp trilling yanked Melloryn's attention upward, to a trio of glowing amber eyes the size of gold pieces. To the other four sets of eyes, watching from the treetops. Raccoons—but no, they were as big as Davros, their hands like a human's, their fingers too long for comfort. Clutching the air as if they were grasping at some invisible sphere, approximately the size of her skull. Spikes like silver needles stuck out of their thick fur.

The center one climbed down the tree partway, headfirst—*heads* first. Its face split into two sharp-toothed muzzles, and nestled in the canyon of them, an unblinking center eye. Both mouths hissed, not quite in unison.

And they all began to descend.

Melloryn pulled her sword out. "Davros, get back. Aghi, here's your—"

A rustle from the underbrush. Melloryn broke off, looking back over her shoulder. Davros loosing arrows into the trees, no eye for the other four beasts slinking out of the bushes toward his back. She hardly had time to curse.

Then a roar shook the leaves overhead, as if the trees rattled in fear of the *orog* raging in their midst. Aghi tore down a branch from one of the oaks, ripped it down as easily as if it were a leaf she'd plucked, eyes on the four climbing down. Melloryn darted past Davros—sword through the nearest one, right through the eye, the momentum of her body driving the blade. She kicked out, catching the next in the teeth—stunned, long enough to pull her weapon free of the dead one. Green blood smeared the blade as she sliced down, into the raccoon-thing's neck, then stabbed deep into its chest. A third leapt on her, the broken nails of its hands scrabbling against her leather breastplate. Elbow to its growling, bifurcated face—

The fourth creature reached for Davros, as he turned, noticed, reached into his quiver for another arrow. The glint of silver against the arrowhead…

"No!" Melloryn shoved the raccoon-creature off and sprinted toward Davros.

The charm tied on the arrow began glowing red as he nocked it, the air vibrating as the magic built. He seemed to realize his mistake, heartbeats before she reached him—before the air around the charm surged with power—before she slammed the hilt of her blade into the back of his hand, forcing him to release the string.

She tackled Davros, bearing him to the ground.

The charm-arrow spun toward the raccoon-creature and, inches from its center eye, imploded. The creature seemed to simply vanish in a fine green mist, along with half of the creature beside it. The left-hand face bared its teeth, mouth snapping twice as it collapsed over on the green, pulpy mess of its missing right side.

Melloryn's arms held Davros tight, refusing to let him go, no matter how much she wanted to scream at him. "*No* shekking—"

"No shekking magic," Davros gasped. "Blistered Modren, thank you."

"Up!" she barked.

Aghi bellowed again, the tandem screech of a raccoon-creature dwindling to a gurgle even as the *orog*'s roar faded. The monster's body sailed overhead, its narrow spikes embedding in the trunk of a tree, so that it hung in place there for a moment before they snapped off. Melloryn marked her, lingering a bit too long at the sight of the *orog* seizing one beast by the throat, slamming it into a second like a living club.

Melloryn released Davros and rolled to her feet, cutting across another raccoon-creature as it leaped toward them. As Darvos gained his feet, she shoved him back, away from the monsters. Give him room, get him safe—if anything was going to take her friend, it would be the gray and the creep of age, not some deeping raccoon-things—

One of the deeping raccoon-things snapped its jaws on her sword arm, hard enough to bruise her through the thick leather. It yanked her away, like a dog with a toy, and down to the forest floor. Melloryn fell. She heard Davros shout, then the *twang* of a bow.

Aghi roared again. The raccoon-creature lifted sharply away. Melloryn came with it, up a few feet before its grip failed, one tooth tearing from its jaw. The roar that shook Melloryn's bones, made the raccoon-creature twist, and suddenly Aghi smashed it into the last of its fellows—again and again. Her great feet crashed down on the corpses, splattering green blood like mud. Then the orog turned to the elf.

Melloryn scrabbled for her sword.

Red blood, green blood, Aghi had been painted in pain. Four silvery spines stuck out of her shoulder. Panting, heaving, she looked ready to tear the two of them in half just as she had the raccoon-creatures. Her dark eyes blazed at Melloryn, and animal panic scrabbled up the elf's chest.

Aghi blinked. "Are you all right?"

"I'm not the bloody one." Melloryn shook her head, shook off the fear. "Give me your bags."

Aghi shook her head. "I can bear it. We are made for such things." She reached up and snapped off the spikes before pulling open the bag. "You two are more delicate. Especially Davros."

Davros bled from a cut on his cheek, and now favored his left knee. "If I'm delicate," he said lightly, "what's Mell?"

"What's Tulbeth?" Melloryn said, getting slowly to her feet, burning with an anger, a fear she had to find a home for. "Dead. Dead is the answer. Why do we take these shekking jobs? Why does D'Addarian *bother* with rescuing him?"

"Coin's good." Davros winced as Aghi daubed a tincture on his cut cheek. "Besides, it's his kid. Blood's pretty thick. Thicker than gold, when you get down to it."

Melloryn glanced sidelong at Aghi, whose lopsided face took on an even deeper look of concentration.

THE TRAIL WAS CLEARER AFTER THAT–SOMEONE ELSE HAD fought the raccoon-monsters, and left a track of blood through the brush. It was Tulbeth, or they'd been on the wrong path all this time and were about to rescue someone they hadn't been paid for.

The last of the sunlight gave up on piercing the thick canopy. Aghi pulled torches from her pack and handed them out. The dancing light glimmered on the sweat misting her grayish face. She sniffed roughly as she handed Melloryn a torch, as if she were catching cold.

Whatever Aghi insisted, she wasn't fine.

Melloryn caught Davros' eye, and he shook his head once. They were close—so close—and nowhere he wanted to camp. Melloryn counted the cuts scabbing over on Aghi's broad shoulders. If she called for a stop, Aghi would tell her she was tougher than that. They pressed on.

Aghi kept sniffing.

The trail of blood led them to a crumbling stone building. Once, its shape had been graceful and lifelike—hints of the artistry of Ellor Nyall remained in a column's deft mimicry of a sycamore trunk, the curve of a stone vine. But the catastrophe had not left the structure untouched, and great roots broke apart the stone blocks. An oak tree bigger around than Aghi could reach partially blocked the door.

A good shelter, Melloryn thought. *And a better ambush point.* She edged around the tree and threw her torch into the broken temple. Shadows danced along the walls, shaping faces out of the stone. Carvings.

Elven queens.

Ir'nata Elliyan. Mother of catastrophes. Melloryn's heart threatened to stop her feet. She drew her sword to bolster it, and eased into the space, waiting for her foremothers' worst nightmare to come true. *This is where the darkness comes for you,* she thought. *This is where the Mother of Catastrophes waits.*

She watched the statues. Moss crawled across the stone, mobile with magic and giving expression to the long dead queens. None of them lived in truth. None of them were the trapped queen at the heart of the forest.

None of that made Melloryn's heart slow down.

"Tulbeth?" Her voice echoed strangely. She scooped the torch from the floor, eyeing the eerie carvings. "Tulbeth, it's time to go home."

Something skittered in the shadows. She turned toward the noise, seeing Davros and Aghi come up behind her. Davros nocked an arrow, marking a shadow that moved through the dark between the columns and trees.

"Tulbeth!" Melloryn shouted. "It's dead or alive this time! Come out, or we come in, and I'm *not* in a good mood!"

The shadow's pacing grew shorter. "Dead? Dead?" It sounded like two voices, speaking over each other. "That doesn't sound like Papa. Papa."

Melloryn peered into the darkness. "Tulbeth?"

The shadow peeled away, creeping into the circle of light. For a heartbeat, Melloryn recognized Tulbeth D'Addarian—his shaggy auburn beard, his pale skin, his dark eyes, the frantic expression that said at last he'd realized his folly, and thank the Enaros they were here.

Tulbeth D'Addarian—only twice.

Melloryn jumped back. "Shek!"

Tulbeth's face, split and raw, shaped two mouths, two noses. The beginnings of a third, milky eye budded in his forehead. The shagginess of his beard wasn't a day's growth, but the beginnings of a grayish coat of fur.

"Cursed," Davros said. "Venom off those beasties. Maybe poison."

"Sp-Spines-ines." Tulbeth's right mouth spoke faster than his left, making a disorienting chorus.

"How long?" Melloryn asked.

"Fast. Only hours." His hands grasped at them, as if he couldn't help it. "You have to fix it, or I'll tell Father to keep his coin."

While Geesh's contract hadn't specified what happened if they brought Tulbeth back furry and bifurcated, Melloryn could imagine the specific shade of scarlet pale Lord D'Addarian would turn. She tore her eyes off Tulbeth. "Aghi, tell me you've got something."

"I have a potion," Aghi said. "It's supposed to remove curses. If you think it's a curse."

Melloryn didn't answer—her attention was focused on the tip of Aghi's nose, no longer round and smooth as an river rock, but dimpled by a slow-growing groove.

"Are you all right?" Melloryn whispered. Aghi didn't answer, her dark eyes hard.

"It's a curse," Davros assured her. "Plant-borne, but if it's in progress, we can—"

"You took spines in your shoulder," Melloryn interrupted. "You've got the curse, too."

Aghi held out the metal flask. "And one potion. He's worth a lot of coin."

Melloryn didn't take it, *couldn't* take it. She watched the raw spot in the middle of Aghi's nose widen, like the splitting skin of a plum.

"Give it to me,"Tulbeth demanded, "and take me home, Ydrithe. You can get another *orog*."

Aghi's expression grew harder.

One potion, one cure. Aghi or Tulbeth. By morning, Tulbeth would be completely transformed. By the time they got back to the Free Kingdoms, Aghi would be gone—and if there were a cure, she wouldn't have the coin to cover it. One or the other, and Tulbeth had a contract.

"Are you *seriously* considering giving that brute my potion?" Tulbeth cried. A muscle in Melloryn's eye began to tic as she considered, in that moment, breaking both of Tulbeth's noses.

It was not the moment her mother would have chosen, she felt sure, for Melloryn to finally understand—in her own way—the tale of Ir'nata Elliyan

"Right?" she said, eyes on Aghi. "Rescue *her*? I mean, she can't even tell which potion is which."

A flash of hurt crossed Aghi's features, but Melloryn snatched the blue-thread wrapped flask from the top of the overstuffed pack. Aghi started to protest, but Melloryn tapped her lips.

"Mell, there's—" She glared at Davros, and he fell silent.

"Drink it all," she said to Tulbeth. "We've got a long voyage ahead of us."

The smug little lordling snatched the flask from her without a word of thanks, shot a look of triumph at Aghi, and whatever guilt might have rusted the edges of Melloryn's heart fell away. Tulbeth drank the potion thirstily, took a deep breath, and collapsed, asleep, on the floor.

"Blistered Modren." Davros chuckled. "Lord D'Addarian won't like this."

"He can take it up with the Widow."

"Give it to him," Aghi said. "That's what you agreed to."

"We agreed to bring him back," Melloryn corrected. "And we'll bring him back." She uncorked the potion. "Are you going to drink this, or am I going to feed it to you?"

Aghi frowned. "Is breaking your word not *gwircalayan?*"

"You know what's deeping *gwircalayan?* Turning your back on your people for a little better footing. You're *our* people now, Aghi. Drink up."

A hesitant, almost shy smile crept across the *orog*'s splitting features as Melloryn pressed the flask into her hand.

BEHIND HER DESK, NAGHEESHYNARIFA TAPPED HER LONG fingers together, considering Melloryn Ianthippe Ydrithe with an expression as smooth and unreadable as an eggshell. "Lord D'Addarian is…displeased with the state of his son."

"He ought to take that up with the idiot who plunged into the Elliyan Wilds without the tools to protect himself," Melloryn replied.

Nothing flickered in the newardin's enormous dark eyes—no guessing if they were in trouble. *Doesn't matter,* Melloryn told herself.

"He is skeptical that you did not have the means to save Tulbeth," Nagheeshynarifa continued. "I find myself…skeptical as well."

"Sorry, did someone change the terms of the agreement?" Melloryn said. "Because all I recall is 'dead or alive.' Seems pretty deeping alive to me, so Lord D'Addarian should consider his terms the next time he hires someone to risk their hides for Tulbeth."

The newardin folded her spidery hands, each short a finger, and leaned toward Melloryn. "It has long been apparent that you have strongly negative feelings about Tulbeth D'Addarian. But there is no denying that his antics bring a great deal of regular coin to myself and to you—a result that has been repeated often enough to suggest its continued truth. Logic dictates that if he were rescued—and I mean that word to the extent both Lord D'Addarian and I used it, initially—then we would all be in a better state economically, apart from Lord D'Addarian."

Melloryn folded her arms. "Then perhaps I'm done rescuing spoiled third sons who want me to sacrifice a friend so they can go on being a useless idiot."

Nagheeshynarifa tilted her head. "This is value assignation beyond what you've historically shown. Apart from Davros, who I assumed was an anomaly. It is more similar to fey values than—"

"Do you intend to hire us again?" Melloryn asked. "That's really the only question I need answered right now."

A smile curved the newardin spymaster's small mouth. "Of course, Melloryn Ianthippe Ydrithe. Though your offers may change, given the circumstances."

"Right," Melloryn said, standing. "Well, we've got an *orog* now, so that much I expected."

MY DOOM MAY COME SOON

ED GREENWOOD

"I FIND YOUR TERMS UNACCEPTABLE," TARLA SAID CALMLY.

"Oh, *do* you, now?" The man with one milk-white eye pulled a long and slightly hooked knife out of his sleeve—its slender blade black and ungleaming as a shadow—in a swift instant, and had his back to the only door of her office in the next. "Think you're worth more, do you?"

"I know it," Tarla told the man coldly, as she sprang.

Straight up, her hand closing on the crumbling stone sill of a long-filled-in window on the wall above and behind her with the deftness of long practice. She was up and out of his reach one swift gasp of effort later.

There was a reason she met clients here, in this walled-off end of a noisome alley in one of the damper and less savory corners of Port Vale, down dark and narrow streets not even the Mayor's armsmen visited willingly. And one of those reasons was now within reach, ready for situations that turned as unpleasant as this one.

"I can climb faster than that," the man said with a smirk. "And throw this—" He waggled the wicked-looking knife in his fingertips. "—even faster. And what it'll do to your face will end your arm-candy money and gown-strutting for good."

Tarla settled back against the rough stone wall and brought one hand up to where she'd have a hope of batting that blade aside if it came whirling up at her face. It would cost her fingers, but... "And scarring me will make me willing to accept your *kind* offer *how*, exactly?"

"I know many, many men—and some women, too—who don't mind paying for the intimate embraces of someone whose face is hooded. Particularly if she's chained and otherwise bare, so they know she has no way to harm them."

"And you consider my being chained up naked to be an inducement I'll *welcome*?"

"I'll take *very* good care of you. There'd be no more meeting unsavory personages—of the likes of me—in stinking corners like this. No more looking behind you at your every step in these mean streets, or everywhere in the dark hours. You'd have plenty to eat, and I can be *very* attentive. We'll soon become...close."

His smirk had become an all-too-predictable leer. Tarla looked down at him calmly, because to give in to anger was almost as perilous as succumbing to fear. So this Carzath Kethur, self-styled Master Thief of Port Vale, thought her home was a stinking corner, did he?

Well, to speak blunt truth, it was. Yet its uppermost level, lost to view in the roofed-over darkness far above, was a comfortable enough sleeping loft that she'd managed to guard with her own effective alarm of old string and scraps of rusty metal and shards of pottery and glass, to awaken her if an intruder climbed too close. It worked, and she'd come to like this dark shaft, even if hatches on one side of its ceiling did bang open all too often to empty the chamberpot-leavings of half a dozen residences above down in a disgusting stream, and remind her why someone had walled off this space in the first place.

"That would almost certainly be too close for my preferences," she murmured her reply, the black cord that triggered her reason now firmly in her grasp.

Her unwelcome visitor's response was to draw a bowgun—a deadly little hand crossbow, that fired needle-sharp darts that would be either drugged or poisoned—out from under his jerkin, cock it with the usual harsh little rattle, and reach back under his jerkin for a dart.

Tarla let him grab it before pulling the cord, hoping that the poison or snakesleep venom or whatever was on its end would get into him when her defenses took effect.

The cord yanked the support away from the hinged shelf above her, and all the broken roof-slates and cracked cobblestones she'd put up there plummeted down in a crashing thunder that smashed Kethur to the floor in a startled instant. Almost before he had time to start swearing.

She rode the dangling cord most of the way back down to him, wanting to separate him from his knife and those darts right now.

How *dare* he invade her very home, and threaten her with slavery and the loss of her chosen livelihood? Precarious it might be, trading on her looks to earn coins as arm candy for ugly old merchants like Narlis Abbarl and Chendor Thoat as they attended feasts and trademoots, or modeling the gowns and daring bedchamber-wear they tried to sell to wealthier Vale women, but it was the life *she'd* chosen, or devised for herself.

Oh, she'd encountered the likes of Kethur before. Anyone who dwelt in the shady alleys and cruel streets of Port Vale, and had her sort of looks, got noticed by someone like him soon enough. Once she'd worked for a thief who'd been as ruthless and as successful as Kethur when he was still a squalling babe. She'd been a lure—a decoy to distract marks while their valuables were stolen by others—but that man had been dead now for too many winters for her to count, considering how relatively few winters she'd been alive, and the world rolled on without him.

The world always rolled on. Until, of course, the day came when you fell out of it, and it rolled on without you. And if she let the likes of Kethur get his knives close to her, that day would come for her all too—

She was on the ground and warily picking her way through the slippery litter of shards and roiling dust toward him when the Master Thief exploded up from under the wrack with a snarl of rage and pain, streaming blood cloaking all of his face but one glaring eye. His hate-filled gaze raked her in the moment it took him to whirl and flee—and then he was gone, broken tiles clattering on cobbles in his wake.

"Upon due and sober reflection," she murmured, mockingly quoting a favorite verbal gambit of Blythorn Blackwick, Mayor of Port Vale—and *there* was a man to be feared more than a dozen Carzath Kethurs, to be sure—"I find I must refuse your offer, Master Thief. *Kind* and *generous* though it is."

She peered up the alley for a long time to make sure he was really gone, ere using a long shard of tile to rake through the debris for his bowgun, darts, or that knife. A search that proved fruitless, of course.

She smiled wryly. Luck was not one of her assets.

She was Tarla Beltarth, and of assets she had just four, two of which passing years would rob her of soon enough: her looks, her wits, a certain agility, and mimicry good enough to enunciate truly dripping sarcasm, even when she felt nothing of the sort. For Port

Vale was full of viciously sarcastic folk to mimic.

She'd stolen things from more than her fair share of them, she had to admit. Yet she'd always done so with great stealth, so none of her victims sought her throat or knew her guilt, not by open threats and menaces like Kethur. And she got along by trusting no one, thinking ahead, and living alone and simply, avoiding the indulgences that felled so many. Drink was not her weakness, nor did she need the warmth and companionship of an ever-present lover—or an ever-changing host of them. In Port Vale, every friend was a weakness. Trust in no one.

She smiled again, and told the familiar dimness around her in a whisper so soft anyone lurking more than three strides away would hear nothing, "I don't even trust *me*."

Which was why, she realized a sour moment later, she would have to find a new lair. At least while Carzath Kethur still lived.

He would be back, and not alone, and wouldn't be making any offers this time.

He would just want her slow and painful death. After he had his cruel fun, of course.

He was, after all, a man of Port Vale.

THE ROOF–DOTTED WITH MISSING TILES AND GREAT MOSS-covered hollows where the timbers had rotted and let everything above them collapse—looked far too decrepit for its lone leaning gable with its warped window to be fitted with traps, but Tarla was not in the business of taking chances. She crept along the roof peak like a cautious spider, examining the ridgetop tiles carefully for signs of spikes that might erupt up into her as she went.

When she reached the gable, she took advantage of the cracked tiles and an exposed roof beam on the opposite slope to drive her sturdiest dagger in to serve as a handle, so she could reach over the peak with the sliding metal pole she'd scavenged years back from the body of an unlucky burglar, and pry open that warped window with the down-bent end of its swivel joint.

It resisted until her shoulders ached and her braced and spread limbs quivered from the strain, and then…finally swung open. With a squeal, of course, that would have done a slit-throat boar in the market proud.

She froze, lying still and silent, listening hard for any reaction to the noise, but there was nothing. Far across the night-shrouded streets, someone shrieked, stopping with a horrible, wet abruptness, and from somewhere nearer came a muffled interior crash and raucous laughter…but from the house and shop below her, nothing.

If it *was* still a house. The upper floors above the glassblower's were all dark, with more boarded-up windows than open ones, and some of the outside walls above those windows bore the dark scorch-scars of a long-ago fire. Usually someone was squatting in even the worst burnt-out rooms, but then again, if someone wanting to store something paid handsomely…

Long breaths later, she dared to creep over the peak and worm down beside the leaning gable, jamming her knees against lifting tiles to keep from sliding headfirst down the spongy roof and off to crash and splatter on unseen alley cobbles far, far below.

Damn Kethur and his too-alert eyes, anyway. She'd much rather have been home in her little loft, drifting into slumber as she stared up into the darkness of the roof so close above her nose, and spun idle fantasies of dancing in finery through huge mountains of sugarfoam cakes and flaming puddings, at a feast like those she'd glimpsed through windows a time or two, when lurking aloft near the houses of those wealthy enough to waste coin on such things—and on hard-eyed guards with ready crossbows and ruthless aim. Candles, there were always candles made with metal powders and spices that turned the flames eerie hues, and gave off pungent smells…cinnamon and applespice candles.

Those remembered smells made her stomach rumble.

Tarla bared her teeth, angry at herself. Yes, she was hungry, but the wrong noise at the wrong moment could mean her swift death. Port Vale was not a forgiving place at the best of times, and now, with this current rash of daring robberies…

The plundered places were all palatial villas of the "Valearr," the self-styled "Those Who Matter" of the city. Wherefore the local wealthy were fearful and the mayor apoplectic, hired blades were everywhere, and no one hesitated to strike first and worry about repercussions later.

And although it would be night in Port Vale if there wasn't blood dripping somewhere, she was just as soon it not be her own.

Enough of such thinking—Tarla thrust the slender burglar's pole cautiously into the dark window. Encountering nothing but air, she moved it cautiously in all directions, feeling for obstacles and listening for anything that might be a catch releasing or a trap about to snap into action.

Nothing. And the little metal rod encountered nothing solid, even when she thrust it so far that she was on the teetering edge of overbalancing and plunging into the alley below. For a moment, she considered doing the prudent thing: going elsewhere in search of other possible lairs, and checking this one in a night or two to see if anyone noticed the opened window and did something about it. Yet Kethur's visit hadn't left her lazing in the lap of prudence, and she hadn't seen anything as good as this leaning and apparently forgotten gable in a long night of searching, certainly nothing nearly as well situated for stealthy approaches and departures—and they, after all, were crucial to a lair being more than a sometime brief refuge.

Time to hazard all. Again.

She telescoped the pole back into its shortest length—about the run of her thigh—and slid it through the two torn rents in her stolen leather breeches, holes that lined up enough to serve as a carry-sleeve for such things. Then she reclaimed her sturdiest dagger, checked all of her knives and the waxed black cord she kept ready as a garrote—and swung boldly through the window-frame, catching one side of it so she could sit on the sill and try to gauge what was where in the darkness in front of her.

Hoping, of course, it didn't include rusty old blades on a spring-catch or other trigger set to thrust up through the body of anyone putting their weight on the sill.

Not that such a trap was all that likely in such a decaying, neglected attic, but this was Port Vale, and—

There was a stealthy sound in the blackness ahead. Movement, coming quickly closer.

Tarla launched herself off the sill in a frantic instant, to avoid being shoved back out the window by whoever was charging at her. Sharply to the right, and clawing out a knife to slice her unseen foe—

Who cursed and shouted, "Keep *back!* I have nothing to steal!"

A man's voice—a young man who sounded wild with fear. Tarla turned her knife blade down, brought her arm up to eye level to protect her face from unseen sharp obstacles, and sidestepped away from that voice.

Right into a table large and stout enough not to move. Her hip struck it hard enough to jostle what was on it, and a light flared momentarily as a lantern-hood jiggled.

Enough to show her clutter around the walls of an open attic open but for a worn stool on the far side of this old, littered table, and a lone dark figure retreating from her, backing around the table to put it between them.

She ducked under the table and came up on the other side in time to spin, unhood the lantern, and face the man, her knife up in front of her.

"Don't shout or scream," she told him gently. "I hate loud noises so much that my knife hand is apt to…go wild."

"Ah-ah—all right!" the dark-skinned man managed to chirp. He was young, and actually trembled with fear, his eyes fixed on the gleaming point of her blade. She wasn't in Kethur's league, to be able to afford blackened steel. She waved it at the stool, bidding him sit down, and he whimpered. She waved again, and he scurried and sat.

"Suppose you tell me," she said in that same gentle voice, "who you are, and what all of *this* is." The table was littered with vials, glass vessels held upright in metal cradles, many of them holding liquids of all manner of vivid hues—colors not even the priciest cloth-merchants dealt in. Colors that seemed to glow in the lantern light, colors she'd never seen before.

"I—I—uh—"

Tarla soothed him with a quelling gesture. "Name."

"I—Jalandar Faelren."

"You live here?"

"No, I rent this…workshop." He pointed at fire-scars and out-and-out holes in the roof. "Enough gone that if I—uh—there's a—"

He moved his hands apart in a pantomime of an explosion, and added a sickly smile.

Tarla decided to return it, reassuringly.

"You're an alchemist." She looked again at the vials, then swiftly at him again. "Poisons?"

"Uh—ah, well, some are, but only because they happen to be. That is, nothing is intended to kill or melt metal or, ah, uh—"

"So tell me, alchemist Jalandar Faelren, what you *are* working on here."

"Soothing tinctures."

"And what are soothing tinctures?"

"Liquids that, ah, kill pain. When you're pricked or scratched with something sharp coated in them. That is, uh, I mean to say: none of these are, uh, meant to be drunk."

"And who lives or works on the floor below us?"

"No one. But rats. Burnt out and empty for three floors down, to the glassblower's."

"And who knows you're working on this? Who's paying you? Who're you working with?"

"No one, no one yet, and no one on this. By day I make ointments that fade scars and scents for Master Blaethnar."

"Who has no idea you're up to this," Tarla said confidently. Master Blaethnar liked to own people down to their last clipped fingernail, and make sure that everything they had or did enriched his coffers, or Master Blaethnar's strong silent men with big knives and bigger fists saw to changing attitudes in blunt, painful haste.

The young alchemist nodded unhappily. In Port Vale, gaining a hold over someone was what one did—but surrendering one was never pleasant. "If you tell him…"

"You're doomed. So the price of my silence is more answers, alchemist. When you have your soothing tinctures, what then? What're you doing this for? Or rather, you're doing it for coin, of course, but how will you make that coin? Sell the tinctures to who, and for what?"

Faelren regarded her with unhappy eyes.

"If I tell you…"

"You live," Tarla told him, as softly and gently as ever. Commanding this man, she was discovering, gave great pleasure.

This must be what power felt like. Racing through her like a rising warmth, making her feel she should be striding grandly with a cloak swirling in her wake as even Valearr gave ground with respect on their faces, and a little fear. No wonder the likes of Kethur behaved so foolishly.

"I already sell my earlier, lesser efforts to some of the gladiators. If these on the table work, and quell all pain, and I sell them to just one gladiator at a time…"

"Entirely free of pain, they may last a little longer in the fray—and if you've wagered on them…"

"Yes," the alchemist almost whispered, looking down at his hands. His palms were as dark as the backs of his hands, Tarla noticed…and that wasn't all she noticed.

"Clever," she granted, and without pause added, "but what *isn't* clever is trying to get out that vial you're so slyly reaching for, and doing something to me with it. *Stop*—or die."

Faelren stopped. "I—I wasn't—"

"Of *course* not, and I wasn't born yestermorn. Yet I see a bowgun yonder that's cocked and loaded and ready to slay me—or would be, if you hadn't put the quarrel in *over* the guard. You don't know how to use a bowgun, do you?"

The alchemist looked miserable.

"I—no. No."

"And it looks as shiny and new as if it came out of oilcloths this very day."

"It…did."

"So, you're expecting trouble, but as I'm not it, tell me now: just who is going to come up here after you?"

"Oh, we're already here," said a gleefully baleful voice from beneath Tarla's feet—as a long, slim blade thrust up through one of the many lightless gaps in the floorboards less than the thickness of a hand from the inside of her left foot.

With a startled *eeep*, Tarla sprang onto the table. The alchemist shrank hastily back into a corner as heavy-booted men thundered up the attic stairs. Tarla thrust her knife back into its sheath and leaped for the windowsill, caught the frame with frantic fingers, and—

Froze as a cold and unfamiliar voice snapped, "Jump, woman, and you'll be wearing two crossbow quarrels as you go down. Face first onto the alleyway cobbles, most likely. It would be wiser to turn around. Slowly."

So this is what it feels like, when the taletellers prate of "the icy hand of fear closing around your heart." Tarla found her throat as dry as old bone in an instant. Swallowing hard, she found herself looking into faces that grinned coldly, or sneered, or just measured her with a lack of expression that was somehow hostile indeed.

"Ah, you're *that* playpretty-for-hire. I hear you bested Carzath Kethur earlier," said one of the expressionless men. He looked older than the rest, and was the only one not holding a ready crossbow aimed right at her.

"So you hear much, and swiftly," Tarla replied. That meant this had to be someone with coin to spare, to pay for what people in the worst alleys—like the one she'd fought Kethur in—saw. "If it's not too bold a question, who are you?"

"Tarla Beltarth, I am called Gursk Gurdanth," came the flat reply. "I see you've heard of me. And this—" He nodded at the second-oldest man, the one holding the fanciest crossbow. "—is Indurs Heskor. We're here to relieve this young fool of an alchemist of his work, but it's always nice to take care of loose ends that helpfully present themselves. Overbold sneak-thief tries to rob alchemist and tastes the crossbow she didn't know he had...a touching tragedy."

Tarla couldn't keep dismay off her face. She was facing two of the most fell men in Port Vale, true Master Thieves in every sense of the title. Crime lords who commanded shadow armies of alleyknives, the men who murdered in the streets daily as well as nightly.

"Yes," Gurdanth said pleasantly, as if he was reading her thoughts, "you *are* doomed."

Crouched on the windowsill, Tarla said nothing. He was so right. Three crossbow quarrels could be through her in an instant.

"Yet your doom could come years from now, if you do the right things," he added.

"And what might those right things be?" Tarla asked, trying to make her voice calm and level, and almost succeeding.

"You have agility enough to find your way into the unguarded upper windows of grand mansions in our fair city," Gurdanth replied, "and looks enough to be memorable. Especially when you wear a mask of, say, flame-hued silk."

"You want me to be *seen* stealing?"

"Yes. While the lengthened fights made possible by our capable alchemist here enable bolder thefts at the homes of the wealthiest bettors. You show yourself to the passing public and the servants—while we do the real thieving."

"So the mayor's armsmen will be seeking me, not you. That doesn't sound like a doom years off," Tarla said dryly. "And bone white, not flame silk, *please*."

Gurdanth chuckled. "Bone white it is, and I have every confidence in your agility, my dear. And your wits. I'm even prepared to be generous."

"Oh?" Tarla asked softly, dreading what might come next.

"So that you have the leisure to properly scout and prepare for our first theft, which will happen the moment Faelren here has his painquench ready, we will take care of Kethur for you. Permanently."

"That is generous," Tarla agreed. "And so that I may begin

scouting, where is this first theft to take place?"

Gurdanth's smile was as sudden as it was sunny. "Why, at the home of Mayor Blythorn Blackwick, of course."

FAELREN DIDN'T EVEN GLANCE UP AS SHE CAME THROUGH the gable window. Perhaps he was getting used to seeing her in the skin-tight, dark-red leather thieving suit and bone white mask she had insisted on wearing during her outings. Or perhaps he was just concentrating very hard, biting his lip as he peered into the bubbling depths of a steaming flask that was clouding over and giving off a *very* evil smell.

He knew she was there, though. As he scribbled a note and reached for a small wooden bowl to add just a few grains of reddish-brown ithkel powder to the brew in the flask, and turned the wheel that would raise it a little farther from the brazier's heat, he asked rather distantly, "How'd it go?"

Tarla deliberately stopped, putting her curvaceous self right in front of his nose as she leaned over with one long arm to steal a swallow of his broth from the mug the black man was never far from. Ugh; he'd let it go cold. "Not as bad as the Mayor's place," she told him. "Only two guards had crossbows, and neither could have hit a horse rearing right in front of them. Gurdanth's dogs seemed pleased with their haul, and I—"

She reached into her left boot and drew a slender glass bottle out. "—plucked this from a *covered* sideboard—never *seen* so many bottles, all together—before I got out. Blade Sea Black; want some?"

The alchemist blinked, lifted his head from his notes, saw what was right in front of him and recoiled in an embarrassed storm of blinkings and ahems and hand-wavings, then managed to stammer, "Y-yes, I would. Very much. Ah, thank you."

Surprisingly, Faelren kept his eyes on hers after that, until he asked suddenly. "Is…is it hard for you, doing this?" He sipped cautiously from the bottle, gasped, shook his head as if he'd been slapped, and handed it back. "Strong stuff." Watching her smile in agreement and take a swig, he asked, "Seriously, Tarla; how are you holding up? What's this, now, the twelfth robbery?"

"Sixteenth," she replied with a shrug. "And I'm doing well enough, for now. Just the one scar." Involuntarily, the alchemist glanced down at her leather-clad left side—but that drew his eyes perilously close to other places, and he whirled hastily away.

"I don't have much choice, do I?" Tarla added, following him and reaching around him with the bottle to offer it again. The alchemist stiffened as she pressed against him, her arm around them both, then shifted nervously from foot to foot, almost snatching the bottle and putting a stumblingly-swift two strides between them as he drank.

"I'm—" The strong drink made him gasp again, and swipe tears from his eyes with the back of his sleeve before blurting, "I'm working as fast as I can, I promise you! I—it's not easy. The paralytic's done, but the vapor…"

Tarla nodded sympathetically, grabbed his hand, and shook it as if they were two merchants closing a deal, trying to ease his embarrassment. He really wasn't used to being close and easy with women.

"I understand. Believe me, Jalandar, I know you're doing your best, and that these things take time. I can hold out."

To save her skin, Tarla needed to expose the Master Thieves, or better, bring them down.

So between thefts, she and Faelren were working desperately to create a sleep-inducing gas and a paralytic she could coat her weapons and some of her fingernails with, so she could take down

Gurdanth and Heskor and their armies of men. Or rather, the alchemist worked, and she fetched him all the strange ingredients he thought he'd need, not to mention food and drink and clean chamber pots.

For her part, Tarla did just as she was told by Gurdanth, and tried to count and name and learn the dwelling-places of every one of the alleyknives and skulkers who worked for the two Master Thieves. When the time came, she'd have to know every last one of them; her life might very well depend on it.

After all, it only took one knife...

Or crossbow quarrel. She rubbed at the still-healing scar on her side. As usual, it had started to *itch* abominably.

There was a muffled crash from the littered table. Faelren slumped to the floor, the bottle of Blade Sea Black he'd just set down toppling in his wake. Tarla snatched it up and put it back before too much spilled, then looked down at the alchemist—just as a whiff of what was bubbling up out of the flask caught her in the face.

She staggered back, her legs giving way, as the attic rafters swam into dimness above her, and everything went...dark.

"OHHH..." FAELREN GROANED, CLUTCHING HIS HEAD. HIS black skin looked oddly pale.

Tarla tugged him up into a sitting position—and kissed him thoroughly. "You *did it!*"

"Ah, whaaa?"

She plucked the flask off the table, waved it under his nose, and caught him before his eyes finished rolling up and he started to sag again.

"It *works!*" she hissed while lowering him gently to the floor.

"Sleeping gas! You've done it, Jalandar!"

The alchemist, senseless again, his mouth gaping open like a fish, stared unseeing at the attic rafters and made no reply.

"I just hope you remember everything when you wake up," Tarla added as she searched out a cork to stopper the flask. Most of its contents had bubbled away while she'd been asleep atop the snoring alchemist, but hopefully enough remained that she'd be able to go to war.

"Let your dooms come first, Master Thieves," she whispered, so softly that only she heard herself, and put the flask carefully down in a corner, behind the dusty litter of old furniture lining those walls. "Oh, let it be so!"

TONIGHT, TARLA HAD A RARE EVENING OFF, FOR THE Mayor's armsmen buzzed about the streets like angry bees in the wake of their six bold snatchings in as many nights, searching the city for long-haired women in bone white masks and red leather, swinging in high windows and disappearing before any could lay hands on them. Gurdanth had no need for her tonight.

Tarla shrugged. If this worked, he'd soon have need for nothing and no one. She'd cached darts and knives coated with the paralytic—*selver*, Jalandar called it—on several rooftops, and covered all of her weapons with it. The effects didn't last long, but in a fight or when fleeing, their fleeting efficacy was an eternity. The sleepbringer gas didn't bring sleep for long either, but it hit hard, and that might be all she needed.

She'd been stealing crossbows whenever she saw the chance, from the Mayor's armsmen as well as from everyone else in Port Vale whose defenses weren't strong enough, and had assembled a small arsenal of those, too, on a nearby rooftop, under a tarp she covered with dead pigeons every time she left it, to dissuade the curious. There weren't likely to be too many people curious enough to risk their necks scaling that steep a roof, but after all, this *was* Port Vale; she wasn't the only one who came stealing in through windows and onto balconies high above the unforgiving cobbles.

Yes, tonight would host her first move, and very soon now. Gurdanth might be taking it off to wallow on silken pillows with some drunken doxy, but he'd left firm orders to keep his men hard at work, in a warehouse very few in the city knew belonged to him, and one that her rooftop that housed the crossbow arsenal overlooked.

Which meant it was time to go moonlighting. She'd gotten her breath back from spiking all the doors Gurdanth's unwitting men had already barred from the inside, and from climbing up here, so it was time to…

"Let the fun begin," Tarla murmured, and rose from cocking and loading the last crossbow—fourteen of them in all, now all pointing carefully out over the rooftops—to grab her swing-line. She tested it carefully to make sure no one had cut or untied it, or otherwise made mischief…no one had.

She drew in a deep breath, settled her now-notorious mask securely into place, and told the absent alchemist, "Wish me luck, Jalandar!" Then she took two swift running strides, and *kicked.*

Off from the tiles and out over the dark street, the air rushing softly past her ears to a clumsy but fairly quiet landing on the roof, above the heads of the alleyknives busily crating the bodies of villa guards and an armsman or two they'd slain. Amid all the grain sacks and other crated warehouse cargo, the corpses would be shipped out of Port Vale to somewhere less incriminating. Yes, it was time to clean up incriminating leavings and make room for the new.

Tarla smiled wickedly and dropped the first flask down the warehouse chimney. And then the second.

Then she crawled across the warehouse roof to her first oil-soaked bundle, and set to work with her striker and dry curled bark. A spark became a flame almost instantly, and she got the bundle well and truly going before lifting the tile she'd prised out and put back in place three nights ago—and shoved the flaming bundle of oil-soaked rags and twigs down into the warehouse, to rain down on a great heap of sacks of grain.

She tossed a few more flasks after it, angling her arm to fling them well to the sides, then put the tile back down and headed for the next bundle as the first shouts arose from below.

Two more bundles, and it would be time to clamber down from roof to wagon-top and then street, and get back over and up to her waiting crossbows. They'd only be able to force open the one door she could readily fire at, but she didn't want them escaping too soon.

"Your dooms could come a few moments from now, dogs," she murmured, "if you do the wrong things."

These would not be pleasant deaths, but then, how many throats had these ruthless men slit, how many lives had they drenched in fear, how many savings had they seized? "Is the ratcatcher evil, who kills the rats that spread horrid, slaying disease?" she murmured as she dropped another lit bundle into the warehouse. "I think *not*."

Smoke curled out of a score or more gaps in the walls, and from under roof tiles, and the shouts were growing fearful. Heavy thudding crashes arose, as the great beams serving as door-bars were hurled aside, and doors groaned under desperate shoulder-rending charges. Groaned, and bulged, and held.

In a moment, they'd think of using a door-bar beam as a ram… but that moment was all it took Tarla to finish sowing fire and drop from the roof onto one of the three wagons drawn up along its wall. Usually bored guards lounged by these wagons, but they had all fled now—not to try to aid their fellows trapped inside, but off in great haste to take word to their masters.

Tarla smiled as she swarmed down to the street and sprinted across it. She happened to know that Gurdanth had just stored several coffers of gems in this warehouse, that would be taken to purchase large cargoes that would enrich both Master Thieves mightily in the days ahead, particularly when brought into a city experiencing some temporary shortages of those very goods—thanks to the carefully-targeted thefts of men working for those same two Master Thieves.

So men *would* come running, to try to rescue those gems—and it was those targets she was after.

They were no fools; after just a few quarrels from on high they'd know where they were being attacked from, and she'd have to relocate in swift haste. Panting her way to the waiting bows, she checked the lines she'd strung to adjacent rooftops one more time. Doomed she might still be—but not, if she could do anything to prevent it, this night.

Not before Gursk Gurdanth paid a high price for forcing her to become his decoy. The man was a fat pig, and sooner or later, pigs that got fat enough got butchered for the table.

It was past Gurdanth's time to be served up on a platter.

She'd regained breath enough that her hands no longer trembled, and down below, men were arriving down side-alleys at a run. She peered hard, looking for hardened faces she knew. It was too much to hope that either Master Thief would put in a personal appearance—when there were public skirmishes or debacles, they were somehow never to be found—but if their most capable hands paid the price…

She started seeing faces she knew. Calmly she took up a crossbow and laid it across her knees until she was ready to aim carefully at a good shot.

Now. She sent death hissing into an unsuspecting neck, flung herself flat on the roof, and reached for the next loaded weapon.

"Doombringer am I," she whispered in sudden, fierce exultation.

"TARLA," GURSK GURDANTH SNAPPED, "I'VE A SPECIAL TASK for you."

Did he know, or suspect, and so was sending her to certain death?

Tarla swallowed, knowing she looked afraid, but glad of it. If he noticed the barest hint of glee, she was doomed right here and now.

Oh, but the two Master Thieves were icily furious.

She hadn't slain many, but the fire and the uproar it had caused had brought the Mayor's armsmen in swarms, and they'd fought the alleyknives—every last one of whom had been captured or killed.

And under Mayor Blackwick's gentle hand, captives had a way of talking.

Which meant that not only were the Master Thieves' plans in disarray; they now lacked warehouse, contents—including those gems—and almost two score men, they had also been forced to go into hiding, where they would remain until Blackwick was gone from office or had been bought off—or was dead.

When Gurdanth had sent for her, she'd wondered if she was reporting to her own cruel execution—but no, it seemed his rage and lost coins had goaded him to send her and some of his surviving alleyknives on suicidally unlikely-to-succeed snatch-thefts, like this one.

As he snapped out instructions, Tarla listened glumly. Gurdanth *was* desperate. She would have to succeed spectacularly at the nigh-impossible, or die.

"Go," he said coldly, and she nodded, turned, and went.

THE ONE GOOD FEATURE OF GURDANTH'S PLAN WAS THAT he'd ordered Tarla to serve as a distraction in relative isolation from his other forces. In her distinctive mask and leathers, she was to leap boldly from balcony to balcony above a feast where wealthy Valearr ate, laughing and taunting the gawking diners below, while a small band of alleyknives swarmed some guards and servants in a distant corner of a sprawling, palatial villa.

Which meant that, unless Gurdanth had reliable spies among the servants waiting tables, she could abbreviate her performance and flee.

Which is exactly what she did.

Watchful hired swords stood around the walls of the feasting hall, bodyguards with little to do. At her first appearance, they charged to the stairs that led up to her. Tarla gave the wealthy feasters in their finery one long peal of mocking laughter, and made for the nearest window.

Swiftly enough that she got away from the walled villa grounds with her life, hotly pursued by a lumbering band of heavily armed mercenaries.

They pounded along the streets as she leaped from steep and dangerous roof to steep and dangerous roof, annoyingly persistent, even when she headed into dark and dangerous areas of the city, where lanterns were few and sharp knives lurked in the darkness.

By the time she got within sight of the alchemist's attic, her pursuers had dwindled slightly in numbers, but those that remained were as determined, as cruelly grinning, and as large and well-armed as ever.

She sought the leaning gable in haste that almost killed her, in her hurry to get through the window before the hired swords could run around the last corner into the alley below and see where she vanished to.

And she'd barely fetched up panting on the floor, with a startled Faelren cursing and rising from his stool to make sure his sudden visitor was her and not some other crazed woman who leaped around Port Vale rooftops by night, when they heard the crash of doors yielding several floors below, and heavy boots mounting the stairs.

Tarla rolled her eyes and struggled to her feet, breathing hard and drawing her knives, but the alchemist raised his hand in a gesture that would have been more reassuring if it hadn't trembled so much, turned back to littered-as-ever table, and started lining up vials.

The last door crashed open just below them, and men erupted up the stairs with hard glares and swords up—and Jalandar Faelren greeted them with vials hurled hard and accurately into their faces.

They howled and slashed out viciously—but blindly—with their blades, and the alchemist gave ground with a whimper. They hacked the air as they charged in the direction of that sound—but before they could drive the frightened man back against a wall and butcher him against it, Tarla got to them, caught sword arms behind the elbows, and ran, hard and low.

Steering the foremost sightless pair—who tried to rid themselves of her unwanted grasp by turning and hewing, but succeeded in carving each other just above Tarla's ducking head.

And by then, Tarla had rushed the two mercenaries to the window she'd come in by, and slammed them against its sill.

They were big, tall men, and struggling, twisting to lay about them in all directions with their sharp steel, so the sill caught them low, and it was relatively easy to rush up their legs, ram a fist where it does no man much good, and keep shoving.

One man exited the room precipitously, with a startled shout, and then the other. Tarla didn't wait to hear the dull, wet thuds of their deaths in the alley below, but whirled back in time to intercept a slashing sword that would have sent many vials flying. The mercenary on the other end of that blade could see dimly, and was driving Faelren back; Tarla shoved the alchemist under the table and parried desperately, wondering if she'd have strength enough to hold back this third hiresword's blade for long. She had to get the table between them…

Whereupon the alchemist surprised her by coming back out from under the table, snatching a vial, and smashing it against the side of the mercenary's face. The man went down with a shriek, and Faelren snatched two more vials and flung them into the faces of the last two mercenaries.

Who staggered, sidestepped wildly, and crashed to the floor, dazed and rapidly falling into slumber.

When Tarla finished feeding the window, she turned and found Jalandar Faelren giving her a tentative but widening grin.

She gathered the blushing alchemist into her arms and murmured, "I believe we've become trusted friends. Thank you for my life, Jalandar."

SIX NIGHTS LATER BROUGHT A LIGHT RAIN, AND A FIRM disagreement between Gurdanth and Heskor over a theft—but Gurdanth went ahead with it anyway, using only his seven remaining alleyknives, and Tarla.

Or rather, *not* Tarla. The moment she was well away from his lair, she slipped away. Then she proceeded cautiously to where the robbery was to take place, but only as far as a nearby rooftop that afforded a good view. She had a bad feeling about this scheme.

And her instincts were soon proven right. Armsmen streamed

out of side alleys, leaving the alleyknives only one escape: straight back the way they'd come. As they turned and fled, Tarla saw more armsmen waiting in side alleys along the route. Gurdanth's snatch team had run straight into a trap set by the Mayor.

The Master Thief had chosen his lair well; if he kept silent and within, it would be hard for the Mayor's forces to find him before he slipped away through the cellars.

But if he thought the cellar route was cut off...

Tarla raced from roof to roof faster than she'd leaped in a long time, taking one of the tavern-slop-chute ways down into the cellars and coming up past a startled bodyguard to burst in on Gurdanth in his bedchamber, panting, "Mayor's armsmen, swarming up through the cellars! They've found us!"

Cursing, Gurdanth snatched up a dagger from the table, banged out through a door, and was gone.

Shouts and the clash of swords were coming from rooms all around the bedchamber, so she made for the room's large chimney. The fire had gone out, but the shaft was still hot and slick with soot—and when she emerged from the next hearth, on the floor above, she was caked with it.

And had so much of it on her slippered feet that she slipped and slid—straight into an astonished armsman. She punched him in the throat before he could do more than start to curse, then ducked back into the chimney and climbed higher.

"My doom may come a little sooner than I'd like," she panted as she came out into a thankfully deserted room, and made for its window.

Yet for once, it seemed, luck was with her. There was neither thief nor armsman in sight to stop her as she fled out into the night.

ALL AROUND HER, PORT VALE WAS IN AN UPROAR AS TARLA made for the attic. Armsmen were everywhere, rounding up thief after thief from what was left of Gurdanth's and Heskor's bands. The Mayor's men seemed to know exactly who worked for the two Master Thieves.

By the time Tarla slipped through the window, squads of armsmen with lanterns were in the streets just below. Faelren barely had time to greet her and ask what was afoot when they heard doors being flung open down below, and feet on the stairs. Again.

With a sigh, Tarla looked back out the window, peering at rooftops to plan her best escape—and then looked back at the frightened alchemist. If he got out on a roof, he'd fall to his death even if there was no one after him and he had all the time in the world. And she'd remember his face, fall or be left behind here, forever.

She started to curse—and the last door burst open, and several large, heavily-armed, and glowering armsmen ascended the stairs, visors down and shields up. Behind them were two men Tarla recognized with more than a little astonishment.

The first was Indurs Heskor. The second was Blythorn Blackwick, the Mayor of Port Vale.

"Tarla Beltarth," he greeted her crisply, then looked at the alchemist. "Jalandar Faelren."

Tarla and Jalandar both stared back at him, dumbfounded.

The Mayor smiled. "From time to time it becomes necessary to curb the worst excesses of Port Vale's criminal element. So, one makes deals." He and Heskor exchanged smiles.

Then Blackwick turned back to Tarla and Faelren. "I keep the city in my grip by treating the right people properly. Beheadings for some, tortures for others—and some useful individuals, I employ. For the greater good of Port Vale, of course. And pay handsomely, for I have found that loyalty has a price. A high price."

He spilled the contents of a purse full of gold coins out into his palm, and set them on the table in front of Tarla. Then put another purse-full in front of Faelren. "I find I have need for a peerless alchemist and an acrobatic and daring roof-climber. What do you say?"

Tarla thrust aside her amazement long enough to put a smile on her face and reach for the coins. It was her best false smile, because if she didn't fool this cold, shrewd snake of a Mayor, she'd last no longer than the crime lords who'd crossed him.

So when she did move against him—as she knew she'd have to, sooner or later—it would she who triumphed, and Blackwick who fell.

She would have to be very, very patient, and even more cunning than the man now smiling softly back at her.

Not to mention very, very careful.

For if I do the right things, my doom may come years from now…

THE BRIDGE

LARRY CORREIA

LAVRO COULD HAVE SAT IN THE SHADE OF A NEARBY TREE, but Droth had blessed this day with miserable heat and a merciless sun, so he gave thanks for his sunburn and discomfort, and remained standing in the middle of the bridge.

He did loosen the straps of his armor a bit, so he wouldn't boil in his own sweat. Droth taught through suffering, but it would be difficult to fulfill his guard duty if he became delirious from heat exhaustion. Summer in the Free Kingdoms was nothing like the northern wastes where his clan wandered. This place was green instead of grey. The water in the river below wasn't choked with ice. It was a good thing this land was so plagued with perpetual warfare, otherwise those who lived here would be in danger of becoming soft.

This portion of the Serenth River was sluggish. The shores on both sides of the bridge were mud and reeds, so Lavro was continually bitten and stung by hungry insects all day. At night, it was cool, but that was when the beast men liked to sneak up and try to murder him.

Praise Droth.

It had been many days since he had spoken to anyone, not that Lavro cared much for speaking even when there were others around. Most things a drothmal wanted to communicate were better shared with steel than words. He had been all by himself since the rest of the mercenaries had fled.

Lavro the drothmal did not flee. He had accepted a contract, and would fulfill his duty until relieved or killed. Mercenaries had been hired to hold this bridge because one petty lord was feuding with another petty lord, and someone somewhere had seen this crossing on a map and decided it might be of strategic importance. Sure, they'd camped here for weeks without seeing so much as a single refugee, in a forsaken part of the Free Kingdoms abandoned by civilization and reclaimed by nature and monsters, where they had been neglected, unsupplied, and forgotten…but a promise was a promise.

So, long after the others had left, Lavro continued guarding the bridge. He slept beneath it so that he would wake up should anyone attempt to cross. The hardest part of this duty was foraging for food in the reeds while still keeping an eye on the crossing. It was hard for a three hundred pound drothmal to find sufficient nourishment in such a small area. He was very tired of eating frogs. If he never ate another damned frog again, that would be fine by him. Especially these miserable, stinking swamp frogs that tasted like mud.

Praise Droth.

Boredom was just another form of blessed suffering, but Lavro couldn't help but hope that if the war was over, eventually someone would remember to tell him.

COULD IT BE? LAVRO LIFTED A HAND TO SHIELD HIS EYES from the glare of the setting sun. Someone was approaching his bridge. At first he thought it was just another vicious beast man, coming to throw rocks at him, but this one wasn't running on all fours or howling for his blood. It walked like a normal, boring, civilized traveler.

The man was tall for an atlan, but still tiny compared to Lavro. He wore simple, baggy clothing, a straw hat, and carried a large traveling pack. Despite looking like a farmer, the man wore a pair of swords through an orange sash on his waist. The stranger also had a confident walk. He certainly didn't carry himself like a refugee. Lavro knew refugees. You couldn't work as a mercenary in the Free Kingdoms for long without becoming very familiar with the look of refugees. They were always either shocked, skittish, or defeated. This man was confident, and walked with purpose.

Excited, Lavro adjusted the straps of his armor, and dusted off his steel breastplate so that he would look respectable. Since he'd been wallowing in mud and insects for a month, that wasn't very respectable at all, but Lavro put his great sword over one shoulder, drew himself to his full seven foot-height, and tried to be as intimidating as possible.

"Hello," said the man.

"You will not pass!" Lavro bellowed.

"Oh..." the man stopped and looked around. There really wasn't much to see, except for a rickety old bridge and a whole lot of mud. He lifted the straw hat and wiped his face with one sleeve. Lavro was not good at guessing atlan ages, but this one was no longer young, but not yet old, though his long hair was turning grey. "Why?"

"I have orders to hold this bridge. Only the forces of Lord Wainbrook may cross here."

"I don't know who that is." He pointed at the Donarzheis

Mountains on the other side of the river. "I need to go there."

"Well, you can't cross here," Lavro said with grim finality. "If you try, I will bleed you."

"Bleed? Interesting choice of words."

"Whether you live or die is the will of Droth. But when I hit somebody with this sword, they usually die. More often than not."

The man nodded thoughtfully. "That would be terribly inconvenient. Do you mind if I have a seat while we debate this?"

"There is no debate. Those are my orders." But the atlan had already taken off his heavy pack, placed it in the dirt road, and sat on it. As long as he didn't try to cross, Lavro didn't mind the company. "Fine."

"What a miserable day." The atlan paused to swat a mosquito on his neck. "Normally, your people are as deathly pale as your tundra. I didn't know you could get so red in the sun. May I ask your name, drothmal?"

"I am Lavro, son of Ulm."

"A pleasure to meet you. I am Decimus." He held out his straw hat. "If you let me use your bridge, in trade, I will give you my hat. It would make that sunburn far more bearable."

"We learn through suffering," Lavro muttered, though he wished he'd brought a hat. He'd been so bored he tried making one out of reeds, but given up when he discovered his large fingers were no good for weaving. "There is another bridge ten miles that way." He nodded downstream, toward the village of Korval.

"I'd rather not. I am on an important quest."

Lavro didn't care. A contract had been made. "No."

"What if I were to offer you a real bribe? I have money. I could probably pay you more than you accepted to guard this bridge, just to look the other way for a moment."

It wasn't about money. Lavro shook his head.

"I suppose I could swim across."

Lavro shrugged. His orders didn't say anything about intercepting swimmers. He'd only seen a couple of scaled gillcutters swim by the entire time he'd been here, so he might even make it.

Decimus looked at the river suspiciously. "Or, I could just fight you and get it over with. Only killing you over something so trivial seems like a waste. I will take the middle path and beat you soundly. I will do my best not to kill or maim you, and this way you will learn a valuable lesson about etiquette."

The drothmal snorted. The little atlan could try. Life was cheap in the Free Kingdoms. "Come on then."

"Very well, Lavro, son of Ulm." He stood up. "It is nothing personal, but I really do have important things to do." He didn't even bother to draw either of his little swords as he started across the bridge. Decimus didn't seem intimidated. In fact, he seemed rather calm about the whole thing.

"I'm not kidding, atlan."

"You don't strike me as the joking type, drothmal." Decimus stopped a few feet away, bent at the waist, and bowed respectfully. "Shall we begin?"

Lavro lifted his sword high overhead, roared his battle cry, and brought the blade crashing down with the fury of an avalanche.

Decimus moved aside and let the blade embed itself deeply into the wood. *Nobody's that fast*— Before Lavro could tug his sword free, Decimus stepped on the steel with his sandal and trapped it. Lavro didn't even see the punch coming, but the small man hit him in the chest so surprisingly hard that Lavro found himself sailing back through the air. He landed flat on his back several feet away.

The drothmal clambered back to his feet. The knuckles of the atlan's fist had left dents in the steel. "What manner of magic was that?" he snarled.

"No magic. Just focus…You lost your sword." Decimus grunted as he pulled the heavy blade free. "This isn't a proper sword. This is a log splitter some delusional smith welded a handle onto." He lifted it in both hands and tossed it toward Lavro.

Lavro caught it by the grip, and spun the sword to show that he meant business. "I was not ready. Now I am ready."

"Good. It's hard to tell what a drothmal is thinking with such a cat-like face, but I thought you remained unconvinced. Let us try this again."

It angered him that Decimus hadn't even bothered to draw his own blade. That seemed incredibly insulting. Lavro roared and swung his sword, this time from the shoulder, so fast it whistled through the air. Decimus ducked beneath it. Lavro recovered and brought it back around, hacking at the atlan's legs, but this time Decimus jumped over it.

"Fight me, cowar—" but Decimus stepped inside the next swing, caught Lavro's wrist with a grip as hard as iron, and somehow, the next thing Lavro knew he was flipping through the air. This time when he hit the bridge, it knocked the air from his lungs.

Praise Droth, that hurt, Lavro thought as he desperately got back to his feet, gasping.

"I find your fighting stance fascinating. I will call it Lumbering Ox style," Decimus said. "May I be on my way now?"

Lavro didn't bother to respond, he just hurled himself at Decimus, counting on his extra mass and weight to crush the atlan. Decimus caught his arm again and rolled Lavro over his hip, using his momentum to hurl him across the bridge again. He hit in a clang of metal and a rattle of chain.

"You do not give up easily, do you?" Decimus asked as Lavro got up again.

"Easily? I do not give up period."

"It's only a bridge," Decimus said.

"It is my duty." Lavro was wary this time, and he led with the tip of his sword. He would use his reach advantage to impale the obnoxious atlan. He thrust, and was glad to see that Decimus actually had to move back. Lavro had him now.

Decimus snap kicked his sword aside. The next kick hit him in the thigh, which caused his leg to buckle, and the next spinning kick hit him in the teeth. For just a moment, Lavro saw a cloud of spit and road dust floating in the sunlight, but then he was somersaulting through the air again. The drothmal found himself face down on his precious bridge, bleeding onto the wood.

"Now may I pass?"

Shaking, dizzy, Lavro got up and looked for his sword. "No." He couldn't find his damned sword. Decimus offered it to him helpfully. Annoyed, Lavro snatched it. "You will have to kill me."

"I respect your dedication," Decimus said as he drew his sword. It was a simple, thin blade. The atlan could have just run him through while he was dazed, but he waited for Lavro to collect himself. "Are you sure you want to do this?"

Lavro was young, but he was no stranger to war. He'd survived many battles. He'd fought monsters, Dark beasts, and other soldiers, but he'd never fought anyone this skilled. There was no doubt Decimus would kill him.

He attacked anyway.

Decimus moved effortlessly around the blow. His counter-attack stung Lavro's arm. Lavro crashed forward, desperate, and Decimus slashed him in the neck. The drothmal gasped in pain, and flinched away, touching one hand to his throat. It came away clean. Both times Decimus had struck him with the flat of his blade. "Are you trying to mock me?"

"I'm trying to convince you to step aside."

"I'll be convinced when I'm dead." Lavro brought his sword up, but Decimus smacked it aside with his smaller blade, and with his other hand stabbed two fingers hard into Lavro's wrist. The great sword dropped from his suddenly numb hand. Before he could do anything else, the tip of Decimus' sword was pressed beneath his chin. He could feel the steel against his jugular.

He was doomed. "Praise Droth," Lavro whispered, totally prepared for his spirit to move on to Lensae.

Decimus frowned, stepped back, and sheathed his sword. "Fascinating."

"Aren't you going to kill me?"

"I'll decide in the morning," the atlan muttered as he walked off the bridge and returned to his travelling pack. Decimus pulled out his bedroll.

"What are you doing?"

"What does it look like I'm doing? Making camp here for the night. Or is that against your arbitrary rules as well, drothmal?"

"Just keep it on that side of the bridge, and I don't care what you do, atlan."

THE FOOD DECIMUS WAS COOKING SMELLED MUCH BETTER than the raw frogs and berries Lavro had eaten for lunch. Because of the visitor, he'd not been able to leave his post long enough to forage for supper. His stomach ached with hunger.

Praise Droth.

Decimus squatted next to his small fire, checking the trio of small animals roasting on spits. "Are you hungry, Lavro?"

"It is not unbearable."

"Oh, do all drothmal stomachs rumble so loudly they can be heard from ten feet away?"

"It is not safe to travel these roads alone, atlan. These little kingdoms are always at war, but this part is worse than most. Your fire will surely attract monsters. Only a fool would be alone here."

"You're alone. Are you a fool?"

Probably. But Lavro dismissed those thoughts of weakness. "I am mighty Lavro, son of Ulm, hired to guard this bridge, and I will not shirk my duty. Why are you here?"

Decimus ignored his question. "I've got plenty of food. I caught these rabbits along the road earlier," he said as he turned the sticks.

The atlan had no bow or sling. "How?"

"By hand," Decimus said. "It is easy, really. You just need to be faster than the rabbit."

Lavro had a hard enough catching the damned frogs. "Where I am from, we use spears. I am a great hunter of mighty beasts… Delicious, tasty beasts."

Decimus took one of the rabbits from the fire and tossed it to Lavro. The drothmal caught it, fumbled, and managed to burn his fingers.

Praise Droth.

He thought it might have been the best meal he'd ever had.

AFTER SUPPER, DECIMUS HAD SAT CROSS-LEGGED, STRAIGHT backed, and eyes closed for a very long time. Lavro had thought it was some sort of strange manner of prayer, but Decimus had called it centering, and then politely shushed him, saying he needed to focus. Lavro watched him carefully the whole time, to make sure this wasn't some manner of trick.

However, once Decimus had finished his centering, he'd gotten into this bedroll, wished him a good night, and promptly gone to sleep. The man snored like an orog. He thought about bashing his head in while he slept, but that seemed dishonorable. So Lavro went about his duties, lighting torches of sticks wrapped in dried reeds on both sides of the bridge, so he could see anything coming. Then he grudgingly sat and rested his back against a wooden bridge support, great sword resting across his legs. He would stay awake as long as it took for this strange man to leave him to his duty.

A few hours later, the beast men attacked.

Lavro had broken his vow and nodded off, but the instant their bare feet whispered across the wooden bridge, he woke up. The beast men should have known better. The bridge had become his whole world, and he had no patience for trespassers. As Lavro lumbered to his feet, the beast men who'd intended to quietly slit his throat realized they'd been seen, and a cry went up. The noise was answered from the reeds and surrounding trees.

He'd only ever faced a few at a time before. There were a lot of angry bellows all around the bridge. This time they'd brought their whole tribe.

A huge number of the creatures rushed, screaming, from the darkness.

They were misshapen, hideous things, dressed in rags and filth, armed with sharpened bones, sticks, and rocks. As they climbed over the edge of the bridge, Lavro swung his great sword and embedded it in the boards. A severed arm landed at his feet, and the beast man splashed into the mud with a scream.

"This is my bridge," he warned the approaching mob.

They came at him in a rush of jabbing sticks and hurled rocks. Lavro split one in half.

In the heat of the moment, Lavro had forgotten his annoying visitor. The strange atlan was probably already dead. He risked a quick glance, and sure enough, the improvised camp was covered in blood and swarming with beast men.

But then he realized all the blood was from the monsters. Decimus was spinning through their midst, sword in hand, turning and cutting so incredibly fast Lavro couldn't believe his eyes. Each strike was precise, dropping another beast man. It was like Decimus was dancing between their attacks. He had been holding back when they'd fought earlier. The sword flashed back and forth, so quickly that the blade seemed to glow.

Quicker and quicker, Decimus took down the beast men. The stupid creatures never even realized what was happening. He used their momentum against them, guiding them into each other's weapons simply by shifting his stance. Every single movement dispensed crippling injury or death, all while Decimus wore a mask of serene calm.

Lavro was fascinated by the display, but he had to pay attention to the monsters swarming the bridge. His technique was much simpler than the atlan's. Be stronger than your opponent. Hit harder. It had worked well enough for most of his life, and sweeping his sword in a wide arc sent several monsters over the side and hurled them down into the mud.

It had worked well before. Only he'd never been attacked by so many of the terrible things at once before. It wasn't working nearly as well while surrounded. A club splintered over his shoulder, and another slammed into the back of his leg. Lavro roared in pain as he cleaved through a beast man's chest.

For each one he knocked down, two more took its place. Lavro tripped over corpses. Thrown rocks clanged off his armor. One split his lip. A bone dagger pierced deep into his hip. It was incredibly painful.

Praise Droth.

Since his sword was stuck in a beast man's ribs, he grabbed the beast man who'd stabbed him by the hair, and slammed his skull against a bridge support. He was surrounded by screeching, chattering nightmares. More beast men hit him around his legs. One leaped from the rail and landed on his back, scratching at his eyes with its filthy, diseased claws. Lavro took that one by its pointy ear, yanked it off, and hurled it into the night.

But then he was hit with several more stinking bodies. Off balance, the mighty drothmal found himself on his knees, being beaten with rocks and sticks as the monsters cackled and jabbered.

Lavro wasn't afraid of dying, but eaten by beast men while guarding a bridge to nowhere was embarrassing. It was good that his clan would never know about this.

A white light was coming toward him, spinning across the bridge. Lavro realized it was the sword of Decimus just as the atlan lifted the glowing blade high overhead, then slammed it point first into the wood of the bridge.

The flash was blinding.

IT WAS LATE IN THE MORNING, AND ALREADY MISERABLY muggy and hot when Lavro, son of Ulm woke up with a throbbing headache. Every muscle in his body hurt. It felt like he was covered in bruises. It had been a very educational combat.

Praise Droth.

Sitting up took a few tries, but he managed. There was wood beneath him. He was still on his bridge. He reached up, and found that someone had bandaged his head.

Decimus sat cross-legged on the road, running a rag across the blade of his sword. "I wouldn't dignify evil with a proper burial, so I pushed all the bodies into the river and let the current take them. I didn't think it was wise to leave them out to attract scavengers."

"Fish must eat too," Lavro muttered. Maybe someone in

the village of Korval would get curious as to why there were so many beast men corpses floating past, and someone would remember he was still here. His throat was parched, but when he went for his canteen, he discovered it had a hole in it from a beast man spear. "Blast."

"I apologize for stepping onto your bridge last night, but I did not think you would mind, considering the situation." Decimus got up, went to his pack and found a wineskin. He carried it the bridge, but politely stopped before stepping onto the boards. He tossed it the last few feet so that it landed in Lavro's lap. "There you go."

Lavro glared at the wineskin suspiciously. Suffering was a blessing, but he couldn't fight again if he was dehydrated. He took it and drank greedily. The wine was much better than swamp water. He tossed the skin back when it was empty. "You saved my life."

Decimus squatted at the edge of the bridge. "Don't worry. I'm passingly familiar with the beliefs of your people. I didn't intervene until I thought you had suffered everything you could on your own. I didn't want to deprive you of the experience."

"Thank you..." It was rare to hear such wisdom from an outsider.

"I don't worship any of the Enaros, but I can respect them," the atlan continued. "Especially the one who gave the gift of challenges to this world. I'm told Droth believes in trials. My school taught that we are the sum of our trials. I spent most of my life preparing and training, then testing myself and correcting my assumptions, all to become what I am today. We're probably not that different, you and I."

Disturbingly, Lavro thought that might actually be true. "Why didn't you cross while I was unconscious?"

"That seemed dishonest."

"I have never seen anyone fight like you." It is said that the Enaros and their servants sometimes walked among the mortal world in disguise. "Are you an avatar?"

"I'm only a man."

"Then you are a wizard?"

"I am Kinjatsi."

Lavro had heard of them, mostly whispered rumors of the mystical atlan warriors who could disappear into one shadow and come out of another, or ride the winds, or stop a heart with a touch. "You don't look like you eat children."

"I haven't heard that one for a while!" Decimus laughed. "Some of our schools are more secretive than others, but I'm afraid there's nothing lurid about the source of our power, Lavro, son of Ulm. It comes from here." He touched the side of his head. "If you train hard enough, and learn to center yourself sufficiently, you can call upon energies that most warriors will never understand."

"You are an assassin." The very concept offended Lavro. Killing should be done face to face.

"Me? No. That isn't my path. It is doubtless, though, that some Kinjatsi are the deadliest assassins on Aetaltis, but there are also those who study the way of the open hand, the fist, or those who follow the path of the sword like me. There are as many styles as there are teachers now. Before the destruction of the world gates, the Atlan Alliance crossed many worlds, and we could pass freely between them. The Kinjatsi were the ones who studied the various martial traditions we came across. We collected the best and made them our own. Kinjatsi was the pure distillation of the arts of conflict."

"Sounds impressive."

"It was." Decimus sighed. "It was said that through mastering the one true path, a Kinjatsi could overcome any obstacle. Sadly, all of our grand masters and many of our practitioners were killed during the cataclysm. Techniques, feats, whole schools were lost. We have been rebuilding ever since. There have been disagreements between schools as to the true path. It has been…fractious."

"Your schools fight each other?"

"Too much. Pride has become a distraction from our search for enlightenment." Decimus didn't seem to want to talk about that further. "You should rest, drothmal." The atlan began walking toward the forest. "I will find us some more food."

Not that he wasn't starving, but that act of kindness begged the question, "Why are you helping me?"

"Because you will need to be at your best when I try to cross this bridge."

THE ATLAN WAS A STRANGE ONE, BUT LAVRO WAS GLAD FOR the company. Decimus spent the next few days hunting—he was rather efficient at it—and practicing with his sword. The Kinjatsi techniques were unlike anything he'd ever seen before. Instead of brute strength and wild attacks, they were about speed, grace, and anticipation. He would move through hundreds of complex movements, stances, and attacks, all from memory, without ever seeming to think about it.

The last straw was when Decimus took up handfuls of grass, tossed them into the air around him, drew his sword, and then cut every individual blade before any could touch the ground.

Lavro finally swallowed his pride and asked, "Could you teach me to fight like that?"

"I can teach, but I don't know if you can learn."

"I am smart."

"It isn't about being able to think, drothmal, it is about being able to *not* think. Before we can reach our true potential, a Kinjatsi must be able to clear his mind and truly think about nothing. Only then can you begin to understand everything."

"Fine." Lavro was already sitting on the bridge. He wasn't flexible enough to cross his legs, but he closed his eyes, like he'd seen Decimus do when he'd been centering, and then he thought about absolutely nothing.

He opened his eyes an hour later. "Was that sufficient?"

Decimus had gone back to working on his shelter. "Seriously? You cleared your mind of all thought that whole time?"

"Yes." Honestly, Lavro didn't see what was so difficult about it.

"Hmm…that is unexpected. It seems there is much I could learn from the drothmal." Decimus actually seemed impressed. "Stand up. Let's work on your footwork."

"My feet are fine. I want to learn to sword fight better."

"Your stance is fine for your current style, such as it is, but Lumbering Ox is insufficient to learn the way of the Kinjatsi. Now be silent and do what I do."

AFTER A WEEK OF TRAINING, LAVRO WAS JUST BEGINNING to understand how little he actually understood about the fighting arts. The Kinjatsi had taught him much, but it was obvious his teacher was becoming impatient. The bridge was Lavro's world, and now Decimus was his only friend. Soon, his friend would need to kill him so that he could continue on his mysterious mission. That seemed like a particularly profound method of suffering.

Praise Droth.

Now they built the campfire at the edge of the bridge. Lavro trusted Decimus, and knew he no longer needed to physically block the way, but it made him uncomfortable to stray too far from his duty.

The normally serene Decimus seemed sad tonight. "You are healed from your wounds, you're no longer weak from hunger, and you have improved greatly."

"You are leaving?"

"I've procrastinated too long already. Tomorrow I must continue on my way."

"You intend to cross the bridge?"

Decimus nodded as he stared into the fire.

He could have easily gone on to the next crossing. In the time he'd wasted here, he could have already reached the Donarzheis. But Droth had brought them both to this bridge for a reason.

"You have never spoken of this important quest of yours, Decimus. Why do you have to go to the haunted mountains?"

"I swore to avenge the murder of my teacher."

That was a worthy quest. "You do not seem to be in much of a hurry to get your revenge."

"That's because it was my sister who murdered him."

"Oh…"

Decimus placed another log on the fire. The smoke kept away the mosquitos. "A Kinjatsi master has a duty to his students, and the students to their master. A rival school desired a forbidden technique from an old world. Our teacher refused to share it… It is a long story. Just know there is no greater crime than treachery… I am the last of my school, and though they're all gone, my duty remains."

Lavro was a warrior. He understood perfectly well what that meant.

Which was why he was prepared to die in the morning.

Praise Droth.

He centered his mind and thought of nothing.

AT FIRST LIGHT, LAVRO OPENED HIS EYES.

"I know now why you atlans clear your heads. It isn't just for battle. After there is no noise, it is easier to think."

Decimus was already packing his gear. He didn't look pleased to be doing so, but a promise was a promise. "That's true," he agreed. "Clarity helps in all aspects of life."

Which was why Lavro had an idea. "What will you do after you get your vengeance?"

"I don't know if I'll survive. Aurelia was always the better student."

"But say you do…"

"In that unlikely event?" Decimus paused as he rolled up his blanket. "Too much has been lost as it is. Kinjatsi should be a force for good. I would rebuild my master's school."

Lavro stood up, took one of his unlit torches and stuck it into the remains of their fire. The dried reeds quickly caught. Decimus watched him curiously as Lavro carried the burning torch over to the bridge.

"Then I will be your first student."

As the two Kinjatsi walked downstream toward the next crossing, the burning bridge collapsed into the Serenth River.

ASHES OF VICTORY

ELIZABETH A. VAUGHAN

CHIEF MAGISTERIUM ADELPHUS, HEAD OF THE HIGH Council of Magisteriums of the Free Kingdom of Tegea observed the lengthening shadows along the wall of his court with both satisfaction and anticipation.

Satisfaction, because the day's petitioners had been few. Their conflicts had been resolved quickly. The scrolls and parchments recording his decisions had been handed to his clerks with alacrity. The room was clear of everything but the dusty scent of the law, the murmurs of the bailiffs at their posts, and the scratch of the styluses transcribing his orders.

Anticipation because his wife had promised a fine haunch of lamb for his evening meal, the fat well crusted with her garlic and herb rub.

Not that the Chief and eldest Magisterium of the Prince's Court of Justice would ever do less than his full duty for the day of open petitions. But perhaps there was little harm in closing the doors a trifle earlier than the norm.

He flexed his stiff fingers, preparing to signal the door clerk. 'Old Man's Creaking,' his healer had called it in a condescending tone, claiming no spell could touch it. *Well, old I might be,* Adelphus snorted softly to himself, *but not yet in my dotage.*

He lifted his gaze, catching the eye of the clerk and raising his hand—

—when the doors flew open with a *crash* that shook the dust from the ancient cast-iron chandeliers as a small group of angry dwarves invaded the room.

Adelphus had sat the high bench too many years to allow himself to display any outward, artless signs of surprise or disappointment. He folded his hands on his bench with every appearance of patience.

His oaths were to justice, not to his supper, after all.

The small crowd was vehement and loud, and the door clerks were embroiled in learning the 'whos' and the 'wherefores' of their unscheduled appearance. Adelphus elected to pull one of his law books close and study it while watching covertly. It seemed the eldest dwarf was the petitioner, and Adelphus noted the man's ink-stained hands, braided beard, rich garments, and guild symbols.

It was quite rare for dwarves to bring their disputes to the courts. They usually avoided them, resolving their issues within the law, but outside of the purview of the Enaros of Justice, with the aid of mediators or guildmasters. When they did come, it was usually as a last resort.

But he knew this particular dwarf, and searched his memory until he had a name for the face and beard. Ah, now he had it. Guildmaster Scribe Valtos Wanesa, Patriarch of the Wanesa Family…

Adelphus frowned at his book. He'd had few dealings with the gentleman, but they had all been in aid of resolving disputes between guildmembers, and all calm and reasonable. Now the elder dwarf was red-faced and furious, shaking in his wrath. Those who attended him were agitated as well. All bore various guild marks of different ranks. Whatever was at issue, it was an emotional one, and the guildmaster clearly had their support.

That did not bode well. Highly emotional matters were not easily resolved by the calm application of reason and logic.

"Stand forth," the clerk intoned, the traditional start to a case. "Stand forth, and your complaint will be heard in the name of King Polonus, who promises justice at his hand and the hand of his judges in the name of Toletren, the Enaros of Truth."

The Guildmaster stepped forward, but Adelphus didn't miss the wince at the mention of the Enaros. Given dwarven history, he was not surprised at the other man's reaction. But coming from a race that had rejected the divine nature of the Enaros, why was he standing before Adelphus' bench now?

Curious.

"State your name and your cause," the clerk continued, and the scribes close at hand started to scribble.

"I am Guildmaster Scribe Valtos Wanesa Sinarkett and I cry a charge of sacrilege against one Roncrate, adventurer, and thief." The dwarf spoke with a voice so deep as to rattle the windows.

"I—" the clerk sputtered to a halt. "Did you say 'sacrilege'?"

"I did."

Adelphus enjoyed the rare sight of his most experienced clerk struck speechless. Not that it lasted long.

The clerk cleared his throat. "I do not believe you are using the correct term," he said cautiously.

The scribes paused, their styluses poised over their parchments.

"I know full well what that word means." Guildmaster Valtos quivered with rage. "Sacrilege! Blasphemy! The desecration and profanation of our sacred relics by that worthless human trash!"

Adelphus made a point of lifting his head to catch the dwarf's eye. "Guildmaster Wanesa," he said in his calmest tone, given the delicate nature of the topic. He hadn't missed the Guildmaster's use of his Clan name. "I would point out that your people do not espouse a faith in the Enaros. Such a charge coming from you is rather…" *hypocritical,* he thought, "…inconsistent…with your people's stated beliefs."

The Guildmaster swelled up, turning an even deeper shade of red. But instead of the explosion Adelphus expected, the dwarf took a deep, angry breath. "The sacred relics date from the time before the Betrayal."

Inwardly, Adelphus flinched at the reference, as any devout follower of the Enaros would. The dwarves had turned from the Enaros upon their decision to imprison Endroren, the Enaros of Darkness, within the Deeplands, driving the dwarves from their ancient homes. All knew their disdain or worse, and the refusal of any dwarf to have dealings with divine magics.

Yet here stood a Guildmaster of a powerful clan, claiming sacrilege.

Odd.

Wanesa drew another breath in the silence of the courtroom and continued. "Roncrate looted the relics on his most recent foray into the depths, and dared to brag of it upon his return to this city. He tells the tale in low taverns, and wears the sacred pieces with whores in his lap and scavengers at his side. He refuses to return or relinquish the relics, although offered full value in gold and precious gems." The dwarf drew another breath, and planted his feet. "I cry offense under the sacrilege laws, and demand trial by combat to the death so that the sacrilege can be brought to an end."

"There is no right to trial by combat here," Adelphus said harshly. "Such has been eliminated from our Code under the reign of the late King Cramac."

Cunning flashed in the dwarf's eyes for just a moment. Adelphus suddenly got a sinking feeling in his belly. The same he'd felt as a young clerk, when he'd missed an important point of law.

"Not for this offense," Wanesa said firmly. "The current edicts of King Cramac adopted the laws under the late Queen Piyaga."

Adelphus bristled slightly and narrowed his eyes at that.

"Still," Wanesa set his shoulders, "that is a matter yet to be determined. Roncrate must answer for his crime against me and mine."

Adelphus didn't care for this turn of events, but the religious laws demanded immediate action. "Send forth the bailiffs to bring one Roncrate before this court, to answer to this charge," he instructed the clerks.

"He spends his time drinking and whoring at the Farting Oxen Inn," Wanesa announced loudly as he and his escort settled on the back benches to wait. "You'll find him there."

The clerks summoned the bailiffs, and Adelphus used the distraction wisely. He leaned over to his assistant, and lowered his voice. "See if any of the other magisterium are in their chambers, and bid them here immediately. Bring me the edicts of Queen Piyaga and King Cramac, and any scrolls that pertain to the laws of sacrilege and the rights of the infringed. Oh, and—"

The clerk paused just before he would have hurried off.

"Please send word to my wife that I won't be home for supper."

Any thought of succulent roast lamb was crushed under the weight of the law.

WHEN LORD DRAKEWYN OF NEW ERINOR MADE HIS Declaration at Talimane, he had made it clear that adventurers were to be held as honored warriors fighting against the evil forces threatening the world. In an effort to curry favor with New Erinor, many of the Free Kingdoms adopted the same stance, and Tegea was no different. But that didn't make adventurers any more or less than what they were.

Roncrate, for example, was a fitting example of the type. He was a young human, muscular and solid. Not much taller than the dwarf, really. He looked like he'd been pulled from his bed by the bailiffs, never mind that the sun was just heading into the west. His adventuring companions stood behind him, of various races and professions. The party's representative of the Enaros, holy symbol displayed prominently on a chain, looked particularly annoyed, and all of them appeared a trifle worse for wear.

Bleary-eyed, rumpled, and unshaven, Roncrate blinked up at the high bench, and then gazed about the court. "What's this all about, then? I paid for the room and the whore and—" he broke off to look at his comrades. "Were there damages? I don't remember breaking—"

"The charge is sacrilege," the clerk cut him off hastily. "Brought by—"

"*You*," Roncrate came fully awake, glaring at Guildmaster Wanesa as he came forward. "You miserable little dwarf—"

"Filthy miscreant," Wanesa roared. "Unworthy to bear those items you stole—"

"Stole?" Roncrate roared back, fully awake and focused. "Do you know how many of the orc scum we cleared from those halls before we found that treasure? It's mine by right of—"

Adelphus gestured.

"SILENCE!" bellowed one of his young bailiffs.

Adelphus waited while order was restored. He and his staff had used the time to their best advantage while waiting for Roncrate to appear, researching laws and seeking information. Those dwarves with Wanesa were all Guildmasters, or Masters in good standing with their guild and the community, of the highest reputation.

Roncrate was also an adventurer of reputation, 'good' only when one considered his occupation. Still, within the confines of the city he held to civilized behavior, and was reputed to pay well for his drink and any damages caused by his carousing. He had a fierce reputation as a warrior, and he and his companions were known to risk the deepest depths in search of treasures.

Guildmaster Wanesa's reputation was also of high standing, and his skills acknowledged, but there was more to that dwarf than the ink-stains of a scribe. Adelphus had looked at the various passages of the edicts, and his fellow magisterium were reviewing his findings as quickly as they could to verify them. Inconceivable as it was, in this day and age, but—

The courtroom was silent, and the parties were staring at him. Enough contemplation. The case was not to judgment. There were burdens of proof, requirements to be met… Adelphus cleared his throat, and leaned forward on the bench.

"Guildmaster Valtos, here in the presence of Roncrate, state your accusation before this Court."

"I cry a charge of sacrilege against this one, Roncrate, for his desecration and profanation of our sacred relics. He has, and continues to, profane a breastplate and shield, used by ancient warrior clerics of my clan, sworn to the service—" there was a distinct pause, "—of Modren, Enaros of fire and the forge." Wanesa lifted his chin in defiance. "Roncrate has, and continues to, appropriate to secular use what is consecrated to the Enaros. Roncrate has, and continues to, intentionally disrespect these sacred items. Such is my cry and my charge, and under the law I demand to prove my words with blood and flesh."

Adelphus sat, maintaining his placid and solemn decorum as the accusations were set forth. But the rustle of scrolls off to the side let him know that his fellow Magisterium had taken note.

Whatever else he knew, Guildmaster Valtos also knew the standards of sacrilege.

That gave Adelphus pause. Of late, there had been a few that styled themselves orators that had dared to enter his court, claiming to speak for their clients, and to *argue* on their behalf. He'd given them short shrift indeed. Petitioners appeared, and made their charges. He and the clerks applied the law, as guided by the writs and edicts of King Polonus. So it was, and so it would always be.

But a petitioner that *knew* the law? That was a rarity.

And a dangerous one.

Roncrate was sputtering now, his face screwed up in anger, his hand clenching for the hilt of the sword he'd been forced to leave at the door. "You fat, hairy son of a troll—" he hissed.

"Those relics are of my Family Wanesa and Clan Sinarkett!" Wanesa bellowed. "Do you deny my charge?"

"I deny your charge, you rat-bastard." Roncrate yelled. "I wrestled those items from the depths of the Deeplands, and I'll use them as I see fit to go back and delve even deeper." He crossed his muscular arms over his chest and scowled. "And it won't take but half a minute and one stroke to gut you, old worm."

From there, the arguments continued, growing louder and even more vehement, as Valtos pressed his case. Roncrate acknowledged possession of the shield and breastplate, and denied any insult to the Enaros or the Clan Sinarkett. But Guildmaster Valtos would have none of that, insisting that the offense was grievous, and warranted immediate action.

Adelphus pressed on, allowing the parties to express their grievances, and vent their indignation and anger. Resolving disputes was as much about allowing the parties to be heard as it was applying the law. But as the presentation continued, it became clear to him that there would be no resolution. The dwarf was inciting Roncrate, using words and insults designed to bring the young adventurer to a frothing rage.

"The dwarves have stated many times that the riches pulled from ancient and abandoned halls are there for the taking, for they are of no use to the dead," Roncrate howled. "I won their use through my blood and sweat, and the strength of my—"

"You insult my Family and Clan, and profane sacred relics older than recorded time itself!" Valtos roared back. "If you would see them, Chief Magisterium, you would know in an instant that they are items to be protected and cherished, and not to be in the hands of this rabble."

Adelphus glanced over to his fellow magisteriums. Each and every one nodded his head gravely.

Adelphus sighed. "We are in an enlightened era, and I have a duty to try to resolve this dispute. Roncrate, you admit to having these items in your possession. Were Valtos Wansae to offer recompense, would you relinquish them to him and his family?"

"I already did," Valtos growled and named a sum.

Eyebrows went up around the room.

Adelphus looked at Roncrate, who crossed his arms over his chest, a mulish look on his face. "No," was all he said.

"Valtos Wansae, will you withdraw your charge of sacrilege against Roncrate, for his use of these items?"

"No." Valtos had almost the same mulish look.

"Guildmaster Valtos, I would remind you that the law does not permit the use of champions in this matter. If I rule that the trial by combat goes forward, you must be the one to enter the circle and prove your allegations."

"I understand that fully," Valtos said. "I stand prepared to prove my charge."

Adelphus leaned forward. "Why?"

There were sounds of disapproval from his fellow magisteriums. He was outside the bounds of questioning, but he itched to know. "Why pursue these charges when it goes against a thousand years of dwarven history? The 'Rise and Fall of the Deeplands' clearly states that the dwarves have rejected the worship of the Enaros."

"Which translation?" The dwarf stared at him intently.

"Odeel," Adelphus said, and there was throat clearing and a distinct cough from the side.

"To my knowledge," Valtos responded, stiff and almost wary. "The law does not require a 'why', Chief Magisterium."

Adelphus settled back in his chair, stung by the truth of that statement. "Very well, then. I hereby find that you are both members in good standing in our community, with the support of your peers. I further find that the sacrilege alleged is both ongoing and continuing, and involves the use of sacred items for a profane use. You will meet at dawn in the designated arena, and prove your charges with the strength of your hands and the edge of your weapons."

DAWN. AN UNGODLY HOUR FOR ANYTHING, MUCH LESS a fight.

Chief Magisterium Adelphus took his position by the stone combat ring, and tried not to lean on his cane overmuch. The chill was a damp one, and cut through his cloak. He was stiff as a board, but his role was to stand and supervise the challenge, and stand he would, for as long as this took.

Not that he'd had much sleep. He'd read the law books deep into the night, and had kept his fellow magisteriums and clerks scouring the scrolls and books as far back as he dared. But there was no getting around the law as it stood.

Adelphus watched the parties approach, even as his stomach roiled at the very idea of resolving conflicts with violence.

There were no death arenas, not since the time of Queen Piyaga. After consulting with the clerks and bailiffs, Adelphus had decided to use a practice circle within the Guards' Barracks Courtyard.

The Guardmaster had agreed, and had offered to provide security for the ring, but Adelphus had declined. It was a Court matter, and the bailiffs would be sufficient.

Less of a spectacle with any luck, other than the parties and their chosen witnesses. If any of the Guard saw fit to watch, well, at least it would be respectful gawkers.

They had gathered, of course, held back from the ring itself by his bailiffs. The Guardmaster stood off to Adelphus's left, a respectful step back.

The dwarf entered the area first, escorted by the bailiffs. Valtos Wansae strode at the head of the group, armored, and carrying a mace. His armor was worn, scrapped and dented, but he moved in it easily.

The crowd parted, and Roncrate stepped forward, followed by his party.

Adelphus caught his breath, even as the guards murmured in admiration.

Roncrate carried a shield before him of amazing quality that shimmered in the light, as if newly forged and polished. Emblazoned on the shield was the symbolic hammer of Modren.

Then the warrior shifted slightly, and the breastplate appeared—

Adelphus dropped his gaze, pressed his lips together and used every moment of his long career on the bench not to laugh right out loud.

The breastplate too was a thing of wonder, with a sheen that seemed to hold the dawn light, etched with Modren's hammer and forge and runes of protection.

But no one had mentioned that it had been made for a female dwarf.

Or that the elderly dwarf's ancestor had been a rather buxom lass. Roncrate had adapted it to himself with the clever use of straps and chainmail to cover the gaps at the sides. Still…

Even as he sought control, Adelphus risked a glance at Valtos. He caught a glimpse of the dwarf's expression and it took him by surprise.

It was one of relief.

But in the next instant it was gone, and a deep scowl appeared as he glared at the human.

There was humor in the murmuring around him, but no real laughter. Instead, Adelphus saw speculation in the eyes of the guards around them. Money was changing hands, and he turned a complete blind eye to the bets being placed.

Thankfully, the ritual of the combat was not a complex one. "Valtos Wansae, stand forth."

The dwarf stepped into the ring and faced Adelphus.

"Roncrate, stand forth."

The young human stepped into the ring with a cocky grin.

"Valtos of Wansae, does the sacrilege against your Enaros continue?"

"It does," the voice was strong as he glared at the human.

"Roncrate, are you willing to cease your actions as requested?"

Roncrate lifted the shield slightly. "Hells, no."

"Declare your weapons," Adelphus instructed.

"My sword and shield," Roncrate pulled his blade from the scabbard.

"My mace and my inks," Valtos said. He gestured to a leather pouch at his belt.

"Ink?" Roncrate glared.

Valtos shrugged. "Am I not a scribe? And is not ink my weapon?"

"Let the field and contestants be tested, that there be no magic to aid the strength of your hands." Adelphus gestured to the Court Cleric of Toletren, the Enaros of Justice. The cleric stepped forward, hand raised to call upon Toletren's power.

Valtos scowled, opening his mouth as if to protest. Adelphus waited, intending to use that to stop this farce in an instant if he could. Just let the dwarf protest the use of divine—

Valtos closed his mouth into a grimace as the cleric recited his spell.

"There is no magic," the cleric said. "But the shield and breastplate give off a faint glow, such as I have not seen before. I can't tell—"

"I waive any concerns," Valtos cut him off quickly.

Adelphus pulled in a deep breath of disgust, and despair, and resignation. "So be it. Let the combat begin, and let no one enter the circle until such time as you have proved your cause on the body of the other." At his gesture a horn rang out, and the fight began.

Adelphus was surprised to discover his own heart racing, and he wasn't sure if it was fear or excitement.

Roncrate held his position at the edge of the ring, bringing up his shield, his sword held low beside his hip.

Valtos slapped his chest with his free hand. "Come at me, boy. Or we'll be here all day!" he roared.

Roncrate charged, the sand lifting behind his heels as he sprinted across the ring.

Valtos dodged, bringing his mace down with a mighty *WHAM* on the shield, then twisting to the left, keeping the shield between him and Roncrate.

Roncrate spun, following him, and lunged with the sword. But Valtos never stopped, just continued around behind him, and managed to smack the human's backside before backing off.

That brought a spate of laughter from the guards, and a few of Roncrate's own party, but Roncrate was focused, and he followed up, again bringing the sword forward, aiming at the dwarf's chest.

Valtos backpedaled, waited until Roncrate's arm was extended , then moved in and threw…ink.

Adelphus blinked, fully expecting some type of missile to rattle against the shield. But instead the black fluid ran down, filling in the etchings, running over the metal like water, dripping to the ground.

Roncrate swore.

Valtos seemed short of breath, but he laughed at the human. "Told you ink was my weapon, why so surprised? No wits in that thick skull of yours?"

Roncrate had backed off, wary now, shield high, considering his opponent.

Adelphus looked at the cleric of Toletren, but he indicated there was no magic. No reason to stop the fight.

Roncrate continued to retreat. Now Valtos stalked him around the circle. "Afraid?" he taunted.

The warrior stopped, watching his every move.

"The one that first wore that armor had more balls than you," Valtos hooted.

There was laughter at that, enough that Roncrate's eyes flickered to the crowd. Valtos sprinted forward, feinting an attack, then backing off with a laugh as Roncrate took a defensive stance.

The dwarf's next comment referred to farm animals and Roncrate's preferences for certain types of sexual congress. Adelphus had too many years of experience to actually blush, but he doubted that act was even physically possible.

The raucous laughter enraged Roncrate. He roared his anger and charged across the field, clearly intent on bashing Valtos with his shield.

Valtos met him head on, using his mace to batter the shield, staying to the left, using the shield against the human, roaring with laughter as ink splattering everywhere. But the dwarf's voice was hoarse with insults, his breathing heavier. It was only a matter of—

Valtos stumbled and crashed back to the ground, losing his mace.

Roncrate's sword bit into his knee. With a cry of triumph, he threw back his shield arm and brought his sword overhand for the final stroke.

Valtos surged up to his knees, his hand thrust high, all five fingers splayed out on the breastplate, and with a harsh tongue, shouted out three sharp words.

The breastplate and shield burst into a cloud of silvery dust.

For Adelphus it seemed that every heart, every breath froze in that moment. The glittering specks hovered in the morning light, before they softly, slowly drifted to the ground.

Roncrate stood there stunned, then screamed, grasping the hilt of his sword with both hands, fully intent on—

"HOLD!" Adelphus cried out, his pulse thrumming in his throat. The bailiffs echoed his cry as well.

"No!" Roncrate spun, furious. "No—"

"The items that were the source of this conflict are gone," Adelphus said. "The sacrilege is at an end. The matter has been resolved—"

"No!" Roncrate spat. "I demand recompense. He tricked—"

"You shall have it," Valtos rasped from the ground, holding his bloody knee. "You shall have the sum I first named."

Roncrate stared at him, spat in the sand, and strode off, sheathing his sword.

The other dwarves flooded into the circle, carrying Valtos off.

Adelphus stood for a moment, letting his heart settle. When he felt he could move, he gathered his robes about him, and with his staff, headed for the carriages that would take them to the courthouse. As he limped along, cane in hand, the Guardmaster fell in with him, bouncing a small purse in his hand.

"If you don't mind," Adelphus admonished.

"'Tis only a small wager." The Guardmaster chuckled as he tucked the purse away. "Although the dwarf didn't win in the traditional sense. And permissible, since you used your own bailiffs for the matter."

"You bet on the dwarf, then?" Adelphus asked.

"Of course," the man lifted an eyebrow. "You saw the fit of his armor? The wear?"

"He is a scribe," Adelphus said. "And the elder."

"Dwarves train until they die," the Guardmaster replied. "Even scribes." He opened the door to Adelphus's carriage, and kindly did not offer assistance. "I'll back experience over youth any day."

Adelphus settled in as he shut the door, and called out to the driver. The carriage jolted forward, offering him one last look at the practice yard.

Only to see the remaining dwarves sweeping the circle clean with unusual reverence.

THAT ITCH TO KNOW, TO UNDERSTAND THE 'WHY' BURNED to such a degree that it forced him to an action he'd never taken before. Adelphus waited for two days before sending a note asking to speak to Guildmaster Valtos.

It was, to a degree, inappropriate. But he had to know.

The message was returned later that same day, scrawled in a fierce hand. *'Any time,'* it read. *'I'm stuck in my damned chair, with none but nursemaids and healers hovering about. You are more than welcome.'*

Adelphus wasted no time in sending for his cloak and his carriage.

He was greeted at the gates of the Wansae compound by young dwarven warriors, bright eyed and fiercely armored. In the courtyard, more young dwarves were training, their axes flashing in the afternoon sun as they took turns at the pells.

A young dwarven woman took his cloak at the door, and ushered him into a large library, filled with scrolls and journals.

Adelphus paused as a wave of warmth hit his face, easing his chill. The welcome heat also brought the familiar scent of old papers, wood polish, with just a hint of medicinal herbs to tickle the back of his throat.

"Welcome." Guildmaster Valtos sat in the center of the room in a chair stuffed with pillows, his leg propped up on a footrest. He'd been placed by a large iron stove, radiating heat. "Come in, come in," he said. "Forgive me for not rising, but as you can see—" He gestured to his bandaged leg. "—they will not let me put weight on it yet."

Adelphus moved stiffly, suddenly uncomfortable. It wasn't done, to talk to petitioners after a judgment. Yet, as he took his seat, he couldn't help admiring his surroundings. The warm glow of candles in glass sconces lit the wooden shelves and floors. There were books and journals, and maps and scrolls everywhere. Thick patterned rugs covered the floor, tables and cushioned benches sat off to the sides, and a desk with ink pots, parchments, and quills littering the top. Much like his own desk, in his own library.

And above it all, a delicately woven silvery chandelier cast a warm glow.

"Not what you thought of as a *tsverg*'s chambers, eh?" Valtos's voice rang with good humor. Adelphus noted the use of the name the dwarves preferred to call themselves He leaned forward as the woman fussed with his pillows. "Expecting more weapons, perhaps?"

"At least a boar's head or two on the walls." Adelphus focused on his host, seeing more of a kindred spirit then he'd first thought.

Valtos wrinkled his nose and shook his head. "Hate those things. The eyes always seem to follow me around the room." He leaned back in his chair and lifted his head. "Leave off your fussing, woman, and bring us ale," he said. "The Chief Magisterium is one that will appreciate good ale. Hard crackers, too, with slices of cheese, and some of that spicy sausage."

The woman folded her arms with a huff.

"It's for our guest," Valtos growled at her. "Let it not be said that this family stints on its hospitality, eh?"

The woman rolled her eyes and turned away.

"Besides," Valtos lowered his voice as she left the room, "What do rune healers know, eh?" He chuckled, his eyes twinkling. "Make yourself comfortable, and pull that chair closer to the stove."

Adelphus adjusted his chair, basking in the warmth. "A fine stove, Guildmaster. It gives out a great deal of heat. Better than an open hearth."

"No open flames in my library," Valtos said with a nod. "Notice too, that we diffuse the sunlight as it comes within. Direct sunlight isn't good for the inks and parchments of old works."

"How does it work?" Adelphus looked at the iron work of the stove, wrought with fine details of what appeared to be a dwarven warrior procession.

"Trade secrets." Valtos clasped his hands together and set them on his stomach. "If you wish, apply to my daughter's forge. She'd be happy to install one for you."

"At a price." Adelphus smiled.

Valtos returned it, somehow managing to look solemn at the same time. "Everything has a price. Everything."

The woman returned with a tray that she set between them on a clever, folding stand. On it were two tankards of foaming ale, and a plate heaped high with thin crackers, slabs of yellow cheese and sausage sliced thick. She offered them both napkins, rolled her eyes at Valtos, and left.

The dwarf leaned forward and helped himself. "You'll want to take a bite of sausage, cheese, and cracker first, then a sip of the ale."

Adelphus did as he was told, surprised by the explosion of spices at the back of his throat, delicious with the sharp cheese and cracker. But his real shock lay with the taste of the ale. A sweet, nutty flavor that sat pleasant on the tongue and past the throat.

He swallowed and cleared his throat in astonishment. "This is Gold Ale," he said in a hush. "I've heard of it."

Valtos had his eyes closed, relishing the taste. "Aye," he said simply. "It is."

"You honor me," Adelphus said, taking yet another sip.

"Nay, Chief Magisterium," Valtos murmured. "The honor is mine. If your wits had been a bit slower, this—" he gestured to his leg, "would have been much worse." He lifted his tankard. "To your health, sir."

"To yours as well." Adelphus lifted his in reply, and then reached for more of the crackers and sausage. His host was quick to follow.

They ate and talked for a bit, as Adelphus danced around the real reason he had come. Instead he complimented the ale again, and nodded as Valtos boasted of the sausage and cheese made by his sister's sons.

Valtos finished his first, with a quiet burp, brushing crumbs from his beard onto his napkin. "So what brings you to my home, Chief Magisterium?"

"Please," Adelphus gestured with his mug. "I am not here in any official capacity, Guildmaster."

"Valtos," the dwarf offered.

"Adelphus," he returned. "I am here strictly as a private person."

“So?”

“You promised me a ‘why’,” Adelphus said.

“Ah, but I didn’t.” Valtos gave him a sly, mercantile smile. “If you check your records, I said it wasn’t a requirement under the law that I explain my reasoning.”

The door flew open, and two of the smallest dwarves Adelphus had ever seen ran into the room, giggling madly, all black curls and pudgy arms. Both wielded wooden swords and shields and they chased each other around the chairs with high-pitched battle cries.

“Here now,” Valtos laughed, a warm deep sound. “What are you lads about?”

Another female dwarf appeared in the doorway, hands on her hips, her face alight even as she scolded. “Oh no, you don’t,” she said, striding forward to capture both of them, one under each arm, under their vigorous protests. “Your Grandsire has a guest. Is this how we greet a visitor?”

“Hullo,” The one peeked up at Adelphus, his sword and shield still dangling from pudgy hands.

“Grans, Grans, it’s time to play,” the other squirmed, less impressed with the visitor.

“Not today, lads. Be off with you now,” Valtos said, his voice stern, but his eyes merry.

“Have you all that you need?” The woman asked, raising her eyebrows at their plates even as her sons tried to wriggle free while voicing their disappointment.

“More ale,” Valtos said. “And sausage.”

She raised an eyebrow.

“We need it to finish the crackers,” Valtos pointed out.

She kept the arched eyebrow, but said nothing as she left with her burdens.

“The youngest of my grandchildren,” Valtos explained with a

proud smile, even as he reached for more food.

"A blessing to your Family," Adelphus observed, then winced internally at his slip.

Valtos just shrugged and nodded. "We would say they are the rewards of our labors," he observed, but with no insult in his tone. He took a bite, chewed for a moment, then cleared his throat. "Young Roncrate came by yesterday, to visit me."

"He did?" Adelphus paused, surprised.

"He did. Poor lad was in a bit of pain. Seems his cleric wasn't too pleased with him, and had decided that bruised ribs would teach him a thing or two." Valtos snorted. "Roncrate accepted the recompense for his loss." He continued. "I complimented him on his fighting style, dodged his questions about the relics, and placed the funds into his hands myself." Valtos gave Adelphus that sly look. "He also offered me four tomes they'd found within the bowels of that old temple." He gestured over to one of the tables.

"Really?" Adelphus couldn't suppress a surge of excitement. "Have you been able to read them?" He rose and went to the table where four old and abused books sat on a white cloth, eagerly leaning over, but careful not to touch. The leather covers were cracked and faded, the pages browned on the edges and crumbling.

"Aye," Valtos said. "Three of them appear to be ancient lore books, but the fourth, that is a tsvergic history book. He gifted them to me, but I told him if he came across any such other tomes or documents, I would gladly take them. And pay well." The old dwarf laughed. "Don't think he understood that the books are worth more to us than the gold and gems he finds, but we parted on good terms. At the very least, he's less likely to use old papers to start fires now, or worse."

"When you have them restored, I'd much appreciate a chance to purchase copies," Adelphus returned to his chair.

"I'll see to it," Valtos said. "And that's yet another reason."

"Reason?" Adelphus picked up his tankard, intent on the last sip.

"I didn't answer young Roncrate's 'why'." Valtos settled back in his chair. "But I'll answer yours."

The door opened, and the young dwarven mother returned with two full tankards in each hand. She served them both, taking the empty mugs, then cast a pointed look at the remaining scraps of cheese and sausage on the plate. "Anything else, Grandsire?"

"Nay," Valtos scowled. "But close the door behind you, and see to it we are not interrupted. We'll be having a private word."

"The Healers are due later," she warned.

"Aye, aye," Valtos grumbled.

She dropped a kiss on his head, then pulled the door quietly closed behind her.

Adelphus took another sip, and closed his eyes. Just as smooth as the last.

"You referred to the Odeel translation in court," Valtos said. "Have you read the Lenear?"

"I haven't been able to obtain a copy." Adelphus lowered his mug. "Although I understood the Odeel was more complete in its meaning."

Valtos laughed. "We can talk that out another day." He paused, taking a sip of his ale. "You have a reputation, Chief Magisterium. When word came of what Roncrate had found, I specifically chose your court to make my charges. You are known for your interest in the history and lore of all of the cultures of Aetaltis, and more so, that you respect them. So I chose your doors to stomp through and cry out my charges."

"The Council of Magisteriums is considering having the law stricken from the books," Adelphus said. "Trial by combat is a holdover from the Age of Shadow, and has no place in our world today."

"Hmm," Valtos said. "It matters not, now. The circumstance was a rare one, and word will spread that those types of artifacts can be dissolved with runes. The next adventurer to stumble on such pieces will probably seek recompense first." He winced, shifting his leg.

"A cleric of Alantra could fix that with a single spell," Adelphus observed mildly.

"I'll not be touched with divine magic," Valtos growled.

"Yet you risked your life and welfare to cry sacrilege," Adelphus leaned forward. "Why?"

The humor returned to Valtos's eyes. "I would not tell the Chief Magisterium. But I will tell Adelphus, student of history. So let me tell you a tale, eh? For what is history if not stories?"

The dwarf belched quietly and leaned back in his chair. "I will ask your indulgence, Adelphus, for I would start my tale in the years before the Betrayal and some of this you will already know. My family is an old one, and our line stretches back over long centuries. The Wanesa Family tradition was of the forges and the sword. Our family is a strong line of smiths, best known for our weapons and armor. But we also had a tradition of war, and those of our family that took up the sword were sworn into the service of the Cursed One—Modren, you call him—as battle clerics.

"Tradition has it that we would arm those that heeded the call with the best we had to offer." Valtos shook his head. "We were proud and strong, and blessed before others..."

Adelphus waited, barely daring to breathe.

"Wanesa developed a special art to honor our dead, beyond the traditions of other Families. We used the dead to forge what came to be called soulsteel."

"Used the—" Adelphus asked, not quite understanding.

"The bodies of the deceased were given to the fires of the forge, and then the ash and bone were collected and used in the forging of glorious things. There are family legends of brilliant diamonds created from the ashes, and the metal created…" Valtos heaved a deep sigh. "Well, you saw. The metal was light as air and held a sweet sheen that had never been seen before, each one unique and different. Strong as anything known and light as feathers against your skin. Soulsteel warded kith and kin for lifetimes and beyond. It was an honor to forge such an item. An honor to bear such a thing into battle. And arrogance to think such things would never be lost to us."

"That's astonishing," Adelphus breathed.

"Then came our—Betrayal." Valtos's voice shook, and his breath caught in his throat.

"It was thousands of years ago," Adelphus said softly. "Yet you speak of it as if it was yesterday."

"Because it was," Valtos raised his head, his eyes filled with anger and pain. "And this is where those not of our race do not, *cannot* comprehend."

"Forgive me, but—" Adelphus settled his tankard in both hands.

"No fault of yours, friend." Valtos said. "You are not *tsverg*. For when I tell this tale to my kith and kin, when I recite the tale of the Betrayal, and I do at every sacred meal, every rite, I say 'This is what the Cursed One did to me. This is how he betrayed my home and hall, my hopes and dreams'. And so he did to my parents, and my parents' parents in a long, unbroken chain. It is a living, breathing betrayal. We, the *Tsverg*, will never forget, and we will *never* forgive."

Adelphus's mouth dried, and he sipped his ale, unable to look away from the determination and strength in Valtos's stare.

And then dropped his gaze as the dwarf wiped the tears from his eyes.

"So it was that the Enaros, in their 'goodness' and 'mercy,' betrayed us and destroyed our homes and halls."

"It was said—" Adelphus found he had to clear his throat. "It was said that the Halls were destroyed beyond redemption."

"No," Valtos said firmly. "We have never doubted that with the work of our hands, and the strength of our hearts, we could have reclaimed and rebuilt." He shifted in his chair, grimacing slightly as he moved his leg. "Having been abandoned by those we worshiped, we turned to our ancestors for guidance. We rejoiced that we honored them with our crafting. We believed that their wisdom was contained within the metal, protecting their loved ones."

A tapping at the door, and a sturdy dwarf entered with wood in his arms and a hopeful expression.

"Come, quickly, and be done," Valtos said, and the young one did, adding the logs to the wood box, and opening the stove to place two on the fire.

"Well done, lad," Valtos said.

The boy squared his shoulders. "Every task needs doing," he recited solemnly then scooted from the room as quick as he came, and closed the door behind him.

Valtos sighed and took up his tale. "So the Betrayal came, and we fled our homes and our Halls, with as much as we could carry. But, as is wont to happen under such circumstances, some items were lost.

"My family was one of the first to strike back at the foul scum. To pledge its warriors to liberate those Halls, its crafters to support them in every way. For the forges of the Liberators can only repair, not create. For their every hour is spent in defense or planning their offense, to destroy Endroren's foul spawn. They have little time to see to their needs. So we send food and supplies—whatever they need.

"In turn, the Liberators send us the precious things they find, and not the gold and gems Roncrate thinks of," Valtos said. "The texts—the lost knowledge of our people—even the religious tomes, for they drive home even harder our love and faith returned with tears and pain. So it has been for season after season, year after year."

"For a thousand years," Adelphus said.

"Aye," Valtos said. "But as we strove, as we fought and died for every inch, we came to understand that soulsteel wasn't the honor we thought it was. We came to understand that we had bound our ancestor's souls into the fabric of the metal."

Adelphus sucked in a breath.

"Legends have grown that soulsteel can not be used against us, but the truth is they can, and are, and the sorrow keens from the very metal as it cleaves our flesh and bone."

"So whoever's ashes were used to create that armor, was bound to it?" Adelphus asked.

"Such was not our intent." Valtos protested, but nodded in agreement. "But then, so many things in this world have consequences unforeseen and unknown. Such is our sorrow. Such is our pain."

"And without records, without histories, there's no way to know…" Adelphus let his voice trail off.

"By our own hands, we were grieved to learn, we had injured the very ancestors we revered." Valtos said. "And there's no way of knowing how many remain bound, serving the likes of the *endrori*."

"That must have been a terrible blow to your hearts," Adelphus said.

Valtos nodded and heaved a sigh. "But everything can be unmade. We developed the Runes of unmaking, and carried ink with us into combat. It was as safe as anything might be in this world. For who carries ink into battle?

"The Liberators of our family are pledged to a two-fold task. To restore our homelands. And to retrieve any souls still locked within, to ensure the tainted ones never touch them or wield them against kin.

"Where once we crafted weapons and armor, now we craft

stoves and pots and grand chandeliers that lend light and grace to our halls. So the Family strives, and the Family endures, and such it has been since the Betrayal, and so shall it ever be. By our own hands, through our own efforts."

"You risked much, Valtos." Adelphus said.

"I did. But so much more than my life, to my way of thinking." Valtos smiled. "I wasn't afraid of dying, you see. I was far more afraid that—"

"That the soul within would remain a captive?" Adelphus asked.

"That Roncrate wouldn't wear the items to the fight," Valtos laughed. "You have to admit, he looked a bit of the fool with—" He cupped his hands a fair distance from his chest, and laughed again. "—out to here."

"It took some doing," Adelphus confided. "To keep a straight face at that."

"The idiot told me he had the idea he could beat them down with a hammer." Valtos grinned. "Ridiculous notion."

The door opened. "The healers are here, Grandsire," a lovely young dwarf entered with a smile, her robes and fingers as ink-stained as Valtos's. Behind her hustled in three dwarves, their Healing Guild symbols embroidered in their robes, with a wooden chest and satchels of supplies. They wasted no time, shedding their outer garments to reveal the white robes beneath.

"And how are we today?" the eldest asked.

"Fine, fine," Valtos winced as one of the healers pulled what seemed to be a rune-covered wire brush from his bag.

"I'd best be on my way," Adelphus said and pushed himself up. He'd been sitting too long, and his knees creaked and groaned in protest.

All three healers jerked their heads around and stared at him with frowns.

"This is Chief Magisterium Adelphus of the High Council of Magisteriums," Valtos said.

Adelphus nodded to all three, but none seemed impressed.

"These are my healers," Valtos gestured toward the oldest. "Guildmaster Healer—"

"Do your knees always sound like that?" The Eldest asked pointedly.

Adelphus blinked at the rudeness, glancing at Valtos. The dwarf shrugged, as if to say 'what can you do?'.

"Well?" the Healer asked again.

"Yes, but—"

"Your hands too, no doubt. Apprentice," the Healer barked. "Third shelf from the right, two jars in. The little jar of green paste."

The youngest of them leaped to his command, rattling the wooden chest, producing a jar.

The Guildmaster slapped it into Adelphus's hand. "Use this once upon rising, and rub it in well around the fingers and knees. Let it absorb into the skin."

"My thanks," Adelphus said. "What do I owe for this—"

But the Guildmaster Healer was already waving him away. "Consider it my thanks for preserving the life of my Great Uncle." He said shortly. "Now, if you don't mind—"

"Come back again, another day," Valtos called as he was escorted to the door. "After these bone-cutters are done with me." A deep, thunderous burp caught the dwarf by surprise, and he pressed his fist to his chest as he continued. "We'll compare those translations and have a good long talk then!"

"I will," Adelphus said, pleased at the invitation.

Just before the door shut behind him, he heard the condescending tone of disapproval from the Guildmaster Healer. "And what did we say about eating so much spicy sausage?"

THE TOWER OF THE GOLDEN GOD

STEVEN S. LONG

TORVIN COLLAPSED AGAINST ONE OF THE KNOBBY ROOTS of a huge *barayan* tree, unable to run any further. His breath came in ragged gasps; sweat covered his well-muscled body. His legs felt as if they might fold under him at any moment.

This was not what he'd expected today.

He and his band of spice-hunters had entered the Zhamayen Jungle a little after dawn in search of the flowers, leaves, and roots so desired by Calliosan merchants. Like always, they kept a wary eye out for any of the hundred dangers lurking within the thick jungle's gloom. When they had no luck at their usual hunting spots, they decided to explore further into the green.

Fortune favored them, or so they thought. They found a rich patch of redspice flowers—rich in both senses of the word, since the patch had enough blossoms to keep them all in women and ale for a sixmonth once they sold the petals. But in their eagerness to pick the flowers they didn't pay enough attention to the jungle around them, and the Zhamayen rarely forgives such folly.

The *endrori* ambush killed three of them before they could fight back. Torvin had chosen his men well, though. They reacted swiftly, and soon several green-skinned corpses, orcs and goblins mostly, joined those of their comrades on the ground. But fight as fiercely as they could, Torvin realized he and his men had no hope of victory—the *endrori* were too many, and they could see better beneath the thick jungle canopy. As the last of his spice-hunters fell to an orc's axe, Torvin grabbed the fattest sack of redspice petals, hacked his way through three of the foul creatures, and fled for his life. But the ferocity of his attack had cost him his *balshara,* the thin-bladed sword that was as much a tool for chopping paths in the jungle undergrowth as a weapon; it had snapped when he plunged it deep into a goblin's skull. That left him only his heavy fighting dagger, the one he'd brought all the way from his homeland in the distant north. And now he was deeper than he'd ever gone into the Zhamayen, far deeper—with no idea of the quickest way out, or what other dangers he might face.

As he got his breath back, he wondered how the *endrori* had stayed on his trail so long. He'd used every trick he knew—running along fallen logs, wading through streams, stepping on stones—and still they followed. Then he glanced down at his prized sack of redspice flowers and had his answer. Somewhere during his headlong flight he'd torn a hole in the cloth, leaving a trail of distinctive red petals every step of the way.

Cursing, he almost threw the nearly empty sack away, but stopped himself. He could use the few remaining petals to lure his pursuers away—or better yet, set a trap for them.

The idea came not a moment too soon: in the distance he heard guttural *endrori* voices. Quickly taking in his surroundings, Torvin saw a patch of dim sunlight not far away—a clearing. The *endrori* hated sunlight; that might give him an edge. He headed that way, swift and silent as a panther, dropping a redspice petal every few steps. When he got to the edge of the clearing—really just a place where the trees grew shorter and sparser for some reason, allowing a few shafts of sunlight to fight their way through to the jungle floor—he hid behind a thick *golura* tree and waited, dagger in hand.

The voices got closer. He risked a glimpse around the tree trunk and smiled when he saw only two *endrori*: a short, stooped goblin armed with a bow, and a big orc carrying a battle axe. He couldn't understand their language, but he knew what they intended to do to him. Unfortunately for them, now it was his turn to strike from ambush. He crouched behind the *golura* tree and waited for the right moment.

The two *endrori* entered the clearing and paused, not liking the sunlight. Torvin stepped up behind them without a sound, jerked the goblin's head back, and savagely slashed his dagger through the creature's throat, cutting almost to the spine. As the goblin collapsed, the orc shouted and swung his axe, reacting more quickly than Torvin expected. He threw himself backward to avoid the blow; the orc pursued, bellowing in triumph.

Before the orc could swing again, Torvin recovered his footing. He grabbed the axe haft with his left hand; his muscles bulged as he struggled for control of the weapon while jabbing at the orc with his dagger. The orc, unable to bring his full strength to bear while dodging dagger thrusts, couldn't free the axe.

As they grappled, the two stepped into a shaft of sunlight. The orc roared in pain and fury as the light of Lensae blinded him, leaving him vulnerable. Torvin stabbed him in the gut, then again in his chest and arms, and as the orc tried to crawl away in his back as well. Dark blood flowed from both corpses to soak into the jungle floor.

Hefting his newly-won axe, Torvin listened carefully to the

jungle around him. He heard nothing: no *endrori* voices, no one charging through the brush to continue the fight. At first the silence comforted him, but then he realized that he truly heard *nothing*—no birds singing, no insects buzzing, no chattering monkeys.

Frowning, he looked around warily. It didn't take long for him to realize this "clearing" was some ancient plaza. Tree roots had cracked many of the flagstones, often pushing them upward, while the covering of moss and leaves made it even harder to discern where the jungle ended and the square began. But it was still a plaza.

Torvin shook his head. He'd heard stories about ruins in the Zhamayen Jungle, but he'd scoffed at them, having never found any in all the time he'd hunted spice. Now he could scoff no longer.

Then he saw something even more astonishing. On one edge of the plaza, nearly hidden by the gloom of the jungle, stood a tower of green-grey stone. Behind it, an upthrust rock wall created a sort of cliff, and the tower almost seemed to grow out of the base of the rock as if it were a part of it, but rose higher than the clifftop. Unlike the plaza, it seemed untouched by the ravages of time and nature.

To Droth with the lost redspice petals! A tower like that might contain the treasure of a forgotten king, the possessions of some long-dead sorcerer, or relics not seen by human eyes for a thousand years. Unable to resist the lure of either curiosity or avarice, Torvin moved toward the tower, stepping with stealth and care, hiding behind trees.

The doors leading into the tower were made of stone and sealed with a large bronze disk that displayed a scene Torvin didn't understand—a sun god blessing his worshippers? A conqueror receiving the obeisance of his new subjects? A wizard cowing a demonic horde? Whatever its decoration, the seal held the doors firmly shut. Torvin stepped back to look for windows he could enter through instead. He saw several, but stone shutters covered each one—and in any event the sides of the tower looked too smooth and slippery for even him to climb.

He returned to the door. In his frustration he lashed out at the bronze seal with his axe, but a blow that would have beheaded an ogre barely scratched the bronze and left the blade badly notched.

Where force would not work, perhaps other methods would do the trick. Torvin took out his dagger and began trying to pry off the seal by digging at the substance attaching it to the doors: a sticky, foul-smelling stuff that stained his blade and clung to his fingers. But he persevered, and after an hour of tedious work he freed the top third of the seal.

Using a rock as a makeshift hammer, he wedged the axe's blade behind the seal as far down as it would go. Then he grasped the back of the axe head and pulled. As he strained his warrior's muscles to their utmost, he felt the substance slowly begin to give way. Just when he thought his arms and back couldn't take any more, the seal came free from the door. The sudden release made him stumble backward and fall down in a patch of weeds.

Beneath the seal were incised hand-holds, partly filled with the stinking glue. He placed his hands in them and pulled. At first the doors resisted, held in place by who knew how many years of immobility, but soon they gave way before his strength and opened with a *whoosh.*

The room beyond was empty but for one item that caught Torvin's attention: a golden statue of a god, holding a crystal-topped staff in one hand and gazing benevolently down. The warrior advanced toward it, alert and wary, axe at the ready, but he sensed no threats. He reached out to touch the statue, hesitating only at the last second. It seemed solid, and far too heavy for even an ox to carry. Perhaps he could pry off some of the gems or small pieces of gold and use those to convince some adventuring wizard to help him come back and retrieve the rest; he couldn't imagine getting a wagon and team through the Zhamayen.

He examined the room more carefully now that his eyes had adjusted to the dimness. Murals or mosaics of some sort decorated the walls, but he couldn't make out what they showed. Other than that all he saw in the room were two staircases: one leading upward into the gloom; the other boring into the ground beneath the tower. From the latter came a miasma that offended his nostrils. Having no desire to find out what created such a stench, he took the upward stair.

One circuit up the stairs he faced a choice: continue up the tower, or take a corridor that led back into the rock of the cliff. At the end of the corridor he glimpsed a glow around a door; above him he saw only shadow, and he had no torch. He took the corridor.

The light around the edges of the door was strong enough for his eyes to make out a few details. The door was bronze, and like the seal he'd pried loose it showed no verdigris or other sign of age. Elaborate designs covered its surface, but he didn't have enough light to make out the details.

He touched the bird-shaped doorknob cautiously, not knowing what to expect, but nothing happened. It turned freely and he pushed open the door.

On the other side was a room of wonders lit by crystal lamps that held bright, smokeless flames. Another statue of the golden god, this one seated on a throne with his crystal-topped staff across his knees, occupied the center of the room. To Torvin's left a bizarre device of slowly-turning golden rods and crystal spheres occupied an alcove. But the larger alcove on his right captured more of his attention, for it held a kingdom's pricc in treasure behind a wall of glass: pyramids of gold bars; jars filled to brimming with silver and gold coins; closed chests, tantalizing in their mystery; statuettes of jade, lapis, marble, chalcedony; and most beguiling of all, a mail hauberk and a longsword, their silver shine undimmed by dust or tarnish.

Torvin looked around, up and down and into the far reaches of the room, but he saw no dangers, sensed no movement. But for the gold-and-crystal thing to his left, the room had the stillness of a tomb. He saw two other doors, each made of iron-bound oak instead of bronze, but no light or sound came from beyond them.

One cautious step at a time, Torvin approached the glass wall. Nothing happened; no traps sprang, no unseen guardian attacked. He touched the glass; it felt icy cold, but no mist condensed where his fingers made contact. On the other side the treasure glittered in the lamplight.

Torvin raised his axe and struck the glass a swift, strong blow. The haft shivered in his hands, and the glass remained intact and unmarred. He smashed it again, this time bracing himself and using all his strength—but again he had no more effect on the glass than if he'd hit it with a feather.

He looked around the room to find something better to attack the glass with, but what he saw instead chilled him to the bone: the golden god was coming to life! "Droth's blood!" Torvin said, backing toward the open door and holding his axe ready to attack.

The tips of the statue's fingers were no longer gold. Now they had the color of living flesh. The hue of life slowly spread up the fingers, then to the backs of the hands and wrists. For a time Torvin lost sight of the transformation beneath the god's golden robes, but it re-appeared on his neck and flowed upward until all the visible flesh looked like skin instead of gold.

The god breathed in deeply, like a man awakening from sleep, and opened his eyes. They, too, were golden-colored, and looked at Torvin with piercing intelligence and deep wisdom. With the aid of his staff the god rose to his feet, and as he did strange colors coruscated around the staff's crystal.

"Who are you, man, and why have you come to the Tower of the Vault?" the god asked.

Torvin fell to his knees and placed his axe on the floor. "I am Torvin, son of Toroth, Holy One, a man of the Free Kingdoms far to the north across the Amethyst Sea. I came here fleeing the *endrori* who attacked me and my men."

"Be welcome here, then, and have no fear of me," the golden-robed one said. "My name is Daramanthes Aspar, and I am no god—only a Morogani wizard, the last of all of us, old and tired but ready to perform my final duty."

Torvin stood, still wary. "Morogani? I have not heard of them."

"Have men forgotten the Morogani Empire already? Once we ruled half the world, and Ormenos, the City of Emperors, was the most beautiful city ever built. But being forgotten is no more than we deserve, I suppose, and the world better for its lack of memory."

"What do you mean? Were you cursed?" Torvin asked, covertly glancing at the hoard behind the glass wall. Perhaps if the wizard kept talking he would reveal how to get to the treasure.

"In a way, we were. The Morogani grew complacent and decadent, interested only in satisfying their own desires and lusts. They turned their back on our traditions, and began worshipping strange, dark gods from the worlds of shadow and chaos. To please their new masters they willingly—even gladly—committed the foulest sins. In time, evil so corrupted their souls that they became *mogorh,* horrific beast-men with a malign intelligence and cruel cunning.

"Only the few of us who held true to the Thirty Gods of the Morogani remained free from the *mogorh* taint. Some counseled that we should slay them and so cleanse the world of their evil. But most of us could not turn our backs on our own people, and believed we should do whatever we could to save them.

"As the *mogorh* ravaged Ormenos we worked a great ritual in haste. We had crafted a spell to undo the transformation, but it could only be cast when the stars were right and the dark gods' power was at its ebb—thousands of years in the future. The others sacrificed their lives so I could place the *mogorh* into a trance from which I would revive them when the time came. They sleep still in the great vault beneath this tower. I also put myself and my daughter apprentice into a sorcerous slumber to preserve our lives in anticipation of the great day of the liberation of the Morogani.

"And now that day has arrived! My enchanted orrery has tracked the movements of the stars and sounded the mystical chime to awaken me because they've reached the proper position for the invocation. Come, I will show you."

Daramanthes walked over to the alcove containing the device of spinning gold rods and crystal spheres and observed it intently. A frown creased his brow, and it grew darker the longer he watched the spheres move.

He turned to Torvin. "The orrery did not awaken me—it will be centuries until the stars align for the Ritual of Profound Return! Why did you bring me out of my long sleep?"

"I did nothing, old man," Torvin said, preferring not to mention his efforts to break the glass wall. "I found the tower, I came in, you returned to life."

"Tell me everything that happened as you approached and entered the tower," Daramanthes said in a more placating tone. "Leave out no detail."

"My men and I entered the jungle in search of spice plants, as we have many times before. But a band of *endrori* ambushed us and killed all of them; I fled before they could cut me down, too."

"What are these *endrori?* You mentioned them before."

"Evil beings, the spawn of the shadow god Endroren: orcs, trolls, goblins, and worse."

"They are his creatures—his hounds, his beasts of war?"

"No, they're shaped like you or I, but hideous, and they think only of destruction and cruelty."

"They sound much like the *mogorh.* Continue, please."

"Two of them pursued me, and I discovered that I'd foolishly left a trail for them to follow as I ran. So I hid behind one of the trees outside, surprised them, and killed them."

Daramanthes paled. "You did this in the plaza before the Tower?"

"Aye, though it's no longer a plaza."

"By the Seven Fires, now I understand. I awakened because *you* aroused the *mogorh.*"

"You're wrong, old man. I've never even seen these *mogorh* you speak of."

"You did it unwittingly. Spilling the blood of thinking beings—and evil ones at that—above the Vault that holds the mogorh will break their long trance. But the fault is mine, not yours. Never did I imagine such a thing could happen or that anyone would ever dare enter Ormenos again."

From below came a sound Torvin couldn't identify: part howl, part snarl. With a warrior's reflexes he spun to face the bronze door, axe held at the ready.

"May the Thirty Gods help us!" Daramanthes said. "Some of them are already awake. I can renew the spell that makes them sleep, but it will take time."

"Hurry, wizard! I'll hold them as long as I can, but one man with a notched axe and no shield or armor can't stand long against a horde."

Daramanthes paused. "I have no shield to give you, but the

notched axe at least I can remedy." He gestured, and the silver sword in the treasure hoard flew through the glass wall as if it weren't there and into the startled northman's grasp.

"That is Ulsingbrand, the Three-Edged Blade. I forged it long ago for Marentius, the last and greatest hero of the Morogani Empire. It has slain *mogorh* aplenty in its time, and now you can add to that count."

Flinging his axe aside, Torvin examined the blade. It was marvelously made, with edges sharp enough to cut fog. Its curved guard had a red stone set at each end, with a matching stone in the pommel. Despite its size it felt as light as a rapier, but had a hilt long enough for two hands if need be. Engraved onto the ricasso was a single, complex rune whose arcs and angles Torvin's eyes couldn't quite follow.

Another howl-snarl echoed up from below. "Get to it, wizard!" Torvin said. Daramanthes took a silver wand from his sleeve and began drawing circles and runes on the floor with light the color of the moon.

Torvin turned back to face the door, Ulsingbrand at the ready. He could hear them moving below now, and the same stench he'd smelled before reached his nostrils. "Droth's dogs take you!" he shouted as the bronze door burst open and a half-dozen creatures charged into the room. They had the forms of men, but their hairy skin was a sickening purple-grey, and their faces seemed as much simian as human. Their teeth were fangs, and claws tipped their fingers.

Seeing their prey, the *mogorh* howled and rushed forward. Torvin's first swing chopped through the lead one's neck so easily he nearly lost his balance. He scrambled to the side as another came after him, but didn't move swiftly enough. He felt fire along his side as the *mogorh* raked him with its claws. The others surged past him.

He heard a shrill scream from the wizard and gritted his teeth in frustration. The *mogorh* avoided his next blow with bestial speed and moved in for the kill. But now Torvin knew Ulsingbrand's balance. His swift return blow came before the *mogorh* reached him and cut deep into the fiend's chest. Hissing and spitting, it tried to claw its way up the blade to reach him, but with a vengeful smile Torvin twisted the blade, and it died.

As he freed the sword so he could go to the wizard's aid, a flare of heat and light filled the room, half-blinding him. When his eyes cleared, he saw Daramanthes lying on the floor in a pool of blood, his golden robes in scarlet tatters. The charred corpses of the other four mogorh surrounded him.

"Can you stand, wizard?" Torvin asked as he hurried to the old man's side, but as he got closer, he saw the answer was no.

Daramanthes's eyes fluttered open. "They were on me too quickly. I called on the Fifth Fire to destroy them, but…too late."

"Come on, old man, finish your spell!"

The wizard shook his head and gestured feebly at the door behind his throne. "No…no time. Dying, after…so many centuries. But my daughter…apprentice…she knows…what to do. Awaken her with the words *anthuren scaru bilata.* Give her my staff, it… holds the…magics that support us and this place, the power she will need to…to…" His eyes shut, his head fell back to the floor, and he became silent forevermore.

Torvin looked around cautiously, listened with the careful ears of a hunted man. He heard no more *mogorh* approaching, but these six wouldn't be the only ones who'd been roused from their long sleep. His instincts screamed at him to flee, to get far away before that happened. But the *mogorh*—how many were there? Could they ravage the land as the *endrori* did so long ago? What use might the Lord of Shadow make of them? If he had the chance to stop them now, he had to take it.

Cursing his own foolishness, he took the crystal-topped staff from the hands of Daramanthes and placed it on the throne. Then he tore down a wall hanging and covered the body so the wizard's daughter wouldn't see how *mogorh* claws had torn at her father. He winced as the motion tore open the bloody crust forming over his own wound, but by Droth's grace it was a shallow cut that would heal quickly and hinder him little.

The chamber beyond the wooden door was a much simpler room containing only one thing of note: a catafalque upon which lay a woman in peaceful repose. Raven-haired and wearing a purple gown, she was beautiful, but Torvin had no time to stop and admire her. Stepping close, he leaned over her and said, softly but clearly, "*Anthuren scaru bilata.*"

Almost at once her eyes, a lambent violet matching the color of her dress, snapped open. "Who are you?" she said, her voice betraying no fear at the close presence of an armed stranger. "Where is Daramanthes?"

"I am Torvin, a spice hunter who got lost in the jungle and found his way here," he said, stepping back from the catafalque. "Your father is dead, slain by the *mogorh,* who are awakening. He told me you could cast the spell to return them to sleep."

She swung her legs off the edge of her sleeping-platform and stood up. "Where is his staff?" she asked, her face showing no grief, no concern. Torvin led her out to the throne.

She snatched up the staff and her expression became exultant. Colors flared around the crystal atop the staff: lightning blue, blood red, fire orange, a dozen shades of purple, crimson. "At last!" she said. "The power is mine after so many years!"

"My lady, you should cast the spell to put the *mogorh* back to sleep as soon as you can. The rest of them may return to life at any moment."

She looked at him more closely this time, and a touch of

craftiness tinged her features. "Put them back to sleep? No. That was Daramanthes's plan, for he was a fool who had no ambition. With the magic in this staff, I can *control* the *mogorh* and make of them an army to conquer empires! All the people of the world shall kneel at the feet of Zharana the Great and worship me as if I were a goddess!"

"Control them? My lady, is that…wise? They're savage devils, no better than *endrori!* They'll slaughter every living thing they see—starting with us!"

She stepped closer. Before, when she'd just awakened from her millennia-long slumber, she had seemed merely beautiful. Now, come fully to life and power, her regal magnificence gave her an allure that would make men fight and die for her. Her charisma held him like golden shackles, and when she smiled at him it seemed as if his heart stopped beating for a moment.

"I possess the magic to control them, have no fear of that, Torvin." She placed her left hand gently on his chest and a warmth spread through his flesh. "But I cannot rule the lands I will conquer by myself. For that I need a king by my side—handsome, strong, skilled in war."

Torvin's eyes widened. Him, a king? With the most beautiful woman in Aetaltis as his queen? The thought intoxicated him. His gaze darted once more to the treasure confined behind the glass wall.

"Yes, Torvin!" she said, divining his desire. "All that wealth of ancient Morogani, and more, will be yours. The richest merchants will seem like paupers compared to you. Stand aside and let me cast my spell, and you will have everything you ever dreamed of."

"My lady, I… I…—"

"The bold warrior hesitates?" Zharana said, a hint of playful scorn creeping into her voice. "Think on this, then," she said, leaning even closer and looking up into his eyes. "Besides all that, you will have *me* as well. Do you not desire me beyond all other things?"

"All...all but one, my lady."

"And what is *that?*"

"My freedom." Before she could move, he snatched the staff from her grasp and hurled it like a spear at the enchanted glass wall. The crystal struck the barrier and exploded in a blaze of colors that dazzled his brain and a cacophony of sound like every temple chime he'd ever heard playing at once. With a distinct, indefinable sound of its own, the glass wall shattered. The entire tower rumbled and shook, almost throwing Torvin off his feet.

"Nooooo!" Zharana screamed, falling to her knees. "The power in the staff supports this Tower and those who watch over it! You've doomed us both!" Before his eyes the years, long kept at bay by sorcery, took hold of her. In mere seconds she went from being a score of years old, to two score, to a crone. Soon she looked older than anyone Torvin had ever seen, and her frame began collapsing in on itself. She toppled over, her body turning into dust as it hit the floor.

Another tremor, this one even stronger, rocked the tower; stones began falling from the walls and roof. Torvin started toward the treasure alcove, eager to take anything he could put his hands on. Then half of the archway leading into it collapsed, along with more of the ceiling. Some of the stones missed him by only a hand's-breadth.

"Droth's dogs!" he said, fists and jaw clenching at the sight of so much gold just beyond his grasp. He turned and ran for the stairs. Stumbling as the tower shook, clambering over the rubble that already filled half the hallway, he made it there. Luck or the gods were with him, for none of the falling stones that hit him were large enough to cave in his skull or break his limbs.

He practically threw himself down the stairs. With the floor tilting beneath him like the deck of a ship at sea, he staggered to the entrance and out into the golden afternoon sunlight. But the ground outside the tower rumbled and shook almost as badly as the tower itself. Running as best he could, he made it across the clearing and into the trees beyond, where the jungle floor stayed firm beneath his feet.

He looked back to see the mighty Tower and the Vault it guarded fall, collapsing into the ground until nothing remained but a vast, sheer-sided hole lined with boulders and soil at the bottom. He kept watching, getting as close to the edge of the pit as he dared, but nothing moved anywhere. Were the *mogorh* dead, crushed by the vault they'd slept in, so that Daramanthes hadn't died in vain? Torvin prayed to the Enaros that it be so.

He trudged away. He didn't know which direction would lead him out of the Zhamayen the quickest, but he cared more about getting as far away from the ruins of the tower as he could. "Droth's dogs!" he muttered. To have come so close to such riches, but walk away empty-handed! *Well, not entirely,* he thought, reaching up to touch Ulsingbrand's hilt above his left shoulder. *With a blade like this, a man could win gold aplenty—or make himself a king.*

Now he just had to do it…

BELLAR'S THORN

JEAN RABE

WITH A SHARP CRACK! THE EASTERN SUNSET LISTED HARD to port, spilling sailors across the deck and setting the main sail flapping like a wounded bird. A second *crack!* shook the hull, and the ship stopped as though it had struck a rock wall.

"Curse your deadlights, Volkin!" Captain Bellar Graydelver pulled himself up by the wheel and glared at the crow's nest. "Aground! You shout no warning, damn you!"

Volkin Firmfist peered over the nest and flailed his stubby arms. "'Tis not a ridge we struck, Cap'n! 'Tis a—"

The rest was lost in a piercing howl and another *crack!* as something rammed the stalled ship again.

"Huller! Huller, Cap'n!" This came from the first mate, Rakgar Ironbeard. He'd drawn a cutlass, and made ready to leap over the railing. "A brace of 'em, Cap'n! They're right on us! To arms!"

"Mind the grass!" another sailor hollered.

"Two! We've never faced two before!"

"All to arms!" Captain Bellar shouted, fear clawing at his heart.

Indeed, hullers were solitary beasts, or so he'd always believed. "Hullers upon us! All to arms!"

"To arms!" called Volkin. He climbed out of the nest. "Huller!"

"Huller!" became an echoed buzz that raced through the dwarven crew. Each man clambered to the rail, pulling weapons—swords, axes, hammers, pikes—and jumping over the side with angry war cries: "Hullers! To arms!"

"Mind ye the grass!" shouted bosun's mate Agamm Chertheart. Then he leaped, too.

As the last of his crew went over the side, Captain Bellar noted that only Sanill, the tall, grizzled drothmal barbarian, remained on board. He held tight to the fife rail, the strong wind tugging at his braided, gray-streaked topknot and implacable expression on his faintly feline-looking face.

Advanced age was no excuse for inaction as far as Bellar was concerned. He snarled at Sanill. "Get down there and fight with my men!" The barbarian didn't move, and Bellar joined his crew, landing on the ground amid the bloody chaos and narrowly missing one of the sapling high blades of lethal grass. Fortunate there were gaps in the greensward wide enough to pass through, else Bellar's men could not have come to ground to fight their enemy.

The hullers must have burrowed up beneath the *Eastern Sunset,* or Volkin would have spotted their approach through the prairie. As large as elephants, but with piglike snouts and thick hide as tough as dwarven-made armor, the pair had rammed the keel and shattered the port forward wheel, rendering the ship dead on the plains. The beasts were so close against the hull, the ship's great crossbows—mounted for distance shots—could not be used.

Twenty dwarves, the *Eastern Sunset's* entire complement, now battled the hullers. Captain Bellar weaved through gaps in the grass and swung his cutlass hard against the nearest huller's leg. The blade bounced off, and he swung again. The stink from the behemoth was horrid, like rancid meat in his mouth. It was redolent of things dead and rotting, and the wind whipping across the plains only made the stench worse, stirring it stronger, and making Bellar's eyes water.

Volkin waded in next to him, short sword leading and finding a gap in the plates and drawing blood. He was a bloody mess; his wide, ruddy face scratched; the backs of his hands shredded and bleeding; he'd not taken care when he charged through the grass, and had been lacerated for his bravery.

The hullers were immune to the razor-edged grass—and largely to most weapons—so the dwarves wielded barbed spears and long blades that could slip between the plates. War cries, huller howls, the clang of weapons, and the sails flapping futilely in the strong summer wind…the sounds of a cacophonic lance that drove painfully into Bellar's skull. Bellar shouted orders to his crew, though he suspected none of them could hear him. Reflex—a captain always barked orders.

Volkin darted under the beast and rammed his long sword straight up at a seam in the belly plating, rewarded with a splatter of dark blood that added to the awful stink. The huller felt that, its howling shriller as it kicked a front leg back into Volkin's chest, knocking him down. Bellar watched in horror as the beast took a step back and crushed the young dwarf.

"Nooooooo!" he screamed. His slashes came faster now, eyes locked on the space between plates, where Volkin had injured the beast. He couldn't see how his other sailors fared; it was all huller legs and grass from his underbelly vantage point.

The beast keened again, a pitch that set the captain's teeth to aching. If Bellar was the pious sort, he would have prayed to one of Aetaltis' many gods. But his race put no stock in them. Whether they would survive this day was on their own shoulders.

The huller's snaky tongue shot out, acid dripping from it and sizzling on the ground. Bellar felt something slice into his leg, sharp like a sword—a blade of grass bent low to the ground by the huller and springing up as the beast moved. Bellar ignored the pain and drove his cutlass up again and again, his arm a piston fueled by anger. Blood poured from the wound like he'd tapped a barrel. The creature wailed in obvious agony now, and even as angry as he was, Bellar hoped it wasn't all his doing, that his men were inflicting wounds elsewhere on the beast. The blood, dark as coal, gushed from the rent and made his hands so slippery he had trouble gripping the pommel. Again and again he jabbed along the seam, moving with the huller so he'd not share young Volkin's fate, then rushing out from beneath the beast when it started swaying.

Bellar now saw other dwarves fighting this huller with him. Svrul Bronzefoot, Cathal Earthminer, and Thomru Firespike, fine sailors who been with him the better part of a decade—men with sand, who'd taken on a huller before. But hullers were solitary beasts—Bellar had never encountered more than one at a time, and never had the behemoths crippled his ship. Never had they been so close he'd not first got off a few shots from his ship's ballistae to wound them. More often than not, they'd chased the beasts away.

His arms ached, so much effort he'd put into his blows, and his stomach churned from the overpowering odor. Still, he couldn't pick through the noises, everything a hurtful miasma. How much time had passed… Bellar thought it felt like years, that he'd aged to a point of utter weakness. Moments, heartbeats, time on a razor's edge that split life and death. His father once said a man was never more alive than when he was close to death. Bellar wondered what the huller felt right now.

"Die!" he shouted, not hearing himself, but feeling the word rumble up from his bucking stomach. "Die!" He blinked the sticky, fetid blood from his eyes and spotted another seam between plates, scuttling toward it, seeing Thomru do the same. "Die! Die! *Die!*"

The captain rallied his nearest men by his actions, somehow throwing off his exhaustion and willing his arm to keep stabbing, leaping with each jab so he could reach the tantalizing spot on the huller's chest, a space between plates where it looked like it had been wounded before. The blade sunk deep, and Bellar dropped back, crouched, and sprung again. Blood rained down, and Thomru alternated jabs, both of them dodging to avoid the creature's lashing, acid-coated tongue.

The ground seized and Thomru lost his balance, falling back and being impaled by a blade of grass. Bellar continued working on the huller's wound, leaping and stabbing, crouching to spring again, maintaining his balance when the earth trembled. There was a rhythm to the tremors, and through the noise—thankfully lessening now—he heard *throm! throm! throm!*

Footsteps! The other huller was retreating, the tremors were from its footfalls and grew softer as it hurried away.

A cheer cut through the din, his men victorious.

But the huller in front of him was not yielding.

"To the death!" Bellar cried. "Yours or mine!"

Rakgar was at his shoulder now, wielding a pike and driving it up. The pike wasn't his first mate's weapon of choice, and so Bellar knew that it had come from a downed sailor. How many men had they lost?

"To the death!" Rakgar howled.

More sailors joined them, swinging, cursing, most of the blows powered by fear and anger and largely ineffectual against the hide. But enough got through, and as Rakgar crumpled from injury and exhaustion, the huller did too, dropping to its knobby knees as dwarves skittered back—some straight into blades of the hateful grass, one pinned beneath the behemoth as it listed like a ship before toppling to its side. The dwarves continued hacking at it to make sure it was dead.

There were no cheers this time, but Bellar felt the shared bone-numbing sense of relief.

The dead were tended to first: Durthic the Blue, Rakgar Ironbeard, Thomru Firespike, young Volkin Firmfist, and Rakgar's brother, Eldar. The survivors were all wounded, Cathal the most severe; he would not live to see the stars come out. So six down, the remaining crew counted fourteen, including Bellar. It would be enough—the captain had left port with twice the number essential to man the *Eastern Sunset*, as he knew this voyage might be deadly.

Even so, he could only afford to lose four more.

"Agamm, you are first mate," Bellar pronounced after the dead had been burned far off the starboard side on a barren patch of earth—the blaze carefully managed, as the dwarves could not risk the plains catching fire. That would be the end of all of them, given the constant wind.

"Svrul, you are bosun's now." The promotions were not cause for celebration. There'd been no religious ceremony or prayers for the dead, it was not dwarven custom, nor was there thought given to any afterlife. There wasn't one as far as Bellar was concerned—a dwarf existed or did not. He knew some, though, who worshipped their ancestors—ghost gods. Bellar did not believe in such specters either.

The damage to the ship was significant.

A gaping hole in the ground near the center point of the keel showed where the hullers had burrowed up. Agamm speculated that the beasts must have been tunneling, sensed the ship rolling across the plains, and had surfaced to investigate. They'd shattered the port wheel and smashed through a section of hull. The *Eastern*

Sunset always carried wood for repairs—every stoneship did—but there wasn't enough for the scope of this. Bellar ordered the men to harvest more—from some of the quarter deck supports, from crates in the hold, and using all the furnishings in the galley; meals would be eaten on the floor for the remainder of the journey.

Half the sailors carefully cleared the grass directly around the ship and tackled repairs under Agamm's direction. Agamm was the *Sunset's* only speller, and used his rune magic to strengthen the sections. The rest of the men rendered the massive huller, while large carrion birds struggled to circle overhead in the strong wind. Flanks were cut and would be roasted for dinner. Despite its stink when alive, huller meat was rich and sweet. Strips of it would dry on deck, then be seasoned for jerky. But there was too much to manage, and so the carrion would feast on the carcass for a long while.

The smaller armor plates were culled and cleaned, and later would be fashioned into shields or sold. The tusks and claws would bring a good price in a big market—much too valuable to leave behind.

It was far into the evening before the repaired wheel was affixed and the ship righted. Lantern held close, Bellar circled the *Eastern Sunset*, inspecting it. The *Sunset* was a large, old stoneship, named not because it was made of stone, it was made of wood brought from the forests around Port Vale, but named because it traveled over stone and earth, across the plains between the mountains and plateaus. Long years ago, dwarven craftsmen wanting to cross the stretches of deadly blade grass came up with the notion of wheeled ships, and the whipping winds that coursed across the land had been harnessed to propel the vessels at great speed. Like most of the stoneships, *Eastern Sunset* was built in Razor's Edge, a settlement near Stonegate Pass on the Blade Sea. No body of water this sea, just an immense tract dotted with the tall lethal grass and populated with dangerous beasts—the hullers among the worst of them.

"If this wind holds, Cap'n, we should reach the mountains in less than three days." Agamm was at the wheel. Bellar had come back on board and was to his side, face tipped up and letting the rushing air play across his craggy features.

"And will it hold, Agamm?"

"I could cast runes to be certain, Cap'n, and—"

"My question was foolish. It doesn't really matter, does it?" Bellar shook his head. "It doesn't matter at all. The wind will hold strong, or it will lull. The wind will do what it will do. And I do not need your runes to tell me it will rain soon. I can smell it."

The rain came at dawn, and the dwarves stripped naked on the deck, letting the deluge wash the blood from their hides and their clothes and out of their caked beards. Bellar ordered the sails down; no reason to risk the rigging and masts in this serious blow. Clean and on the mend, bandages showing on all of them, they gathered on the floor in the galley, riding out the rest of the storm and alternately dozing and reminiscing about their dead fellows.

Bellar fought sleep and sat cross-legged near the barbarian. The captain was oddly tall for a dwarf, just shy of five feet, but the barbarian was easily seven—and had been taller before the years rounded his shoulders and stooped his back. The drothmal was *old*...sixty years at least...young for a dwarf, but ancient for the barbarian, a decade past the expectancy of his life. Sanill's pale skin gave him the complexion of a scholar, and it was so deeply wrinkled it reminded Bellar of tree bark. His eyes were an odd cast; gray one moment, winter-sky blue the next, and then almost colorless, as if he could change them on a whim.

"I have not been a warrior for a long, long time." Sanill's voice was soft and breathy, as if talking was an effort. "They grumble that I should have joined the fight, your sailors. But my bones are too weak for that, and I carry no weapon." A pause: "And you are not paying me to swing a sword, are you?"

Bellar listened to the sailors chatter.

"Some of the treasure to the sister of Rakgar and Eldar, agreed?" This from Agamm, who had been immediately accepted by the others as first mate.

"Aye, and some set aside for the family of Volkin," Svrul added. "I know his father. Any coin would be welcome there. Thomru, Cathal, the Blue…they never spoke of relations."

"The Blue, he would have hated this storm," Agamm chuckled. "He would have kept all the blood in his beard, proud of it. Strung some of the beasties' teeth around his fat neck." The first mate raised a tankard and the rest joined him in a toast.

Svrul drained his mug and passed if for a refill. "Let us hope there is plenty of treasure at the end of this. More coins than this ship can carry."

Those awake heartily agreed.

"I am paying you well." Bellar kept his voice low, not in secrecy, but so not to intrude on his sailors' conversations. "So much coin you'll not have enough years left to spend it in. All the coin I had, I gave you."

"It is for my children's children," Sanill returned in his age-soft voice. "I've no need of your gold."

"But I've great need of you—your mind for the ancient language." Bellar had found Sanill in New Black Cliff nearly two weeks past. The captain had been visiting settlements in search of someone able to read the primitive drothmalen language—little more than curious scratching, the words seemed—and held in a book with pages made of an unidentifiable kind of skin. Rather, the pages were *part* of a book, a collection stitched together with gut threads, rolled and presented in a scroll case to Bellar. The rest of the book, penned during the Age of Darkness, had been lost to the centuries, and even the drothmal known to the clan had been able to decipher only a few phrases…these hinting at a "treasure of all treasures," and a broken weapon that could be rejoined. Bellar had to find a drothmal who could read it.

Then fate had given him Sanill.

"You find the ancient weapon rumored in this book," the dwarf clan leader had said to Bellar, "the weapon this piece I give you has broken away from. You bring me that prize of a whole weapon, Bellar Graydelver, and I will not stand in your way." Currently the clan leader stood firmly in the way of Bellar joining with his youngest daughter, Rurli, an incredibly beautiful dwarf the captain loved even more than the *Eastern Sunset*. The dwarf clan leader had said that since Bellar owned no lands, and had no home, save this ship, he had nothing to offer. But if he could gain the prize that matched the hook piece, a thorn a weaponsmith would call it…

"For your children's children, eh?" Bellar mused. "I do this for sweet Rurli. Perhaps with her I will have children, too. Perhaps my children will have children. But I must find the weapon first." The elder dwarf was demanding the rumored prize in exchange for permission to take Rurli's hand. Any treasure beyond that weapon was for Bellar and his crew.

If Bellar had believed in the gods, he would have prayed that there truly would be treasure at the end of all of this, and that the broken weapon existed. But since he had no faith in any supposed deities, he closed his eyes and listened to the crew's chatter until he fell into a well-needed sleep, wherein he dreamed of sweet Rurli.

THREE DAYS LATER, THE EASTERN SUNSET ANCHORED AT the foothills. Agamm had worked closely with Sanill in that time, who translated sections of the book and gave directions. It was as if the complement followed some old trade route and used all the navigation tools they had, coupled with the speller's runes.

"Svrull, the *Sunset* is under your watch." Normally Bellar would leave his first mate in charge, but Agamm's runes might be necessary on the mountainside. The captain selected three others to accompany them—Gradon and Halmett Oresplitter, and the strongest of his crew, Orok the Oak, who he entrusted to escort Sanill. Bellar worried the ancient barbarian might need to be carried up the mountain, and the Oak would be up to the task.

They stopped often so Sanill could rest. The Oresplitters were anxious, the promise of treasure making their feet itch.

"Cannot we be on up?" Gradon pressed. "Let the Oak bring the drothmal as he will?"

Bellar scowled. "We go together. Enjoy the slow journey, my friend. Enjoy the crunch of rock under our heels and the burn in our legs from all this climbing. Soon enough we will be back on our ship."

Gradon paced as much as he could on the mountainside, his brother sitting nearby, mumbling and ticking off something on his fingers. Bellar listened close and made out: "Sandstone, siltstone, basalt, quartz, granite—" The dwarf was counting the types of rock he saw along this trail.

And trail was a generous word, Bellar considered. The course they traveled was a mere suggestion of one; it looked like a path great horned goats had set down by infrequent passage rather than one caused by men. It was difficult going, and he didn't mind taking the rests to accommodate Sanill, who refused to be carried. Bellar sat near the barbarian now and pulled out the scroll case. The Oak leaned close as his captain unrolled the book and held it carefully. Sanill turned to the third page and pointed to the marks.

"Are we going true?" the Oak asked. "It's like a treasure map, isn't it? That book is a map."

Sanill turned to the fourth page. "The book is a history, and so thereby is a map of my people's ancestors. One tribe's history. It is incomplete, as if a storyteller caught his audience with a grand tale, but walked away before finishing it. And he left out some of the middle story, too." He studied the fifth page. "But yes to your question. We are going true. When the sun drops below the head of the eagle, we should find your treasure."

"Treasure!" The Oak straightened his shoulders and shook a big leather sack that was filled with other empty sacks. "Cap'n, if I can ask—"

Bellar nodded.

"—if this treasure we're after belonged to your people, drothmal—"

"Sanill."

"Fine. If there's any treasure here, Sanill, your ancestors placed it. Why is it you've not staked a claim for a share, asked to be part of the crew, demanded—"

"I will have these pages, and the ample coins the captain already gave me. I do not need riches from a time that my people would rather forget." Sanill closed the book and rerolled it. His voice took on strength. "The Age of Darkness was our punishment for being decadent on the eve of the Dark Hordes. Our ancestors suffered for their severe greed and wrong-living. Forgiveness took centuries to achieve. I took the captain's coins for my children's children. Divided, the wealth will not burden them, but will provide them a good future. I will take this book to share with them so they can learn the ancient language. If any treasure from the dark time still rests at the end of this map… I want no part of it."

The Oak stabbed a finger toward the ground. "But you're here," he said, "not because of the Cap'n's coins or that ugly book…you're here 'cause you're curious, aren't you? I can see it on your face."

Sanill raised his eyes, colorless at the moment, and fixed his gaze on a puffy cloud. "Your thoughts are true, Oaken dwarf. I would see what brought about our punishment with my own eyes. So I revel in the hardship of this climb and this search, and I pray to Droth, the god of trials, that my limbs endure. Yes, Oaken dwarf, I have come to sate my curiosity."

IT SHOULD HAVE TAKEN ONLY SEVERAL HOURS, BUT IT TOOK three days, the Oak and the Oresplitters quietly grumbling because they'd not brought enough food and were forced to ration their strips of jerked huller. Agamm used his runes to create enough water to sustain them, and he caught a small goat, which filled their bellies one evening. They'd meandered along the side of the mountain, searching for "the right spot to ascend to the eagle," according to Sanill. Then they had to wait for the sun to slip behind the formations at the top of the tallest ridge, discovering their first path did not match the book's instructions. They searched again because some of the formations looked similar, and they chose wrong twice more. Bellar thought the outcropping Sanill selected this time might have truly looked like an eagle's head centuries past, but time and the weather had worn it down, and perhaps some quake had destroyed what the drothmalen book said was a "pronounced stone beak." Nothing suggested a beak now.

"Cap'n!" the Oak gestured furiously at a cleft in the rock beneath the formation. In sunlight they'd not noticed it, the rent in stone. But in shadow it was clearly visible, looking like the black pupil in a cat's eye.

"Magic," Bellar said. No other explanation for its emergence. "Did your people have magic, Sanill? Strong enough to last so many years to hide this place from common eyes?"

Sanill leaned against the Oak as if the dwarf were a crutch. "Greedy in wealth, greedy in magic…the shamans, at least in those long ago times, practiced strong magic." The barbarian looked even older this day, the journey clearly wearing on his frail bones. "The shamans had magic so powerful they could have cracked the world with it and tossed us all into oblivion. Today, our shamans still have magic. But we are not so greedy about it, and we are no longer so foolish as to challenge the gods."

"The gods. Hah!" Bellar spat at the ground. "Your people were and still are foolish enough to worship them."

The captain had brought a small lantern in his pack. He filled it with oil as the Oresplitters rocked anxiously one foot to the next, then passed it to the Oak. The dwarves didn't need the light for the tunnel ahead; their keen eyes accepted the darkness. But he knew the drothmal was not so blessed.

"We cannot tarry in there," Sanill advised. "The pages say the shadow keeps the door open. If we lose the shadow, we might well be trapped inside the mountain. Not so much concern for me. I've lived a long life. But for you—"

The Oak laughed. "You don't know dwarves, drothmal. We like mountains. If we go in, we'll find a way back out."

"Or make one," Agamm added.

Bellar started in, but Agamm grabbed his shoulder. "Cap'n," he whispered. "If magic hid this cave, protecting it from nosy eyes, maybe there's more magic about. Best to let me go first." The dwarf pulled four stones out of his pocket and stirred them in his palm. After a moment he added a fifth, closed his eyes, and spoke words that sounded dwarven, but Bellar couldn't attach any meaning he knew to them.

The Oresplitters rocked back and forth on their heels, and the

Oak let out a long hissing breath and shifted the lantern to his other hand.

"Follow me." Agamm said. He held the stones out, symbols on them glowing the color of embers. "But not too close."

Bellar was next, and motioned the Oak and Sanill to come behind him.

"Last," Halmett grumbled.

"Aye," said Gradon. "Last to the treasure, but last to find any trouble hidden magic might cause." He patted his brother on the back. "Cap'n, maybe we can find something to eat in here, eh?"

Bellar tamped their talk down and focused on Agamm. The first mate continued mumbling his mystical words, and Bellar could tell the rune rocks were glowing brighter without seeing them; the ember-color reflected off crystals in the passage walls as they went. The place reeked of age and had a mustiness to it, and the air was filled with stone dust that hung suspended. Bellar could smell the rock under all of it. Rocks carried scent, as much as flowers and the salty sea did, but not all races were able to discern it. These rocks were rich with minerals, silver buried somewhere inside, it had that tang to it.

Agamm stopped and faced the larboard wall, so abruptly Bellar bumped into him.

"I said not to follow too close, Cap'n." Agamm held the runes near the wall and whispered something. The rune stones glowed brighter and revealed a myriad of scratches from floor to ceiling. "That's writing I think. Drothmal?"

"Sanill," Bellar said. "His name is Sanill."

The Oak tipped the lantern high so the old barbarian could read it. "Like the book, this is not complete," Sanill said, raising a bony finger to trace a section. "See here, and here." He pointed to a place where the stone had been chipped away. "A quake maybe.

Maybe someone obscured this on purpose."

"What can you read?" the Oak jiggled the lantern. "The words that are there, what do they say?"

"We miss something by being last," Gradon grumbled. "I cannot see what is so interesting."

"These words, they refer to the Sea of Swords, before it was called that, and before the Age of Darkness. This place is very old." He traced more of the marks. "Here is reference to what came to be called the Icebound Plain. And here and here are references to Droth, the god of trial. But this is more incomplete than the pages. Any meaning is lost."

"Think someone was here before us?" Gradon asked.

"Obviously," the Oak returned. "Someone carved this." He jiggled the lantern near the words. "Carved this tunnel, too. Someone was here before us, you fool."

"I meant after that. After this was dug. Someone came and already got the treasure, do you think? My feet might be aching, my belly might be growling for nothing."

"You worry too much, Gradon." The Oak resumed his place behind the captain, and the group edged deeper into the mountain. "The treasure is here or it isn't. Someone came before us or they didn't. But we're here, foolish not to see it through, right Cap'n?"

"Aye." Bellar could sense their depth, not in the precise measurement of feet or fathoms, but in relation to ridge. They were halfway between the eagle's head formation at the top and the base of the foothills. The air was even staler, still filled with stone dust, and the walls were smoother—save for the places where someone or nature had ruined sections that had writing on them.

"Wards," Agamm decided. "They have that feel to 'em, Cap'n. Speller words that were either meant to protect what's below or keep intruders away."

"That's the same thing," the Oak said.

"No, I don't believe it is," Agamm returned. He went faster now, the passage sloping at a steeper angle.

Bellar kept pace, but the Oak and Sanill lost ground. The old barbarian was having a difficult time managing the grade. In his impatience, Gradon passed them, and in his rush tripped over rubble along the wall and fell.

"Damn. Damn!" Gradon cursed. "Damn and—"

Bellar wheeled around and stared at the rubble Gradon had landed in. "Bones."

"Aye, Cap'n," Agamm said. "Man-sized."

"The bones of two men. Two skulls, parts of skulls. The jawbones are missing." Bellar extended a hand and helped Gradon up, and with a finger wag indicated the dwarf should retreat to the back of the line. The captain knelt, bracing himself against the wall and poking through the bones, instantly pulling his fingers back. The bones were unnaturally cold and he could see his breath as he bent low over them. "Drothmal bones. Too thick to be elves, too long to be dwarves. Too old to be humans."

Despite the cold, he prodded one of the leg bones and turned it over, noticing scratches on it like those on the wall. "Did someone write on these?" He shook his head. "No, just scratches from the rocks. No one would write on bones."

Unnerved, he pushed himself up and waggled his fingers. "Get moving, Agamm." Turning to the Oak: "And help Sanill move faster. Carry him if you have to." What he did not add: *I do not wish to be down here longer than necessary.*

It was the cold bones. Bellar was more than a little unsettled by this place, even though he usually felt a sense of peace in the mountains. The course curved now, back upon itself and ever down; they passed two more scatterings of bones—and these Bellar did not pause to examine.

"Curiosity, it is a foolish thing," he heard the old barbarian mutter. "Wise to leave the dead alone."

"As is love foolish," Bellar whispered. Were it not for fair Rurli, he would be on the deck of his ship, sailing back and forth between settlements along the Blade Sea to satisfy trading contracts.

The passage ended at a point Bellar guessed was a mainmast's length below the surface in front of a stone door covered with a riot of the ancient drothmalen scratchings.

Agamm raised his rune stones and the ancient words on the door glowed bright.

"Don't," Bellar said. "I don't want them read."

"But Cap'n, they could be a warning or a ward," Agamm argued. "You brought me here to use my magic. These letters are not scratched out. Perhaps Sanill can—"

Bellar pushed him aside. "If it is a warning, I'll not heed it, and if it is a ward, I'll weather it. Come too far to turn around. I smell gold."

"I do too," Agamm said softly. "Gold and something else."

Bellar put his shoulder to the door and shoved. Again, and Agamm joined him. It finally budged, and a swirl of dust drifted out.

"Again," Bellar said, coughing. He felt the dry dust on his tongue.

Two more shoves and there was an opening just wide enough to squeeze through.

Agamm pulled the rune stones out of his pocket again. As the first mate consulted them, Bellar went inside. "Follow when I call for you."

"And if you don't call?" Gradon wondered.

Though dwarven eyes were keen in darkness, it took minutes for Bellar's vision to adjust and pick through the shadows. He would need the lantern to better see this place, but his senses told him quite a bit. It was cold, colder than it should be, given the time of year and that they were not so deep into the earth. It was a cold like he'd felt touching the bones. The chill seemed to have a presence. He shook off that notion; such a thing was not possible.

More interesting to him were the scents of gold and silver, a trace of platinum—he smelled those things, and rotted wood and cloth. Focusing and picking through the shadows, he saw mounds of coins, the pieces larger than current currency. Some had been contained in chests, but the wood had yielded to the centuries, leaving only strips of the metal that had once bound them together. There were totems two dwarves high, carved of a stone Bellar had no name for, but it smelled valuable. The pieces of jewelry were large, and would be considered ugly by present standards—but what they were made of could be broken apart and refashioned, gold, gems. There were countless gems, but in rough states; a jeweler would be needed to facet them. The drothmal of centuries past likely lacked skilled artisans to give them a proper cut and sparkle.

"Bring all the sacks," Bellar said. And they wouldn't be enough. On the following trip he would bring the entire crew, and it would require still more visits. The wealth of a kingdom, of several kingdoms perhaps, and Sanill had said it belonged to only one tribe. And now it belonged to the crew of the *Eastern Sunset*. "This is amazing. Take care where you step. Destroy nothing with your big feet. Agamm! We need light."

The lantern the Oak carried wasn't bright enough; it revealed only Sanill's weary, pale face. The Oak helped the barbarian sit on the only flat piece of ground in the large chamber. The old drothmal set his back against a wall covered with the ancient writing and closed his eyes.

Agamm stood at Bellar's shoulder. "I smell magic, Cap'n, the scent as strong as that of the gold. Can't tell if it's good or for ill, but—"

"Can you give us some good light? And can you find magic

weapons, with those runes?" Agamm had sailed with Bellar long enough that the captain figured he should know what his first mate was capable of. But he didn't all that often ask for runes to be cast, and in truth he wasn't all that interested in magic. Bellar reached into his pack and retrieved a cloth envelope the size of a pie plate. He unwrapped it while Agamm worked.

The first mate knelt and placed his rune stones on the ground. He had to nudge some coins away to find an empty piece of floor. Nine stones, flipped this way and that, then he added four more. The runes on them glowed blue this time, and he arranged them in a star pattern. One more stone added, and a ball of light a big as an ale keg appeared in mid-air, so bright Bellar had too look away. The light spread throughout the cavern.

"By my beard!" the Oak shouted. "Cap'n, we are forever rich!" Mounds of gold and silver, uncut gems everywhere—everything coated with stone dust, yet there were spots that glimmered brightly nonetheless. "My heart! My heart!"

The Oresplitters started filling their sacks, scooping the riches in without bothering to pick through anything. The Oak followed suit.

Agamm and Bellar watched them.

"Can you find magic weapons?" the captain persisted. He could see weapons scattered in the mix of everything…sword pommels visible in a hill of coins, spearheads laying atop wood that had rotted. A bone sticking out. "The runes, your nose, Agamm. I want something in particular. Can you find me a magic weapon?" Bellar had thought he'd wanted only the axe head that went with the thorn, but the sight of all this wealth was making his mouth water. He'd take a share of riches, too. It would give Rurli a very good life.

Bellar showed Agamm the thorn that he'd carried so carefully in the envelope. It was a piece of citrine, snapped off from the axe blade head of a halberd. "I need to find the rest of this, Agamm.

Can your runes—"

Agamm took the thorn and glanced between it and the men scooping up the coins.

"There's so much here, they'll not get more than you. Find the rest of this, Agamm, then fill your own sacks."

"I smell the magic, Cap'n, in this thorn and in this place. You must smell it, too."

"I smell the gold, and minerals, the stone, things I can't put names to. Find the rest of this." He stabbed a finger at the thorn.

"Aye Cap'n." Agamm retrieved three small stones from his pocket, along with a finger-length piece of tusk, all with symbols etched on them. He turned the pieces over so the runes were against his skin, and he talked softly. Bellar barely heard him over the sound of coins being scooped.

"We'll have to come back with more sacks," Gradon said. "Empty the ale barrels and roll them down here. Fill 'em up. It could take us a week or more!"

"So much gold," the Oak said. "So very, very much. Too good to be true."

A part of Bellar shared that sentiment. It all seemed too good, unreal.

"So easy, this treasure," Gradon gushed.

Bellar didn't think it had been easy at all. It had cost the lives of four sailors...and the life of the old barbarian. He realized minutes ago that Sanill's chest had stopped rising and falling, and that the old man's head was canted unnaturally to the side. The journey had been too much for the drothmal's advanced years. What to do with the body? Bellar didn't know drothmalen custom. Should it be returned to the settlement where he'd come from, given over to the children of Sanill's children?

Easier to leave it here, he decided. They had enough to carry out of this chamber…more than enough. "Can you find—"

"Yes, Cap'n. I think I have found something." Agamm shuffled forward, pushing coins aside with his feet as he went. Citrine thorn in one hand, runes in the other, he headed straight to a mound in a far niche of the cavern. "The thorn is tugging me, Cap'n. The magic smells stronger here."

Bellar followed and saw it—sitting atop a pile of coins and gems, the axe blade that had snapped off from the thorn. No dust had dared settle on it, and the citrine glowed warmly.

"Give it here." He reached for the thorn and held it out. He felt a pull, as if the piece wanted to be next to its other half. "Can your runes…can your magic…put it back together?" He realized as soon as he asked the question that Agamm's mystic skills weren't needed.

Bellar set the thorn against the axe blade and the pieces joined together with a sharp *hiss!* "There's no haft," he said. "Rotted away. Rurli's father will need to replace it."

"So beautiful," Agamm said. "A weapon head made of crystal, edged in platinum." Agamm whistled. "A fortune, it's worth."

For the briefest of moments Bellar considered keeping it, forgetting Rurli and the clan, sailing away and battling hullers with this ancient magical blade. But love was more powerful than his greed. This weapon would not keep him warm at night. With a sigh, he edged the citrine blade into the cloth envelope and put it inside his pack. "I've won a bride today, Agamm."

"And we've won a fortune." Agamm started scooping coins into a sack. "It's so cold here, Cap'n."

Unnaturally so, Bellar thought. Colder than when they'd first entered. He could see his breath puffing away from his face and the tips of his fingers felt numb. He reached to his side and tugged an empty sack loose from his belt, bent and started filling it with coin.

"Sanill is dead," Bellar said after a few moments. "All of this was too much for him."

"Dead? Leave him here?" Agamm looked behind him and gestured to the dead drothmal. "Aye, leave him here, Cap'n. There are other bones in this place. He'd have company." He pointed to the base of another mound, a leg bone protruded. He indicated more bones under another pile. "Let him rest with his ancestors?"

"Aye," Bellar said. He was more choosy than his men, scooping in only the gold coins, and plucking only the largest uncut gems. "We should leave soon. I remember Sanill saying the entrance could disappear when the shadows go. Easy to find this cavern now, we can come back another day."

"He said something to that notion, about the entrance, Sanill did. Something about it disappearing." Agamm bobbed his head and worked to fill a second sack. "Though my runes could open whatever magic closes this place. I'm strong with earth magic." But the first mate was not so strong physically as the other dwarves, and wasn't filling his sacks all the way full. "Leave in a little while and—"

"Gradon!" Halmett's howl caught Bellar's attention. The younger Oresplitter had stepped away from his sacks and drawn his short sword. A few feet away Gradon had collapsed on a pile of treasure.

Bellar rushed toward the Oresplitters, abandoning his sack—but not his satchel, drawing his short sword and fixing his eyes on the bones protruding from the pile Gradon had fallen on. The light Agamm had called was so bright the motes of stone dust looked like hovering gnats here, easily seen…as was the drothmal-shaped mist that had risen from the bones and that hovered over the fallen dwarf. Gradon was dead.

"Undead!" Bellar shouted. "To arms!"

Halmett swung first, his blade passing through the ghostly image.

"Your runes!" Bellar ordered Agamm. "Do something! The spirit ignores our steel. Use your runes. Weapons are useless." But the captain swung anyway, watching the blade pass through the undead, seeing Halmett pull back for another swing and stop, eyes bulging. The sword fell from Halmett's fingers and he grabbed for his throat. A pair of ghostly hands was around his neck. "Agamm! Your runes!" A second spirit appeared.

Agamm stirred rocks on his palm, chattering fast and sounding like he rushed through a child's song. "True undead, Cap'n. Their spirits haven't severed the connection with the bones."

"Sever them!" Bellar barked. He dropped his pack and reached inside, pulling out the pouch that held the ancient weapon head. If their steel did nothing, perhaps this artifact might. "Sever them now!"

"Trying," Agamm cast his rune stones at the bones near Gradon's body. One of the spirits writhed and rose to the ceiling, disappeared in the motes of stone dust. Then the first mate was chattering again, drawing out more stones. "I've only these stones left, Cap'n, and—"

"Another one here!" This came from the Oak, who stood not far from Sanill's corpse.

Perhaps the drothmal did not die from exertion and old age, Bellar thought, as he felt the ancient weapon head warm against his fingers. He hadn't needed to swing it, the edge glimmered and a bolt of lightning shot out, striking the spirit choking Halmett.

At the same time Agamm cast his stones again, and the target spirit dissolved before it reached the ceiling. Then the first mate reached down and grabbed at the sacks that Gradon had filled and started tugging it toward the cavern entrance. "I've no more runes, Cap'n."

"Retreat!" Bellar howled, gesturing wildly to the Oak and Halmett, and somehow coaxing another bolt of lightning from the weapon. The latter dwarf was bent and coughing, trying to regain his breath. "Now!" Bellar tucked the weapon in his shirt, grabbed another of Gradon's sacks and managed to hoist it over his shoulder. "Now if you want to live!"

That jolted Halmett into action, and the dwarf bolted toward the doorway, not bothering with any treasure. The Oak was already there, sweeping his sword in front of him, breath fanning away from his face. In the bright light, Bellar could see his lips had turned blue.

"Leave!" Bellar shouted. He watched the Oak grab a sack and follow Halmett through the doorway. The captain paused only long enough for Agamm to slip out. Bellar had always prided himself on being the last one to leave a place—his ship, a tavern, even this accursed cavern.

"Get behind me!" Agamm shouted in the corridor. The first mate slammed the stone door shut and ran his fingers along the edge, more of the sing-song words from some spell. "Using the door, Cap'n. Enough runes on it, pulling their magic. Pulling—" The stone seam sealed, and from behind it came an eerie wail. "The undead, Cap'n. They want us."

"Move!" Bellar gestured up the rocky tunnel. The Oak and Halmett were already out of sight. The treasure in his sack was heavy and clinked together with every step, weighing him down. He could move faster without it, leave it and come back later. But there might not be a later, and so he gritted his teeth and refused to drop it, sucked in the frigid stone dust that continued to swirl. "Move, Agamm! Move for all that's in you!"

Chest burning despite the wintry air, legs feeling like anchors, Bellar pushed himself up the steep grade and around the turns, in the back of his mind registering where he was within the mountain. Too deep, so very far to go. He thought he saw some of the ancient drothmalen scratchings on the wall glow like Agamm's rune stones had, but it could have been a trick of his exhaustion.

He refused to let go of the treasure, even when his fingers ached from the cold. This voyage had been too costly to discard the coins—Durthic the Blue, Rakgar and Eldar Ironbeard, Thomru Firespike, young Volkin Firmfist, Gradon Oresplitter, Sanill the drotheen. They had paid for this treasure, and paid dearly.

The Oak was added to that list, taken down by another spirit that swirled around bones—the pile that Gradon had disturbed when he'd fallen on their way in. Perhaps that was what had awakened the spirits, moving the treasure and jostling their remains. Perhaps if the dwarves had been more careful, not so overcome with greed…as the ancient drothmal had been overcome with greed for wealth and power long centuries past.

The writhing spirit released the falling Oak and stretched a misty arm toward Agamm, who had paused to gape at it. Bellar pushed his first mate forward, and in reward felt the icy insubstantial fingers close on his flesh instead. Bellar screamed, the pain so intense it threatened to render him boneless. Once more he retrieved the weapon and coaxed a bolt of lightning to destroy the spirit, then felt the blade cool.

"Move, Cap'n!" Agamm cried. "Move! There's another one. No, two!"

Bellar again tucked the weapon under his shirt and grabbed the Oak's dropped sack with his free hand and forced his legs to pump faster. The air swirled even colder against the back of his neck, and he didn't pause to turn around. He knew more wraiths were following, felt the bone-numbing chill right behind him.

He burst out the tunnel opening and fell on a patch of gravel, Agamm and Halmett picking him up and nervously looking at the slit in the rock. A patch of milky white haze hovered inside the opening, the undead waiting.

But the undead did not venture outside.

Four large sacks of gold and gems had made it out with them—an impressive treasure, though merely a suggestion of wealth in comparison to the ancient drothmal horde below the mountain.

"For another day, another year, Cap'n." Agamm gestured at the slit and then tipped his head back. A host of stars were out; they'd been inside the mountain for hours. "When I've replenished my strength and my runes and can come back and sever the spirits. You can use that axe blade, too."

"Don't know how many spirits are down there," Halmett said. He bent and tried to catch his breath, dropped to his knees and shook. "Don't know how many bones are hiding under those coins."

"Too many," Bellar said. He started down the mountain, shouldering the largest sack, and dragging another. "Don't tarry," he warned them. "We've our dead to toast, and I'll be sailing for Rurli at dawn."

THE WARLADY'S DAUGHTER

LUCY A. SNYDER

LULLED BY THE STEADY SWAYING OF THE MULE-DRAWN wagon, Elyria stared at the shimmering green sea of grass surrounding Oakengrove. It seemed to stretch on forever; a terrible, dull, oppressive expanse of green, relieved only by the occasional drab field of barley or wheat farmers had carved through the deep sod. Grass and grain, grain and grass! Would she ever get to see a real ocean? Would anything ever *happen* here?

Her miserable teenage reverie was broken by her uncle's voice: "Ria, are you listening to me?"

"Yes, Uncle Bevard." She sat up straighter on the wagon bench, then realized she hadn't any clue what he'd said. "I'm sorry; what did you say?"

He gave an exasperated sigh. "We're almost at the Iron Fist Tavern. What's on their order?"

She spread the coarse, grass-pulp paper out on her lap. Its paleness contrasted prettily with the new purple skirt her aunt had sewed for her 16th birthday. Elyria had gathered a whole quart of pokeberries to make the dye, but of course her aunt had hidden the reason she needed them. The smooth fabric had come out a gorgeous, vibrant hue that made her think of royalty, which in turn made her imagine the traveling bards' tales of court intrigue and sword duels in the Northern palaces…

"Ria! The order?"

"Sorry, Uncle," she mumbled, forcing herself to focus on the dull list scrawled in his nearly indecipherable handwriting. "They ordered ten loaves of honey white, five loaves of dark rye, and five loaves of the nutberry."

He shook his head at her, his long rust-colored beard sweeping across the front of his plain work tunic. "Was that so difficult? We'd be finished already if it weren't for your constant woolgathering!"

She hung her head. "Sorry, Uncle."

"You told me you didn't want to be cooped up in the bakery all day." His frustrated tone made her want to jump out of the cart, dash into the shoulder-high grass and keep running until she got to the Amethyst Sea somewhere in the unfathomable Southern distance. "You *begged* me to let you come out here and help me with deliveries. Why can't you pay attention to what we're doing?"

A tiny, frantic voice in the back of her head wanted her to scream, *"Because it's all so bloody boring!"* But she knew saying it would be disastrous. Her uncle wasn't the kind of brutal man to backhand her for talking back to him. But he almost certainly would punish her with a month of scrubbing floors, chopping wood for the fires, and scraping ashes in the name of giving her a fresh appreciation for delivery duty.

So she meekly said, "I'm sorry, Uncle Bevard. You have been very patient with me, and I'm sorry."

"You need to spend more time in the real world and less time in your head." He pulled up on the mules' reins to halt them in the shade of the three-story public house at the edge of the town. The Iron Fist Tavern was built from clay bricks, thatch, field rock, plaster, and wooden beams secured with iron bands and huge iron nails with heads the size of a man's fist.

"Once you're married, your husband will expect you to be attentive to his needs at all times! If you turn out to be a poor wife, it will reflect badly on your Aunt Ruth and I, and you wouldn't want that, would you?"

It felt as though something inside her soul had been impaled on a spit and was being roasted, squirming and kicking, over a hot coal fire.

Don't say what you're thinking, she warned herself. *It'll be floors and ashes for sure!* "I…I don't think anyone will be wanting me as a wife, at least not soon—"

"Oh, nonsense!" He laughed. "You're a fine-looking female, healthy…you have the bloom of a girl who'd birth a fine, strong son!"

Oh, ye sweet and fuzzy gods, she thought. *Babies.*

Other peoples' babies were cute. And if cuteness were their sum total, bearing them would be fine! But then there was the staying up all night with a crying infant, the endless dirty diapers, the colic. She'd been at Ruth's side when she gave birth to her little cousin Sky; her aunt had been in labor for two solid days. She nearly died of fever afterward! And to see the agony of a baby tearing through such a woefully small part of the body…oh no. She didn't know what malign curse the Enaros had put upon women to have to go through all that, but she wanted no part of it!

"There are plenty of lads and men who'd want a girl like you," her uncle continued, oblivious to her discomfort. "The blacksmith's son, what's his name?"

Oh gods, that brainless lunk, she thought.

"Corlis," she muttered. Being married to him would be like

being married to an orc, except perhaps an orc might have better personal grooming habits.

"Ah, yes, Corlis! I've seen how he looks at you," her uncle sing-songed.

Have you also seen how he digs in his ears and eats what he finds? Have you heard how he can't pronounce words with more than two syllables? Elyria wanted to ask. She blushed, wishing the ground would open so she could tumble into a chasm and be lost forever.

"And there are right proper men in this community who could do well for you. *And* give our family's reputation a real boost in the bargain! Like Grainger Tevis; he's got at least fifty acres of the richest land around, and since his wife died last year, every woman in town seems to be trying to get his attention. I admit he's not much to look at…and he's a bit gruff…but that land!"

Grainger Tevis? He had to be at least fifty years old! She shuddered at the thought of his old, cold hands touching her in a marriage bed. It was just…just *nasty* for a man his age to want a girl her age. If Corlis was unappealing, Tevis was so many leagues beyond that she couldn't plumb the depths of her dismay.

"Well, it'll be at least another year before finding you a husband becomes a critical matter," her uncle mused aloud. "Wouldn't want you turning 18 and finding yourself an old maid, would you?"

"No. Of course not," she replied through gritted teeth.

He laughed. "Ah, we can worry about it later. The bread's getting stale while we sit here yammering!"

IT TOOK THEM ANOTHER TWO HOURS TO WEND THEIR WAY back to their family's thatched brick building in the center of town. The bakery and small rooms for the apprentices occupied the first floor, and Elyria and her family lived on the second floor. It had cost a pretty pile of silver to build, but her uncle had inherited a decent sum when Elyria's parents died. Their hard work at the bakery had turned him into one of the wealthier men in town. Not as wealthy as landed gentry such as Grainger Tevis, of course, but he did well.

"Stack the baskets and fold the linens, then wash up for supper." He unhitched the mules, and started leading them around to the barn behind the bakery. "I'll tell the apprentices to carry everything into the storeroom."

"Yes, sir." She set to shaking the crumbs off the cream-colored cloths and folding them into neat squares in one of the empty reed baskets.

She'd almost finished the last cloth when she heard a hubbub and the sound of heavy horses' hoofbeats coming down the thoroughfare.

Her mouth fell open when she saw a wedge of armored warriors atop huge black horses thundering down the cobblestones. Five, seven, nine…a whole dozen of them! With their fierce face paints and black swirling tattoos, they looked like something out of a fever dream. Where could such warriors as these have come from?

Elyria's jaw dropped further when she realized the warriors were all women! How was it possible? Girls simply weren't allowed to fight in Oakengrove. Her 12-year-old cousin Stone got into fisticuffs with the other boys all the time, but the *one* time Elyria had given a bully a well-earned kick in his nethers, she'd had to scrub floors for a week! And take endless manners lessons at Lady Stufflebeam's house! How had these mighty-looking women been able to take up arms, ride horses, and learn the arts of war? One look at their hard faces and battle scars told her that if these women had husbands, those men would dare not treat them as chattel.

And in fact, she saw no signs of wedding jewelry or other marks of marriage. If these women had avoided that dreadful fate, perhaps she could, too? Hope and fear swelled in her heart.

The warriors clattered to a stop in front of the bakery. A tall warrior with black braids curling from beneath her battered steel helmet dismounted and clomped forward in her hobnail boots.

"Bevard of Oakengrove!" she bellowed. "I am Radulla of the Nemain! Come forth and parley, or we shall drag ye forth!"

A moment later, her uncle came through the door into the courtyard, wiping his hands on his apron. His face was ashen, and he shot Elyria a worried, ashamed look that she didn't understand.

"I am Bevard." His voice shook. "What is your business?"

"Our lady Aetiane has sent us to retrieve her daughter. It is her 16th year, and it is time for her to join our riders, as you agreed when we left her in your care."

Daughter? Elyria wondered. *This must be a mistake. He doesn't have any girls in his care, except…*

Her whole world suddenly seemed to tilt at the realization of what this strange amazing warrior-woman was saying.

"Ah." He paled and shifted his feet nervously. "Yes. Well…"

"Where is the girl?" Radulla stepped forward, scowling, and pulled off her heavy leather gauntlets as if she intended to beat or throttle him with her bare hands. "You were paid to keep her safe. If anything has happened to her—"

Her uncle took a step back, terror plain on his face. "No! No, she's fine…she's right there!" He pointed at Elyria, who felt as though she'd been thrown under a runaway cart.

Radulla turned and gave the girl an appraising up-and-down stare. Her dark eyes were disapproving and concerned. "You're Elyria?"

"Yes, ma'am." She gavc the warrior a quick, uncertain curtsey.

"Let me see your hands."

Elyria held her hands out. The warrior stepped forward to scowl at her palms and knuckles.

"You don't have the proper calluses." Radulla sounded disgusted. "How skilled are you with the sword and bow?"

"Sword and bow?" Elyra stammered. "I'm…I'm sorry, but girls aren't allowed—"

Radulla whirled on her uncle with alarming speed. "*You have not trained her?*"

Bevard flinched and backed up against the brick wall of the bakery. "I…I didn't think Aetiane would come back. She's in such a dangerous line of work—"

"You had but one job to do! One!" Radulla stepped forward until she was right in Bevard's face. "You were to hire a weapons tutor from Castle Port and make sure that your daughter was properly trained when we came for her! Our lady gave you a handsome sum to ensure that!"

Daughter? Elyria wondered, heat rising in her face. *He's really my father? Why did he lie? Was he ashamed of me?*

Meanwhile, Radulla was still shouting, her spittle lashing Bevard's face. He cowered lower and lower under her tirade.

"I have seen *many* worthless sires in my time," Radulla snarled, "but you are by far the most incompetent. Even the most sodden drunks of the bowery know better than to cross the Nemain! We should make an example of you that none shall forget!"

The warrior's tone promised terrible violence.

"No!" Elyria shouted. "No, stop! Please have mercy on him. *Please.*"

Radulla straightened up and gave Elyria another appraising stare. "I have many qualities but mercifulness is not among them. You *will* be trained, and trained *properly*, and if anyone interferes, there will be dire consequences. Your mother will test you herself to be certain."

Elyria's throat suddenly went dry. "How will I be trained?

Who will do it?"

"My lieutenant will stay behind to train you. Six months of *nothing* but training. If you have a beau, say goodbye to him this evening, because you will *not* be spending time with him after today."

She turned on her heel and pointed a stern finger at Bevard. "And *you* will provide our lieutenant with quarters, food, and anything she needs for your daughter's training. You will supply them without resistance or remark, and you will *not* interfere. Or your life will end in fire. Is this clear to you?"

"Yes." His face was ashen, and his voice was a broken whisper.

"Good." Radulla turned to face the other warriors, who had been waiting atop their steeds. "Korraine! Are you ready?"

"I am," replied a voice that rolled like a summer storm.

The other warriors reined their horses aside to allow Korraine through. Elyria's breath caught in her throat. Korraine was like a mountain made flesh and poured into leather and chainmail, and she rode atop a mighty dappled gray warhorse that had to be at least 17 hands tall. And she wasn't atlan. Her features were coarse, and her dark skin had a strange greenish hue, like copper that had just begun to patina. Her neck and shoulders were corded with muscle, and her lower canines jutted up over her lip like small tusks.

"Baker-man," Korraine rumbled. "Have you a barn with a hayloft?"

Bevard nodded, looking miserable and embarrassed; several dozen townspeople had gathered at a safe distance and were whispering in each others' ears and pointing. "Around back."

"Good." Her golden eyes flicked to Elyria. "Tomorrow you shall also sleep in the barn. Find a sturdy bedroll. Some nights we shall sleep in the field."

"But my bed is right here above the bakery—"

"You must get your bones used to sleeping on the ground." Korraine's tone left no room for negotiation. "There won't always be fine linens or a hearth where you're going. Meet me at the barn at first cocks-crow and wear sturdy clothes. Spend the night as you prefer."

Korraine gave Bevard a pointed stare, her lip curling back from wolfish teeth. "I expect you have questions only *he* should answer."

ELYRIA FINALLY BROKE THE TENSE SILENCE AT DINNER: "WHY did you say you were my uncle when you were really my father?"

Bevard bowed his head and clenched the edge of the broad oak dinner table, his knuckles going white. Her cousins Sky and Stone—*no, half-sister and half-brother*, Elyria corrected herself—looked wide-eyed from her to their father.

"I..." Bevard's voice faltered.

"Just tell her." Her stepmother Ruth sounded and looked as if the weight of the entire world had fallen on her shoulders. "Just tell her, and be done with it."

Her father set down his fork. "Eighteen years ago, I and some friends travelled to the Orchard Festival in Castle Port. I was betrothed to Ruth, but because we had not yet married, her parents did not let her travel with us. Had they relented...well, they did not."

He cleared his throat, looking deeply ashamed. "My friends and I drank a great deal of cider and perry at the festival. I had sworn faithfulness to Ruth, but at a tavern I met a young warrior woman named Aetiane, and the drink made me forget my vow that night. I was still in a stupor the next morning; my friends carried me out of the inn, and I put what little I could remember out of my mind and focused on my love for Ruth. I returned to Oakengrove, and the next month she and I married.

"Then, ten months later, Aetiane and one of her lieutenants rode into town after dark. They carried an infant—you, Elyria—and they told me they were going to war, and that I was your father, and that I had to keep you and raise you. They gave me the money I used to purchase this bakery. Ruth and I decided that the best thing to do was to make up a story about a brother of mine who'd died and left behind an orphaned daughter. Such things happen all the time, and the townsfolk would not bring whispering shame down upon our house. Shame that I now cannot avoid facing."

Everyone was silent for several moments. Elyria tried to make sense of the storm of emotions and questions inside her. She'd been told she was an orphan when her own father was the one raising her. How could he be so ashamed of her? Why did the townsfolk's opinions matter so much more to him than being honest with his own child? He could have told her, and she'd have kept it a secret. Did he not trust her to keep their family's reputation safe? Did he not really love her as a father was supposed to love a child?

But then, her mother was still alive, too. Why hadn't she come to get her? Was she still off at war? Was she having some grand, dangerous adventure? Was *she* ashamed of Elyria, too, because her father wasn't even brave enough to tell the truth? Would Elyria ever be good enough for her, or would she look at her with dismay, as Radulla and Korraine had? How could she ever be good enough when her father hadn't prepared her to do anything but cook?

"Radulla said you were given the money to train me. And you didn't," she finally replied.

"But you were a girl!" her father exclaimed, as if this were the most obvious thing in the world. "Seeking a warrior's training for you would make people ask questions!"

He frowned, looking troubled. "Besides, to hear Aetiane talk, I expected she'd be dead on the end of an orc's pike within a year, two at the most. I *swear* I never thought she'd actually send for you, and that you would spend your life in Oakengrove. And so

Ruth and I decided that we would raise you just as we'd raise any daughter of ours."

"But you didn't." Elyria felt a flush of anger. "I was always the orphaned niece. Not your daughter. You *never* would have admitted I was your daughter if they hadn't turned up today, would you?"

"Elyria! Don't speak to your uncle that way!" Ruth said, and then caught herself. "I mean, your father."

Elyria stared down at the rabbit stew and bread on her plate. *I am the daughter of a warrior woman,* she thought. Not just a woman; her mother had enough money to purchase a whole bakery. She was a warrior lady, the captain of her people.

"Apologize to your father," Ruth warned.

"I don't think I owe anyone an apology for speaking the truth." Heart pounding with anger, Elyria stood and picked up her plate and fork. "Good night to you all. I'll be in the barn."

"Don't you dare get up and leave!" Ruth's face was red with fury, but her voice was shrill with terror. "If you leave, you'll not be allowed back in this house!"

Elyria was too angry to care whether her stepmother feared the loss of her adopted child or was simply upset that she'd been disobeyed. She carried her dinner out into the darkness.

Korraine was on a folding camp chair beside a fire she'd built in the dirt in front of the barn. "That went as well as could have been expected." The orcish warrior's golden eyes gleamed in the firelight.

Elyria stopped short. "You heard us?"

The massive woman smiled and tapped her pointed ear; it reminded Elyria of a bat's. "I have unusual good hearing, thanks to my sire, may Endroren devour his blackened, worthless soul."

The curse shocked Elyria. "What did he do to make you say such things about him?"

"He was an orc chieftain. I do not know his name, nor do I wish to know it. He captured my mother, Lady Ariale…she was your mother's sister. He tortured and debased her. When the Nemain rescued her, she was pregnant with me, and her body was too broken to survive childbirth. Because there was no other family to take me, your mother and Radulla raised me on the backs of their warhorses. I teethed on arrow shafts and leather scabbards, and my first toy was a wooden dagger."

Korraine threw another log onto the fire. "It is my eternal regret that Radulla and Aetiane slaughtered my sire and his gang, because I would have liked that opportunity myself. I would have liked it *very* much."

"I'm…I'm sorry." Elyria didn't know what else to say.

"Sorry? There is nothing to be sorry about." Korraine stood and brushed off her leather tunic. "The Nemain saved me when any other atlan would have burned me with my mother's corpse, or left me on a hillside for the wolves. I have never known children's games or had a beau take me to a town dance, but I have known a mother's fiercest love, and I have learned everything I can about fighting and surviving. And I am respected by our sisterhood; the Nemain look to me to train daughters whose fathers have failed them, and I do that as well as I possibly can. I live, so that you and your cousins might live."

Elyria stared into Korraine's campfire for several moments. "I have a question," she finally asked.

"Yes?"

"Do I have a choice? About training to become a warrior, I mean."

Korraine gave her a sidelong glance. "I know you'll be expected to marry soon if you stay here. I got a good look at the lads here on our ride through the town, and if they have any outstanding qualities at all, they *must* be hiding them beneath their trousers.

Do you really prefer become a scullery-slave wife to one of these grassland bumpkins instead of seeking fortune and glory with your mother?"

"No," Elyria replied, blushing. She paused, trying to figure out how to voice the turmoil in her mind. "But Radulla didn't speak as if any of us here had a choice. If this is something I'm forced to do because my mother paid my father money, I'm still a slave, aren't I?"

Korraine laughed. "Few of us get to do exactly what we wish! Even the most powerful kings and queens are born into duty. But your mother would not want you to be forced into a dangerous life that doesn't fit you. Radulla…spoke *strongly* to aid your father's comprehension and stir his sense of urgency."

"So if I decide I don't wish to do this . . ?"

Korraine spread her scarred, calloused hands. "I was sent here to train you. That's the only duty I have right now. I have trained girls who were eager students, but I have trained girls who resisted and whined and feigned injury. I much prefer willing students! But I will not simply forget my duty in the face of your reluctance. Besides, you cannot know what life with the Nemain might be like until after I've trained you, can you? So why not learn what I have to teach you?"

"All right. That sounds fair." Elyria paused. "Have you never trained boys?"

Korraine shook her head. "Almost never. The Nemain only conceive girls, but every once in a while a girl decides she'd rather be a boy. And even more rarely, a boy wants to join us after he sees his father's daughter in training. The boys are welcome; it's handy to have some bearded chins around when we negotiate with clans that don't respect females."

Elyria frowned in confusion. "How is it possible that the Nemain only have girl children?"

"The story is that long ago, a princess named Nemae was married to a proud war king who got into a quarrel with a powerful wizard. The wizard, instead of attacking the king directly, decided to cast a spell upon Nemae so that she could bear no sons who could be heirs to the throne. The king discovered this after his twin daughters were born. Though it was entirely the sorcerer's doing, he blamed his wife. He planned to have Nemae arrested for witchcraft so that she would be executed and he could remarry. Nemae learned of the plot and fled in the night with her daughters, swearing that she would never again be at the mercy of a king's good will. She raised her daughters in the wilderness and taught them to fight, and our tribe grew from there."

"The Nemain don't marry?"

"Sometimes they do. Love is powerful, and leaving a child behind to be raised by strangers is by far the most difficult thing any of the sisters have to do. Some do marry and leave us to raise families; some later return to us. Some fall in love with warrior men and women who join us for a few months or their whole lives." Korraine shrugged. "To me, the Nemain are all the family I need, and I see no reason to leave."

THE NEXT MORNING, KORRAINE TOOK ELYRIA THROUGH a battery of lung-bursting calisthenics at the barn and in a nearby fallow field until the girl lay gasping in the dirt.

"You did better than many," Korraine said cheerfully. "You can't climb a rope or pull yourself up onto a branch, but you can press a good-sided log overhead and your balance is excellent. We'll work on the rest until you're fit. Now, let's go over to that orchard, and I'll show you how to care for a sword."

"Is…is it this hard for everyone?" Elyria gasped.

"At first it is. Everything gets easier with practice. Particularly the killing."

Elyria felt a chill. She sat up. "I…I don't like hunting," she admitted. "What if I can't kill?"

"Is it the blood and guts you dislike, or do you simply dislike hurting doves and deer and other gentle forest creatures?"

"I don't mind handling guts. And I certainly don't mind making sausage…but I just don't care for the killing part," Elyria replied, thinking of all the times her mother had told her to go wring a chicken's neck for dinner and the nearly-equal number times she'd given Sky or Stone a sweet biscuit to do it for her. "It seems…cruel."

"It's different when you look into a goblin's yellow eyes and see the violence it wants to commit upon you and your sisters. I think you'll find they're *quite* killable."

"But—what if I don't," Elyria pressed. "What if I'm rubbish at it?"

"Well, you must learn how to fight properly, first! And then see. But if it turns out you just don't have the spirit for killing, well. We always need sisters to care for the horses and tend to the sick. I can't train you in those arts, but Galetta can."

Korraine leaned in and spoke in a conspiratorial tone. "And frankly our cook Venia only knows how to make stew. Her biscuits are best loaded into the catapults and flung at the enemy. If you were to replace her, few of us would weep."

Elyria smiled in spite of her doubts.

Korraine slapped her on the back, nearly knocking her into the dirt again. "I'm turning black as a kettle out here, and I feel like I might boil. Let's go under the trees and put some sword-lore into that questioning head of yours . . "

THAT NIGHT, ELYRIA COLLAPSED INTO HER BEDROLL IN THE hayloft, utterly exhausted. She thought she would surely pass right out...but falling asleep just seemed too difficult, somehow. The bedroll was lumpy, and the hay smelled musty. So she just lay there in a daze with her eyes shut, hoping that Nature would eventually take its course.

Meanwhile, Korraine's lantern was still lit, and the orcish warrior was digging around in her bag, making rustling noises in the straw. Elyria cracked open an eye and turned her head. In the flickering light, she saw Korraine threading tiny, brightly colored beads onto a length of sinew.

"What are you doing?" Elyria asked.

"Jewelry." Korraine held up the half-finished piece. The beads glittered, colorful as a field of summer flowers. "It'll be an anklet for me, if I keep it. Probably a necklace for anyone else!"

"You...make jewelry?" Elyria's tired mind couldn't seem to wrap itself around the idea that this hulking, dangerous warrior would spend her time creating dainty baubles.

"It's an ugly world, so I like to make something pretty at night. It helps me rest." She paused. "Someday, maybe, if we can help Lord Drakewyn defeat Endroren's minions once and for all, we can lay down our swords for good. And spend our days creating beauty instead of destroying evil."

THE NEXT TWO MONTHS WERE A BLUR OF TRAINING, EATING, and sleeping. Korraine spent a great deal of time teaching Elyria different forms of unarmed combat, some she'd learned from the fabled Kinjatsi monks. When she wasn't studying fighting or armor-making, Elyria had to run or climb ropes or lift stones. She quickly got used to being sore, bruised, blistered, and filthy pretty much all the time. Neither her father nor her stepmother visited her at the barn. Stone and Sky were practically mute when they brought out the food and house supplies at Korraine's command, refusing to meet their half-sister's gaze, and speaking only to give short, terse answers to questions.

"This happens," Korraine said sympathetically as they both watched Stone scamper back to the safety of the bakery as if a shadowman was chasing him. "They might feel differently later."

"And if they don't?"

"Then it will be all the easier for you to leave this place when the time comes." Korraine slapped her on the back. "Fetch us some water from the pump; let's get cleaned up, and I'll buy you an ale at the tavern."

They departed the bakery just as the sun was starting to set. Elyria wasn't prepared for the dirty looks the townspeople gave her and Korraine as they walked down the main street towards the tavern.

"Orcish filth," an old man growled, and spat at their feet. "Mingers!"

Elyria felt a surge of anger flush her face, and she'd half-turned, fists raised, but Korraine grabbed her elbow and smoothly led her on down the road.

"Let it go," she whispered, looking calm as a windless lake. "He'd just bleed all over your good boots."

It was only after Korraine spoke that Elyria realized the insulting old man was Grainger Tevis. *So much for my father's plan to marry me off to the old bastard*, she thought.

The Iron Fist Tavern wasn't as crowded as it was on Aleday nights, but a good fifty men were seated at the round oak tables or standing at the bar. Everybody turned to stare at them as they pushed through the swinging doors.

"Two pints of dark ale, please." Korraine slapped two silver pieces down on the lacquered bar.

The bartender met Korraine's gaze as he polished a pewter mug with a rag. An unspoken conversation based on pointed looks seemed to move between them, and Korraine's hand casually dropped to the hilt of her sword.

"Two ales, coming up," the bartender replied. His eyes turned to Elyria and he smiled uncomfortably. "Your uncle farin' well?"

"Well enough," she replied.

"Ain't this a pretty sight," announced an alcohol-slurred voice to her left.

Elyria turned. The blacksmith's son stood there with a look of distaste on his face. He wore a sleeveless leather tunic that showed off the corded muscles in his arms and shoulders; no doubt he'd been strutting around town trying to impress girls most of the day. He was sweating as if he'd already had quite a lot to drink, but his legs were steady.

She nodded in cautious greeting. "Corlis. Good to see you."

He grinned at her unpleasantly. "So, I hear this *mudbeast* is showin' ya fightin'. Ya shoulda come t' me instead. All a girl needs to know is how t' swallow a sword."

He grabbed his crotch in an exaggerated, obscene gesture and hooted at Elyria. Half the bar laughed along with him as if he'd just told the cleverest knee-slapper of a joke they'd ever heard. The other half sat back in silence, nervously eyeing Korraine, whose expression was a studied blankness. She might have been bored, or sleepy, or calculating how to slaughter every man-jack in the tavern. It was hard to tell.

"Oh, Corlis. Always so witty." Elyria smiled sweetly at him. "*So* nice chatting with you."

She turned to get her drink at the bar, but Corlis roughly

grabbed at her shoulder. She easily shook him off.

"I wasn't done with you, *bitch*."

"I'm quite sure I'm done with you, though."

"No fighting in the tavern!" the barkeep bellowed at her. "Take it outside!"

"I'm not fighting," Elyria shot back, annoyed.

"What, you scared?" Corlis sneered at her and gave her shoulder a shove.

In a well-practiced move, Elyria grabbed his outstretched right hand and yanked hard. He weighed a good three stones more than she did, but Korraine had shown her how to use what mass she had for excellent effect. Her quick yank jerked him forward onto his knees, and then he sprawled onto his belly with a curse of surprise. She twisted his wrist up and back, and pressed down on his elbow until he cried out and beat the floor with his left fist.

"You'll stop being a jackass and let me drink in peace?" She pressed harder on the sensitive nerve bundle at the base of his trapped elbow for emphasis.

"Yes, ow, goldamn, yes!"

She flung his arm down into his face. "Next time you try to put your hands on me, I'll break your bones."

Swearing, Corlis crab-crawled backward until one of his buddies helped him up. Nobody else stepped forward to challenge her.

"Oi, fightin's against the rules," someone in the back complained loudly. "Throw 'em out!"

"That *wasn't* a fight." Elyria glared at the crowd, unable to see who had spoken.

"The lad put his hands on her and that's not proper," the bartender said. "I don't see that she broke any rules teaching him some manners. They stay."

Korraine pulled out a nearby stool and sat down at her drink, a smile playing on her lips.

Elyria frowned at her. "What are you grinning about?"

"You're certainly your mother's daughter!" Korraine toasted her with the pewter mug and drank deeply.

THE COLD BITE OF AUTUMN WAS IN THE RESTDAY AIR WHEN Elyria's day of testing arrived. One of her mother's pet crows arrived two hours before at first light, heralding their impending arrival in a squawking monotone. That gave Elyria time to bolt down a quick breakfast, do some exercises and stretches to warm up, and get her gear on as her mentor stood by offering calm encouragements. Elyria tried hard to not think about what would happen if she failed: namely, that she'd have to stay in Oakengrove and make some kind of peace with her family and the disapproving townsfolk. The prospect of being stuck here, friendless and without prospects, seemed nearly worse than death.

"You can do this," Korraine said. "Just keep your head about you. Always defend yourself; easy openings will be traps."

Elyria stood on the cobblestones in front of the bakery dressed in leather armor Korraine had showed her how to craft herself. A wooden longsword she'd made from a fallen oak branch waited inside the scabbard at her hip; if she did well in her test, her mother would gift her with live steel. Her hands quivered inside her heavy leather gauntlets, and she vainly tried to still them. She still felt uncomfortable in the steel helmet Korraine had bought from a traveling vendor; it was a little too big, and the extra padding she'd added muffled her hearing and made it even heavier.

If anyone was still sleeping when the Nemain rode down the main street, the war cries, clop of hooves, snort of warhorses, and clank and jingle of armor surely awakened them all. Korraine had told Elyria that the Nemain usually rode quietly as a spring breeze, but they could thunder in like a hurricane when they wanted to make their presence known. And clearly this morning they wanted all of Oakengrove to know they had arrived. There were at least three times as many warriors as had come to deliver Korraine, and Elyra saw a few male faces as well as massive orogs and fey-looking folk she guessed had to be elves.

And at the front, a proud-looking warrior in fine plate armor fit for any queen. Was it Aetiane? Elyria scanned her features, looking for any resemblance. It was possible—the curl of hair escaping her helmet was the color of hay, the same as Elyria's, and her eyes were the same river green. But the warrior queen looked directly at her—practically looked *through* her—and showed no sign of recognition.

Don't think about it, Elyria told herself. *Put her out of your mind. Just focus on the fight.*

Townspeople, some still in their nightdress, trailed after the warriors like the tail on a kite, but all kept to a safe distance. Above, Elyria heard the shutters of her parents' bedroom creak open. She didn't look up.

The Nemain pulled up and fanned out in a big half-circle around the front of the bakery. There was perhaps thirty yards between Elyria and the nearest warrior.

"Elyria of Oakengrove!" Aetiane called out. "Do you stand ready for the test of combat?"

"I stand ready," she called back, heart pounding.

A tall warrior in leather and scale armor dismounted and pulled a wooden sword from a scabbard strapped behind her saddle. Elyria flipped her visor down, drew her sword, and took a ready stance.

"On your guard, apprentice!" The warrior came in swinging, her wooden blade a blur.

Elyria parried the blows before she'd even had time to think.

The crack of wood on wood echoed down the streets. Korraine grunted approvingly.

The warrior swung hard, seemingly trying to knock the sword from Elyria's hands, but Elyria's muscles were strong after Korraine's training, and her body easily absorbed the shock of the blows. They soon fell into a violent, fast rhythm of strikes and parries. Anything the warrior tried, Elyria found she could parry. Elyria thoroughly enjoyed it, even as the battle started to wind her, and she could see frustration gleaming in the warrior's eyes.

"I *know* you saw that opening!" Korraine barked. "This isn't dance class! You're faster; take her!"

Elyria parried hard, knocking her opponent's sword wide, and lunged in hard and fast, jabbing the point into the padded leather over the warrior's ribs. The warrior swore loudly and fell to one knee.

"Hold!" Korraine shouted.

Elyria stepped back, keeping her sword at the ready.

"Goldammit, I think she broke me rib," the warrior complained.

"I mark that as a killing blow, were this a match of live steel," Korraine called to the Nemain. "What say you?"

"I mark it as but a flesh wound," came an amused reply. "And your apprentice dragged things out so long that reinforcements have arrived!"

Two new warriors in leather armor dismounted and charged Elyria. She braced herself for the impact of her new opponent's heavy wooden weapons. The one on the left was fleeter of foot, and would arrive first—

Crack! Elyria parried the first blow, pivoted and drove her shin into the warrior's midsection. She heard the air *whoof* out of the warrior's lungs and she raised her sword again to meet the second warrior, but she couldn't lift her weapon quickly enough and the other tackled her and threw her to the cobblestones. Her helmet took the worst of the impact, but sparks still bloomed in her eyes like festival day fireworks.

When her vision cleared, she saw the two warriors standing above her, the points of their wooden swords inches above her throat.

"What happens now?" Elyria asked.

"Step aside and let her stand," Aetiane ordered.

The warriors fell back, and Elyria climbed to her feet, back and neck aching.

"Did…did I pass?" she asked.

Aetiane smiled and called out to the thronged warriors around her: "What say you, Nemain? Does this girl belong with us? All in favor, say 'Aye'!"

A thunderous *"AYE!"* arose.

"And so she is one of us!" Aetiane declared. "Welcome, daughter!"

Elyria suddenly felt light as a magician's balloon.

"Come forward and claim your prize," said Aetiane.

Elyria stepped up to her mother's warhorse, and Aetiane handed her a sheathed longsword wrapped in a fine belt.

"It's a good solid weapon," her mother said. "No doubt you'll find something finer on your adventures, but it won't fail you."

"Thank you, ma'am." Elyria buckled the sword around her slender hips. Her very own sword! She'd have never imagined that this could really happen. "When do we leave?"

"Just as soon as you gather up your things; we have a few extra horses, and you can choose whichever you prefer."

"Elyria, wait." It was her father's voice.

She turned. Bevard the Baker stood there in his Restday best, but his hair was still mussed, as if he'd quickly awakened and dressed in a hurry.

"Yes, Father?" she asked uncertainly.

He looked from Elyria to Aetiane, a thousand emotions playing across his face. "I…I'm sorry. I failed you. I failed *both* of you. I was a fool. And I wasted precious time."

"Make it up to her when she comes back next year," Aetiane said.

"I'm coming back here?" Elyria asked.

"Just to visit," Aetiane said. "And only if you want to."

"I…I think I'd like that," she said.

THE NEMAIN CRESTED THE DUNES ABOVE THE COVE, WHERE the *Dawn Fortune* awaited at anchor. Beyond the clear blue waters of the bay, the Amethyst Sea rippled like a vast, endless expanse of cerulean satin. The sea! Elyria's heart soared. She'd dreamed of seeing it ever since the first traveling bard entertained her and the other children with pirate tales.

"The sea's not usually this calm," her mother remarked. "I take it as a good sign."

"There's a thousand kingdoms out there," Korraine said. "The minions of Endroren want them all. Are you ready to stop them?"

"I'm ready," Elyria replied.

Her mother smiled. "Then let's go…"

UPON REFLECTION DARK AND DEEP

AARON ROSENBERG

"REMIND ME AGAIN," LESSANDRALINDA GRUMBLED, LEANING back on her haunches to inspect her delicate, jewel-adorned hands, "why I am risking my lovely nails to dig through rock and stone for something that, even if we find it, will not in any way reward me for my efforts?"

Thalgon blew rock dust from his mouth and beard, then shook his head to scatter it from reaching his eyes before laughing at his companion. "You're not exactly digging with your bare hands," he pointed out with a deep, rumbling chuckle. The little cheebat had a small but sturdy shovel, in fact, which she'd been using to chip away at the rubble, though admittedly to little effect. "Besides, I'm the one doing the heavy lifting."

As if to prove that point, Thalgon raised his pickaxe again and took a solid swing, sending the sharpened pick end slamming into a small boulder jammed in the midst of the small rockslide blocking their path. The blow shattered the rock, and its sudden disappearance crumbled that entire section of debris, allowing them to see a sliver of darkness beyond the rock pile.

"I still fail to understand how you can do that," Lessa insisted, cooling herself with an intricately carved hand fan she'd produced from the elaborate coif of her long red hair. "How do you know exactly where to strike?"

Thalgon shrugged. "I just do," he answered. "It's the Stonecleave way." Which was how his own father had explained it to him when he was just a youngling. "All *tsverg* have gifts with stone and rock," his father had said, "and each *kett*'s is different. We are stonecutters and always have been. To us is given the knowledge of how and where to strike in order to shatter the stone just so, to cleave it along the lines we desire."

A skittering, scraping sound from behind them distracted Thalgon from his memories, and he whirled about, raising his pickaxe while Lessa ducked behind his legs, her own hands rising and arcing in preparation of casting. But the figure emerging from the shadows was familiar, slender and garbed in loose-fitting clothing, and despite the mask and hood obscuring their features, Thalgon relaxed.

"Ho, Sagash," he called out as the figure approached. "What news?"

"Goblins," the wiry scythaa spat in reply, long, curved daggers already in its hands. "Right behind me."

"Filth!" Thalgon slid the pickaxe into its loop at his belt and drew his short, broad-bladed double axe instead, hefting it in his gauntleted hands. "Let them come! They shall see why the *tsverg* were once and will again be masters of the Deeplands!"

He felt as much as saw his cheebat friend shake her head behind him. "There is no profit in any of this," she muttered, yet she did not even try to suggest they leave, or avoid the approaching fight, and for that Thalgon was grateful. It was why, of all their companions, she and Sagash were the only two he had asked to join him on this quest.

The only two to whom he had confided his vision.

"GANTHIKETT!"

The voice had woken Thalgon from a deep sleep, and he'd staggered to his feet, blinking as he looked about.

He and his friends had recently returned from dispatching a band of brigands preying upon anyone trying to use the passes through the Donarzheis Mountains, and had retired to the finest tavern in the region to celebrate their victory—and the wealth it had brought them—so he had not only a full belly to contend with, but also a head muzzy from ale and a body that did not wish to relinquish the first real bed he'd enjoyed for weeks.

Still, the voice had been insistent, calling out to him again. *"Ganthikett!"*

"Who is there?" Thalgon had demanded, reaching for his axe where it leaned against the bedside table. "Who disturbs me?" *And who knows to call out my clan name?* he wondered as well, though he did not say such. To most of the world he was only Thalgon Stonecleave, an adventurer, explorer, warrior, and occasional stonecutter. Very few still kept to the old ways well enough to know of the *kett*, the dwarven clans, and even fewer would know of his family.

"Kin," the voice had replied, that single word sending shivers down Thalgon's spine. *"Long-lost kin, in need of aid."*

The room was dark, the single candle long since having burnt out, and Thalgon had squinted about, trying to find the source of that pleading voice. Slowly, ever so slowly, he began to make out a patch in the middle of the room that was not as dark as the rest. And as the seconds ticked by, that patch had taken on more shape and detail, transforming from a mere lighter region into something resembling a body and, finally, into a clear figure.

The figure of a fellow dwarf.

And not just any dwarf. This one had all the earmarks of the Ganthikett clan—the flared eyebrows, the hooked nose, the wide, full mouth. His hair was streaked with white but still thick, as was his full beard, and both had been braided in a style Thalgon remembered seeing his grandfather wear on festive occasions. Everything about this strange apparition had suggested that it truly was kin.

"Who are you?" Thalgon had demanded again. "Name yourself!"

"I am Dromund," the visitor replied, drawing himself up to his full height, on a level with Thalgon's own. "Dromund Rockfist Ganthikett."

"Rockfist?" Thalgon had rubbed a rough hand over his face, trying to force himself more awake. It was a Ganthikett tribal name, sure enough, but— "The Rockfists are long gone," he'd argued. "All died out during the—"

"The Age of Darkness," his supposed relative had interrupted, spitting out the words like they were poison. "Aye, we were severed from the rest of you then. But not dead, no. We were trapped down here, laddie. Trapped in the Deeplands."

"No!" Thalgon had stared at this distant cousin. There had always been rumors that not everyone had made it out of the mountains and the Deeplands beneath them before the Enaros had sealed the underground kingdoms, imprisoning Endoren and his creatures inside. But no one had ever been able to confirm that. Yet here was one who claimed he could. "How did you survive?"

Dromund had given him a weary half-smile. "A tale for another time, lad," he'd insisted. "Provided there is another time. That is why I've reached out to you, my kin on the surface. All manner of monsters inhabit the Deeplands now." He'd shuddered. "The rest of my family were captured, and I cannot evade the creatures for long, nor can I win the rest of my tribe free alone. Help me, cousin—I beg you!"

Thalgon had been fully awake then, the call to action singing in his blood. "How may I help?"

"I am deep down, very deep," his kin had replied. "You would not be able to reach me in time, even if the wards would allow you through. But there is another way. A mirror, a mystic portal between the Far Deep and one of the Great Halls just below the surface, near the Lightning Pass. Find the Great Hall, locate the mirror, and recite these words—*Uurshk Barkamot Ganthikett Hardunach.* The mirror will open a portal between us. Then I will able to escape to your side, and together we can return and free the rest of my people. Our people."

"Yes!" Thalgon had roared with excitement. "I shall leave at once!"

He had been halfway through donning his armor when he realized that, zeal and family loyalty aside, it might be best to not go alone. Just in case.

Which was why he had sought out both Lessa and Sagash. "This is something I must do," he had told them both, "and I cannot wait for the others to recover, or endlessly discuss and debate our course of action, plus a larger group would take too long to marshal regardless. I am leaving now, and would welcome your companionship and your aid, if you were so inclined."

Both the cheebat and the scythaa had eyed him for a moment, no more, before nodding. "You are our boon companion," Sagash had stated in his rough, pebbly voice, "and you have requested our aid. No more need be said. We are with you."

Lessa had nodded. "Of course," she'd agreed. Then she'd grinned.

"Though maybe we can figure out a way to turn a tidy profit on the way?"

The Lightning Pass had been simple enough to locate—it was one of only a handful of passes that cut through the Donarzheis Mountains. Finding an entrance to the underground had taken more work, but finally they had spotted a small, low-ceilinged cave that had dropped back and away into shadow, and had ventured into its hidden depths.

And now here they were, unable to move forward, unwilling to fall back, about to battle monsters that should been on the opposite side of the wards so they could then try rescuing someone who belonged on this side with them.

Thalgon had never felt so alive.

"IS THAT THE BEST YOU HAVE, ENDRORI?" THALGON ROARED as his axe bit deep into a leaping goblin, arresting the vicious fiend's mid-air charge and knocking it backward in a spray of blood. The goblin crashed into one of its fellows, knocking the second creature to the ground, where an eldritch bolt from Lessa finished it off. The one Thalgon had struck down twitched a few times, as if attempting to rise, but those feeble efforts quickly subsided, and soon it too was still.

Thalgon glanced around, taking in their situation. Lessa was still behind him, the rubble serving as a bulwark for them both. That and the narrow walls of this natural passage forced the goblins to attack from either directly ahead or just to the sides. Sagash had taken up position ahead and slightly to their left, his paired daggers flashing in the dim light Lessa had conjured overhead. The scythaa fought with his usual grace and silence, weaving through attackers like a ribbon of light amid shadow, blood and death spilling in his wake. Already a dozen goblins lay dead or dying upon the rough stone floor, and only a handful still remained.

A handful of breaths and lunges and dagger-strikes and axe-blows and spells later, the last of the creatures had been dispatched.

"There, now," Thalgon declared, leaning down to wipe his axe clean on one of the bodies, "that was invigorating." He laughed, the battle-surge still singing through his veins, his every nerve and sense afire with the joy of combat.

"If you say so," Lessa grumbled, sliding past him to give the dead goblins a cursory glance. The little cheebat shook her head. "Useless," she declared. "No gold, no jewelry, not even any decent equipment. What's the point of killing them if they don't have anything worth taking?"

"It kept them from killing us," Sagash pointed out, having cleaned and sheathed his daggers. "Surely you find value in that?"

That earned him a sour look from their tiny companion, and another laugh from Thalgon. The three of them had traveled together, adventured together, for almost a year now, and he'd grown accustomed to the way these two sniped at each other. In many ways, their good-natured ribbing reminded him of growing up with his cousins and siblings, picking on each other but never meanly, more as a way of showing attention and affection—and of keeping each other on their toes. In all this time, he had yet to see these two have a real disagreement, which was far more than he could say for some of their other companions who, to a casual observer, seemed to argue far less.

Now that the brief skirmish had ended, Thalgon returned his attention to the makeshift wall blocking his path. Before the goblins had arrived, they'd spent at least an hour, perhaps more, digging and chipping and picking at the rocks jumbled together here, but beyond that one tiny gap near the top, they hadn't made much progress. He estimated that, at this rate, it would take several more hours before there was even enough room for Lessa to wiggle through, and then they would still have to work more before Sagash could fit, much less him.

Well, he thought, swinging his arm to loosen it as he drew his pickaxe again, *best to get back to it.*

But a small, long-fingered hand on his gauntlet arrested his first swing. "A thought, my worthy friend," Lessa chirped up at him, her eyes alight. "Where did those goblins come from?"

"Hm? From the Deeplands, of course," Thalgon answered, frowning through his beard. "Why?"

"Yes, from the Deeplands," the cheebat agreed. "And yet, they attacked us from behind, did they not? Which must mean—"

Now Thalgon did lower the pickaxe, even as he broke into a broad grin. "That they circled around us somehow," he finished, staring anew at their fallen foes. "And that means there's another way down than this rubble-infested hole!"

He could have kissed Lessa. This was one of the reasons he had asked her to accompany him, because for all her avarice and vanity, there was little her sharp eyes missed or her sharp mind did not comprehend. Sagash was already nodding as well, thin tongue flickering slightly from his wide, lipless mouth.

"I can track them back," the scythaa confirmed, turning back the way they had come. "Follow." Without another word he had slipped down the passageway, only the faint *click* of his clawed toes on the stone indicating his movement. Thalgon and Lessa hurried to keep up.

"IT IS...AMAZING," LESSA ADMITTED, FOR ONCE UNABLE TO come up with anything more grandiose to say.

Standing there beside her, Thalgon had to agree.

Sagash had led them through narrow, winding tunnels, along ledges and ravines, across wide caverns, all the while tracking the goblins back toward their own deeply buried homes. And at last, they had squeezed through a narrow crevice in the rocks to emerge here, upon this broad ledge, facing a cavern so wide they could not see the other side of it. The floor was lost from sight as well, as was the ceiling.

But that did not mean they saw nothing.

Not at all.

Before them stretched a chaotic jumble of rock and stone, high and low, level and angled, flat and pointed. Down below was what looked much like a frozen sea carved from the very bowels of the earth; platforms and ledges and rises and peaks jutting up out of the shadows below in such profusion as to create a patchwork surface of sorts. That was matched by the jagged array of spikes lancing down from above, like a series of thunderclouds aburst with lightning, petrified in the very act of arcing down toward the waiting ground. There were stalagmites there that looked wide enough to fit a small army across their flat tops, and stalactites large enough to spear through the mightiest giant.

And, jutting up right in the center of all that tumult of earth and rock, lit by the soft glow of lichen clinging here and there, was a monstrous barb of stone that gleamed and glistened as if carved of ice instead of rock, its facets clear and precise—

—and readily visible through those crystalline planes was a perfectly shaped rectangle, tall as a large man and half as wide, its surface reflecting back both the dim light around it and the rough shapes of its neighbors.

It was the mirror Dromund had spoken of. It was real, and it was right there before them.

"Thalgon," Lessa murmured, her eyes also on that eerie, hanging portal, "I know your cousin told you of this, but don't you think it's just a little too…convenient?"

"Nonsense," Thalgon replied, his gaze still fixed on the mirror. "It is a *tsverg* artifact, placed here for protection and access, nothing more." He glared at his small companion for a second before once again turning toward his objective. "I am coming, Dromund," he called out, his words echoing off the many surfaces around them. "I am coming, kinsman. Soon you shall be free!"

He stomped toward a spot where the ledge had crumbled, creating a step down from which he could jump to the nearest plateau. With a wary grumble, Lessa followed behind him. Sagash accompanied them without a sound, save for the clicking of his claws upon the floor.

THOUGH MARCHING ACROSS A COMPARABLE DISTANCE might have taken even Lessa only the better part of an hour, navigating the jutting stone of the cavern was far more treacherous, even for one with Thalgon's rock knowledge and Lessa and Sagash's agility, and it was several hours before they finally reached the last plateau, the one that placed them directly in front of the mirror itself.

The bottom edge of its crystalline prison just barely scraped the plateau, and the enchanted portal itself stood a few feet higher, so that Thalgon had to peer up to see its top. He noticed that the mirror did not show him or his companions, nor indeed the rocks behind them—it seemed to reveal a different, darker landscape, one more cave than cavern, with a rough stone floor and sloping walls and jumbles of rocks or boulders all about.

And, now that he was closer, Thalgon could see a stocky figure there as well. One with features very much like his own.

Dromund!

"Kinsman!" His long-lost relative called out, evidently spying him as well. "At last!" The other dwarf turned away for a second, and it was only then, upon seeing a flash of motion, that Thalgon realized his cousin was not alone. What he had mistaken for boulders was, in fact, bodies.

The bodies of goblins, to be precise.

And the majority of them were still moving.

Straight for Dromund.

It was one of these advancing creatures the other dwarf had just turned away to face, hefting a massive stone mace whose end had been carved into an enormous fist. *The Rockfist way,* Thalgon realized as his cousin swung the weapon and crushed the goblin's chest, hurling the monster into several of its fellows. That tribe had been weaponsmiths, crafting fine maces and clubs and hammers from rock. Clearly that skill lived on among them.

"The words, cousin!" Dromund bellowed over his shoulder, dispatching several more goblins with a single great sweep. "Quickly, say the words!"

"Uurshk—" Thalgon began, but stopped as Lessa laid a hand upon his forearm.

"Are you sure this is wise, Thalgon?" she asked. "We have only his word that—"

"He is kin," Thalgon replied sharply, pulling away from her touch. "And he is in need."

The little cheebat studied him for a second, then shrugged and stepped back. "Then do what you must, my friend," she told him. "I will stand at the ready."

Returning his attention to his beleaguered cousin, Thalgon began again. *"Uurshk,"* he intoned, his arms spread wide. *"Barkamot!"* The mirror began to glow, brighter and brighter. *"Ganthikett Hardunach!"*

As the last word left his lips, there was a great burst of light, and the mirror shone as if someone had pulled a thin veil from its surface, revealing its true luster. Dromund was as sharp and clear as if he were standing there beside them. Then he took a great leap forward—

—and burst from the mirror, right through its crystal emplacement, to land with a heavy thud upon the plateau directly before Thalgon.

"At last!" the other dwarf declared, raising his mace high above his head with both hands, his shout filling the cavern. *"At last!"*

But as Thalgon stared, his kinsman began to change.

The color leeched from Dromund's skin, leaving it a cold, sullen grey. His hair darkened, turning black as the depths below, and taking on an unpleasant oily sheen. His eyes grew darker as well, becoming gaping holes of pure darkness beneath his brows. And his smile widened, revealing sharp teeth like those of a hungry beast.

"No..." Thalgon cried, though the denial trickled forth as a mere whisper, for there was no denying the evidence of his own eyes.

Dromund was a darkholder.

"My thanks, cousin," the Fallen dwarf crowed, clapping a heavy hand upon Thalgon's shoulder. "For many years have I labored to break through those accursed wards, to no avail. Then I discovered the mirror—and knew that with it, I could finally be free, and bring my master's will back to the surface world." His vicious grin grew, if anything, even broader, nastier, more predatory. "But in order to activate it, the words had to be said from this side. And only one of our clan could use them. Thus it was truly a gift from Endoren when I felt you nearby." He laughed, the sound like rocks grinding against one another. "And now I am free!"

"No," Thalgon replied, finding his voice again. He shrugged off the Fallen dwarf's hand and raised his axe. "You are not. Because

I will not allow you to pass."

But Dromund only laughed again. "I think you will find that you and your two friends are not equal to that task," he ground out, and spat a word in some dark tongue.

Goblins began pouring through the mirror behind him, charging Thalgon and Lessa and Sagash, claws out and mouths open wide.

"Die, traitor!" Thalgon roared, swinging his axe in a powerful blow that would have taken his cousin's head clean off at the shoulders if Dromund had not blocked it with his mace, the force of the impact sending a shiver down Thalgon's arms. He swung again, and again his evil kinsman countered. Dromund was shorter, though not by much, but he was as strong as Thalgon, if not stronger, and neither of them was able to land a solid blow.

And more goblins were emerging with every second.

"Thalgon!" Lessa shouted, drawing his attention. "We need to close that portal!" She waved a hand, and two goblins turned and attacked each other.

"Aye," Sagash agreed. He slit the throat of one goblin as it tried to claw him, then slid past and spun to open another from belly to throat. "You must do this. We will deal with your kin and his foul pets." Another swipe of his daggers, and a third goblin dropped, its head rolling free.

Dromund had not missed that exchange. "And how will you stop me, scythaa?" he sneered, stepping back and swirling his heavy mace about him. "I will crush you to powder!"

"You must land the blow first," Sagash replied, darting in and stabbing the darkholder in the shoulder with a dagger before the shadowy dwarf could react, then springing back out of reach so that Dromund's return blow smashed into one of his goblins instead.

"Go!" Lessa urged again, and Thalgon nodded. He knew he could trust his friends to have his back. But the mirror—that was his responsibility.

Turning away from the fight, though it tore at his instincts to do so, Thalgon crossed the short distance to the gleaming spike hanging before him. It was so wide he could not have wrapped his arms around it if he were twice as tall, and at least three feet of solid crystal stood between him and the mirror.

Behind him, Dromund laughed. "That is a fool's errand!" the dark dwarf cried. "You will never be able to break through that!"

But Thalgon was studying the stalactite, frowning. He stroked his beard, eyeing the angles, his hands automatically returning his double-bladed axe to its belt loop and drawing the pickaxe instead. A goblin tried taking advantage of his momentary distraction to attack, and Thalgon speared it with the pick, then hurled it away from him in a single sweep, launching the creature into the void between plateaus and ridges, without ever ceasing his study of the object before him.

Finally he nodded and took a step back, to give himself space to swing.

"Surrender this notion!" his kinsman called out, still trying to hit the scythaa flitting about him like a deadly moth. "You cannot break through!"

"I don't need to break *through*," Thalgon replied over his shoulder, raising his pickaxe in both hands and cocking it back. "I am a Stonecleave. And this is our way."

And then he swung, putting every bit of power he possessed, every ounce of strength, into the arc of his pickaxe. It curved up and out, well above his head, forcing him to stretch up onto the tips of his toes, his shoulders aching from the strain—

—and finally connected, right at the upper corner of the frontmost facet, where the angles jutted forth sharp enough to cut flesh.

There was a massive peal as the pickaxe struck, like the ringing of an enormous bell—

—and, with a shudder and a sigh, the entire facet slid free, to crash to the ground at Thalgon's feet and shatter into a thousand pieces.

Leaving the mirror before him, still embedded in crystal, but with its face now exposed to the open air.

"NO!" This time it was Dromund who shouted. Wheeling about, he dove in front of the portal, mace raised to shield it from harm—

—and Lessa threw herself at his feet, tripping the darkholder so that he stumbled, reeling, desperately trying to reclaim his balance—

—only to have Thalgon's shoulder collide with his chest, hard enough to lift the Fallen dwarf clear off his feet—

—and send him plunging back through the portal, his bulk scattering goblins from the opening as he passed through.

"Back to the depths with you!" Thalgon shouted, and his pickaxe came up again. This time it impacted in the exact center of the mirror, and with a resounding thunderclap the portal shattered, shards flying free.

When the last piece had hit the ground, and the tinkling of broken glass faded, nothing remained but the halved stalactite and glittering rubble at its base.

Of Dromund and his goblin army, there was no sign.

"Well struck," Sagash noted, nodding to Thalgon before turning to dispatch the last few goblins, who were even now trying to creep away unnoticed.

"Aye, but if not for my foolishness there would have been no need," Thalgon replied wearily. He leaned on his pickaxe. "I brought us down here with hopes of rescuing my kin, reclaiming our ancestral home, and restoring our family honor. Instead I nearly doomed us all, and many more besides."

"It isn't your fault," Lessa assured him, her face free of mirth or greed for once. "He knew exactly how to lure you in. You thought you were doing the right thing."

"Perhaps." Thalgon sighed. "You attempted to warn me," he acknowledged sadly. "I was too blind to listen."

"But you listened when it mattered," Sagash pointed out, wiping his daggers and sheathing them. "You sent him back, and prevented him from ever escaping again."

"Ever?" Thalgon shook his head. "Perhaps. Or perhaps he will find another way." He toed one of the mirror shards. "But you are right, at least he will not be able to use this path again." He smiled at his two companions. "And if not for you, he surely would have overwhelmed me, and even now be leading his army of goblins to the surface. Thank you, my friends."

"No, thank you," Lessa replied, her nose quivering with delight. In her hands was one of the pieces that had broken free of the stalactite when that facet had fallen. "Did you even notice what this was? It's diamond! The whole thing! We're going to be rich!"

Despite his anguish at what had almost happened, and his guilt at having been so easily tricked and nearly used to unleash a wave of evil upon the world, Thalgon laughed. "You see," he told his little friend as she began frantically gathering as many diamond shards as she could carry, "you were rewarded for your actions after all."

And he was glad of that, because truly, he now realized, their friendship was precious to him, and truly worthy of any reward he could name.

A WHOLE-HEARTED HALFLING

MELANIE R. MEADORS

KENDRA STUMBLED HOME IN A HAZE OF CONFUSION AND dismay. Ma had warned her curiosity would be her ruin, but Kendra had assumed once she reached adulthood, she needn't worry about such things.

What a fool she'd been.

If other halflings spoke to her as she numbly made her way through Cider Dale, she didn't notice. She didn't feel the weight of their usual judgmental glares as they wondered why she wasn't practicing her cooking or cleaning, as a fine halfling maiden should. Not today. Not now.

The only thing she could see was Master Gaeben's handwriting on a piece of parchment.

Toby, age 15. Passed. The staff is stronger than I expected. Difficult to control.

Daisy, age 37. Recovered, barely. Told family illness had weakened her.

Jonnan, age 23. Passed.

Raggin, age 62. Passed.

Siggi, age 35. Recovered. Felt things more clearly. Learning.

And finally, *Lumo, age 56. Passed. So close.*

Master Gaeben's voice echoed through her mind. *"I only experimented with those who were well along on the path to Numos anyway. They would have died even without my help. You shouldn't bother telling the others. They'll never believe you. They know that everything I've done, I've done to help this village."*

They'll never believe you.

He was right, of course. Who was she but the odd one in the village, the one who spent her days working as Master Gaeben's apprentice? The one who spent her evenings poring over her even odder grandfather's adventure journals. The one with ideas. If she said anything she'd be accused, yet again, of having an overactive imagination.

No, the best thing would be to go home and organize her thoughts. Lumo's remembrance was tonight, and she would be expected to be there. She didn't want to cause a commotion that would distract from that. It was the least he deserved. After all, he'd given his life to save the village from the ogre's fires of last night, even if things hadn't quite happened the way Master Gaeben said they did.

THE TRUTH GNAWED AT KENDRA ALL DAY, STILLING HER usually over-active tongue, and causing her family to worry. Everyone was too busy cleaning up from last night's catastrophe to intervene, however, which came as a relief. She wasn't ready to explain Gaeben's treachery yet. Not only would she be speaking against one who the villagers trusted, but she would be affirming the villagers' fear of strangers. She wanted them to open up a bit more to the outside world, not close down entirely.

No, she needed a way to tell them the truth without feeding their paranoia, though at this point, how could she fault them for it?

That night, the halflings feasted under the stars on the grassy mound in the center of the village that served as their meeting place. Everyone brought food or drink from their stores and took a place at the long, wooden table beside their friends and neighbors. They remembered Lumo and paid their respects by sharing memories of him.

When Kendra's turn came, words failed her.

"May his death remind us of the importance of life," she managed. She could have said, "Taken before his time," or, "Heed his words, don't trust overly kind wizards," but she wasn't ready to part with the truth just yet. Lumo had been suspicious of Gaeben's magic from the beginning. It was only because Kendra convinced him that the wizard was trying to help that he finally gave in and trusted him. Could she have been partially to blame for his death? Sould the other halflings blame her? If she spoke too soon, she, rather than Gaeben, could end up the object of the halflings' ire.

A young halfling had been sent to fetch the wizard for the feast, but Gaeben was nowhere to be found. The others assumed he was busy, but Kendra knew better. He didn't want to show his face in case she had reported him.

As stomachs got full, talk turned to what would happen next. While it was easier to set aside the larger issue in their grief, ignoring a problem never made it go away. The halflings debated.

"We can't let that ogre continue to harass us," Old Man Sloane said. "What will be next? Will he set our homes ablaze? Eat folks who wander too close to his cave?"

Kendra's own father, Jorah, stood and spoke up. "And what's he doing in these parts, anyway? Surely he didn't come all this way to just set our orchards on fire and torture our sheep for fun."

"How are we supposed to stop a ogre?" Lorie said. "We're

farmers and shepherds, not warriors."

"Well," Corrin said, silencing them with his gavel. Everyone hushed, and paid the head councilman heed. "You forget. We do have a wizard to help us."

"You know," Kendra said suddenly, surprising even herself. "Winterkeep is not so far away. We could send there for help."

Everyone at the long table looked at her. Amazing, how heavy stares could be.

"Or," she said with a shrug, "we could defeat the ogre ourselves."

This caused a general uproar. Kendra was shaken by it at first, but the more the halflings shouted at her and asked her if she was mad, the more she realized something.

"What if Master Gaeben wasn't here?" she said, raising her voice to be heard over the tumult. "What if we were on our own? Yes, we're a village, same as any other. But that doesn't mean we're helpless."

"Against an ogre?" Corrin's son Jax spat from across the table.

"Well, ogres aren't exactly the most intelligent of creatures," she replied.

"I'm surprised a high and mighty wizard's apprentice thinks halflings are smarter," Jax said.

"I'm as much a halfling as any of you," she snapped. "My grandfather would have fought. He went on adventures. He studied things to help our people survive in the larger world. There are many entries about ogres in his journals." Kendra's cheeks burned, and once her words started, she couldn't stop them. "We are halflings. *Tsaals*! We are an ancient people who have made it this far for a reason. And not because we rely on the strength and smarts of others."

The entire table exploded into a cacophony of shouting, and while Kendra was heartened to hear some cheers mixed with the cursing, on the whole, it was not friendly.

Corrin banged his gavel on the table and asked for order. Still the crowd clamored on. It was only when he stood on the table and shouted, "If you please!" that folks finally calmed to the point where he could be heard.

"Quiet now. We'll accomplish nothing by shouting at each other." He turned to Kendra. "Your grandfather was…different," he said. "He did things no other halfling did before, and no one has done since."

"But he proved they *can* be done. We don't need a wizard to save us all the time." Kendra swept the table with her gaze. "Do we not have any self-respect?"

At this, everyone at the table was quiet. Every eye was downcast, and every body fidgeted.

"I know it's easier to be helped, but think how great it would be if we managed to take care of this ourselves. Think how impressed other villages would be. Even Master Gaeben. If he were truly our friend, he would want to see us grow."

"He wouldn't want us risking ourselves in that way," Lorie said, pounding the table with a hammy fist.

"He wouldn't want us to be self-sufficient? Help is one thing, control another. If we let him take on all responsibility for us, are we truly a village? Or are we merely servants to his whim?"

"Ogres are very large," Corrin said, his voice tinged with doubt.

"Ogres also have weaknesses," Kendra said. "We just have to figure out what they are and how to exploit them."

THE NEXT DAY, KENDRA SAT IN THE SMALL LIBRARY OF her family's home and scoured her grandfather's journals for any mention of ogres, to be sure she hadn't missed anything. Even before she looked at the journals, however, she knew what they would have to do.

"We need to trick the thing. Capture it, somehow, taking advantage of its greed and stupidity. Direct combat would never work," she told the others later, at the central mound.

How would they do that? That led to hours of debate. Did they trap it? Fight it? Maybe a huge pit, or a giant snare.

Kendra shook her head. "We aren't thinking about this in the right way. We aren't big humans. We're halflings."

"And we're proud!" someone proclaimed from the far edge of the congregation.

Kendra smiled at the declaration. "Then let's behave that way," she said. "What are halflings good at?"

"Eating!"

"And drinking," someone else added.

"Don't forget smoking," another said. "But only the finest leaf will do."

Kendra clenched her hands into fists in her apron pockets. It wasn't the first time she felt inadequate as a leader. She was far too impatient. How much easier would it have been to wave a cursed staff and kill the thing on the spot?

She mustn't have been the only one getting short on temper, however, for Corrin said, "What are you lot planning to do, invite him to tea?"

Amidst the laughter and snorts that followed, Kendra caught herself wondering what Master Gaeben would do. A smart, worldly man, someone she looked up to because he always had the answers. What would Master Gaeben do?

He'd kill people, she thought. *He'd suck the life out of them to use for his own ends, and pretend it was for the good of the village.*

For the first time, the true emotional impact of his betrayal fully hit her, as real as a punch to the stomach. Was anything she'd ever known true anymore? Would she find everything to be as false as her faith in Gaeben?

She swallowed. It was time she did as she had told the others to do. Have faith in herself. Kendra looked down the long table at the people she had grown up around, the people who'd raised her and the younger people she'd helped raise. Yes, it would have been easier to look the other way, to pretend she hadn't understood what the notes had meant. But she knew there was no way she could let another of her people die. She could not let them be used as tools, at the whim of someone who fancied himself more powerful than they.

Hadn't her grandfather said repeatedly that halflings were stout and hardy, that they could rise to any challenge? Hadn't he worked so they could use his knowledge to make themselves a race to be reckoned with? The other halflings dismissed him as peculiar and an outsider, but that didn't negate his words. Why should they bow to a human who used them as experiments and literally sucked the life out of their village? In his notes he said he did it to help the village, but at the same time, he mentioned how impressed those at Winterkeep, the tower of the mages, would be at his accomplishments.

No. Not at the expense of her village.

What would her grandfather have done? He'd have used his strengths as a halfling. What were those? Eating and drinking? Was that really all they were?

"Wait." Kendra stood up, shaking the table and almost upsetting mugs of cider. "Wait, listen," she said, loud enough to get everyone's attention. "What if we *did* invite him to tea?"

Ignoring the baffled looks from the other villagers, she went on. "The ogre only does his mischief at night. What if…"

She hesitated. Saying it aloud, it did sound insane. But everyone looked at her expectantly. She took a deep breath. Grandfather wouldn't have been afraid.

"What if we set up a large table? A huge, ogre-sized spread. Show him the hospitality only halflings can offer."

"Yes," Lorie said. "Then what?"

"It'll be dark. We can do things to distract him. Keep bringing more food and drink until he's groggy and drunk and relaxed. Then, we can trick him."

It was mad, but if Kendra had learned anything from her grandfather's journals, it was that the safe, sane plans never worked. Or if they did, it was at a dear cost.

"We can do this," she said. "But be sure not to tell Gaeben. Imagine his surprise when he sees we can be as brave and strong as he can."

Imagine his surprise when he sees he can't use us as his pawns anymore, she thought.

THE NEXT DAY, KENDRA TRIED TO SPEND HER DAY AS Gaeben's apprentice as normally as possible, so the wizard wouldn't suspect anything was happening. When he mentioned the ogre, she told him some of the halflings had tracked the beast and could find no trace of it, which was true. Of course, halflings weren't the best of trackers, but she left that detail out.

"We have scouts looking out for him," Kendra said. "He won't catch us by surprise again. We'll send for you if we need you."

Of course, the subject of the staff was never brought up. Kendra had so many questions, but she was afraid if she asked them, Gaeben would cast her out, and the halflings' plan of helping themselves would be in jeopardy. She had to be sure they were confident in their independence before they learned of their beloved wizard's betrayal. Her village may have been hard-headed, but they were still her family, and she wanted to protect them from heartbreak.

She wanted to be sure they had the tools with which to deal with the bad news.

No one knew exactly when the ogre would come back, but they were certain he would. Even Gaeben had commented that it was odd he'd left after just setting some fires. True to their guesses, it was sooner rather than later.

They smelled him before they saw him. His reek wafted across the entire village just as the halflings were convinced it was too late for him to come that night.

Things happened differently from what Kendra imagined. She thought since they had a plan, everything would work that way. Of course she wasn't a fool. She knew danger always existed, and plans failed, but it wasn't until the ogre approached, snorting and grunting, talking to himself and spreading his stench, that she realized the true magnitude of what they were attempting.

They were halflings, however, and halflings meant good company. They might have been terrified, but they were terrified together.

From the shadows, they watched the bulging, hairy monster approach the village, hauling his huge stone club behind him. Kendra was glad she'd thought of evacuation plans. Instead of staying to the outskirts of the village, as he had the first time, he stomped directly down the path that led to the village center. Every now and then he swung his club and pummeled the roof or wall of a house. He kept sniffing and snorting, knocking his club through fences and kicking his foot through windows.

The halflings stayed in their hiding place in one of the cider cellars, peering through the narrow space of the open trapdoor. They knew what he was sniffing for. According to Kendra's grandfather's journals, there was only one thing ogres liked more than destroying things, and that was a feast.

A feast of the flesh of sentient beings.

"Ock!" he suddenly exclaimed, and he dashed, as much as an ogre could, toward the center of the village, where a different feast from the one he'd been hunting had been laid out.

The other halflings had despaired over leaving food out indefinitely until he arrived. "He'll think we serve garbage. The food won't last." But of course, ogres were not picky eaters. Kendra just hoped the food smelled better than a cellar of fresh halflings. It would be easier to catch, at any rate.

"This be a grand feast," the ogre said, not bothering to wipe the drool that streamed down his chin. "A grand feast left all alone. Poor dopes that left it. It's mine now. I'll find them later."

The ogre began gorging himself. Ham after ham disappeared into his wide mouth. Potatoes, cheese. Mrs. Potsley's prize meat pie, a week's worth of bread from the baker. Tarts, cakes, and more cakes. Apples, though he grew restless after eating a couple bushels. More than one halfling's stomach growled as they watched, unable to try even a morsel of their favorite foods. Kendra tried not to think about the cost of the feast vanishing into the ogre's seemingly bottomless gullet, nor of the fact that Gaeben could have finished it off with one swing of his staff. She tried not to feel disappointed that she'd been such a poor student that all she could manage under Gaeben's tutelage were a few charms to confuse people or make them sleepy. Her spells weren't nearly strong enough for an ogre, and she knew better than to try.

"Why doesn't Gaeben come?" one of the halflings asked from the darkness of the cellar. "He can usually tell when something is happening. He could kill this ogre right."

It was a fair question. Was it possible the wizard knew of the plan? That he was simply watching to let them fail? Then he could swoop in to the rescue, and the villagers would all be on his side. They would never question his motives again, but they would eye her with suspicion.

There was only one thing for it. They would not fail. They *could* not.

"What yous got to drink here?" the ogre asked, letting out a belch that surely could be heard in the next village. "I knows youse ones are over there. I ain't stupid, ya know."

Drink.

Drink! Of course! Kendra didn't waste time reacting to his knowledge of their spying on him. "Cider," she hissed. "All the cider. Every cask we've got!"

"But that's for trade!" Corrin argued.

"Would you rather it burn? Or perhaps he drank it after finishing us off first?"

Much to the ogre's delight, they rolled barrel after barrel from the cellar to him. To Kendra's delight, after about six, the ogre began to move more sluggishly than before.

"More, more. Keep it coming," she insisted.

After ten barrels, the ogre wiped drool from his chin. "How much night's left, anyway?"

"No need to worry about that," Kendra said, her voice higher than usual. "Why don't you lay your head down on the table for a spell? You look quite sleepy."

"What?" he said, jerking his head up. "I ain't tired. Need to get back. Light hurts me eyes."

"But you've barely sampled our hospitality," Kendra said, feeling a bit braver. Or reckless, perhaps. What did it matter? If they didn't succeed, all would be lost. She chased away the nagging thought that all could be solved quickly if they just called Gaeben. She *had* to be right. They had to be able to do this on their own. Otherwise, they'd never be willing to let the wizard go, even if it was for their own good.

"Whas' dis hospito-thing?" the ogre slurred. "Jus' wanna go

home. Wanna sleep."

"Oh, you'll sleep well at the end of this night," Kendra said. "But surely you'd like to taste some of the best wine us halflings have to offer."

A strangled voice of protest sounded from the darkness. The ogre's ears perked up at the sound.

"Don' wanna part wi' that, do dey?" He scratched at something large and lumpy on his head, then examined his fingernails. "Awright. Lessee it."

"I don't know," Kendra said. "It's awfully strong. And you've had all that cider."

The ogre spat. "Ya think I can' handle a bita drink. *Youse* ants can't drink dat. I can. I'll show youse."

Kendra turned and glared at Corrin, who shook his head. "That's for my finest company," he hissed.

A flash of anger jolted Kendra into action. She arrived at Corrin's side before even realizing she had moved. "Our *whole village* will burn," she hissed. "The vineyard, the orchard, the sheep will be gone. Is all that worth your precious cask of wine? You would trade entire your village just to impress company?"

Without taking his glare from her, Corrin ordered his son to grab the cask from the cellar.

"Is Hondo here?" she whispered.

The halfling pushed passed the others to stand in front of her. "Yes, Miss Kendra?"

"Your whistle. Is it handy?"

He pulled it from his belt. "Always, Miss. A tune?"

Kendra found calm in giving orders, helping her people to organize. "A lullaby. The sleepiest tune you know."

Gentle notes soon rode on the breeze into the ears of the tipsy monster now lounging at the table. He grunted, but said nothing.

His head nodded. His eyes started to close, only to jolt open again.

"Where's 'at wine?" he asked. His mouth sounded like it was full of cotton.

"Right here," Corrin's son Jax said, rolling the cask up the hill. Not wanting to get too close, he pushed it hard so it rolled right up to the ogre.

The ogre snorted. "This be but a mouthful."

"But a lovely mouthful it will be," Kendra said. "This wine is from Bottomland, the best vineyard in the country. Even the tiniest glass is more than most can afford."

The ogre let out a laugh that ended in a belch. "I'll drink dis, and if i's as good as you say, then go I'll to dat wretched vineyard and schteal me sommore." He broke the top of the cask and took a deep slurp. "Thish jus' juice. Imma drrrnk allvthish…"

He spoke as he drank, and his words became completely unintelligible. When he drained the cask, he lowered it and looked at its empty interior.

"Wait," he muttered. "Why'd you give me this? Why halflings give me good food?" He stared blearily at Kendra and the other villagers, who watched him eagerly.

Kendra took a deep breath. "We halflings pride ourselves on our ability to host any guest. We wanted to see how we measured up to ogre standards. Are we doing a fair job?"

"Yer doin' a fair job if halflin' pudding's fer dessert," he answered. "Made from real halflin's. No tricks."

"Oh, how did you guess?" Kendra said with mock surprise.

The ogre scowled at her. "Ants, the lot of you. Thinks I'm stupid."

"Oh, we don't think you're stupid. You just might not be strong enough or fast enough to catch the halflings that will make your dessert."

"What you mean?" The ogre stood, club in hand, and the

halflings standing nearby retreated a bit. "I plenty strong to get food. I can rip trees from the ground with me bare hands."

Kendra's stomach clenched. This would be the true test of their plot, and the most dangerous part.

"Well then, you must go down the hill," she said. "Quickly! Before they all get away!"

His eyes narrowed. "Who?"

"Only the best and fattest halflings we have." She turned to glance down the hill. Even by torchlight, she could tell the looks of fear on the villagers' faces were genuine. "We have truly outdone ourselves. Halfling Surprise, we call it. And we only give it to the most worthy of ogres."

"Worthy. Thas' right," he said. "I show youse who's fast enough fer Halfling S'prize."

He dropped his club to the ground with a *thud* and followed Kendra's lead as she tore down the hill, the other villagers scattering in their wake. The ground shook under the ogre's flat feet, and Kendra could hear the destruction from his drunken swerving into fences. Kendra ignored the irrational fear that suddenly filled her, that despite their planning and testing, the lid to the old dried up well would somehow not be as weak as they thought it would be, that the ogre would not be as heavy. Straight toward the well she ran, and then sprang over it, feeling the wind from his huge hands as they grabbed for her at the same moment there was a loud *crack*.

A roar of rage echoed over through the ruined orchard. The ground stopped quaking beneath her feet. Kendra dared to stop her sprint and turned just in time to see the tips of the ogre's fingers disappear into the depths of their deepest, oldest well.

Something drew her gaze to the hillock. There, in the pale dawn light, stood Gaeben, a look of confusion, betrayal, and disappointment on his face as he glared at her.

Such a look would have shamed her just days before, but now, she forced her attention away from him and to the group of halflings who ran to her, shouting with joy.

THE HALFLINGS COLLAPSED ON THE DEWY GRASS AS THE SUN fully dawned upon the hillock, still laughing and crying in mingled relief and excitement. It was safe now to admit how frightening the night had been, to admit that they had no idea if the plan would work, to acknowledge they actually stood a chance.

And they had done it without the wizard's help.

Kendra ignored the wizard's presence as long as she could. They had proven it; they didn't need a wizard to defend them. She looked at her villagemates who, though exhausted, clapped each other on the back. Several shook her hand, and she nodded numbly to them. When she looked back at where Gaeben stood, he was gone.

"We should go home and get some rest. Then tonight we can celebrate as this village never has before!" Jax said.

"With what, though?" his wife said. "We gave everything we had to defeat this thing."

Kendra might have been tired, but that didn't stop the thoughts from flying about her head. "Perhaps we've allowed ourselves to be isolated too long. Remember, there was a time halfling villages would work *and* celebrate together. My grandfather spoke fondly of the bonfires and feasts in his day. You know that once the ogre had finished with our village, he would have moved on to the next. Why not send to Shepherd Dale and invite them to celebrate with us? It's been too long since we've seen our friends there. Tell them what we've done, and invite them to share in our feast."

Corrin shook his head. "And have them see our village in this state? We'd seem like charity cases. Let it never be said that Cider

Dale must rely on help from others."

Kendra almost smirked, but kept it inside. Secretly, she was overjoyed to hear the pride in Corrin's voice. "Look at it as community building, not as charity. We still have some food, and we have plenty of leaf left."

"Plenty of leaf, eh?" Corrin's peaked face brightened a bit. "Indeed, yes. Shepherd Dale grows weak, smoky leaf from what I remember. Jax, you and Hondo can go. Hondo can tell a story like no other. Bring along some pipe leaf to warm the telling and listening, and two barrels besides to share with the village." His face took on a strange, faraway look. "Yes, it's been too long."

No one mentioned the wizard. Kendra knew she wasn't the only one to glance south and wonder where he'd gone, and why he hadn't been happy in their triumph.

WHEN SHE WOKE UP SEVERAL HOURS LATER, KENDRA wandered back to the hillock. Though she knew it had really happened, part of her couldn't help but check. Had they truly defeated the ogre, or was it just a dream?

She joined other villagers who stared at the giant stone club the ogre had left near the table, yet no one stepped close to it, either from fear or reverence of its significance.

Yes, they had really done it.

After a while, she became aware of a presence beside her. She didn't turn to look at Gaeben. They stood in silence for several moments.

It was the children who were brave enough to approach the club first. Of course, they had all been safely in bed at the emergency camp during the entire encounter. They didn't know enough to fear it. Perhaps that was a good thing. Perhaps they would grow up to know monsters could be conquered. Their children would view ogres as stupid beings, and their children would use their massive clubs and helms as playthings. *Indeed,* Kendra thought as she watched a boy try to lift the club to no avail, *some already are.*

Not able to stand the silence between them, Kendra finally glanced up at Gaeben. She'd never really noticed how very tall he was. He wasn't a wizened old wizard, but he was worldly enough to command respect. His ever-present staff was in his hand, and Kendra was now well aware of what he was capable of doing with it.

"So, am I to believe the villagers rallied together on their own to defeat the ogre?"

It took her a moment to muster her courage. "I encouraged them. I didn't tell them why."

"I see."

Kendra was afraid to move. Inside, every bit of her seemed to tremble. She knew if she made the slightest motion, her hands would shake or her knees would knock together. Nevertheless, she had to speak.

"I think—I think you should leave. Let one of us deliver the staff to Winterkeep where it can do no further harm. I don't have to tell the others anything. I'll allow them to remember you fondly, if that's your wish. I know they'd be happier not knowing how long they were used by you."

He stood silently, his expression stoic. Kendra forced herself to breathe evenly and keep her mouth shut. There was nothing more to be said.

"Do you think he will be the last evil thing to come to your village? Do you truly believe that no more servants of Endroren will come to trouble you?" he asked. "Fools. If you send me away, you'll only invite death in."

It wasn't until Kendra's cheeks burned with fury that she realized how afraid she had been of this moment. Afraid she would be too fearful of Gaeben to do the right thing. Her anger surprised her, and she drew strength from it.

"Death? More than *you* have already brought upon this village?" She felt her courage grow with every word. "That ogre didn't kill a single one of us, yet how many of our lives have you claimed?"

"Everything I've ever done has been for this village."

"But why?" Kendra finally turned to look at him. "Why did you feel the need to help a village of strangers, of a different race? Was it pity or ambition? Or was it because we were weak, and therefore easy to control?"

Gaeben's mouth fell open and his eyes seemed like they would pop from his head. "What are you getting at? How can you fault me for wanting to protect you from monsters like that? Or the raiders from before? The epidemic a couple years ago? I only wanted to stop evil from inflicting itself upon this village."

"And who will stop *your* evil?" Kendra asked, her voice raw. "I've seen nothing so evil befall our village as the one who would pretend to be our friend, only to further his own ambition. I've seen your wishes spelled out on parchment. We're but a means to an end to you, nothing more. And I repeat: You must leave."

"Leave?" he spat, anger finally lighting up his eyes. "I should leave. Leave all of you to your deaths. You can do nothing without me." He gestured wildly at the club with his staff. "That was nothing. I heard how you fools behaved." "Do you think you could defeat a dragon like that? Do you think you could defeat a horde of goblins?"

"Is that what you'd hoped to accomplish?" Kendra asked. "To render us useless, powerless without you?"

"You *are* powerless on your own," he replied.

Dozens of retorts popped into Kendra's head, each more angry than the last. Then she glanced at Gaeben's staff, and a realization came to her: "So are you."

The mage suddenly seemed even taller than his usual head and shoulders over Kendra. His rage took up space around him, invisible yet detectable just the same. "How *dare* you. You ungrateful—"

"Tell me, would someone who was truly wanting to help be so angry when those people helped themselves? How is keeping us weak and convincing our people they can't defend themselves helpful? And you call me ungrateful. Tell me, was Lumo grateful after you sucked the life out of him? Were any of the others?"

Kendra shook her head. "I think it's you who is ungrateful. This village has given you enough. No wonder you couldn't teach me more than the simplest charms. It is not I who was lacking in skill. It was you."

For the first time, Gaeben glanced around and saw the halflings surrounding them. There was no escape for him. He could claim she was lying, but it wouldn't be so simple to hide what would become obvious if anyone really thought about it. Kendra could see the rage slowly drain from his face as he realized the people he claimed to care about were on the verge of completely losing faith in him.

"I'll leave," he said. "I'll go without a fight, but I beseech you, reconsider. You've always been fascinated by my workings. I'm not a strong wizard, I'll grant, but I do have abilities. I wouldn't be able to use the staff otherwise. And I can teach you more. I can teach you to use it, too. Remember how you loved to come for lessons, how you begged me to teach you just one more thing? Do you really think you can get that somewhere else? Together, we can defeat any evil that comes to this village and beyond."

"And who will defeat you?" Kendra asked in a whisper. She didn't trust her voice. She remembered. And she knew no one else would spend the time teaching a halfling to use magic. She knew the price of sending him away. This was her only chance—but she had no choice.

"I worshipped you," she continued. "You were everything I wanted to be, but you've brought a greater evil here than any ogre or goblin. I don't know where that staff is from or who created it, but it doesn't work for the powers of any but those who would steal essence and use it for their own ends."

"I won't give it up."

"Then you'll have to answer to me."

Kendra gasped as Corrin took a step closer. She was so wrapped in her shell of torn emotions she'd forgotten they were not alone.

"And me." Lumo's wife Smee stepped forward. "I wish I'd never brought my husband to you. If I had known—"

"You people don't understand," Gaeben protested. "I had to take life to replenish mine. The staff needs power to work. Life essence is its raw material. Through my will, that raw material becomes what I need. It can extinguish fire, heal illness, make crops grow. It can defeat enemies and turn water to the cider you halflings love so much. I can replace the crop you lost in the fire. I can replenish your stores after you wasted them on that ogre."

"And how many lives would that cost?" Lorie asked.

Gaeben looked from halfling to halfling. "You act as if I'm using dark arts. I simply found a way to use magic. Of course those arrogant fools in Winterkeep would say I am practicing evil. They don't want anyone else to know their secrets. They'd make me out to be as bad as Endroren himself!"

"Corrin," Kendra said. "I was a very small child the last time we had a Winterkeep mage come to our aid. What was the body count after they left?"

"None. We lost not a single halfling under their watch."

"I'm not a murderer," Gaeben said, sweat dripping down his temples. "I eased their passing to Numos."

"You steal the essence of innocent people," Corrin said.

More halflings approached from all sides. Gaeben glanced around. His mouth was open, yet he seemed to have run out of excuses.

Kendra searched for any courage remaining after the ordeal of the night before. She had to get his staff away from him, yet there was so much she didn't understand. The one thing she knew for certain was that magical items were nothing to be handled lightly. Hadn't her grandfather related several tales of people being corrupted by them? Unable to control themselves?

Sudden tears prickled her eyes.

"You know, I believe you," she said as she blinked and cursed her weakness. "I believe that in your heart, you thought you were doing the right thing. But you have to understand, Gaeben, the most evil thing that has ever befallen our village..." She swallowed hard, determined to continue to the end, despite the tears that fell to her cheeks. "Is you."

Gaeben looked as if she'd slapped him.

Memories flooded through her; of childhood teasing, of being an outcast, being taunted by her kind for asking too many questions, for wanting to know things that were "none of a proper halfling's business." Memories of open arms, of comforting words, of understanding. Of her Gaeben. The only one who understood her. The only one who could help her find the answers she sought. The only one.

She fell to her knees in their wake, the unbidden images still haunting her. What would life be like without her Gaeben?

Her Gaeben...

She shook her head. He had never been her Gaeben.

"Even me?" she asked in a broken voice. "You would enchant even me? Who will pay for that bit of sorcery?"

"No one," he said. "Only me." He stared down at the staff. A smooth, black piece of wood, so dark it seemed to swallow light. Yet so much more.

Then he knelt before Kendra, still taller than her, but lowering himself to the same level. "I don't know how to live without it," he said. "I can't put it down."

They made eye contact, and he was just Gaeben then; the atlan who stole her heart when she was little. The atlan she'd tried to impress when she was a teenager. The atlan, the only being she'd ever felt a kinship with, the only one who knew what it was like to want more from life than what was handed to her. More.

Would this happen to her, too? Could she be corrupted as well?

She held out her hands, not fully comprehending why, only knowing there was a question in her heart she couldn't put into words.

She waited. He would make the right choice. He would see.

She waited while the halflings of the village closed in on them.

She waited. Then she broke from his gaze. She stood, and at the same moment the halflings were within arm distance, she grabbed the staff.

Immediately, she felt a clarity she'd never felt before. She could see *everything*. She could see more than everything. The world was too full. Light, darkness, and every hue between. Life and death, good and evil. She could see it all.

It fascinated her. It drew her. It wanted her.

It frightened her.

Her gaze traveled back to Gaeben's. They both still held the staff, but when she saw how dark his essence had grown, she jerked it from his hand. He looked at his appendage as if it had somehow betrayed him by relinquishing his most precious belonging.

How dare he? How dare he look at her as if she had taken from him? Had he not taken everything from her? Her hopes, dreams? Her childhood? For when she should have been learning halfling-like things, he had shown her wonders to make ordinary, practical life pale in comparison.

The halflings grabbed his arms and tied his wrists behind him. Still Kendra held the staff. She felt hatred well up inside of her. And she knew. Oh, she knew how to use that staff.

It had taught her.

Her chest rose and fell with her breathing, every breath deliberate. Every heartbeat deliberate. Her loathing burned through her, searing her veins. The only way she'd find relief was to draw the life from him. Draw away every ounce of his essence. Make him pay for every bit he took from others.

The others…

Hadn't they all laughed at her, teased her all her life for wanting more? She could hear them in her mind even now, taunting her, asking her how she'd ever find a husband, scowling at her failed pies while ignoring that so much evil existed in the world. Mean, spiteful, and nasty beings. She could show them now. She would show them all, now that the staff belonged to her. Its power coursed through her, just waiting to be used.

Then she heard a faint laugh.

A giggle.

Kendra blinked. The breeze felt cool on her cheeks, and she saw only Gaeben tied before her. Only regular halflings. Birds calling, and the children laughing as they played.

She dropped the staff and rubbed her tainted hands on her apron. "Take him to the village hall and keep him locked there until the mage from Winterkeep can come. He won't fight you," she said. True to her words, he stood weakly, his gaze cast to the ground. "No one is to touch this staff," she added.

Kendra didn't know what the others had witnessed, exactly. But Corrin, their leader, deferred to her. "Do as she says," he said.

"And we shall have three halflings watching this staff constantly until the mages arrive. The true mages."

Gaeben began walking with his guards, but stopped and turned to her. "Kendra, you must believe me. I never meant to harm anyone."

Kendra found herself constantly drawn to the staff. It wanted her to pick it up. It wanted her to use it. "I'll be taking the journey to Winterkeep with you," she said, still staring at it. She didn't know what gave her this knowledge, but once she'd said the words, she knew no other alternative existed for her.

The staff would call to her forever after this. She must learn how to resist. She must learn how to control whatever it had awoken within her, lest she become just another version of Gaeben.

She would be her grandfather's descendent. She would protect her kind, and inspire those younger than her.

She would be the hero her people needed.

VENDETTA

RICHARD LEE BYERS

ARON MARCHWARD REACHED THE VILLAGE WELL AFTER dark. He'd spotted it from higher ground just before dusk, and trusting that between them, he and his horse could avoid straying from the trail, chose to press onward. It seemed preferable to another night of gnawing hardtack and sleeping on the ground.

But as he looked around, he started to wonder whether that had been such a good idea. The problem wasn't the lack of an inn. He'd hoped for one, but hadn't expected it. It was the lack of people. In other such isolated hamlets, some of the inhabitants would be emerging from the small houses with their plaster facades to gawk at a stranger or, if they were enterprising, try to sell him supper and a bed. Not here. He had no doubt people *were* peeking at him—he could feel the pressure of their gazes—but they were taking care not to be spotted.

Perhaps experience had given them cause to be wary of men-at-arms. He pondered how best to reassure them that, his saber, swordbreaker, and brigandine notwithstanding, he was no bandit or slaver, just a weary traveler with a few copper gates left to spend. Then voices screamed. A moment after that, a door banged open, and a woman and a little boy, both in their nightclothes, stumbled out into the street.

Aron started to dismount, then hesitated. The last six demoralizing years had convinced him to leave the Duchy of Vaun and head south to Callios. Now that he'd arrived, he meant to stay clear of trouble unless he was well compensated. But it was a mother and child in distress, and how much trouble was a domestic altercation likely to be? It should be easy enough to intimidate or subdue the irate and likely drunken husband, and win the village's trust thereby.

He swung down from the saddle, tied the roan mare to a hitching post, and strode toward the woman and the little boy. He also made sure his blades were loose in their scabbards. He'd be surprised if he needed them, but caution had kept him alive until now, and he had no intention of abandoning it.

He drew breath to ask the woman what was going on. Then a shadow appeared in the doorway. Mother and child shrieked anew as they retreated farther away, and Aron scrambled to interpose himself between them and their pursuer. That was when he noticed the sickly green phosphorescence in the dark figure's eyes.

When the father-thing sprang into the street, its other abnormalities became apparent; the snout, a wide mouth full of jagged fangs, crooked spine and limbs, and the bloody lesions that were apparently a byproduct of its transformation. Like the woman and child, it wore nightclothes. Unlike them, it bore a woodcutter's axe in its oversized hands.

Aron faltered, but only for an instant. He'd fought unnatural creatures before, and when the axe leaped at his head, he simultaneously spun aside and drew his weapons. He slashed to the knee, and the father-thing pivoted, parried with the axe, and struck back at his midsection.

Aron took a half step back, and the horizontal stroke missed by an inch. He then cut to the hand, severing tendons, and his adversary fumbled its grip on its weapon. He lunged, and the saber plunged into its chest. That would have been the death of a human foe, but the father-thing dropped the axe and, heedless that the action drove the sword deeper into its body, bulled forward. Using its undamaged hand, it caught Aron's extended arm and jerked him close. Its jaws opened wide.

Aron stabbed the swordbreaker between the rows of fangs and up through the roof of the mouth. The father-thing froze, and then crumpled. The green glow faded from its eyes, and the woman's screams turned into gasping sobs.

Panting, Aron studied his foe, making very sure it was truly done. Then he turned to speak to the woman and discovered that, to their credit, some of the villagers had come rushing with weapons in hand to help her and her son. They just hadn't reached the trouble as quickly as he had.

Someone moved to take charge of the anguished mother and child, and, judging that a neighbor was apt to prove more comforting than a stranger, Aron left that compassionate fellow to the task. He turned his attention to the other villagers.

"My name is Aron Marchward," he said. "I'm a mercenary on my way to Filicos to seek employment. I stopped here hoping to find food and lodging, heard the screams, and, well, you know what happened after that."

"Thank Alantra you happened by," an old woman said. White-haired and plump, she had an apple-cheeked face made for smiling and entertaining grandchildren, although her expression was grim enough at the moment.

"Has this happened before?" Aron asked. "Your village is closed up like a fortress."

"Yes," said a short man gripping a shovel. "Not that it does much good when the evil can reach out and possess any of us no matter where we are."

"We don't know that it's done with us even now," the old woman said. "We should burn the body immediately."

"No!" wailed the bereaved son. Thrashing, he fought to make his way to the corpse, while his mother and the man who'd sought to comfort them both struggled to restrain him.

The old woman hurried to him and put her hands on his shoulders. "I'm sorry, Tevis," she said. "So sorry. But that's not your papa anymore, and we have to make sure it won't get up again, and that the curse won't spread to any of the rest of us."

Using tools, gloves, and a tarp, the villagers conveyed the body to a burn pile without ever touching it. The fresh wood lay atop the ash and charred sticks of previous pyres, and atop pieces of blackened bone as well.

As a big, barrel-chested man with a curly grizzled beard lit the new fire, the plump woman said, "We should move back. For all we know, even breathing the smoke might be poisonous."

Aron backed away a few steps. But he kept watching as the nightshirt charred away to reveal the lesions beneath, some of which looked like glyphs sliced into the flesh above the heart. Perhaps part of him still needed convincing that the monstrous thing was dead.

Apparently believing they'd retreated far enough for safety's sake, the old woman stayed at his side. "May I know your name?" he asked her.

"Medelyl Fisher." She offered her hand, and he clasped it.

"What's going on in this town, Medelyl?"

Before she could answer, the man with the curly black beard

interrupted. "Several of us would like to talk to you about that," he said, his manner that of a person accustomed to getting his way. "We'll be happy to do it over that supper you wanted, and we'll open some wine to wash it down."

Aron nodded. "If someone will help me see to my horse, it's a bargain."

THE MEAL TURNED OUT TO BE A MIX OF VEGETABLES AND noodles, with just a few overlooked scraps of goat meat left in the cauldron. Though a far cry from the gourmet fare reportedly available in Filicos, it was tasty enough, and Aron made his contributions to the conversation between mouthfuls.

Judging from the absence of youthful faces, it was a conversation with the half-dozen village elders, the circle who made decisions affecting the community as a whole. The man with the curly beard was Dornus Fisher—many people hereabouts seemed to be Fishers, with the familial prominent nose to prove it—and Medelyl and the other elders deferred to him as their chief.

Popping the cork from an earthenware jug, Dornus said, "You have to understand, there's us, and there are the Hightreaders up on the ridge. We don't get along."

Riding down from the Dragon Tail Mountains to the northwest, Aron hadn't seen any signs of nearby habitations, but he'd noticed that the land rose again to the east. That must be where the Hightreaders made their homes. "What does that have to do with men who suddenly turn into monsters?"

"The Hightreaders have a sorcerer," Dornus said, "Ullinar Hightreader." Some of the elders made a sign to avert evil at the utterance of the name. "He's the one cursing us. There's no else it could be."

Aron wasn't any sort of spell caster, but since taking up the sword, he'd known his share, and through simple propinquity, had absorbed a little something about their art. "Then this Ullinar is practicing a dark form of magic indeed. Not that you need me to tell you that. But even evil men generally need a motive above and beyond pure wickedness to undertake a campaign of destruction like this seems to be. What's he trying to accomplish?"

"What the Hightreaders have always wanted to accomplish," Dornus said. "To kill us or drive us from our land, and take all the most fertile fields and the most abundant streams and hunting grounds for themselves."

Aron nodded. The city-states of Callios were as wealthy as they were contentious. That was why he'd crossed a fair piece of the world to come here. But the riches came from trade, not this rocky, hardscrabble countryside, and it was easy to imagine competing clans of rustics feuding over its limited resources, easy, too, to imagine that if someone possessed a talent for tainted magic, he might use it to settle such a vendetta once and for all.

"How many have fallen prey to the curse so far?" he asked.

"Four to the sorcerer's magic," Medelyl said, "and two to the arrows and spears of his kin."

"We went up the hill to kill him," Dornus said, "but the Hightreaders saw us coming."

"I tended the wounded as best I could," Medelyl said, "but there was only so much I could do." She sniffed and knuckled away the start of a tear.

"So we were thinking," said Dornus to Aron, "that perhaps the Enaros brought you here tonight."

Aron cocked his head. "I'm afraid it was Rosie. My horse."

Dornus waved the quip away. "We Fishers have brave men among us, but none of us is a trained soldier. Fortunately, none of the Hightreaders are, either. If you lead us back up onto the ridge, things will fall out differently."

"I'm sorry," Aron said. "I was happy to keep that mother and child from coming to harm, and I'm grateful for your hospitality. But this isn't my fight."

Dornus grunted. "When true evil is hurting innocent people, isn't that everybody's fight?"

Aron sighed. Once upon a time, when he'd run away from his father's farm to become a mercenary, he'd believed as Dornus did. He'd imagined that in his new trade, he'd fight to earn his living, but also for what was right and true. But that naiveté had faded over time, and the last six years of watching his employers and their rivals wage war and betray one another for the most venal and petty of reasons had extinguished it utterly. He now understood that looking out for oneself was the way of the world, and he meant to act on that realization and make himself a man of means.

"I need to get to Filicos," he said.

Medelyl put her hand on top of his. "We understand. We aren't your kin, and you have your own path to walk."

Her absolution made Aron feel more guilty rather than less.

"Wait here." Dornus rose and tramped into the next room. A piece of furniture grated against the floorboards as he evidently shifted it from one spot to another.

When he returned, he had a bag in his hand. He dumped the clinking contents on the table amid the jug and the clay and wooden cups. The majority of the coins were copper caravels, but there were a fair number of silver towers as well, and one of the other elders caught his breath. The hoard apparently represented an impressive amount of money by village standards, and Dornus's neighbors hadn't suspected he had it stashed away.

"Help us," said the big man, "and it's all yours."

Aron wondered if there was any tactful way to explain that while the sum might be a lot of money to the Fishers, it wasn't to him. Not when the job under discussion was to deal with a formidable sorcerer and his brothers and cousins, too.

"You might not think it to look at me," Dornus continued, "but I've been to Filicos in my time. Food and lodging cost plenty there, and you don't know that you'll find a job right away."

That gave Aron pause. The coins on the table might seem a meager sum compared to his aspirations, or the danger of the task at hand, but they would still constitute a substantial addition to his depleted stake.

"All right," he said, "it's a bargain. But I'm not leading a force up onto the ridge. I'll go alone."

Dornus frowned. "That's madness."

"Forgive me, but you said it yourself: Your men aren't trained soldiers. I couldn't count on them to understand what I'd want them to do or how I'd need it done. I *can* count on my own skills, however."

SURELY, IF THE HIGHTREADERS HADN'T KEPT A REGULAR watch on the Fishers' village before, they were doing so in the wake of the failed assault. Accordingly, Aron had ridden out of the settlement on the trail that would take a traveler to Filicos, then swung wide to come at the ridge from the east.

In rugged, unfamiliar terrain, that took time, especially after he left Rosie tied to a holly oak to travel more quietly. It was mid-afternoon when the first sod-roofed Hightreader shack came into view. The field adjacent and the scraped deer hide drying on a rack suggested it belonged to a farmer and hunter rather than a spell caster, and so, slipping from one patch of cover to the next, he prowled onward.

Though the Hightreaders' dwellings were more scattered than those of their neighbors below the ridge, a dozen cottages stood in proximity to one another, and someone had painted the walls of one with sigils of green and white. Aron crouched in a stand of gorse to watch and wait.

People came and went. Shouting, laughing children played tag, and a pair of young sweethearts quarreled while other folk pretended not to eavesdrop. In time, the aroma of roasting meat made Aron's stomach rumble, and set him reaching for a chunk of hardtack.

To his disappointment, though, no one came out of the house daubed with mystic symbols or went into it, either. Perhaps Ullinar was busy inside preparing another curse. If so, Aron hoped to get to him before he cast it.

Eventually, night shrouded the ridge, but still Aron waited. While one by one, the shacks darkened as the occupants extinguished the pungent tallow candles burning within.

At last, when it was reasonable to hope everyone had retired for the night, he rose from his place of concealment and headed toward the cottage with the glyphs. Then a voice called, "Velnin?"

Aron turned. A man was approaching. Numos's silvery crescent shed enough light to reveal the javelin in one hand and the dead rabbit dangling in the other. A hunter or trapper, then, returning late from the heath. Who'd mistaken Aron for someone else in the dark.

Raising his hand, Aron advanced on the Hightreader. He made it most of the way before the other man, whose night sight plainly was nowhere near as keen as his own, stiffened and gasped.

Aron drew his blades and charged. Correctly judging that a shout wouldn't bring help in time to save him, the Hightreader didn't bother. He simply dropped the rabbit, leveled the javelin, and thrust.

The mercenary parried with the swordbreaker, then twisted it when the notched edge of the knife caught the spearhead between two of the teeth. The action failed to snap the javelin's point, but it did immobilize the Hightreader's weapon and leave him open.

Aron stepped forward to cut the other man down. Then he slammed the guard of his saber into his face instead. The Hightreader lurched backward and fell down, unconscious.

Afterward, Aron wasn't sure why he'd shown mercy. Perhaps it was because he'd observed too much of the mundane life of the Hightreaders and that made it more difficult to view them as nothing more than the confederates of a diabolical sorcerer, but he hoped not. That kind of softness wouldn't commend him to a merchant prince. He'd rather believe he'd refrained from killing because Dornus hadn't purchased the hunter's life.

After a moment, he pushed such reflections away. Whatever was responsible for his forbearance, he'd neutralized the immediate threat and needed to proceed with his mission. He dragged the hunter into the patch of shadow beside the nearest shack, then stalked on to Ullinar's home.

The door cracked open when he tried the handle. Perhaps people rarely bothered to bar them up here on the ridge. Or maybe Ullinar preferred magical safeguards. As Aron eased the door farther open, he watched for a first flicker of flame leaping up around his feet, or a guardian imp taking form in the gloom. But there was nothing.

The inside of the hut was all one room, and its walls positively swarmed with painted symbols. They weren't writing in any language Aron had ever seen, and he suspected that, growing up where he had, Ullinar was illiterate. He himself hadn't mastered his letters until well into adulthood, after he'd realized that officers should be able to read and write dispatches.

Perhaps the occult symbols simply popped into Ullinar's mind after his natural gift for magic began to manifest. Or else some vile familiar had risen from the Deeplands to tutor him.

The moonlight spilling through the door also revealed the sorcerer himself snoring on a pallet. Ullinar appeared to be in his thirties, which was to say, about the same age as Aron. His face, with its cleft chin and drooping mustache, was slack and unremarkable in slumber.

Aron raised the saber. Killing a sleeping man felt like the act of an assassin, not a soldier. But he'd done it before when it was the sensible way to accomplish an objective, and that was surely the case now. The alternative was to give Ullinar a chance to either blast him with magic or scream for help.

Intent on his quarry, he crept forward.

CRUMBLING AND ABANDONED, THE HOUSE STOOD AMONG fields that tares and brush were rapidly reclaiming. Seen by moonlight, it looked like a dwelling where everyone's luck had always run bad, perhaps even one where misery had twisted people's minds until they did horrible things to one another. A place the neighbors whispered about and shunned after the occupants died out.

Maybe it was. As Aron understood it, spell casters sometimes set up shop in locations where the atmosphere was of a piece with the rituals they intended to perform, and though he'd lost sight of his quarry in the dark, it hadn't been until the low, swaybacked form of the house appeared among the blighted trees that he realized where she was going. Now, it seemed obvious this was her destination.

No one had struck a light inside, but that didn't astonish him. Wizards and their ilk knew magic that allowed them to see in the dark, and one engaging in nefarious deeds wouldn't want a late-night passerby to detect her presence.

Unfortunately, Aron didn't know such a charm, but perhaps he could peek through a window and still glean something of what the spell caster was up to. He skulked forward, and then pain ripped through his back.

He grunted, staggered, and cast about in vain for the source of the attack. He started to turn—

A second burst of agony slammed into him. Crying out, he fell. A third such assault left him left him rigid, his muscles locked in spasm.

His attacker stepped up to him. Though tears blurred his vision, he could make out white hair gleaming in the moonlight.

Medelyl stooped, grabbed him under the arms, and dragged him toward the house. Every bump was excruciating. He was almost glad when she hauled him over the threshold, even though concealment eliminated any possibility of some potential rescuer observing his plight.

Moonlight shined through holes in the thatched roof. The illumination sufficed to reveal a pentacle scratched on the earthen floor, and the spatters of dried blood inside. It was the gore that gave the space its stench, that and the excreta released by sacrificial animals amid their death throes.

Medelyl dragged him to the center of the pentacle and relieved him of his saber and swordbreaker. She then moved back by the door, set the blades at her feet, and pointed a black wand in his direction.

"I know you're hurting," she said, "but I also know the pain has eased enough to let you talk. So let's. I take it Ullinar Hightreader isn't dead?"

Aron drew a ragged breath. "No."

"Why not?"

"When we burned Tevis' father's body, I spotted the bloody runes on his chest. It happens that as he develops his gift, Ullinar is painting sigils all over his walls. But I didn't see any that looked like the symbols on the corpse. Just as I was moving in for the kill, that struck me as curious, and then it occurred to me that it would take a powerful spell caster indeed to transform a man from miles away. But a witch who lived in proximity to the victim, who could pilfer a personal article of some sort to aid in the casting…well, she'd have an easier time of it, wouldn't she?"

"So your suspicions turned to me."

"You're the village healer. Your craft is bound up with magic. You also wanted the victims' bodies burned quickly, without anyone having a chance to discover the runes sliced into their chests. Symbols that looked like someone rendered the men insensible and then cut them physically, in the same way anybody would carve flesh with a knife. And, you encouraged me to continue on to Filicos, even though I might be able to help the village. *Because* I might."

Medelyl nodded. "With whom have you shared your suspicions?"

Aron wondered if there was anything to be gained by lying. He couldn't see how.

"No one," he said. "I wasn't certain, and even if I had been, I doubted Dornus or any of your other neighbors would believe me without proof."

"So you set out to find it."

"Yes. First, I searched your cottage in the village. There was nothing damning there, but perhaps you considered it safer to work corrupt magic somewhere. I decided to follow you, and here we are."

She smiled. "Because I sensed you skulking after me, gave you the slip, and circled around behind you. I can be sneaky when it suits me."

"Because you're not human. Not anymore."

Her eyes widened. "You even figured out that part."

"Just now. Not soon enough to save me. But I've heard of shadowmen. Unlike many evil creatures, you can bear the sun if you must, and stain masks the gray skin. You delight in suffering, and relish eating human flesh."

"Soon I'll relish eating yours. Entertaining though it is, all this cursing and stirring up the old feud with the Hightreaders doesn't put meat on the table. And since no one will know you ever came back down from the ridge…"

She raised the wand. Plainly, she intended to make sure pain still held Aron helpless before approaching and sticking a dagger in him.

"At least tell me why this is happening," he said. "How did you fall so far?"

"It isn't a 'fall!'" she snapped. "Not in the sense that the ignorant mean! But…a bit at a time, like most of my kind. I loved a boy, but there was another girl, and he liked her better. So she had to go. Later, when he was unfaithful to me, I had to punish him. Later still, there were other sleights, and the need to balance the scales."

"Is that why you want to provoke the Fishers and Hightreaders into slaughtering one another? Or is it just your natural cruelty?"

"It's more than either," Medelyl said. "But I've heard all I need from you, and I'm hungry."

While Aron kept the witch talking, the pain in his back had subsided. But from past experience, he knew that such discomforts could fade when a man was lying still only to erupt into paralyzing agony again as soon as he tried to move. Thus, he had no idea whether he was capable of self-defense or not.

But he did know he had to try. Just as Medelyl mouthed a word of command, he attempted to fling himself to the side.

Pain jabbed through his back, but then the pang was gone, and he was rolling. Better still, no fresh burst of agony pounded him like a mallet. He didn't know how the black wand worked, but apparently Medelyl needed to aim it, and he'd just dodged the discharge.

A clump of slimy, fallen thatch lay beside him. He grabbed it, reared up, and, his back muscles tightening, threatening to seize but not quite doing so, threw it at Medelyl's face.

The soft, rotten stuff was harmless, but the impact flummoxed the shadowwoman's attempt to aim the wand again. Aron scrambled to his feet, snatched a cobweb-covered clay jar from a shelf, and hurled that.

Striking lower than he meant it to, the jar smashed into Medelyl's chest, not her head. But she was still half-blinded by the mucky straw sticking to her face, and the jolt caught her by surprise. She flinched, and her arm cocked upward, pointing the wand at the ceiling.

Aron rushed her and slammed her back against the door. With a *crack*, it broke loose from one of its hinges. He and Medelyl fell on the shards of broken pottery, him on top and her underneath.

She tried to point the wand. He grabbed her wrist and strained to keep the magical weapon averted. With his other hand, he clutched her throat. She seized hold of his forearm and struggled to break his hold.

It seemed to him that as wrestlers, they were equally matched. But perhaps that was all right. He was the one with the death grip, his fingers crushing her windpipe. Then her lips formed words, and green phosphorescence swirled in the depths of her eyes.

A chill surged from the points where their bodies touched to deep inside him. He gasped, and suddenly he was no longer strong enough to keep her from jerking his hand loose from her throat or to prevent the wand from hitching inch-by-inch in his direction.

He twisted his wrist out of her grasp, cast about, and discovered the swordbreaker lying within reach. He jerked the notch-edged knife from its sheath, raised it high, and drove the point deep into her left eye.

She bucked beneath him and then lay still. The glow in the

remaining eye went out.

An instant later, his lower back throbbed. It likely would have been hurting all long if desperation hadn't masked the feeling.

Despite the grinding, pulling spasms, he smiled. Because now he could afford to lie down and rest and let them run their course.

WHEN DORNUS OPENED THE DOOR, ARON SAW THE rest of the villagers had assembled to see him off. The contents of Medelyl's secret lair had gone a long way toward convincing them that she was the true source of the hamlet's ills, and revealing the gray skin beneath her garments, the skin she hadn't bothered to color, had persuaded whatever skeptics remained.

"You see?" Dornus murmured. "You have a place here if you want it."

"As your mercenary in residence," Aron replied.

"I think sheriff would be a better term. Whatever we called you, we could use you. There really is bad blood between the Hightreaders and us, and sometimes there are other problems, too. This is wild country."

"I'm flattered," Aron said. "But my goal is to serve one of your merchant lords, and get rich doing it."

"Is that your true dream?" Dornus asked. "Or have you really been looking for a cause worth serving?"

"The former," Aron said. "Sorry." He clapped the big man on the shoulder and then walked into the crowd.

Clustering around, villagers clasped his hand and gave him fresh-baked viands for the trail. By the time he reached Rosie, his hands were so full of snacks and trinkets that he had to juggle them awkwardly while stowing them in his saddlebags. While he was so engaged, a snatch of his final conversation with Medelyl came back to him.

She'd hinted there was a reason she was trying to set the Fishers and Hightreaders at each other's throats. Something beyond the instinctive malice of her kind, or the need to settle grudges.

What if there was something special about this unassuming patch of earth, something that made the servants of the Lord of Darkness particularly eager to destroy the human population? If such was the case, others would try now that Medelyl had failed, and the Fishers might truly need a soldier.

What's more, in some form, the wealth Aron sought might be right here for the claiming if only he could find it.

He didn't bother pondering which consideration weighed heavier. He simply smiled and turned to inform the villagers that he was staying after all.

TRUE MONSTERS

JOHN HELFERS

THE HARVEST MOON SHONE BRIGHT OVER THE SMALL forest town of Thornwall, its golden rays illuminating quiet rows of shops shuttered for the night and clusters of homes with their fires banked and candles extinguished. Merchants and families alike were all inside, tucked in their beds. Even the famed Green Briar Tavern, renowned for its hospitality, had finally fallen silent, the boisterous cries, laughing boasts, and gleeful songs fading into the night hours ago.

All was still and peaceful, secure behind the tall, unusually thick hedgerow surrounding the village—except for one place.

Near the gleaming white temple of Lensae, on a small hill overlooking the rest of the town, a large humanoid shape, half again as tall as a man, walked toward the graveyard, pulling a rough, two-wheeled cart behind him. The tools of his trade rattled and clanked in the cart's bed, along with the linen-wrapped form that would be laid to rest tonight.

As he trudged along, Torg savored the quiet autumn evening. He tended to stay out of sight of the other townsfolk, either remaining in the ramshackle cottage provided by the temple, or taking long walks in the woods surrounding the town. He liked the nights most of all. The shadows and darkness hid many things…including him.

He paused to wipe his lumpy brow, sweeping a thick tuft of wire-stiff hair out of his eyes. The first frost wasn't far off now, the cool nights eliminating the pesky clawflies and blood-biters that plagued him during the summer months. What he did for the temple and the town wasn't hard, but it was outdoors, and he hated the flies buzzing about his face and ears and tiny little biters stinging through even his thick skin as he worked.

Torg began walking again, passing the neat rows of gravestones, many of them faded and moss-covered after years of exposure. He smiled as he checked the short, neat grass around them; he was also responsible for maintaining the cemetery, and took that duty seriously, trimming the grass around the stones and ensuring that the gravel paths were neat and well kept.

He studied the names carved into the stones, many from Thornwood's founding families. *Bythewater. Endlebry. Patera. Fegel.* He could read them all, although the longer ones were difficult for him. He'd always been puzzled by many people's need to have long names. His name was short and simple, just the way he liked it. A tongue wouldn't trip over "Torg," like it might trying to say some of the other townspersons' names.

Tonight's work was a rare double—he had two bodies to take care of this evening. The first was a drunken traveling merchant who had fallen off his horse outside the Green Briar and broken his neck. Torg had learned from Brother Basil that the mayor had sent word to his next-of-kin, but with no way of knowing how soon they would arrive, the decision had been made to cremate his body and have an urn of ashes ready for any relatives to take with them.

That body had already been prepared in the crematorium, and only awaited Brother Basil to oversee the final cremation.

The second body, a dwarf, was a much more unusual case—the last remaining member of the Dolgenkett family, one of the oldest families of Thornwood, had finally expired at the ripe old age of 292. But instead of the usual cremation, he had requested to be placed in the earth, giving Torg the chance to do something he rarely did nowadays, due to the evil lurking across the land—dig a grave.

Reaching the spot where the body would lie in eternal rest, he set the handles of the cart down and reached for his shovel. A massive tool of steel and wood, its shaft was as tall as his own nine feet, and almost as thick as a sapling's trunk. On the end was an edged spade almost two feet across.

Torg hefted it as he eyed the section of earth he'd be moving. Normally he would have dug by lantern light, but the moon's beams cast a rich yellow glow over everything, making it easy to see.

He pushed the shovel down, its keen edge biting into the black earth. Thick, corded muscles rippling, he heaved up the first spadeful, removing a scoop of dirt the size of a small boulder, and dumping it aside. With the large bites his shovel took, it wouldn't take long to finish the grave. He bent and lifted, turned and dumped, and each time both the hole and the pile grew steadily larger.

Torg settled into his rhythm, smiling as the square hole grew larger from his efforts. He liked all his work for the temple—it was simple, uncomplicated. Brother Basil treated him very well and got supplies for him whenever he needed them. Mostly food—his kind tended to eat a lot.

There was just one problem with working at night—that was often when the Darkness tried to come out.

Torg knew all about the Darkness hidden deep within his soul, a curse each one of his kind shared, and had to resist every day. He dimly remembered stories told around a long-ago campfire when he was just a youngling, tales of those who had surrendered to the Darkness, and the terrible crimes they committed under its sway. Torg and those long-gone others had been warned to always remain vigilant against the ever-creeping, ever-searching Darkness, which would seize upon the smallest pretext to persuade him, to control him, and to make him do terrible things.

The *crack* of a breaking branch made him raise his head and stare toward where the noise had come from. A small copse of trees sat on the cemetery's northern edge, and as he squinted, Torg thought he saw someone—or something—moving near the trunk of the largest one. Shadows flitted underneath its canopy, hidden from the moonlight, and the thick mat of hair on the back of his neck rose in warning, not fear. Torg was not afraid of anything that walked upon the land.

As he half-expected, the Darkness seized that moment to push at him, trying to make him fall upon whoever was out there and tear them limb from limb. It insinuated that whoever was spying on him was an enemy coming to attack him, and therefore he must destroy them before they destroyed him.

It didn't speak to him, but filled his mind with images of a terrible death as the barely-seen shadows left the trees and swarmed over him, clawing and biting. Even though he flung them away in the vision, there were always more, they never stopped coming at him, and were always scratching and chewing—

A low growl welled up from deep within and rumbled out of his mouth. Torg found himself taking a large step forward, huge, gnarled hands knotted into fists that could fell an ox in one swing, before realizing what he was doing. Shaking his head, he turned back to his work, forcing the Darkness away again, back down to that place deep within him that he didn't like thinking about.

Torg knew the Darkness wasn't conquered for good, just held off for a while. He never liked thinking about it, didn't like thinking about what might happen if it got ahold of him, even for a little while. He liked his cottage and his job, liked working among the silent graves in the cool night.

And even though the people of Thornwall hardly ever saw him, he liked them, too. He liked watching over their dead. It made him feel like he was a part of their lives; perhaps unrecognized, but there all the same. He never wanted to do anything to hurt them.

Another twig breaking near the trees drew his attention again, and this time Torg heard whispering as well. He still couldn't make out who was there or what they were doing, but the shadows around the base of the tree seemed to have multiplied since the last time he'd looked.

With the grave nearly finished, he took a hesitant step forward, peering at the small copse.

"SHH!" ELLA ABLEHAND HISSED. "ALL THAT NOISE YOU'RE making, he'll hear us for sure!"

"I'm telling you, it's not us!" replied Kitt, one of the dwarf triplets clustered around her. "Jensen stepped on that last one—"

"Nuh-uh!" The wiry boy shook his head so hard his black hair flopped down across his eyes. "I wasn't anywhere near it!"

"Did too, I saw you!" Keesa, the second dwarven child on this crazy venture, chimed in. She looked like a copy of her brother and sister, with eyes so dark brown they were almost black, and flaxen hair that practically gleamed in the pale moonlight.

"SHH!" Ella hissed again, so loud she clapped a hand over her own mouth. "All of you be quiet right *now*!" she said after taking it away a moment later.

That shut the four other children up right quick. Breathing a soft sigh of relief, she turned back to the hulking figure standing in the middle of the cemetery a dozen paces away—*well, maybe only four or five for him*, she thought—and staring hard in their direction.

"Think he can see us?" Jensen whispered in Ella's ear, startling her.

She turned and frowned at him, catching a glimpse of his startlingly blue eyes staring back at her. Waving him off, she swept a braid of her long, brown hair away from her face. "I don't know, but if you all keep shuffling around like that, he'll spot us for sure."

Hearing a small *click* as Jensen moved away from her, Ella looked down to see him holding a pair of smooth stones in his fingers. Too late, she remembered he was always throwing rocks at things…targets on a wall, birds, other rocks…and occasionally an errant throw through a shop window. She grimaced. "And just *what* are you planning to do with that?"

"Hey, just in case…you know, if he does come after us," he said.

Ella's grimace darkened into a full-blown glare. "Jensen Zirlo, if I catch you tossing even a pebble at him, I'll make you eat every last stone in your pocket, and see if I don't!"

"It's only if we get in trouble, that's all," he protested, but put the rocks back in his pocket. "Who knows that that thing might do?"

About to protest his words, Ella was cut off by another voice.

"I can't see anything!" Kolvin, the shortest of the three dwarven children, balanced on his tiptoes on a thick tree root and stretched as high as he could. "Wow…he's *huge*. So, what is he? A giant? An ogre?"

"We already know what he is, silly," Ella said. "An orog. My da told me that."

In fact, Ella could kind of blame her da—and herself—for why the five children had snuck out in the middle of the night to get a look at the huge gravedigger.

Da had been talking to Frayer and Grimalt Harvenkett in the bakery as the dwarves had arranged a double order of honey cakes for their company, some cousins arriving from Dunbury Castle next week. Ella had been keeping an eye on the triplets, who were playing outside. That's when the trouble had started.

Much like the adults in Thornwall, all of the town's children knew each other. And like their parents, they worked together, played together, formed alliances, feuded with, and gossiped about each other. But in the end, they all usually came together in the face of any challenge or threat.

Ella was no different. In this case, it fell to her to make sure the mischievous dwarves didn't get into any trouble while their parents negotiated. Fortunately, the rambunctious trio was distracted from the moment they'd arrived, each one jockeying to play with a jointed wooden doll that seemed to be Keesa's, but that all three of them wanted. Finally, their squabbling drew the adults' attention.

"Beware, you three!" Da had said as he dusted off his flour-covered hands. He winked at Grimalt, which the other kids hadn't seen, but Ella had caught. "If you don't settle down this instant, we'll send Torg the giant gravedigger out to collect you. He loves snatching naughty children in the night—"

"Dorbold Ablehand, stop that nonsense this instant!" Frayer Harvenkett said, glaring up at him. "Do *not* fill those kids's heads with stories about Torg! He'd never hurt a soul!"

"Aye, Frayer," Da said, lowering his voice, but talking still loud enough for Ella to hear. "I know that, and you know that, but *they* don't know that. Besides, one look at that orog would send 'em all runnin' for your skirts, I figure."

Those last words had garnered the triplets' attention. "What?" Kitt asked, looking around and spotting Ella. "Did your da just call us scared?"

"Well, no, not exactly—" she began.

"'Cause we're not, ya know!" Kolvin said, swaggering up to her with all the toughness an eight-year-old dwarf boy could muster. Even though Ella was two years older than him, they stood face-to-face as he continued. "Us Harvenketts aren't afraid of anything!"

Ella held up her hands, trying to placate the three glowering children. "Look, no one said you were—"

"An' if he thinks we're too scared to go check out old Torg, then he doesn't know the Harvenketts at all!" Keesa chimed in.

It had snowballed from there, and before she knew quite how it happened, Emma had agreed to go with the three smaller children to see the orog that night. She knew they all could get in a fair amount of trouble if they got caught, but she also knew the three kids couldn't be talked out of their plan, and there'd be even more trouble if something happened to them. And, to be honest, a small part of her, peaked by the adults' conversation, also wanted to get a real look at the huge gravedigger.

It was supposed to be just the four of them, but Kolvin must have bragged about their upcoming adventure to Jensen Zirlo during the afternoon. When Ella had met the three dwarves that night, he was standing next to them as well, a knowing smile on his face. Stuck with him—but secretly glad to have another older child along—they'd all set out for the graveyard which, she discovered, looked a lot creepier at night.

Now that they were here, Ella wondered how she'd ever allowed herself to be talked into this. Torg was *enormous*—easily four feet taller than her da. He clutched a huge shovel in his thick fingers that looked big enough to scoop up two of them at a time and dump them into the empty grave he'd been digging.

"Well, now what?" Jensen asked.

"Just be quiet and nobody move," Ella whispered back. "We

can't go until he leaves—if he sees us, who knows what—I mean, we could get in big trouble."

"Uh-oh." Keesa said, pointing at the looming figure. "I think he's coming this way."

Ella turned back to see the orog take another giant step forward. He was much closer now, and she shivered as she imagined trying to run away from him. *It'd be impossible…he'd be on us in three steps and scoop us up—*

"Ella! He sees us!"

Startled, she broke from her reverie to find the orog gravedigger striding toward them. "Ah! Let's get out of—" Heart pounding in her chest, Ella whirled to see the three dwarves already gone, sprinting toward home as fast as their short legs could carry them.

She turned back to see Jensen still beside her. "Come on!" he said. He waited for her to start running, then, with a last panicked glance over his shoulder, he followed her.

Together, the two children ran into the night after the three fleeing dwarves.

SHOULDERS SLUMPING, TORG WATCHED THE CHILDREN RUN away. He wasn't surprised—this wasn't the first time someone had come out to get a look at the "giant gravedigger," and it wouldn't be the last.

He was actually used to it by now. In the four summers he'd been here—or was it five?—there had always been a curious someone or someones who wanted to get a better look at the big, ugly orog at the temple. The encounters were never pleasant. It wasn't because of the townspeople's behavior, for they tended to treat him with either wary respect or ignore him entirely, but the occurrences always seemed to inflame the Darkness, which relentlessly tried to chip away at his resolve for days afterward.

Even so, Torg didn't like that his size and appearance could still cause fear in those who saw him. He wouldn't have hurt those children; he was more concerned about them running around at night. On the whole, Thornwall was a safe place, but accidents still happened, and he would have hated to see something bad happen to any of them.

"Torg? Torg?" A calm voice from behind him made the orog turn to see a halfling approaching. He was dressed in dark green half-sleeved robes, brown leather bracers, and sandals, with a small sun worked in gold, the symbol of the order of Lensae, hanging around his neck. A genial smile brightened the small man's face, and his hands were clasped as he stopped in front of Torg. "Is everything all right?"

Torg grinned upon seeing the tiny cleric. Of all the people in Thornwall, he liked Brother Basil Underwood the most. The halfling had treated him with patient kindness from the very first day he'd found Torg sitting outside the temple as a nervous mob of townspeople had tried to figure out who he was and where he had come from—and what he intended to do.

Brother Basil had been very helpful in allowing Torg to stay in the village, vouching for him and giving him the cottage to live in, and his work in the graveyard. The halfling kept him well supplied in bread, meat, and the occasional bottle of beer, but never too much, for Torg knew the Darkness would take advantage of his muddled head if it could.

Torg cared about the little cleric so much that sometimes he feared what he might do if anything happened to Brother Basil. The stories of the Darkness said it was the most powerful when it could convince an orog to do something because he felt it was the right thing to do, even if that wasn't the best thing to do. He didn't know what he would do if the little halfling ever got hurt.

"I thought…I saw someone…by the trees there." Torg pointed at the now deserted copse.

"And was there?" Brother Basil asked.

"Yes." Torg nodded. "I walked toward them…but they left before…I could get there."

"Do you know who it was?" the cleric asked.

The orog hesitated. He didn't want to lie to the cleric, but he also figured the children were probably just playing, and didn't want to get them in trouble either. Brother Basil was a good man, but that meant he would talk to the kids' parents if he knew who to go to. "I think…they were some children…of the town," he finally said.

"Ah." Brother Basil sighed. "Trying to catch a glimpse of our resident gravedigger again, eh? Did you see who they were? Would you recognize them if you saw them again?"

Relieved, Torg shook his head so hard his bushy, shoulder-length hair whipped back and forth. He hadn't seen them clearly, so he could answer the question honestly. "Nope."

"All right, then," the halfling said with a slight frown. "I'll send a general message to the townspeople to try and keep a more watchful eye on their children, or at least keep them a bit closer to home."

"It…is okay," Torg said. "I…do not mind…if they want…to look at me."

Brother Basil smiled. "I know you wouldn't mind, and that you would never harm a hair on their head. That is not my point. You are a good person, not some curiosity to be stared at for the amusement of others. You deserve their respect, and to be accorded the freedom to live as you wish—basically, the same rights as anyone else in Thornwall. *That* is my point."

Although Torg didn't catch the meaning of some of the halfling's bigger words, he got the general idea of what he was saying, and his smile grew even wider. "Thank you…Brother Basil."

"You're welcome, my friend." The cleric smiled. "Now, we should probably return to our duties tonight, yes? The grave looks to be almost finished—you've done a great job, as always. I will finish the last rites, and then we will see to the arrangements for our other guest in the crematorium. And then, if you'd like, we can take in the sunrise together."

Torg nodded happily. "I would…like that," he said, and turned to head back to the open grave.

Even though he preferred the darkness, he also enjoyed watching the sun come up with Brother Basil. He knew the tiny man assigned a much greater importance to it, given the symbol on his chest, but Torg just liked being there with him as he performed his morning prayers. It was soothing and peaceful.

And although he would never tell Brother Basil, or anyone, Torg, too, saw meaning in the sun rising every day. Each time it did, that was one more day he hadn't given in to the Darkness inside him.

THE CHILDREN'S ENCOUNTER WITH TORG WEIGHED ON Ella's mind for days afterward. They had made it back to their beds that night, although she'd paid for the escapade the next day. Half-dozing through her duties at the bakery, she ended up scorching a dozen loaves of maslin dark. Finally, her exasperated mother had sent Ella with her father to pick up the week's flour order.

The trip to the mill gave her time to think even more about the orog, and Ella found herself regretting her reaction the night before. Although he was certainly large—the biggest person she'd ever seen—he hadn't appeared threatening at all, more curious than anything. She supposed it was her own fear of getting in trouble that had made her run away, and wondered how he might feel about that.

A few days later, Ella ran a late afternoon order to Thornwall's gatekeeper, an ornery old man named Jeb Odano. Gruff and direct with just about everyone, he'd taken a shine to her, and wouldn't accept his orders from anyone else. Ella didn't mind, as it got her out of the shop to see what was happening around town. Plus, Jeb always gave her a copper for her effort.

With the delivery completed, she was about to head back, idly thinking about how she might persuade her mother to let her make more small deliveries. The area in front of the gate was an unusual bustle of activity, with a small line of wagons about to head out. In front of them, Ella spotted one of her friends running past, tears trickling down her face.

"Ressa?" Ella increased her stride to intercept the other girl. "Ressa, what's wrong?"

Ressa Ordlin was one of the butcher's three children, whose shop was near the Ablehand's bakery. Her strawberry-blonde hair was mussed and windblown, and her eyes were red from crying.

"I can't talk, Ella, I've got to go get Da!"

"But why?"

"Because—!" Ressa glanced around and lowered her voice. "Because Owen's lost!"

"*What?* When? Where did this happen?" Ella's questions tumbled over each other in her concern.

"Just now. Ma and Da are smoking hams today, so there's less work than usual," Ressa said. "We were playing stag and hounds near the main gate, and Owen—you know how quick he is—I almost caught him, but then he saw his chance, and got under a departing wagon and left through the gate before I could catch him!"

Ella was all too aware of the boy's slipperiness—the six-year-old was renowned for escaping whoever was watching him and trying to bust out of town every chance he got.

"He thinks we're still playing, but who knows where he'll wander off to if he gets a chance!" she continued.

"Right…you could get your da…" *And get in a hidefull of trouble,* Ella thought as she glanced toward the main gate, where as luck would have it, she saw Jensen with his father, Rokos, who was chatting with Bass Morgan, the village wainwright. "Or maybe we can find him ourselves before he wanders too far off."

"What?" The older girl frowned at her. "What are you talking about?"

"If we look for him together, we can find him quick, and then you won't get into trouble, right? Come with me!"

Before Ressa could protest, Ella grabbed her hand and ran over near Jensen, who looked bored stiff as the two men jawed back and forth. From around the corner of the gatekeeper's hut, she tried to get his attention. "Psst.…*Psst!*"

Hearing her louder hiss, the boy checked on his da—who was still chattering on—then slipped over to her. "Hey Ella, I haven't seen you since—"

"Hush, Jensen, there's no time," she interrupted, then quickly filled him in about Owen.

He got the picture immediately. "It'll be dark soon, and who knows what'll be lurking out there…we should probably tell the folks—"

"You know what Ressa's Da'll do when he finds out," Ella insisted. "Besides, Owen's only six—how far could he have gotten? If the three of us go out now, I bet we can find him and have him back before anyone even knows he's gone."

"Please, Jensen—your help would mean so much to me," Ressa said.

Jensen's chest puffed out a bit at that, and Ella found herself frowning at both of them, although she wasn't sure exactly why.

Shaking her head, she fixed her gaze back on him. "So, are you in?"

Jensen leaned back to check on his father, who was still chewing the fat with the wainwright. "Sure. Like you said, how far could he get?"

AS IT TURNED OUT, AN ENERGETIC SIX-YEAR-OLD COULD get pretty far.

"Are you *sure* he was heading this way?" Jensen asked for the fifth time in as many minutes.

"Yes, I'm sure." Ressa snapped as she glared at him. Any previous warm feelings between the two had quickly vanished under Ressa's worry about her brother and Jensen's increased skepticism that they were going in the right direction.

After using the confusion of the departing caravan to slip through the gate, the three kids had been walking for at least a quarter-hour now, as Ella judged by the internal clock she used to watch the loaves baking, and Thornwall's high hedgerow had disappeared behind the trees long ago. It was also full twilight now, with the sun fast disappearing behind the mountains. In a few more minutes, night would fall, and they'd have to turn back—

"Shh!" Jensen held his hand up as he cocked his head. "Did you hear that?"

Ella was about to say no when she did hear a sound—a rustling in the brush ahead that might have been a child walking—but there was something about it that struck her as wrong. "I did hear something—"

"I bet it's Owen! Come on!" Without waiting for the others, Ressa plunged in toward the heavier brush. "Owen? Owen!"

"Ressa! Ressa, wait!" Ella said, but the girl was already several steps ahead of her. She turned to Jensen, but he was also charging forward. With a groan, she followed them.

"You shouldn't go—" Frustrated, she rounded a huge oak tree and found herself in a large clump of bushes. Ella looked around—Jensen and Ressa were nowhere to be seen.

Suddenly a hand clamped over her mouth and dragged her into the thicket! Terrified, Ella kicked and squirmed, only to hear a voice hiss into her ear, "Stop! Stop it! It's me, Jensen!"

Twisting her head around, Ella stared up at his blanched face and wide, fear-filled eyes. "Whatever you do, don't scream, okay?"

She nodded, and he took his hand away. Ella noticed Ressa was crouched down nearby, tears streaming down her face. "What—what's going on?"

"Look where I point, but whatever you do, do not scream and do not run, do you understand me?" Ella nodded—she'd never heard Jensen sound so serious in her life.

"Okay…" The boy pointed off through a cluster of bushes, and when Ella looked in that direction, she saw a sight that made her stomach clench. "By Lensae's light…"

They had found Owen—but something else had found him first. And this—*monstrosity* was the only word that Ella could think of—would haunt her nightmares for years afterward.

The hunched beast loomed over the sobbing six-year-old was some kind of large, hideous humanoid the likes of which she had never seen before. It sort of resembled the orog back at the graveyard—if he had been warped by the blackest evil. There was a term her mother and father called these things, corrupted by Endroren, the Lord of Darkness: *endrori*.

Tall and gangly, it had abnormally long arms and legs that splayed out from its lean torso. Naked and completely hairless, its dark green skin was completely covered with warts, boils, and running sores. Even several paces away, she could smell its odor—a mixture of slime, rot, and spoiled meat that made her want to gag.

Its face was a mockery of anything civilized; it had the requisite two eyes, beady and cunning; a long nose that dripped snot as it sniffed the air, and a mouth that constantly opened and closed, revealing jagged teeth that looked as long as Ella's hand, with a black-edged tongue that curled out to lick its thin, pale lips. Every so often, it reached out a claw-tipped finger to poke at Owen, who was huddled in front of it.

"What's it doing?" Jensen asked. Ressa huddled mutely nearby, apparently frozen in terror by what she was seeing.

"I don't—" Ella began.

The *endrori* poked Owen again, harder this time. The child yelped, leaped up, and tried to run away. It let him take a few panting steps, then sprang into the air on its spindly legs. It came down in front of its prey, who bleated in terror as it swatted him to the ground with a huge hand. The creature loomed over him again, mouth split open in a hideous mockery of a smile as that disgusting tongue flicked out over its pointed teeth.

"It's—" Jensen began.

"It's *playing* with him—playing with its food!" Ella said, nearly choking on her rage. At that moment, she almost didn't care that going out there would likely mean her death—she wanted to leap out and kick it away from poor Owen.

"What are we gonna do?" Jensen asked, his voice quivering in barely-controlled terror. "We charge in there, and it's gonna have four kids for dinner, not just one!"

"I know, we wouldn't have a chance, and town's too far away to help. Just be quiet and let me think!" Ella hissed, trying to come up with any way they could rescue Owen and get out of this alive.

Hearing a familiar *clicking*, she turned to find Jensen clutching his throwing rocks in both hands. His face was as white as the inside of a fresh-baked loaf, but he still stood firm next to her. "I sure hope you got an idea, Ella."

"Maybe," she replied as the glimmer of one started forming in her mind. "Depends on how well you can throw those rocks—"

Another scream came from the clearing, and Ella glanced back to see Owen sobbing and clutching his arm as the creature swayed back and forth over him, looking like it was about to start devouring the child at any moment.

"I'm going out there to get my brother!" Snapping out of her daze, Ressa suddenly lurched forward, bursting out of the thicket.

"Ressa, wait—Jensen, grab her!" Ella said, but it was too late.

Grabbing a broken branch as thick as her arm, the older girl raised it over her head as she ran toward the monster threatening her little brother.

"NO!" Just like that, Ella's plan fell apart before it could even start. Now she had to somehow stop Ressa from also becoming the *endrori's* next meal. "Jensen, circle around and throw rocks at it! Try to keep it distracted!"

"Okay, but what are you going to do?"

Probably get myself killed, she thought. "I'm gonna save Owen!"

"Hey!" Ressa screamed as she approached the beast, which turned at hearing her shout and raised up to its full height—at least eight feet tall. Ressa slowed a bit upon seeing that, but raised her improvised club like she was about to deliver the mother of all beatings to her family rugs. "Leave him alone!"

She swung the branch wildly as the monster casually swiped at her. Wood met flesh and bone with a resounding *thwack!* and both sides pulled back in surprise.

Ressa stared at her newly-shortened club, which had broken in half on the creature's forearm. The *endrori* also stared at its limb, which it shook with a grimace. Its toothy smile turning into a snarl, it stuck its head down and roared, a guttural, bellowing cry at Ressa that made her scream and skitter backward.

Uh-oh! Ella had used the distraction to try to sneak around to Owen, who was still lying on the ground and holding his arm. But now Ressa was in real danger.

Thwip! Something small and gray blurred through the air from the other side of the clearing, striking the monster in the side of the head. Startled, it half-turned toward this new enemy, leaving the other side of its face exposed.

Ressa didn't hesitate. With a blood-curdling scream, she stepped back up and swung her short club with all her might. The end smashed into the creature's face, hard enough to rock it back on its heels. Growling, the *endrori* slowly turned back to Ressa, a nasty gash dripping dark blood onto the leaves, and its jaw hanging oddly as it glared at her. Then, with a popping noise, its jawbone tightened and moved back into its normal position on the monster's face.

It can heal *itself*... Emma knew that realization spelled their certain deaths. Even if they could somehow manage to bring it down, it wouldn't *stay* down. It would just keep coming after them until they were all dead—

A scream brought her back to the present, and Ella watched the *endrori* backhand Ressa hard. She sailed through the air, hitting a tree trunk yards away hard enough to knock her senseless—or maybe even kill her, she wasn't sure.

Another rock flew out of a different place in the underbrush—Jensen was moving after each throw—and hit the *endrori* full in the face. It roared again and clamped both hands to its head, writhing in pain.

"Come on!" Jensen burst from the brush and ran to Ressa. Although short and wiry, he managed to pick her up and sling her across his shoulders. "Grab Owen and follow me!"

Ella was already running to the little boy and hoisting him to his feet. "Run, Owen, fast as you can!"

Despite his injury, the boy needed no further prodding, and took off after Jensen. Ella followed them, even knowing it was hopeless—they were only putting off their deaths a little longer.

Even so, the three children ran as fast as they could through the forest, although Jensen soon lagged behind, puffing with every step. "Go on—I'll lead him away!"

"No, Jensen, you can't—" Ella began, when the *crunch* of a heavy step behind them made her freeze.

Slowly, dreading what she was about to see, she turned around—

—and saw the orog, Torg, standing there, staring at the four children with a puzzled expression on his homely face.

Ella nearly fainted with relief, but didn't. There was no time. "Torg, please help us—*look out!*"

Out of the forest behind him burst the green-skinned, fang-faced *endrori*. With a rage-filled shriek, it shot straight for the orog.

TORG HAD BEEN OUT ON ONE OF HIS EVENING WALKS WHEN he'd heard a commotion nearby—shouts and yells and screams, along with a strange kind of roar he'd never heard before. He'd tried to figure out where it was coming from, but the forest was tricky, and he couldn't get a fix on where the activity was. So he started walking in its general direction, figuring either he would find it, or it would find him. As it happened, it was a little bit of both.

After coming across the four children, all looking scared out of their wits, he turned to see a walking nightmare charge out of the forest directly at him. It roared and slobbered as it ran, its clawed hands extended to tear into him, intending to rip off his face and tear out his throat and feast on his remains.

Any other person, even a hero of the land, might have been scared at seeing that monstrosity bearing down on them.

But Torg feared no living thing that walked the land.

And he didn't fear this thing, either.

Cocking a huge fist, he set himself, and when the charging *endrori* got close enough, he let it fly, smashing the beast's face hard enough to send it staggering back. Its nose had been pulped into a green-black smear, but as Torg watched, the flesh and bone shifted, realigning itself into its normal position with small *cracks* and *pops*.

"It can heal itself, Torg!" the girl screamed.

He took in this new information with a frown. This might be a little harder than he'd thought. Smelling something burning, he looked around to see what was on fire, then realized it was coming from him. He looked down at his hand, which had gotten cut—probably from the *endrori*'s mouth—but was also red and sizzling, like he had spilled hot water on it.

"Look out, Torg—it's doing something!" the girl screamed again.

He looked up to see the *endrori* convulsing, arching its back and swaying back and forth while a series of deep, belching croaks issued from its gaping mouth. Unsure what was happening, Torg took a large step backward just as the monster vomited a stream of putrid-smelling liquid that splashed down right where he'd just been standing.

The moment it touched the ground, everything it covered—leaves, branches, plants—died, burning up in in the pool of black acid. The stench was horrible, even worse than the *endrori's* already foul odor.

Torg eyed his opponent as he began circling warily around it. It had obviously been chasing the children, and just as obviously meant to hurt them, probably eat them if it got the chance.

That made him angry.

Sensing its chance, the Darkness encroached on him, whispering, convincing, cajoling...

But, it didn't want him to kill the monster.

No, it wanted him to *join* it, to chase down the children and kill them. It even showed him at the *endrori*'s side, grabbing the shrieking, fleeing children and breaking their necks, or dashing their brains out against a tree.

That idea made Torg even madder.

With a low growl, he shoved the Darkness far away, back into its dark place.

The *endrori* was starting to convulse again, its stomach roiling as it prepared to spew more acidic sludge on Torg. As it did, he got an idea. But it would require really good timing, so—

He walked straight toward the beast, which quickened its contortions, trying to prepare its disgusting attack before its prey got too close.

"Torg, what are you doing?!" the girl screamed. "Get away!"

He ignored her, all of his attention on his enemy.

When the *endrori* hunched over, just before it was about to rear back, Torg bent down and swung the hardest uppercut he'd ever thrown in his life at the abomination's face.

He hit it square in the nose again, feeling it pulp and squish under his knuckles.

The *endrori* flew off its feet, its acidic stream fountaining out as it sailed through the air. Torg dodged away, too, but he still got splattered with a few drops of the corrosive stuff, which smoked and sizzled on his skin.

The monster crashed to the ground, its acid vomit pattering down all around it. Smoke rose from its own skin as drops landed on it as well. Seeing that gave Torg his second idea.

Along with the tales of the Darkness he'd heard long ago, his people had also passed down the ways of fighting the largest *endrori*. Chief among them was that in order to ensure one was killed, either the heart or the head had to be removed.

Running to the creature's side as it tried to rise, Torg smashed it in the face again, driving it back down to the ground. Placing a large knee on the its waist to hold it in place, he locked both hands together. Raising them above his head, he brought them down on the monster's chest with all his might.

The *CRACK!* of shattering bone echoed throughout the forest, and the *endrori* howled in agony. Mustering all of his strength again, Torg raised a huge fist and drove it straight down, this time *into* the monster's chest.

Black blood spurted from the wound as Torg felt around, struggling to find the *endrori's* frantically beating source of life. Meanwhile, it thrashed and screamed and beat at the ground with its legs. The *endrori* scrabbled at Torg, trying to scratch his face or claw at his eyes, but he used his free arm to fend off the clutching claws. He still took several deep gashes, until finally he'd had enough, and broke first one arm, then the other, all the while rummaging in its torso until he found what he was looking for.

With a savage roar, Torg grabbed and twisted, ripping the still-beating heart out of the *endrori's* chest and held it in the air, black blood dripping everywhere.

Panting with his efforts, he looked down at the still-moving creature, then walked over to the nearby puddle of acid on the ground.

With one last glance and a feral grin at the *endrori*, Torg dropped the beating heart into the pool. The organ hissed and smoked as it began dissolving, sending the monster into a fresh series of yowls and spasms.

In a few moments, there was nothing left of the heart except a greasy, black smear on the ground. The *endrori*, its chest a gaping hole, also stopped screaming and moving, except for the occasional twitch.

About to go to the children, Torg caught a glimpse of his gore-covered hands, and realized that wouldn't be the best thing to show them. After wiping them off as best as he could on the grass and leaves, he trudged wearily over to the children, all of whom had huddled together while watching the whole thing. "Are you…all right?"

One of them, the girl who had yelled advice to him, slowly nodded. "Are you?"

Torg nodded.

"Is it…really gone?" the boy asked.

Torg nodded again. "Come on…I will take…all of you…home."

Gently taking the unconscious girl from the boy, who sagged in relief at having that weight lifted, he also picked up the smallest one, who seemed to already be forgetting the terror of earlier, and now squealed in delight as Torg set him on his shoulders. "Let's go back…to Thornwall."

"Who are you?" the youngest boy asked as they began walking back to town. "Are you another monster, like the green thing?"

"No, Owen!" the girl said sharply, pointing back at the dirt patches and shattered body of the *endrori*. "That thing back there was a true monster.

"Torg, here—" she said with a smile as she reached up and took his hand, "—is our friend."

BOOKS ARE NO GOOD

CAT RAMBO

IT STARTED, AS SO MANY THINGS DO, WITH A BOOK. IN THIS case, a book of adventure stories authored by one Octavia Viort, entitled *The Curious Peregrinations of a Goat Herder*, in which Octavia, at first a simple goat herder, was swept up by chance into adventure to the point where she circumnavigated the Amethyst Sea, fighting great serpents and cat creatures in the Zhamayen jungle, journeying into the Deeplands for ancient treasures, taking a series of highly unsuitable lovers, including a half-year spent among the elves, and generally leading a much more exciting existence than that of an innkeeper or her maid.

Each adventure had been more exciting—and more improbable—than the last. While Letitia didn't doubt there were seeds of truth hidden here and there within Octavia's pages, most of what sprouted from them were exaggerations, misrepresentations, and on occasion, outright lies. Books were good for nothing.

It was not that Letitia was particularly experienced, but that she was extremely cynical, as might befit a cheebat, orphaned or kidnapped as a babe, and traded to the tenderhearted Poppy, who simply said of the man afterwards that he had not been particularly nice. Letitia freely admitted she had been lucky to end up in Poppy's care, receiving food, clothing, and a warm bed to sleep in, but she was acutely aware that her birth circumstances, through no action of her own, circumscribed her life.

She did consider herself extremely lucky, for the most part, to have been adopted by Poppy, who she considered the most wonderful person in the world.

Poppy's arms were strong and brawny, and as big around as a young birch tree, and capable of swinging the rosewood truncheon she kept behind the Flagon's bar with a solid *thunk* that would stop a belligerent drunk in their tracks, usually at the first blow, always by the second.

She'd inherited the wayside inn—"twice as far as the back of beyond," one traveler had called it—when her parents were slain on a trading trip to the Free Kingdoms, and she'd taken over from old Dad, her mother's father, at the tender age of seventeen. A quarter-century later, old Dad was even older, and had retired to his own little cottage, and Poppy knew everything there was to know about the art of running an inn located somewhat remotely, it was true, but at least on a trade route.

Her hair was colored henna and brass, and she was a big woman with a bigger laugh, one you could hear echoing down the road at night when you were tired of walking and caught it, letting you know the inn was within shouting distance. A dozen bards had tried to teach her one musical instrument or another, and she'd taken to none but the pat-a-pat drums, and even then did not like performing before others. While she'd celebrated lovers enough, she'd never cared to kindle with child, and then one thing happened and another, and before too long, she realized she was no longer capable of having a child in the usual way, and shrugged and accepted it in her own usual way.

Her only flaw was her obsession for books, and travel stories in particular.

While Letitia considered her innkeeper employer's mania unfortunate; the most recent manifestation of it was disastrous. *Curious Peregrinations* was so engrossing that Poppy completely forgot about checking on the Amethyst Flagon's new cook, with the result that tonight's stew was oversalted in a way that was impossible to wash away, and afterwards had been so distracted that she would have charged the only two visitors on this slow night half of what she should have if Letitia hadn't noticed and nudged her.

And it was, quite probably, Octavia Viort's fault that the inn burned down that Laborday night, because although Letitia didn't voice her suspicions aloud, she thought perhaps reading in bed by candlelight might perhaps be conducive to falling asleep and leaving a candle unattended.

All of this went through her head as she picked sadly through the remnants of the inn's kitchen, trying to salvage what she could from the ashes.

"Letitia," Poppy said, "Mark my words, this will turn out to be a good thing."

"Everything is destroyed!" Letitia said. "Nothing's left!"

"Not true," Poppy said with her usual cheerfulness, brandishing a volume. "I managed to get the strongbox and my book out, you saved a number of our belongings, and even Henry the stableboy escaped with the two horses and a mule out of the stable. It's a shame that their owners didn't make it, but I'm sure they would have wanted their horses well tended. So now it's time to go."

Letitia eyed the book with no expression. "Go where?"

"On a quest."

This time she blinked. "A quest for what?"

"Adventure," Poppy said, relishing each syllable. "That is what we're in quest of. We will follow in the footsteps of Octavia Viort, and let her book be our guide."

"That's the worst idea I've ever heard," Letitia said with unaccustomed bluntness.

Poppy's face softened. "I know you're upset," she said, patting the girl's hand. "But we must make the most of things. And this is what books are good for, to give us dreams that let us pull ourselves away from today and look to the future."

Letitia grumbled, "Good for nothing," under her breath, but she followed Poppy away from the ashes. She felt dubious about the whole enterprise, but she knew one thing: Wherever Poppy went, she intended to go as well.

ONE DOES NOT RUN AN INN FOR DECADES WITHOUT learning how to arrange things, and in a remarkably swift time, both of them were outfitted for adventure. Poppy had taken a bow, saying she had been a good shot as a girl, light armor, and had opted, instead of weapons, for the cleavers she had wielded with efficiency in the past, rescued from the inn's ruins, and outfitted with new wooden handles.

Letitia, by contrast, opted entirely for knives, and managed to secrete a satisfyingly large number of them about her person. She'd acquired a new cloak in the process of the outfitting, and better boots than she'd ever owned, both with satisfyingly well-hidden sheathes along the outer seams.

Even their horses, despite their dubious provenance, were suited to the adventuring life and their new owners. Poppy's was a fiery roan that matched her hair, a stallion given to temper and flash.

Letitia much preferred her dove-colored little gelding.

Despite the smell of smoke tangled in her hair, and the scarcity of her belongings, she felt oddly cheerful as she swung into the saddle and headed out after her mistress. Adventure, even real life instead of misleadingly painted on a page, would surely be a satisfying thing. After all, Poppy had never led her astray before.

A few days later, she was not so sure.

At least, that was what was flickering through her mind as they continued along the road. Poppy was expounding on her notion of travel, and why it was to be pursued, and how broadening it would inevitably prove, while Letitia kept an eye open for good kindling for the fire. She was only half listening, because she'd heard all of this before. It was a damp and misty day, so she was leading her horse and walking so she could collect twigs and secret them about her person in order to dry them out enough to make them useful later on when they made camp.

The book, which Poppy insisted on reading aloud from at every campsite, had supplied a hand-colored map of the coastline. Letitita had not seen that many maps in her lifetime, but she thought that this one might have a few shortcomings. For one thing, the area they were heading into was a spot colored a vague green, which turned out to be towering pines and cedars, shaly hills, and tiny streams inevitably at the bottom of steep-walled gullies full of brambles. It was lettered, the amount of lettering sparse in comparison to the amount of blank space provided, "Unexplored Forest." So far, they were three uncomfortable days into changing that into "Partially Explored Forest."

"Pay attention and stop stuffing sticks down your shirt," Poppy said severely.

Letitia sighed, both inwardly and outwardly. "Yes'm," she said, allowing resignation to seep into the words.

"And don't act like that! There are many who would chew their left arms off in order to face an existence full of adventure of the sort you've signed up for."

So far the trip had involved a great degree more physical discomfort and much less excitement than Letitia had hoped. At times like right now, in fact, with the cloud cover showing no sign of breaking up or relenting with the drizzle that had been soaking them for the last four hours, it was downright unpleasant.

"There hasn't been much adventure yet," Letitia pointed out. She was not much given to dampening Poppy's enthusiasm, but they had been walking for hours. It was, according to her way of thinking, far past time to be making camp and starting to think about preparing dinner and above all either finding a dry spot or else figuring out a way to transmute one of the many wet spots into a dry one. There were tarpaulins and tents on the mule, and that would be an excellent place to start.

That was when they heard the first scream.

It came from off the road, among the trees, unseen but close from the volume, the sound of a horse crying out, and then a second echoing noise, like the harsh squeal of an enormous machine wheel.

Poppy's bow was out and in her hand, the other one pulling an arrow from its quiver as she sprinted toward the noises. Letitia followed, pulling daggers from her belt as she went, but moving more cautiously than her mistress, and therefore slower.

She arrived in time to see Poppy's first arrow strike the monstrosity towering over the fallen unicorn, a mass of black fur and teeth and more than one head, each additional one protruding at awkward angles from around the main one with its ferocious canine grin. Every eye in the multitude burned bright as fire, red as madness.

The arrow extinguished one of that pair burning brightest and largest. The beast threw all its heads back. The sound of that tortured clash came again, so loud that it throbbed in Letitia's ears.

Daggers sang from her hands, thrown almost without thinking, *thunk thunking* into that glistening black snout. Annoying wounds at best, but another of Poppy's arrows flew straight and true—had she really merely said she'd been "all right with the bow" when a girl?—putting out the other mad red glare, and as it died so did all the tinier ones, heads slumping awkward as the beast toppled, halfway over its fallen prey.

They circled it warily as they came up. The unicorn let out a tortured breath. Poppy moaned in sympathy and started to step closer, but Letitia tugged her back.

"You can't help it, boss," she said. Her eyes welled with tears, obscuring the gaping belly wound, the entrails fanned out from a savage bite. "It's hurt too bad."

"I can put it out of its misery at least," Poppy said. She tugged one of Letitia's daggers from the monster's corpse, and moved towards the unicorn, speaking softly, calmingly, an ostler's murmur, soothing and nonsensical, *theretheremylove, theretheremypretty.*

The gleaming ivory horn raised an inch from the ground as though in challenge, but was too feeble to move further. Poppy stroked her hand along the broad neck. Letitia held her breath.

"Move no further," a voice said from behind them.

THE ELF LORD WAS MORE ANGULAR THAN ANY HUMAN, and leaner than any human, and above all, more beautiful than any human would ever be. But it was a cold and frightening beauty, not one that kindled any warmth in Letitia's blood. His hair was the silver of a melting icicle, and his lips were perfectly shaped but pale as death in their hue. This was not at like the book, where benevolent queens ruled each kingdom. Where else had it led them astray?

They had been bound and blindfolded, and forced to walk

until Letitia had no idea where they were. She'd felt the giddy stomachdrop of passing some sort of magical barrier. Finally the blindfolds had been ripped from their eyes, and they found themselves in a dazzle of light and silver columns and staring elvish faces, forced to their knees on the chill pearly tiles before the elf lord's throne.

He sneered, ignoring Letitia and focusing on Poppy, and the expression lessened his beauty, made it something petty, in a way that put a little heart in Letitia, *It's a weakness, that sneer,* she thought, and it would have been infinitely more dangerous if he had not cared at all.

"You have trespassed on my domain, and the punishment for trespassers and spies is death," he said. His voice was sweet and clear as a dulcimer, despite the harshness of the words.

"We didn't know we were," Poppy argued. "We're not spies—I'm just a former innkeeper, lord. I've never traveled this far before."

He ignored her. "Moreover, you have been involved in the death of one of our most beloved creatures."

"We were trying to save it!" Poppy protested. Letitia bit her lip and bided her time.

He flicked his fingers in dismissal. "Kill them."

The guards leveled the points of their halberds at the pair.

"Wait," Letitia said. "In the book, it said you have to have a trial." *Please let this be one of the accurate bits.*

For the first time he looked at her. "What book speaks of elvish law?"

"*The Curious Peregrinations of A Goat Herder,*" Letitia said, and held her breath, praying that this was not one of the bits that Octavia had made up, but that it was based on something, anything.

For a long breath, the elf lord considered her. "Very well," he said. "You are correct that—if invoked—a trial must be held."

"A trial by combat," Poppy said steadfastly. Letitia's heart sank.

But the elf lord did not feel like letting himself be directed. "I will not dishonor an elvish blade with your blood. We will find another combat." He smirked at Poppy. "You claim you are an innkeeper?"

"Was," she said.

"Then I will find a trial more fitting to you," he said.

PERHAPS HE WAS TAKING HIS TIME FIGURING OUT THAT trial, or more likely, simply he did not care how long they waited on his pleasure. The cell they were in was spacious and well-lit, but even so, it was still a cell.

From the bed, Poppy said, "I'm so sorry, Letitia. I didn't mean to drag you into this. A little danger, maybe, but I thought it would be more glorious. That our lives would become meaningful."

Letitia was exploring the lock. It was beyond her skill to pick it, but she admired the workmanship nonetheless: it looked as though it had flowed out of the metal naturally into that form, rather than being forced.

"Why should life be meaningful?" she asked. "It seems like it should be its own meaning."

"Very philosophical," Poppy said, and rolled over to lie on her back, staring up at the intricately carved scalloped ceiling.

Letitia shrugged. "We might as well not give up until it's time," she said pragmatically.

But it did seem as though it might be time when they were dragged before the court again. Beside the lord stood a tall elf, her purple eyes downcast, her hands clasped before her, her white hair worn in an intricate netting of braids. At her hip hung a ring of keys, made of silver and ivory and blue-tinted glass.

"This is Elianna, who runs my household," the elf lord said, slouching on his throne. "Rather than having you face a true noble, one of the lowest of our court will defeat you."

Letitia saw a flicker of annoyance tug at Elianna's mouth at the words "lowest of our court" but the elvish woman said nothing.

"There will be three tasks," the elf lord declared. "You said you are a former innkeeper, so Elianna will tailor their cloth to that profession." He smirked, the expression making him seem more human for a second, but just as unpleasant. He gestured to his housekeeper.

Elianna kept her gaze on the opalescent floor, not looking at Poppy or Letitia. Her voice was so low they could barely hear it over the amused whispers of the courtiers.

"We will begin with brewing," she said.

Hope flamed in Letitia's heart. Poppy was an excellent brewmistress, and most of the ales the Amethyst Flagon had served were by her own hand.

A slim servitor came forward, his tray holding a long stemmed glass, filled with golden liquid, a pale pink tint, soft as a blush, hovering in the upper third.

"You will tell me the ingredients," Elianna said.

Poppy took the glass and sipped, closing her eyes. Keeping them closed, she said, certainty in her voice, "Hops and honey..."

Elianna nodded, although Poppy could not see her.

With less certainty, "Cinnamon."

Again, Elianna nodded.

Then, with no conviction at all, "Anise?" Poppy opened her eyes and looked at the elfwoman.

The servitor took the glass from Poppy's hand as Elianna shook her head.

"It is littlestar, a plant that grows only in groves where a unicorn has cast its shadow," she murmured. Was that a trace of apology in her tone? Letitia thought it might be.

"How was she supposed to know that?" she snapped, even as the elf lord exploded in laughter like broken glass shards, with the rest of the court followed suit, drowning out anything else she might add.

Letitia didn't look at the lord or Poppy or anywhere else. Instead she stared directly at Elianna, willing her to look back.

As though she sensed the gaze, the elvish woman's eyes rose to meet Letitia's. The beautiful face was an expressionless mask, no sympathy visible in the serene amethyst gaze. But the housekeeper maintained her stare for only a few seconds beneath Letitia's hot glare before she looked away as the guards took them back to their cell.

Letitia expected the next challenge to occur the following day, but the long wait proved her wrong. They'd been pacing their cell for three days, three days of Letitia tinkering futilely with the lock, and Poppy re-reading *Curious Peregrinations* before the guards reappeared and they stood before the elf lord and Elianna again. This time they had been brought to what seemed to be the keep's kitchens, as vast as the throne hall above, and almost as crowded with onlookers.

"The second challenge," Elianna said, her voice as soft as before, "is cookery."

She indicated the dish that sat steaming on the tray the servitor held. It was a round of wood, as though sawn from the heart of a tree, and on it lay moss and a bird's nest, spun of sugar, with sweetmeats shaped like eggs, each a different color and texture, in its heart.

The arrangement was so exquisite that Letitia's heart sank. Certainly Poppy could cook, and well, but even she knew that candymaking is its own sort of alchemy of molten sugar and browning butter and boiling milk.

But Poppy strode toward the table helped with sugar and spices, the great stove, and the copper pots there with more confidence than ever, and before the hour was up, a second dish of wood sat beside the first, and seemed identical.

"In my youth," Poppy said with pride, "I went to a school of cookery in New Erinor for two years before my father's death called me home to the inn." She smiled, wistful. "I have not tried such dishes in a while."

The elf lord's eyes narrowed as Elianna tasted Poppy's offering, but the room did not erupt until Elianna said, "The human has won this challenge." She inclined her head towards Poppy.

"Then you have failed, and will be punished yourself, so you may have that to think upon before the next challenge," the elf lord barked, and snapped his fingers to have Poppy and Letitia taken away.

Back in the cell, Letitia said, "Did she let you win?"

Poppy shook her head. Despite their bleak situation, a smile still trembled on her lips in the aftermath of the cooking, the sort of smile a practiced lover might leave behind, and her color was still flushed from the stove's heat.

"I haven't had a chance to cook like that for decades—I'm surprised I remembered how." She huffed out a sigh. "But that was an aberration, Letitia, you know that. I'll be just as lost in the third challenge as I was the first. She has even more reason to concoct a test I cannot pass this time."

Letitia shook her head from where she sat by the cell door. "Maybe."

That night, after Poppy's breath had slowed and evened, Letitia finally picked the lock she had been working on all this long while. She knew they would not be able to win free of this place and its guards, and she didn't want to raise her mistress' hopes too far, but still, she had a plan. She slipped the book from beneath Poppy's pillow, and with it under her arm, let herself out of the cell.

Up the stairs she went, and then farther up, and farther up still, to the attics where the servants were housed in narrow chambers chased with silver, their beds long slabs of stone chosen for aesthetics rather than comfort. There she slipped through the shadows, nose twitching as she chased after a specific perfume, until she came to a door, and there she quietly knocked. When she first stepped inside, there was a sound of shock and surprise, but it stopped as Letitia began to speak.

After a while, she stole back down into the cell, teased the lock back into its original configuration, and curled up to sleep beside the unknowing Poppy.

ON THE AFTERNOON OF THE THIRD CHALLENGE, THE ELF lord wore silver and crimson, a great of blazing rubies around his white throat. He saw Letitia looking at it as they were dragged before him and forced once more to their knees, and he grinned at her and drew his finger across his throat, miming her eventual fate.

"The third challenge involves the hardest art of all for one such as us," Elianna's soft voice said. She bore no sign of her punishment other than a hint of blue shadows under her eyes. "Celebration planning. I will tell you the details of the next great ceremonial dance here, and the feast and gifts that accompany it, and the guests from other kingdoms and courts, and then you will tell me how to lay it out as though it were happening a day less than a fortnight from now."

The elf lord looked unimpressed, but stayed silent as Elianna raised her eyes, looked at Poppy, and began to speak.

The soft voice began, first speaking of lodging, of the keep's constraints, of feuds that should be considered in placement in room and at board, of special supplies and arrivals over a span of tomorrow till the last minute. Letitia tried to keep it all in her head, but soon was lost in the flood of needs for the eagle mounts of one group and the great wolves ridden by another contingent.

The elf lord yawned. "You will send for me when all of this is done, and it is time to kill the trespassers," he said. The courtiers trailed him as he left the room, leaving only Elianna, Letitia, and Poppy, and the guards that surrounded them.

As time wore on and Elianna began on feast details, Letitia became aware that the elvish woman was doing more than simply droning—she was stressing some words, glossing others, making the information a little easier, and sorting it in a way that made one detail follow neatly onto another. It was a marvelous feat of mental agility, but it would require just as marvelous a one on Poppy's part to retain it all and make sense of it, then deliver a plan as detailed as these base instructions.

On and on Elianna went. Letitia found herself dozing, despite the tension, dreaming of the festival as organized by Poppy: the careful marshalling of the kitchen staff, the timetable for the meats to be brought to table, the dance to keep the middens clean, and linens changed each night, along with all the rest.

Later—it might have been minutes, it might have been hours—she roused enough to find Poppy speaking now, just as steadily as Elianna, her words measured and careful, precise as the lines in the tiles. Letitia bit her lip and waited.

Finally Poppy spoke of the last things to be done after all the horde had departed, and what was to be laid away back in storage, with dried lavender and other flowers to keep it fresh smelling, for the next year, and then stopped.

Elianna said nothing for a long time, and then dropped a single nod.

Letitia's heart hammered in her throat. Were they truly to be released? But instead, despite her questions, they were dragged back to the cell.

The guards did not speak to them, but a few hours later, a hooded figure came to the cell and unlocked it with one of the keys from the great ring hanging from her belt. Elianna put a finger to her lip for silence, and led them down to the stables, where their horses stood, eying the nearby great white elvish mounts uneasily (Letitia's gelding) or with an overly ambitious lust (Poppy's stallion). Elianna led one of those from its stall and mounted, motioning at them to do the same.

"Are we being freed?" Poppy asked.

"Yes," Elianna said, "by my word. The elf lord is hunting, and was so bored by my recital that he will not remember the challenge at least till evening meal. So I would stay silent, as we go along, until we are past this territory and well into the next."

"We?" Poppy said.

"I thought," Letitia said, "that perhaps Elianna might find her existence in the stronghold unsatisfying. Without meaning. That she might need something to help her look past today and to the future."

Elianna took *The Curious Peregrinations of a Goat Herder* from her saddlebags and held it out. "I will go with you to recreate this journey," she said with a yawn. "I have been reading it all night. Do you have any more like it?"

Poppy looked at Letitia hard. "I thought you said books were good for nothing."

Letitia only shrugged, turning away to hide her smile.

"Maybe *not* all the time."

THE SECRET OF THE HOLY CRYSTAL

MARC TASSIN

FLAMES DANCED ALONG THE EDGE OF THE GLITTERING blade as the dwarven warrior swung it in a wide arc. It struck the shadow creature again, this time biting into the fiend's previously immaterial form. The flames exploded, racing up the creature's side as if the monster were made of oil. Wracked with pain and wreathed in arcane fire, it let out an ear-piercing shriek that shook the stained glass windows around the great hall.

The warrior's muscles strained, and he pushed the blade through the monstrous body, slicing clean to the other side. As it emerged, the monster let out one final cry before it was consumed in an inferno of blue arcane fire. When the last flame winked out—"

"—there was nothing left of the creature but a pile of cold, gray ash," Eathen interrupted, the irritation in his voice clear. He sighed and set his quill pen on the table.

"Is there something wrong in my recounting of the story?" the elderly monk sitting across from him asked.

The young scholar looked at the older man and wondered if he truly didn't know. The gray-haired monk in his night-blue robes looked deeply concerned, and the small, glowing crystal mounted in the silver headband on his forehead dimmed slightly.

"No, nothing is wrong with it," Eathen said, leaning back in his chair and rubbing his forehead. "And that's the problem. You're the fourth member of your order that I've talked to about the battle here, and you've each told me the *exact* same story. Word for word. Without any differences."

The monk looked apologetic. "I am sorry for your frustration. The nature of the Holy Crystal means that all memories are shared between us. It is impossible for any monk to have different memories of the event."

Eathen picked up the blotter and rolled it over the text he'd just written. There seemed little point to the document, since it was no different than the other accounts he'd already taken down, but University protocol demanded that every account be recorded as told. Granted, he doubted they'd ever considered a situation like this one, but it would be much easier to write it each time than to try and explain to Grand Master Wineman back in New Erinor why he'd broken protocol.

"I understand," he said at last. "I just thought that you might at least have different opinions or perceptions of the event. You can't all have experienced the battle the exact same way."

"You are correct," the monk said, "but the crystal has already considered any differences and then shaped the memory into its truest form. All differences of opinion or perception have already been taken into account."

"Well, I think that's all I need for now," Eathen said. "And I don't think I need to interview anyone else at this point. I'll probably head back to the mainland tomorrow morning. Thank you again for taking the time to speak with me."

The monk rose with calm purpose. “It was our pleasure. As adherents of Toletren, we value knowledge above all things. Naturally, we were happy to assist you.”

The monk headed toward the door as Eathen put the stack of paper and his writing tools back into his pack. Before he left, the monk stopped, steadied himself on the doorframe with a gnarled hand, and looked back at Eathen.

“You should really stay here in the main hall. It’s far more comfortable than the servants’ quarters, and we’d be happy for your company.”

“I appreciate the offer, I do,” Eathen replied as he buckled his pack and hefted it onto his back. “But the servants’ quarters are just fine, and Matron Underdown has been lovely to stay with.”

“As you wish.” The crystal on the monk’s forehead pulsed faintly. “Good night, Eathen.”

With that, he left the room.

Eathen breathed a sigh of relief. He’d met all types of people during his travels gathering knowledge for the Royal University in New Erinor, but the monks of the island monastery were by far the strangest. At first they’d seemed normal enough, but the more time he spent with them the more he felt a deep feeling of wrongness around them.

He assumed it was something to do with the crystal that connected the minds of every monk living on the island through their headbands, but he wasn’t sure what bothered him specifically. There was just something in their manner that always left him wanting to look over his shoulder or keep his back to the wall.

He definitely didn’t want to stay in the main hall with them.

Eathen left the small room and headed down the long, arched hallway. He passed a pair of monks, a man and a woman. They smiled and nodded, the crystals in their silver headbands pulsing slightly. Eathen returned the silent greeting and hurried to the door leading to the courtyard.

The cool air of early evening felt fresh and clean. A hint of the sea blew in on the wind, and in the distance he heard the low swish and boom of waves rolling against the base of the cliffs surrounding the island. Except for the strange monks that called the place home, he quite liked it here. The rocky outcropping, with the monastery balanced precariously on top, sat about a mile offshore in the Gulf of Agthor. It had a pleasant, mild climate, as was the norm in the region, and the constant sound of the waves had a hypnotic quality that calmed the mind.

Unfortunately, he'd be leaving in the morning. That was, after all, the nature of his work. Visit some out-of-the-way town or the site of an important event, record what he learned there, and bring it back to the University. It was interesting work, but Eathen looked forward to the day he could return to the University permanently and begin teaching.

As he passed under a high window, he heard the slow monotone of one of the monks reading a book aloud, part of the process that allowed the monks to memorize a text they wished to add to the crystal's shared memory. He wondered what that would feel like, to have a perfect memory of everything that not only you had read, experienced, or thought, but to have access to the thoughts of every other person connected with the crystal as well.

In some ways it was the ultimate expression of what he and the other scholars did at the University—a perfect shared knowledge. On the other hand, the crystal required a sacrifice of one's personal self that Eathen could never imagine submitting to. Even though the monks were blessed by the grace of Toletren, Enaros of Knowledge and Truth, he couldn't shake the feeling that joining the order was a kind of death. Who did you become when you shared and mingled your mind with all those other people? Were you even yourself any longer? Or were you washed away, like a glass of water thrown into the ocean?

Eathen's stomach growled, reminding him that *his* self hadn't eaten dinner yet. Putting the uncomfortable thoughts behind him, he pushed on to the servant's buildings at the far side of the wide lawn of the courtyard. When he pulled open the door of the long, low-slung building, a rush of warm air laced with wonderful smells struck him. Smiling, he entered the room and closed the door behind him.

"Well, there's our houseguest," said Matron Underdown. "We were beginning to wonder if they hadn't convinced you to join the order." The rotund halfling woman laughed, her rosy cheeks shining in the warm lamplight. She gestured with her rolling pin at the small table near the wall. "Don't just stand there like a roof post. Grab a seat, and I'll have Halie bring you something to eat. I'm sure you're famished. Halie!"

A clatter of pots and pans came from the pantry, and a moment later Halie rushed out. Eathen guessed she was in her late teens, but he wasn't entirely sure. She was younger than his own twenty-four years for certain, but the way she moved suggested someone grown beyond youth.

She approached the table, smiling, and Eathen couldn't help but smile back. Something about her freckled cheeks and mop of dusty brown hair, combined with an eternal twinkle in her eyes that spoke of impending mischief, made it impossible to feel anything but joy when she was around.

"Good evening, Master Winswood," she said. She wiped flour from her hands onto the apron she wore over her acolyte's robes. "Dinner and drink for you, sir?"

"Yes, please," he said. "Don't go through any trouble, though.

Whatever you have at hand is fine."

She started pulling plates and cups and jars and jugs from a cabinet. "Oh you needn't worry yourself, Master Winswood. I've too much work to finish before bed tonight to get fancy."

Eathen watched her arrange the dishes on a tray and begin doling out dollops of apple sauce, chunks of dark yellow cheese, slices of fresh bread, and the centerpiece, a bowl of warm stew. The smell made his mouth water.

As she set the food before him, Eathen imagined Halie becoming like the rest of the monks up in the monastery, and it sent a chill down his spine. Would she still have the same energy behind those eyes? Or would it be diluted into the vast sea of memories all the monks shared?

"Tell me, Halie," he said as she handed him his silverware. "Why do you want to join the order?"

She stopped, glanced back at Matron Underdown, who was busy pressing dough into a pie pan, then leaned in conspiratorially. "Can you keep a secret?"

"Of course," Eathen answered.

"The truth is I don't want to join the order. In fact, just between us, I think the monks are all a bit off. I'd never want to live like that."

Eathen's eyes went wide, and he leaned back. "Then, why are you here? As I understand it, you can't be part of the order if you don't, you know…" He tapped his forehead.

"Oh it's not a problem," she stated, dismissing the notion with a wave of her hand. "You have to serve as an acolyte for five years before they accept you, and I've only been here for a little over a year. I expect I'll cause enough trouble that they'll kick me out well before that happens. I'm almost always in trouble already, which is part of the reason I'm always down here working with Matron Underdown."

Eathen picked up a spoon and scooped up a healthy serving of stew, thick with carrots and chunks of beef. Taking a bite, he said, "I'm a bit surprised they even let you become an acolyte. Orders such as this are rather strict about who may join."

"Oh they're choosy, all right," Halie said, grinning. "Choosy about how many of the books from my father's library they'd receive if they agreed to take me on. In the end it wasn't much more than a business deal, really. They got books, I got away from the castle, and my father got rid of me. I think I got the best of the deal. I can read as many books as I like, and no one yells at me to practice my embroidery or train with my dance coach. It's the only place I've ever lived where you're not only allowed to read as much as you like, but it's part of your job. I'll actually miss it when I have to leave."

"I'm not surprised. I've yet to see you without a book close at hand," Eathen said, pointing to a small volume poking out of the pocket of her robe. "What are you reading today?"

"Oh, these are the collected adventures of a scythaan swordfighter named K'lynn. I'm certain most of them are made up, but it doesn't matter to me. I love adventure stories. The action and romance, the danger and thrills. It's wonderful stuff."

Before Eathen could say more the door burst open, and the old sailor that ferried people to and from the island stomped into the room. He must have been at least seventy years old, but he had the energy and demeanor of a man half his age.

"Blessen yer home and blessen yer heart," he called to Matron Underdown and tipped his floppy fisherman's hat to her politely.

"Come on in, Pylas," Underdown called without looking up. "Just keep your fingers out of my apricots. I know you love them, but I'm saving those to make tarts tomorrow."

Pylas stomped his boots clean as he pulled off his hat and jacket. He tossed them over a chair and then clomped over, bent down, and planted a kiss on Matron Underdown's cheek.

"Pylas! What are you doing?" she cried in only slightly veiled mock disapproval.

"Oh, don't get too excited," he said with a cackle. "That was for my luck, not yours. Storm's coming in, and I'm still supposed to sail back to the mainland tonight. It's said that if you surprise a beautiful lady with a kiss before a storm, Larayil will make sure the winds blow your way. I'm just staying safe."

Matron Underdown rolled her eyes and flicked flour at the wrinkled sailor. He laughed again, tromped over to a chair in the corner, and plopped down. Pulling out a clay pipe and a pouch of leaf from his pocket, he began to carefully pack the bowl.

"How goes the scholaring?" he asked Eathen.

Eathen swallowed his bite of bread and washed it down with a sip of ale before answering. "Well, enough, I guess," he answered. "In fact, I think I'll probably be ready to head back as early as tomorrow, if you're coming back out."

"Aye, we can do that," he replied.

Halie came over and collected some of Eathen's empty dishes from the table. "I'm sorry you're leaving tomorrow," she said. "It's been nice having someone closer to my age to talk to."

"Well thank you, Halie."

"If you don't mind me asking," she said, "it didn't sound like you were all that pleased with how things turned out. Did something go wrong?"

Eathen sighed and lifted his pack onto his lap. He pulled it open and removed a few of the papers from inside. Making some space on the table, he laid out the sheets.

"It isn't that something went wrong, exactly. It's just that because of the crystal, every monk gave the exact same accounting of the battle. Hearing different opinions and points of view is one of the best ways to truly understand an event, but here, listen, this is from Brother Rejem's account."

He lifted the first piece of paper and read:

"Flames danced along the edge of the glittering blade as the dwarven warrior swung it in a wide arc. It struck the shadow creature again, this time biting into the fiend's previously immaterial form. The flames exploded, racing up the creature's side as if the monster were made of oil. Wracked with pain and wreathed in arcane fire, it let out an ear-piercing shriek that shook the stained glass windows around the great hall."

"And then this," he said, replacing the first sheet and taking the next, "is Brother Leson's account."

"Flames danced along the edge of the glittering blade as the dwarven warrior swung it in a wide arc. It struck the shadow creature again, this time biting into the fiend's previously immaterial form. The flames exploded, racing up the creature's side as if the monster were made of oil. Wracked with pain and wreathed in arcane fire, it let out an ear-piercing shriek that shook the stained glass windows around the great hall."

Eathen sighed. "They aren't just similar. They're exactly the same. I guess I shouldn't be surprised considering the nature to the crystal but—"

Halie snatched one of the sheets. She narrowed her eyes as she read the account. "Can I read the rest of this?"

"If you like," Eathen answered, pulling the other pages for the account from his pack.

Halie took them and flipped through the pages, mumbling words aloud as she quickly read the account. The more she read, the more worried she looked.

"What is it, Halie?"

Handing him the sheets of paper, she ordered, "Wait here." She rushed out of the room and down the long hall that connected to the sleeping quarters.

"You'd best come right back," Matron Underdown shouted after her. "I need you to swill the floors in the cutting room yet tonight."

Halie reappeared a few moments later carrying a thick, ancient-looking book. She slapped the book on the table in front of Eathen. Throwing open the cover, she flipped through the pages until she appeared to find what she was looking for.

"There," She stabbed at a page. "Read that."

She was so serious and insistent that Eathen couldn't help but to obey. He read aloud.

Flames danced along the edge of the glittering blade as the Ondelvetch swung it in a wide arc. It struck the shadow creature again, this time biting into the fiend's previously immaterial form. The flames exploded, racing up the creature's side as if the monster were made of oil. Wracked with pain and wreathed in arcane fire, it let out an ear-piercing shriek that shook the stained glass windows around the great hall.

EATHEN STALKED BACK AND FORTH IN FRONT OF THE fireplace in the servant quarters sitting room as the others reviewed the passage, comparing it to his notes.

"I don't understand," he said. "Why would they lie? It doesn't make any sense." He looked at Pylas and Matron Underdown, almost pleading now. "Were the adventurers even here? Did anyone see them?"

"Aye," Pylas answered, with Matron Underdown nodding beside him. "They was real as you or me. Four of them. A dwarf gentleman in armor that glittered like gold; a wizard, human lady that one was, all in black, with a staff made outta some kinda stone; a big, monstrous-looking fella, had to be one of them orogs, wearin' nothin' but hide pants and a fur vest and carrying a club as big as a dock post, and a little guy no bigger 'en a child, with big, strange lookin' black eyes and horns coming from his head, a fey of some kind, I think. They got on that dragon-headed boat of theirs and went right out to the island."

Eathen frowned and looked to Matron Underdown. "And the monster, the shadow creature. Did any of you see it?"

"No, thank the Enaros," Matron Underdown replied. "As soon as the thing got loose, Brother Grishen rushed down and had Halie and I go to town with Pylas to get to safety and find help."

"How long did it take to find someone to go out to the island?"

Halie shrugged. "About as long as it took us to get from the docks to the Singing Frog. When we arrived, the adventurers were there. They were talking with Gerill, the tavern keeper, telling him about some grand exploit they'd just come back from. I went straight up to them and told them the trouble. They didn't hesitate. They just grabbed their gear and headed for the island."

"Couldn't it just be coincidence?" Matron Underdown offered. "It's not like the stories are *exactly* the same. The story in Halie's book takes place in a castle back before the Cataclysm, not a monastery. And the four adventurers in her book aren't the same as the four that went out to the island."

"No, it's more than coincidence," Halie replied. She had the book out in front of her along with Eathen's papers. "Except for a few minor details, it's the *exact* same tale from start to finish."

Eathen rubbed his forehead. It didn't make sense. "And the adventurers didn't say anything? After the battle, I mean? No mention of what they fought?"

"We didn't see them after," Halie said. "We saw them go out to the island, but they were gone by morning. They must've left in the night."

"Does that make sense, Pylas? That they'd sail in the dark?"

Pylas ran a hand over his gray chin stubble. "With the shoals 'round here? Not for normal sailors, no sense at all, but these weren't normal sailors. I imagine they had all sorts of magic to help them, and dwarves can see in the dark, so maybe it didn't much matter to them."

Eathen stared into the embers of the dying fire. The monks were followers of Toletren. Truth was one of their most highly prized virtues. To lie outright went against everything they believed in, and yet they *had* lied. Unquestionably. Repeating the text from one of the uncountable number of books they'd memorized, and passing it off as the truth.

"There's only one way I'm going to get to the core of it," Eathen stated. "I have to ask them."

Matron Underdown rose and walked over to Eathen's side, placing a hand on his arm. "Are you sure that's wise? I've known the monks for years, and this doesn't seem like something they'd have done. It would take something, well—something bad to get them to go down this path." She hesitated, as if gathering her courage, and then continued. "They say the Dark One's hand still has reach in the surface world. I dread to think that the good monks might be under his sway, but clearly something is terribly amiss."

Eathen clenched his fists and felt his stomach knot. All the explanations he'd devised involved mortal machinations. A power play of some kind, perhaps to keep some piece of valuable knowledge for themselves? Or maybe an ill-conceived joke, perpetrated by men and women whose minds were so changed by the crystal that their idea of humor was alien to others?

But what if Matron Underdown were right? What if there was a darker explanation? If that were true, the best course of action would be to get to the mainland immediately and send word to the High Temple in New Erinor. Let the priests of Toletren deal with the problem.

What was he thinking? That line of thought was foolish. If

Dark powers were at play, certainly there would have been some clear sign here.

"No, I don't believe this is the work of Endroren," Eathen said.

There was a sharp intake of breath from everyone in the room when he said the name of the fallen Enaros, and Pylas grumbled something under his breath.

"It's just too dark of a possibility for me," he continued. "I am certain something far more ordinary is going on, and as I've said, there's only one way to find out what it is."

Eathen grabbed his cloak from the chair and headed for the door.

"You're not going up there now, are you?" asked Matron Underdown. "I mean, yes, you're probably right, we're probably just double turning the eggs, but if does turn out to be…"

She let the words trail off, seemingly unwilling to continue.

Eathen paused, his hand resting on the door handle, and turned back to them. "If there is a mundane explanation, demanding the truth probably won't hurt. If anything, perhaps I can shake one of them into remembering their vows to Toletren and shining a light on this mystery."

"And if the explanation isn't *mundane*?" Pylas asked, emphasizing the final word in a way that clearly showed what his opinion was.

"Then we need to get off the island as soon as possible, but the only way to know what's going on up there is to confront them."

He pulled the door open and before he stepped out he added, "If I'm not back before that fire dies out, assume the worst. Get off the island at once, and send word to both the University and the High Temple."

As he stalked out the door, pulling it shut behind him, Eathen prayed he had shown more confidence than he felt. He reminded himself that his worries were foolish. Of course the monks weren't under the sway of Endroren. As adherents of the Enaros Toletren, that was impossible, wasn't it? Weren't Toletren's devoted followers protected from the Dark One's power?

A ragged cloud drifted across the moon, and a chill breeze swept through the courtyard. Eathen shivered. Then again, what did he know? He was a scholar, not a theologian. Although he knew a fair amount about the Enaros and a bit about Endroren, could he say with certainty that Matron Underdown's fear was unfounded? And if she was right, was he about to make the worst mistake of his life?

"Eathen!"

Eathen jumped and stumbled over his own feet at the sound of his name. Executing a clumsy skip, he barely managed to regain his balance and at least some of his composure. He turned around and saw Halie running up to meet him.

"What's wrong?" he called, raising his voice, for the wind had picked up quite a bit.

"I'm coming with you," Halie said as she reached his side. "If something is wrong, you may need my help. I know my way around the monastery. You don't."

Eathen considered her offer, then nodded. She was right. As dangerous as this might turn out to be—and he reminded himself that, in all logic, it was probably nothing—if something did go wrong, having her help might be key to his, what, survival? Again, the notion of this being any more than a misunderstanding struck him as foolish.

"You know, maybe we're overthinking this," he said. "I mean, corruption by Endroren? Really? It seems a bit far-fetched."

Even with the moon almost completely covered by clouds, making it difficult to see her features in the darkness, Eathen saw enough to know she didn't agree.

"The men and women of this monastery are the most devoted followers of an Enaros I've ever met," Halie said. "They literally gave up everything that made them an individual to bind their minds to this crystal. I didn't want to worry Matron Underdown and Pylas, but I don't believe for a moment that they'd easily or willingly commit such a serious breach of their vows as to lie to you outright like they have. I don't know what is wrong, but something *is* wrong. I don't think it's wise for you to go in there alone."

The first chilling drops of rain began to fall, and one splattered on Eathen's nose. He wiped it away with his sleeve and said, "This isn't one of your adventure stories, Halie. This is real. If there is something—"

Halie punched him in the shoulder hard enough to make him stagger back a step. "Don't patronize me, you gilt. You sound like my father. Of course this isn't an adventure story. In fact, I'm terrified, if you must know, but that doesn't change what has to be done. If Dark powers are at work here, then time is of the essence, and you need all the help you can get." She paused, shivering. "What's more, I may not want one of those crystals stabbed into my forehead, but those monks have been kind to me. Some of them are my friends. I fear what evil they might be facing even as we speak. And I have friends over in town, too. If something terrible happens here, they'll be the first ones to suffer for it."

She reached out to him, and although he flinched, fearing another blow, this time she placed a hand on his shoulder. "We're both here for the same reason, Eathen. The adventurers are gone, but the monster, whatever it is, remains. If we don't face it, who will?"

Eathen observed the sharp determination in her eyes, and knew it was true. Just like her, he was afraid—very afraid—but also like her, he knew someone had to do something. He still hoped it was all a misunderstanding, but if it weren't? Well, if it weren't, then it was better not to face it alone.

"I'm sorry," he said. "And thank you. I'm glad you're with me."

The rain started falling in earnest, so with no further words, they hurried across the courtyard toward the looming bulk of the ancient monastery.

"YOU'RE SOAKING WET," SAID SISTER DRINDEL. "WHAT IN Lensae was so important to bring you out in this weather?"

They stood together in one of the monastery's small contemplation chambers. Murals of pastoral landscapes in muted colors covered the walls, fragrant vases of fresh-cut flowers sat on pedestals in the corners, and a warm, crackling fire burned in the hearth. A circular bench sat in the center of the room, offering a place to sit and meditate on the paintings.

Eathen cleared his throat and then said, "I have concerns about your account of the shadow creature's attack."

The monk looked at him, eyebrows raised. Her crystal's light wavered before she replied. "I'm not sure I understand. We've given you a complete retelling of everything that happened, more than once, in fact."

Halie stepped forward. "I know I am only an acolyte, but if you will forgive my candor Sister Drindel, the story told to Master Eathen is impossible."

The monk looked at her and pursed her lips. "I do not forgive you for this claim, as it is highly inappropriate, and exactly the sort of behavior that led to your current scullery duties for Matron Underdown. It would appear that you wish to extend your time under her supervision."

Halie started to reply, but the monk raised a palm to cut her off. "But," Sister Drindel continued, "I am curious why you think our account is impossible. It is, after all, what happened, meaning it is anything but impossible."

Eathen noticed the monk's crystal flickering now, as if it were a reflection of her growing agitation. The strange pulsing was unlike anything he'd seen during his interviews with the monks. Glancing at Halie, he noticed her gaze locked firmly on the monk's forehead, a look of deep concern on her face.

Hoping to draw the fire away from Halie, Eathen stepped up. "You see, Sister Drindel, the problem is that the story you told me is precisely the same story as 'The Forgotten Hope' from *Tales of the Western Isles* by Essem Blane. This is what makes the account you and your brethren shared with me impossible. It is almost a word for word retelling of Blane's story."

Sister Drindel tipped her head, clasped her hands behind her back, and let out a long sigh. Eathen and Halie edged closer to one another, and Eathen could hear Halie's breathing quicken in the quiet of the contemplation chamber.

The monk raised her head, her face impassive. The crystal flickered so furiously now that it made Eathen dizzy to look at it. "I'm afraid neither of you are suitable for our purposes," she stated flatly.

Eathen felt his knees weaken, and found himself unable to look away from the crystal. He reached out for something to brace himself with, but his hand found only open air, and he began to fall. Halie stumbled slightly, and he knew she was feeling the strange effect as well. He blinked hard, trying to focus on the monk and keep his footing.

"As such," Sister Drindel continued, "I'm afraid we have no choice but to—"

There was a tremendous crash, and Sister Drindel crumpled to the floor. Like a fresh spring breeze coming in through an open window, Eathen's head cleared, and he regained his footing.

Sister Drindel lay face down amid the shattered remains of a vase. Her head and shoulders were soaked, and the floor around her was strewn with yellow belleyes.

Eathen looked at Halie. She stood over the monk, appearing both terrified and furious all at the same time. "We have to get out of here," she gasped. "What one knows they all know. If they aren't already outside the door, then they're on their way."

They raced to the door and flung it open. As they were about to leave, a weak voice cried out. "Wait!"

They halted and looked back. Sister Drindel rolled to her side, raised her head, and reached a hand out to them. She still wore the silver headband, but her crystal was shattered. Blood trickled from the spot where the crystal had been.

"You can't…go that way," she gasped, blinking rapidly as if she struggled to focus on them.

Halie rushed to Sister Drindel's side and rolled her onto her back, cradling her head.

"Oh, I'm sorry," she choked. "I didn't want to hurt you."

"No…you were right," she said. "Get out…get help…use the grotto."

"We'll take you with us." Eathen hurried over and started to lift the monk. "Can you get to your feet?"

"No time," she gasped. "Go!" The monk's eyes closed, and she slumped in their arms.

"Is she dead?" Eathen asked.

"I don't think so," Halie answered, swallowing hard and choking back a sob. "But she's right. We need to get out of here. Something is terribly wrong."

The sound of footsteps echoed from somewhere not far away. Carefully, they lay the unconscious monk down, and then ran out the door.

"What did she mean about the grotto?" Eathen asked as he

ran down the hall behind Halie.

"There is a sea cave on the east side of the island," she answered. "I'm guessing the monks aren't guarding it."

"A sea cave?" Eathen pictured the waves thundering against the cliffs all around the island. "How are we supposed to escape that way?"

At a t-intersection they cut sharp to the left, only to skid to a stop when they saw a group of four monks armed with iron shod staves charging down the hall toward them. Eathen went right, with Halie close behind.

"We can still get there," she called. "Turn left at the next intersection."

When he reached the next turn, he saw that unlike the other halls, there were no orbs of Aelos or torches lighting the way. He snatched a torch from the wall back in the main hallway, and then hurried after Halie, who was already running off into the darkness.

A moment later, they arrived at a narrow, winding staircase carved into the stone. With the footsteps growing closer behind them, they scurried down the stairs. Eathen's breath burned in his chest.

"There!" Halie shouted.

Eathen saw a small door at the end of the stairs. He could just hear the crash of waves coming from the other side. Halie threw the door open, and they rushed into the cavern beyond.

It was large, as big as a good-sized tavern. The walls bore the sharp, wavelike curves that came from centuries of erosion by the sea. The cavern formed a little cove, and a short passage led out to the open water beyond. At some point in the monastery's ancient history, someone had constructed a stone dock around the walls.

Moored beside the dock was a small ship with a dragon-headed prow.

"Oh no," whispered Halie.

"This is bad. We have to get out of here and warn Matron Underdown and Pylas," Eathen said.

Halie turned to respond but instead pointed at the door and shouted, "They're coming!"

A light was coming down the stairs, growing brighter with each moment. Eathen ran to the door and slammed it shut. He stuffed the torch into a sconce on the nearby wall and then looked around for a way to bar the door. He found nothing. Someone slammed into the door from the other side. Eathen's feet slid across the stone, but he managed to force it back closed. He braced his feet against one of the mooring posts.

"We have to lock it with something!" he cried.

Halie raced around the cavern. "There's nothing here. It's not supposed to lock from this side."

She ran over and grabbed one of the ship's mooring lines and pulled on it. "Maybe I can get one of these loose and we can tie it around the handle!"

Another boom echoed as more bodies crashed against the other side of the door. Eathen pushed as hard as he could, but the door started to open.

"I can't hold it!" he yelled.

Halie rushed to his side. Together they managed to hold the door, but the shoving from the other side didn't relent, slowly forcing them back.

"I'm sorry, Eathen," Halie sobbed as she strained against the door. "This is my fault. I should have noticed something was wrong sooner. I wasn't staying in the monastery, but I helped Matron Underdown serve the meals. I should have known."

"It's not your fault," Eathen said. He groaned with effort as their opponents shoved again, forcing the door open a bit further. "How could you have known? If anyone should have noticed it's me. Every story exactly the same? That's ridiculous. Why wasn't I more suspicious?"

Again their foes pushed, and again the door opened a finger-width further.

"They're going to get in," he grunted, pushing with all his might on the door. "Do you think we can get the ship untied? Get out of the cavern before they stop us?"

Again a push. Again the door edged open a little further.

"We'd never get it free in time," Halie said. "We could swim for it. It'd be difficult, but I don't know that we have any choice."

Somewhere outside, a wave boomed against one of the cliff walls.

"I think it's the only choice we have," he said. "On a count of three?"

Halie nodded.

"One," he said.

The door pressed open further.

"Two."

The door opened far enough that a robed arm reached through the gap and grabbed at their arms, trying to pull them away.

"Three—"

Before he could finish, a scream cut him off, followed by the sounds of battle; thuds and thumps. Crashes and cries. The door slammed shut under their weight as their attackers stopped trying to push through. He and Halie stayed pressed against the door regardless, and stared at each other in wonder.

The sounds of fighting continued for another few moments, but ended abruptly with a clang like a temple bell ringing. For a few long breaths, they didn't move.

Someone knocked on the door. "Hellooo," a voice said.

"Matron—Underwood?" Halie asked, stepping back.

Eathen threw the door open. Standing on the stairs amid a pile of unconscious monks stood Matron Underdown and Pylas.

Matron Underdown wore a strange outfit that looked something like armor, but cobbled together from a variety of kitchen implements. In her right hand she gripped a cast-iron frying pan. Beside her stood Pylas, his face scratched from where someone had clawed at him, but he appeared otherwise unharmed.

The four rushed to one another and embraced.

"How…why?" stammered Eathen and Halie together.

"When you didn't come back, we were worried something might be wrong, so we came in through the dining hall to investigate," said Matron Underdown.

"We ran into a couple of these jesters in the kitchen, but they weren't too much for us to handle," Pylas added. "Calm seas after that, that is until we heard the commotion coming from down here."

Halie looked at Matron Underdown's attire and laughed. "What are you wearing?"

"Now don't you laugh, girl," said Underdown, looking annoyed. "This is the uniform of a Kitchen Ranger, one of the proudest orders in the Grand Army of Gelendor."

"You mean the Kitchen Rangers are real?" asked Eathen. "I thought they were a jok…er…I mean, uh, a legend."

"I wasn't always a cook and a housemaid, boy," she said, puffing out her chest. "In my youth, I served in the frontier army, and fought against the goblin uprising at Windshome. I protected my soldiers, and made sure they fought on a full belly every night. I was even awarded the Golden Ladle for valor."

"Well, that's lucky for us then," laughed Halie. "We thought we were done for. And thank you too, Pylas. Clearly you did your share."

Pylas grunted. "Nothing to it. You're looking at a four-time champion of the Castle Port Knuckle Breaker Tournament. These monkeys ain't nothing compared to the drothmal I beat in '33."

Eathen's joy at being saved faded quickly when he remembered that there were only around five or six monks on the floor there, but the monastery was home to more than fifty.

"There will be more where these came from. We should go. Maybe we can get out using the ship," he said, picking his way over the bodies and toward it.

"Maybe," Halie said, following his lead, "but it's high tide. How are we going to get the ship out of the grotto?"

Pylas joined them, with Matron Underdown close behind. "It'll be a trick, but I can do it," he said. "I've navigated worse than this and lived to tell of it."

Working as fast as they could, Eathen, Halie, and Matron Underdown untied the ship. Meanwhile, Pylas leapt aboard and started making preparations to depart. As Eathen uncoiled the rope from the mooring post, he took a moment to look back at the stairs and wonder how much time they had before more monks came.

At the foot of the stairs, he saw the old monk he'd interviewed earlier that evening. Lying there unconscious, mouth open a bit and his disheveled gray hair framing a thin, wrinkled face, the monk reminded Eathen of his grandfather when he'd fall asleep in his chair reading by the evening fire. Then he remembered Sister Drindle, and the look of pain and fear on her face when she'd been freed from the crystal's power.

Eathan paused, his heart pounding in his chest. At last he said, "I…I can't just leave them."

"What's that?" Matron Underdown asked.

Eathen looked at the stairs, and then back at the ship. This was the moment, he realized, the moment he'd written about so many times when recording the tales of those who had fought back against the Dark. The shepherd who chose to stay and protect his village from a pack of wargs with nothing but his crook. The soldier who remained on the wall in the face of the advancing *endrori* army. The adventurer that plunged into unexplored Deepland halls to hunt the creatures of shadow.

Were they as afraid as he felt now? And was their choice as inevitable as he realized his was?

"I can't leave them," Eathen repeated, his voice firm. "Whatever power is at work here, it has the monks trapped. Who knows what might happen between now and the time we return with help? And what about the adventurers? If the monks were going to kill Halie and I, the adventurers could be here somewhere, and in terrible danger. You said that when you told them about the trouble on the island, they didn't hesitate to come to the monks' aid. How can I leave them now when they might need us?"

Eathen headed for the stairs, grabbing one of the monk's staves along the way.

"I'm going to see what I can do to help. The rest of you get to the mainland and send for help. I'm not sure that I'll be able to do much, but I have to try."

"Aw, hells," groaned Halie. "He's right. I'm going with him."

Halie ran to his side and picked up a staff of her own.

Matron Underdown knitted her brow and nodded solemnly before joining them. "I've got a few scraps left in me still, and I'm not letting the two of you go in there alone."

Pylas, standing alone of the deck of the ship, shrugged his shoulders. "Eh, I'm surprised I'm not dead already. What have I got to lose?"

He hopped off the ship and joined Eathen and the others. Together, with grim determination, they headed back into the monastery.

GRAND MASTER WINEMAN READ ALOUD FROM THE SHEAF of papers he held:

"—With the monks at their heels, they charged into main chapel. Standing on a golden pedestal in the center of the vaulted chamber stood the Holy Crystal. It pulsed with a blue light, and streamers of energy flowed from it, converging on four figures chained to pillars surrounding it.

"The adventurers!" Halie shouted. "That must be how the monks learned to fight so well."

"No time," Pylas coughed, his one arm wrapped around his belly and the other leaning on Eathen for support. "They're here."

A dozen monks armed with swords, flails, staves, and daggers poured into the room.

"Time to put an end to this!" Matron Underwood cried. With unexpected agility, the little halfling charged across the room and leaped into the air. Like a hero from the Age of Shadow, she swung her frying pan in a wide arc. It struck the Holy Crystal like a clapper against a bell and bit into the blue stone of the strange artifact. With a sound like a thousand glasses shattering at once, the Holy Crystal exploded.

As the sound faded, the monks gasped and clapped their hands to their foreheads. They tore off the silver headbands with a cry of both pain and relief. Eathen, Halie, and Pylas ignored them and raced to Matron Underdown's side. The little halfling lay on the floor in a widening pool of blood. The exploding crystal had sliced every area of exposed flesh. At first they feared the worst, but her armor had born the brunt of the blow. She'd require the care of the priests of Alantra, but she would live.

Thus ended the enslavement of the Monks of the Holy Crystal."

Grand Master Wineman set the stack of paper on his desk and looked over at Eathen with narrowed eyes. "Like a hero from the Age of Shadow?"

Eathen swallowed hard. "Yes, sir."

The Grand Master looked at him with raised eyebrows before shaking his head. "And you say that the crystal itself had taken over the monks' minds? That there was no corruption or other evil presence? That the whole 'shadow creature' ruse had been a trap to lure adventurers out to the island?"

"That is correct, sir." Eathen shifted in the chair. It seemed to have padding in all the wrong places. He wondered if Master Wineman had the chairs specially constructed to make visitors uncomfortable, in order to gain an advantage when questioning them.

"As I noted in the report," he continued, pointing at the papers on the Grand Master's desk, "the crystal was originally discovered by explorers in the ruins of Old Erinor. Apparently the monks were attempting to influence the essential pattern of the crystal to make it easier to retrieve memories from it when something went wrong. They remember very little of the time between when the change occurred and when we freed them, and we still don't know what the crystal was trying to accomplish."

The Grand Master steepled his fingers and rested them on his chin. "You haven't made this easy for me, you know. The fact that your story reads more like an adventure story than a scholarly work is the least of the problems we have to deal with." He frowned down at the documents, and then turned his gaze back on Eathen.

"More importantly, your interference was highly inappropriate, and in direct opposition to our mandate to deliver objective and unbiased records. I'm sure you don't need me to tell you that your actions have jeopardized any chance that you'll be given a teaching assignment this year. After all, we are in the business of recording history, Master Winswood, *not* making it." He shook his head and sighed. "As the Grand Master of the University Archive, I must condemn your conduct in this case."

Eathen felt sick. He didn't regret his decision, he'd never regret the decision, but he'd feared this moment for weeks.

The Grand Master lowered his hands and leaned back in his chair. His expression softened. "As a fellow citizen of this great realm, however, I commend you for your actions, Eathen. You showed courage in the face of great danger. I believe Lord Drakewyn would agree with me when I say that if more of our people stood strong against the forces that oppose us, we'd all be better off."

He stood, picked up the papers, and handed them to Eathen. Eathen took them, a sudden sense of relief washing over him. He respected the Grand Master greatly, looked up to him, and knowing he didn't think poorly of Eathen took a huge weight off his shoulders.

"As I've already stated, due to your involvement in this affair, it is unlikely that the council will grant you a teaching position this year," the Grand Master continued. "I'm certain, however, that come next year, you'll find yourself standing before a class of young students, eager for the benefit of your wisdom."

The Grand Master walked around the desk as Eathen rose from his seat. Grand Master Wineman nodded to the door, and Eathen walked in that direction.

"And trust me when I tell you this: another year of travel isn't the worst thing that could happen to you." Grand Master Wineman placed a comforting hand on his shoulder. "You'll find yourself trapped behind a lectern soon enough, my boy. Enjoy this time while you have it."

Eathen turned at the door, smiled, and shook the Grand Master's hand. "Thank you, sir. I truly appreciate it," he said, and stepped out of the Grand Master's office.

As the door closed firmly behind him Eathen let out a huge sigh.

"So, how did it go?" Halie asked eagerly.

Eathen smiled at Halie as she approached from the bench where she'd been waiting. She no longer wore acolyte robes, which made sense, seeing as the order she'd been pledged to no longer existed. Instead she wore a simple dress, perfectly appropriate for a student of the University. “Did he like the part about Matron Underwood looking like a hero of the Age of Shadow?”

“Um, he definitely noticed that part,” Eathen said.

“Ha! I told you he’d like it. Glad you left it in.”

He and Halie started off down the hall. “So, I’m guessing you won’t be getting a teaching post.”

“No, definitely not this year,” he said, and was surprised by the fact that this didn’t seem to bother him anymore.

“What are you going to do next?”

Eathen fished around in his pocket until he found the folded piece of paper there. He pulled it out, unfolded it, and handed it to Halie. It was one of the assignment postings the professors put up on the board for the travelling scholars.

“A complete accounting of the history and inhabitants of the honorable town of Thornwall, in the Duchy of Vaun,” she read aloud. “Vaun? Isn’t that way up in the north? Why would you want to go way up there? It sounds boring.”

“That’s exactly what I’m counting on,” Eathen said.

THE UNDERCITY JOB

DAVE GROSS

"ARE YOU SURE THIS IS THE PLACE?" WREN CLUTCHED NORDA'S arm. Even through armor, the sprite's touch felt warm. Her huge eyes and tufted, fawn-like ears gave her an expression of perpetual innocence—a look balanced by the wicked angles of her coiling horns.

Norda grunted an affirmative. Judging by appearances, they stood at the mouth of Labor Lane.

Human men and women she took for hiring agents stood on either side of the narrow alley. Some operated out of the back doors of shops, others beside tables spotted with bird droppings. A few had posted signs, but most just called out the type of work they had to offer: "Porters," "Carpenters," "Mudders," "Diggers," and so on.

Norda eyed a rosy-cheeked man leaning beside a sign that read *Guards*. Returning her gaze, he noted the headless axe handle dangling from her hip, rolled his eyes, and shook his head. She bit down to suppress a swell of irritation, less directed at the man than at the reminder of her lost blade. It didn't matter. He wasn't the agent they wanted.

A human girl no taller than Norda dashed down the alley, dodging adults on either side of a runnel of waste. She held a scuffed leather ball out of reach of the three younger children chasing her, leaping the filthy stream to evade their grasp.

The children split to either side of Norda and Wren, who had to do a little dance to avoid stepping into the sewage stream. The smallest child bounced off the wooden shield slung over Norda's back.

"Sorry!" she peeped.

"Watch where you're going!" snapped Norda. "There ought to be a rule about children running in the streets.

With a wild grin, Wren started after the children. Norda grabbed the sprite's doe-skin jerkin to hold her back. Wren wriggled out of her grip and pouted. "They were having so much *fun*."

"We're not here for fun," said Norda. She realized she'd lost sight of their other companions. "Where are the Wiseacres?"

"Wherever they went, I bet *they're* having fun."

"That's what I'm afraid of."

Norda glanced up at the blue sky visible between the roofs. It took her a moment to spy Thistle perched on the eaves. The fairy was no bigger than a doll. Folded to her sides, her butterfly wings resembled a blue-and-gold cloak.

Norda crossed her wrists and wriggled her thumbs, their sign for the frisky halfling twins. Thistle pointed down the lane, indicating the side opposite her perch. She held up a number of tiny fingers. Norda squinted to count: eight.

Norda and Wren wound their way down the lane, avoiding the muck and the people seeking work. All of them were human. Norda hadn't noticed anyone but humans since they had entered Hawk's Crest. The dwarf and her diminutive companions stood out.

The only other small person in the lane was another young girl in a dirty frock. Her arms and legs looked as thin and fragile as twigs. She held up a lump that looked like a punctured leather ball to a man calling out for porters. When he shook his head, she tottered over and offered it to Wren.

The sprite ruffled the girl's tangled hair and pointed. "Your friends went that way."

"I'm hiring," said the girl.

Norda eyed the child. Her hollow cheeks spoke of hunger, but that was a loaf of bread in her hands, not a ball. The girl held it to try to conceal the bites she'd taken out of the other end.

Wren was already looking up at Norda with the big, sad eyes routine. With a weary sigh, Norda removed the purse from between her breasts and dug out their last two silver coins. She handed them to the girl. "Go buy something hot to eat."

"But that's not—"

"Somebody gives you a gift, you say thanks," said Norda. "That's the rule."

"Thanks. It's just—"

Norda walked away, pulling Wren by the arm.

The strong smell of stale lager and tobacco wafted from the door Thistle had indicated. Inside, Norda saw a room full of casks, chains of sausage, and wheels of cheese. Through an open door on the far wall, she saw the taproom. Two big figures lounged near the untended bar. Only three other figures resided in the center of the room.

A woman with long flame-red hair leaned back in a chair, her heels hooked over the edge of a table. Beside her, a long spear with a head like a sword blade leaned against a pillar. On the table lay a few parchment pages and a wand with a bulbous head tipped with two horny spikes.

Across from the woman, the Wiseacres took turns interrupting each other as they made their pitch.

Norda cursed. The last thing she needed was for Darbin and Findle Wiseacre to make the first impression on the hiring agent. If they didn't need the money, she might have left them there to humiliate themselves.

She glanced back up to see Thistle fluttering down to perch on the opposite roof. The fairy nodded at Norda, who nodded back. Despite the reputation of fey creatures as flighty things, Thistle was the one lookout she could count on. The others were far too easily distracted, as the boys were proving at that moment.

"Here they are!" said Wren. She dashed in to join the halflings.

Norda followed and took a better look at the men at the bar. Neither was human, and each was taller sitting down than the dwarf was standing up.

The bald orog rested his bulk across three creaking bar stools. A domelike head squatted neckless between round shoulders. The bar groaned under the weight of an iron-studded club. The brute chuckled, a line of spittle connected his two upper teeth with the three remaining on the bottom. "They're all wee things!"

The drothmal leaned against a pillar, his face etched into a leonine snarl exaggerated by the swirls of primal tattoos on his cheeks and forehead. Where his companion was all bulk, the barbarian's lean frame wound like wire around a sword's grip. Norda nodded at him, one warrior to another. He looked away as if bored.

She turned back to the woman at the table, taking her for the hiring agent. The redhead glanced at the new arrivals before turning her amused face back to the halflings, whose body language told Norda the woman had them wrapped around her finger. The dwarf also noted that the woman was barely half a foot taller than she. That was something. In Norda's experience, tall people looked down on her and her friends, figuratively as well as literally.

Norda's relief turned to alarm when she spied the spider perched on the woman's hand. Its hairy legs moved as the woman turned her wrist, but the worst part was the eyes. Instead of the glossy black beads of normal spiders, this one had eight grape-sized eyes with pupils and irises surrounded by bloodshot whites. The irises were matched pairs: two brown, two gray, two blue, and two yellow.

"Is it looking at me?" said Darbin.

"Don't be afraid, little darlin'," said the woman. "They're just having a look-see."

They?! Norda shuddered. She looked down at Wren who was looking up at her, mouthing, *They?!*

"I'm not afraid of spiders," said Findle. He tossed his head to shake the curly hair out of his eyes and held out his hand. "Can I hold it?"

Darbin tossed his own head and held out a hand in echo of his twin's gesture. "No, me first! I'm not afraid either." The more competitive the boys became while trying to impress a pretty woman, the more they seemed connected by invisible strings.

The orog guffawed and slapped the bar top. "They're barely snacks. Better feed it both."

The Wiseacres stepped back in unison.

The redhead giggled and raised the weird spider to her shoulder. It crawled onto her leather pauldron and raised a pair of legs to the woman's neck. She stroked its abdomen and nodded as if listening to its whisper.

"Don't you worry none. They're not hungry. Anyway, I reckon we've got business. Which of you boys is the boss of your little group?"

"Neither of them," said Norda, shoving the halflings aside.

"Aw..." grumbled the Wiseacres.

Wren pushed between them. "Mind your manners, or I'll pinch you both."

Norda left the Wiseacre wrangling to Wren, who relished the

task. "It's a recovery, I hear. Who're you, and what's the item?"

The redhead offered such a pretty smile that Norda could almost forgive the smitten Wiseacres. Despite her brutish companions and that horrible spider, she had a certain charm.

"I'm Haley Green," said the redhead. "And this here's what's missing."

She turned around the top parchment. On it was a pastel sketch of a box inlaid with white gold in web patterns. Red and purple gems nestled between the threads like captured insects. "Contract's for recovery undamaged and—now this is the important thing—unopened. The pay is..." She thought for a moment. "Two hundred."

"I heard it was four."

Haley shrugged. "Half pay for half size."

The orog slapped his thigh and unleashed a terrifying belly laugh. Even the drothmal's grim mouth turned up on one corner.

The spider leaned against Haley's ear, stroking her neck as it whispered. Norda felt bile rise in her throat. She hated spiders.

"Also, they want the thief," said Haley. "Intact."

Norda frowned. "For the city guard?"

Haley shook her head and gave a lopsided smile. "Uh-uh."

The drothmal cracked his knuckles.

Norda didn't like to imagine what those bruisers would do to a thief. She looked straight at the weird spider and said, "We aren't bounty hunters. And we're not cut-rate anything."

Haley glanced at her shoulder. The spider rubbed the tips of its palps together like a moneylender calculating risk. It whispered again. "Bringing them the thief's what you call non-negotiable," the redhead said. "Shame. You're just the right size for where he's run off."

"And where's that?"

"We got a deal?"

Broke as they were, and without better prospects for a job,

Norda shook her head. "No deal."

Haley looked surprised, and perhaps a little impressed. The orog looked confused, the drothmal bored. Before Haley could say something else, Norda walked out, trusting Wren to bring the Wiseacres.

Back out on Labor Lane, they formed a half-circle against the back wall of a chandler's shop. Thistle flew down to perch on the top of Norda's shield. The rustle of her delicate wings reminded Norda of the spider so close to Haley's ear, but the fairy smelled of ripe blackberries.

Darbin wiggled his fingers. "One pass down this street can net us enough coin for supper."

"Not on this street," said Findle, eying the people looking for work. "Everyone looks as broke as us." He peeked through the window of the chandlery. "But if you distract the shop owner, I can crack the cash box and—"

"No cracking cash boxes! No picking pockets!" said Norda. She looked around to see a few of the hiring agents looking her way. She lowered her voice. "No stealing from regular folk."

"What if we take only half the cash?" said Findle.

"No," growled Norda.

"What if we return it after we get a new job?" said Darbin.

"No!"

Wren giggled. Norda shot her a warning glare. The mercurial sprite could shift roles from Norda's enforcer to the Wiseacres' enabler in the wink of an eye. "No stealing from regular folk," said the sprite, mimicking Norda's gruff voice. "That's Norda's rule!"

"You have so many rules," sighed Darbin. "Sometimes I forget them all."

"Not if you know what's good for you," said Norda.

"Hello again, cutie," said Wren, turning outside their circle.

"I'm Wren. What's your name?"

The girl had returned, once again holding the sad-looking loaf in a futile attempt to hide the bites she'd taken—including two new ones. She held up the two silver coins Norda had given her. "I'm Myna. I want to hire you."

Surprise gave way to regret that Norda hadn't paid attention to what the girl had said earlier. Norda hated it when taller people dismissed her; she shouldn't have done the same to Myna. "What's the job?"

"A re-trie-val," said the girl, pronouncing the word carefully, as if she'd only recently learned it. "I want you to re-trieve my big brother, Hebbet."

"Where'd he go?"

The girl pointed down.

Norda glanced down the dirty runnel of waste water to the grate at the end of the lane. Norda frowned. The sewers were bad enough, but she'd heard rumors of the ruined city of Norentor, an ancient Alliance city, lying beneath the foundations of Hawk's Crest. "What's he doing down there?"

"People were chasing him because he was trying to sell a box."

Norda glanced back at the tavern, but no one seemed to be eavesdropping on their conversation.

She took a bite of the pathetic loaf before passing the bread around. Her comrades each took a nibble before passing it back to the girl. Norda took back her silver coins and returned them to her purse.

"Deal."

"I'LL SAY IT AGAIN," ANNOUNCED DARBIN, SQUEEZING OUT of a green-slicked runoff pipe. He plopped to the sewer floor, slimy as a newborn calf and twice as smelly.

"This place stinks," Wren and Findle mimicked Darbin's whine.

They stood in a main sewer channel, all crowding on the same side to avoid the brown stream. Perched on top of Norda's shield, Thistle held up a light-radiating twig that cast their long shadows along the curved masonry. Darbin and Findle had been taking turns slipping through breaks in the walls to scout for an entrance to the city below the sewers.

Darbin pouted. Norda said, "It wasn't funny the last three times you said it. Did you find a way down?"

"Maybe," said Darbin. "Along that way," he pointed. He frowned, closing his eyes to visualize their route.

"Southwest," said Norda. She could always feel which way was north. She'd been tracing a mental image of a map from the point where they had first descended into the sewers a few streets away from where Myna had hired them to find Hebbet.

Darbin nodded. "The storm drains end, but I can hear more water falling below. It's deeper than the sewers. Lots deeper."

They followed the channel until they could all hear the sound of falling water through grates where erosion had eaten away the earth behind the bricks. Norda lifted her axe handle. With the thick iron cap protecting the eye, it still had plenty of heft. She raised the weapon and brought it down on the damaged wall. The first blow cracked the bricks. The second smashed an opening big enough for Thistle to slip through.

The fairy shone her lighted twig on the hole. The muddy shaft beyond was wide enough for a human to slide down. The fairy fluttered out of the way as Norda raised her axe handle again.

The next blow made the hole big enough for Wren. The one after expanded it to Wiseacre size. Three more whacks, and even Norda's broad shoulders could fit.

Findle produced a coil of silk rope from his marvelous waistcoat, in which Norda sometimes suspected he concealed a closet's worth of junk, along with weapons and a vast collection of tools.

While he rummaged, Norda felt an eerie premonition of being watched. She gestured for Thistle to play her light along the walls. A few enormous centipedes scurried into cracks in the walls or ceiling.

Norda drove an iron spike into the sewer floor. They took their time rappelling down to a wet slope, half-mud and half-shattered masonry. Wren sang a fey spell and flicked her fingers. Four will-o'-wisps brightened into existence, the colors inside them swelling and fading by turns.

"Go now!" cried Wren, swirling her arm in a spiral. The globes chased after each other, taking turns in the lead. Norda thought of the children chasing each other through Labor Lane earlier. Her arm rose involuntarily to stop Wren from chasing after them, but the sprite only stared at what the circling lights revealed.

At first the faerie lights shone on high columns tilting to the east. Then they swept past fragments of silvery minerals scattered among dusty fragments of green and yellow glass. The source of the wreckage appeared next, the shattered remains of a stained glass dome toppled from a temple roof.

Despite her rapture, Wren diverted the lights when they met a shapeless mound of earth and stone. She navigated them through the rough terrain to reveal three passages formed between rows of houses whose upper floors had fallen toward each other to form low, narrow lanes. Nearby, the runoff from the storm drains formed a pool of clear water that trickled off in four directions. One of them trailed through a wider passage lined with faintly glowing lichen.

"Tracks," said Norda.

Without need for further instruction, Wren and Thistle each chose a Wiseacre to follow with their magical lights. To the halflings' chagrin, it was the sprite who first found signs of the lost city's inhabitants.

"Rats," she declared.

Moments later, the Wiseacres agreed, pointing at dozens of trails and plentiful droppings. "Lots of rats."

"And that's not all," said Wren. The halflings huffed in irritation that the sprite had beaten them once more. "Some kind of reptile prints here."

Findle knelt beside the tracks. "Crocodile?"

The others joined them. Darbin traced a finger around the edges of the deep print. "More like one of those sand dragons we saw near Callios."

"I don't think so," said Wren. "There's no tail furrow, and it looks like—"

"It's walking on two legs," finished Darbin with a note of triumph.

"Yeah," Wren grinned. Unlike the halflings, the sprite never seemed competitive. She just seemed pleased they saw things the same way.

Thistle waved her twig to draw their attention to a spot farther along. Norda knelt beside the spot and touched a stain on the floor, holding up her gloved fingers to the light.

"Fresh blood," she said with a frown. She looked around the floor but spotted no tracks that might have been left by a human. "Does anyone see any footprints?"

They spread out to search. Norda stood still to avoid trampling the tracks, while Thistle resumed her favored spot on the edge of her shield.

After a while, Wren said, "Nothing." The boys agreed.

"Either he never made it down here, or he came in some other way," said Norda. Only then did she consider that this undercity might be larger than Hawk's Crest above them. Just how much work had she agreed to do in exchange for her own two silver and a bite of bread?

That doesn't matter, she decided. The pay was a formality. No matter how much they needed money, there were some things more important, and finding a girl's lost brother was one of them. Besides, she'd made a deal. And her most important rule was that one never breaks a deal.

"Let's follow the lizard tracks," Norda decided.

She almost told Wren and Thistle to quench their lights. She could see in perfect darkness, but the others couldn't, and she couldn't follow tracks or spot traps the way the boys could. But lights also meant that other people—and things—would see them coming long before they arrived. "Boys, you take the lead. Wren, Thistle, give them some light."

A few hours later, it felt like they had traveled less than the length of three city blocks, but Norda had no complaints. While the Wiseacres acted like idiots around women, they were serious about their scouting. Findle led them around a patch of floor he deemed unstable. After one glance at it, Norda agreed. Later, the Wiseacres found a near-invisible string set to release a cache of jagged rubble on unwitting intruders.

"We're entering somebody's territory," said Wren.

"The lizards'?" asked Norda.

Wren shrugged, but Darbin shook his head. "Not if they have claws on their hands as well as their feet."

Findle nodded. "These were set by somebody—or something—with nimble fingers. Smaller than ours, probably."

"Rats?"

Everyone looked around, hoping someone else would say it first.

"Rats with fingers?" Wren ventured.

Thistle's light dimmed. Norda tensed, knowing what that meant.

The fairy's strange voice unnerved even her friends. She rarely spoke, and her own shyness—or some more enigmatic reason—caused her to cover her tiny face or cloak it in darkness before she uttered a word. She flew up to hover a few feet above the others, and then she spoke.

"The ancient say that after the fall of Norentor, the unleashed energies of the Cataclysm merged the flesh of the survivors, human and beast." As always when the fairy spoke, Norda felt a coolness ripple through her body. "The transformation created new peoples, hardier and more savage, more dangerous than human or animal alone. Some are half-rat, others half-reptile, and still others stranger things yet. They stay down here in their dark kingdom only because they can never stop warring among each other. If ever they should make peace among themselves, say the ancients, then they should swarm the streets of Hawk's Crest, and another city would fall."

For long moments, no one else spoke. Norda felt Thistle's wings brush the back of her head. The fairy's trifling weight settled back onto her shield. She lighted her twig with magic once more.

"So we're thinking rats with fingers?" said Darbin. He gasped at a sudden idea. "What about spiders with fingers?"

"Quit it!" Wren didn't even pinch him. She was trembling too much.

"Let's go on," said Norda. "Just be extra careful."

The boys soon found another trapped passage, which they avoided by entering a tilted marble ruin. The vaults within its walls were all barren, undoubtedly looted of their treasure long ago. With the aid of Thistle's strengthening spell, Norda wrenched tarnished bronze bars out of a window to aid their detour.

Several crooked avenues later, they found the body.

Norda estimated it was only a few inches taller than she, but it was hard to tell while it lay on the ground. The bow by the creature's side was almost as tall as he was, and the arrows spilled from the quiver looked a good six inches longer than her arm. The creature's own arms were disproportionately long, pale green, and scaled.

Judging from the lizard-man's many wounds, he was the source of the blood trail they'd seen earlier. A gash on his side and several on his arms suggested he'd fought enemies wielding blades, but there were also bites. Findle measured one with his fingers and grimaced. "Big rats."

Wren placed a hand on the pebbled skin of the lizard-man's chest. "He feels cool to—Yikes!"

The sprite tumbled backward. She came up in a crouch, a dagger in one hand and a scrolled leaf in the other. "He's alive!"

Gripping her bladeless axe, Norda moved to the lizard-man's side. His shallow chest moved, and she heard a faint wheezing from his toothy maw. Thistle fluttered down on the other side.

"Can you save him?" said Norda.

Thistle sketched a fey sigil in the air, squinted at the brief image that formed above the injured creature, and nodded. She raised a fine eyebrow that asked, *Shall I?*

Norda considered it. Spending Thistle's power on some reptilian monster now could cost the life of one of her friends later. The chance of its knowing how to find Hebbet was small, even assuming they shared a common language.

The creature's jaundiced eyes turned from Thistle to Norda. Despite its bestial face, Norda thought it knew she was deciding its fate.

Half-human or half-monster, Norda pitied it. "Help him."

The fairy's tiny hands were already in motion. As she trilled, she held her thumb and forefinger together and made a series of dipping gestures over the creature's wounds. Norda could just make out the faint glow of divine threads stitching the wounds closed. The magic settled over the torn flesh and turned the lizard's dull skin leaf green. The fey color lingered for a moment before fading, leaving only faint scars where the creature had been slashed and bitten.

The lizard-man stirred, felt his mended flesh, and sat up before Norda began the interrogation. "Have you seen a human boy down here?"

Her question evoked a querulous tilt of the reptilian head and a string of sibilant clucks and pops. Wren began to repeat the question in the fey tongue, but Thistle held up a finger. Rather than extinguish the light again, she covered her mouth with one hand and replied in the lizard's own language. They exchanged a few phrases before Thistle said, "He has seen the boy."

"Is he alive?" said Norda.

Thistle asked. The lizard answered. Thistle translated, "The spider-priests have him."

THE LIZARD'S INSTRUCTIONS PROVED ACCURATE, INCLUDING the sites of two more traps and the methods to disarm them. Norda felt vindicated in her decision to let him find his way back to his people rather than hold him captive. The moment he realized they were heading into rat territory, fear shook his body. It was dangerous to venture close to the lair of the rat-people, Thistle translated the warning.

It was death to enter.

"We made a deal," said Norda. "We've got to find Hebbet."

An hour later, the group gazed down into the shrine of the spider god.

The lair had once been a plaza, judging from the central fountain. The sculpture of a long-legged crustacean rested at the top, its red coral legs and pale green body incongruous to the rest of the fountain's marble construction. No water spilled from its sculpted dolphins and naiads, but several tiers held flicking yellow candles. Along the edges lay skulls, fragments of bas-reliefs, and other decorative objects Norda imagined had been scavenged from the ruins or stolen from surface-dwellers.

Among the offerings she spied a familiar-looking box. A trio of rat-men prostrated themselves before it while hissing prayers and performing the gestures of their unknown god.

"Whew!" whispered Darbin. "From what that lizard said, I thought the spider-priests would be actual spiders."

"They worship a spider," said Findle.

"That's not a spider, you knucklehead. It's a crab."

"Hush, both of you," said Wren. Her voice had lost all trace of whimsy. The Wisacre-herder was back at work.

A throng of rat-people huddled behind their priests. Behind them and all around the shrine, broken windows and doorways of the surrounding buildings cast dark eyes over their worship. Once again, Norda felt that shivering intuition of being watched. She studied the shadowed cavities for signs of watchers. A few times she thought she spied slow, furtive movement.

Beside her, Findle whispered as he counted the rat-people. He trailed off after fifty and said, "We'll never fight our way in there."

"No," agreed Norda.

"We have to," said Wren. She pointed past the central sculpture of the fountain to a cage woven of thick, pale fibers. Norda moved to gain a clearer vantage. The captive was a teenage boy. Even at this distance, she could make out a family resemblance to Myna.

"What are we going to do?" said Darbin.

Norda considered the question. This situation wasn't exactly the same, but they'd faced something similar before. "Remember the cheebat merchant captured by goblins?"

"There weren't this many goblins," said Wren. "But if we run back the way we came and leave something to slow them down..."

"That's it, then," said Norda. "You know what to do."

The Wiseacres moved toward the plaza, quiet as the shadows. Thistle flittered toward the ceiling.

"Here goes nothing," whispered Wren. She took a deep breath, held it, and disappeared. It was a fine trick, as long as she didn't get the giggles. Norda heard the faint crunch of the sprite's footsteps as she moved off to the side.

Norda shrugged the shield onto her arm and hefted her bladeless axe. If everything went perfectly, all of those rat-people would run straight toward her while her friends escaped.

It began with an intruder crawling out of a ruined archway: a cat bigger than a draft horse. Norda groaned as she saw the gigantic orange tabby. Anyone who had seen a lion or tiger would see through the illusion at once.

But when the thing growled, Norda felt the vibration in the pit of her stomach. If Wren's illusion had such an effect on her, she could only hope it did worse to the rat-people.

The rats froze and ceased their hissing, but only for half a second. More than half scattered, vanishing into several passages Norda hadn't detected. The rest squealed, piling into a tangle of fur and claws between the giant intruder and their priests who, after a moment's fumbling, changed their prayers and gesticulations. A faint black halo formed around the high priest, and his beady eyes began to glow deep purple.

On the far side of the fountain, the door to the cage opened. At first Norda couldn't spot Hebbet or the Wiseacres, but a moment later she glimpsed motion on the far side of the lair. There Darbin ran beside the boy, moving fast and low while remaining behind the defending rat-people.

"Where the devil are you, Findle?" Even as she muttered the

question, Norda guessed the answer. She looked back to the rat-priests, whose attentions were fixed on the giant tabby. Mere feet away, Findle crawled around the edge of the fountain, reached up to snatch the stolen box, and stuffed it beneath his waistcoat.

The bravest of the rat-people emerged from their defensive ball to rush the cat. The tabby hissed and raised a paw, extending claws the size of scythes. The rats recoiled, but did not flee. Norda knew that Wren was being careful not to cause the illusion to touch them. If she did, they would realize there was no substance behind the image.

Darbin and Hebbet ran straight into the tunnel from which they had come. Wren backed up toward Norda, still concentrating on controlling the magical image. When the rat-people struck again, she caused the cat to dodge out of the way. Norda winced as she noticed the stony rubble beneath the cat's feet did not shift under its weight.

The rat-people appeared to sense something wrong, too. When they hesitated and looked back to their priests, Wren directed the cat to pounce nearer. The defenders squealed in terror, but it was too late to recapture their attention.

A shriek from one of the rat-priests alerted the others to Findle, caught halfway between the fountain and Norda. Without looking back, the halfling rose from his crouch and sprinted toward her.

Findle was quick, but he couldn't outrun these creatures for long. All but a few of the rat-people abandoned the stand-off with Wren's tabby and swarmed toward him.

Norda took a step forward, but Wren's voice cried out, "Wait!"

Just as the rats closed in on Findle, Thistle swooped down to tap the halfling on his curly head. The pale green light of fey magic covered him as he continued his sprint. The nearest rat-people raised their jagged blades but hesitated, befuddled by the fairy's spell.

Norda breathed a sigh of relief as Findle darted past her. She backed into the passage, Wren following close. They retreated a good thirty feet before Wren dipped her fingers into a pouch and brought them out thick with butter. She called out an arcane phrase, and in a trice the floor behind them glistened with a thick coat of yellow fat.

The rats fell over each other as their feet touched the slippery floor. The first went down flat on their pointed snouts, while those behind tripped over them. The third waved clambered over their comrades and came much closer before succumbing to the greasy surface.

"Better hurry!" shouted Wren.

The dwarf and sprite ran after their friends, spying them across another half-buried plaza just before they disappeared into another narrow passage. Behind them, they heard more rat-people scrambling down the tunnel.

"Go on," Norda said. She turned, raising her shield and axe-handle. There were only three coming for her. This many she knew she could fend off.

A rising sound of squealing and claws on stone shook her confidence. The noise came from all over, not just the tunnel they had escaped. Looking up, she saw a pointed nose poke out of a crack high on the wall. A rat-man pushed out of another unseen hole to the right, and then another from one near the floor. Soon she would face dozens, not just three.

Norda turned and fled, shouting for the others to run faster.

They made it back to the spot where they found the wounded lizard-man before the rat-people surrounded them. There were far more of the vermin than there had been at the shrine. Norda figured their squeals had summoned reinforcements from nearby warrens.

In the center of the chamber, Findle and Darbin stood on either side of the terrified Hebbet, daggers in hand. Above them fluttered

Thistle, fingers dancing in fey gestures while she trilled spells of courage and protection. Wren covered a third side, holding a pair of leaf-scrolls ready to cast. Norda completed the circle, putting her back to the boy before saying, "Sorry, kid. This was supposed to be a rescue."

"I'm sorry," he said. "I'm sorry I'm sorry." He kept repeating himself until Darbin pressed a dagger into his hand.

"Don't make it easy for them," he said. "Slice any that get past me."

"Don't worry," Findle chimed in. "Nothing gets past Darbin."

The rat-people surged toward them. Wren read aloud from her leaf and thrust forth a hand, fingers spread. Dizzying colors shot forth in a cone and half a dozen rat-people tumbled backward, unconscious.

Above them, Thistle intoned a curse in her terrifying voice. One of the rat-priests cried out in defiance, then in horror, and finally in helplessness.

To the sides, the Wiseacres showed the rats just how quick they were, stabbing under their opponents' weapons while ducking their swift but clumsy attacks.

Norda caught a rat-man on her shield, pushing him back while she brained the next attacker with the cap of her axe-handle. He fell like a leaking sack of suet.

Another chorus of squeals rose among the rat-people. Norda felt the humorless grin of battle tighten her face. *A good start,* she thought, *to scare them so early in the fight.* Despite her courage, she knew it was only a matter of time before the rats overwhelmed them.

Instead, the rats scattered once again. To her shock, Norda saw another half-dozen dead on the ground, short arrows protruding from their bodies. She heard the twang of bowstrings she had missed in the earlier clamor, and three more fell as the rest fled.

Findle shouted, "They can't aim worth a rat's—!" A heavy blow from a rat-man's blade cut him off.

Wren cried the halfling's name and slapped a hand on his shoulder. A leather ring around her finger flickered with flame and vanished. The next rat blade to descend on Findle appeared at first to cut him but instead rang out on the stony floor a foot to his left.

Trusting Wren to protect Findle, Norda raised her shield to protect Hebbet from the next volley of arrows. When it came, however, none of the arrows fell near her group, only among the fleeing rats.

It was then that Norda realized they had allies as well as foes in the Undercity.

The lizard-people emerged from the shadows. One pointed an arrow directly at Norda, but one of his fellows pushed his bow aside. Norda recognized the scars on the second figure.

The lizard-man they had healed spoke, and Thistle translated. "Go now," he said. "Do not litter our territory with your corpses."

FILTHY AND EXHAUSTED, THEY EMERGED THROUGH THE same sewer grate they had entered. Shadows pooled in the alley as the setting sun colored the rooftops.

Norda hoisted Hebbet up to the street, where a few local residents saw them emerge, went inside, and closed their doors. Moments later, Norda saw some of them peering down at them through their windows.

Hebbet flopped on the cobblestones, exhausted more from terror than from their escape from the undercity. Unlike the boy, Wren and the Wiseacres seemed exhilarated by their near-death experience. Even Findle had regained his smile after Thistle mended the cut on his scalp. Wren punched Darbin in the arm. Darbin punched Findle. Findle made a fist to punch Wren but thought better of it and hugged her instead.

Thistle fluttered her wings, shaking off the damp of the sewers.

Norda shoved the heavy iron grate back over the sewer hole. "All right, kid," she said. "Tell us about how you stole this box."

Hebbet pushed himself up into a sitting position. His arms and legs were as thin as Myna's, his cheeks just as hollow with hunger. "I didn't steal it. I found it."

"A likely story," said Norda.

"Hmph!" agreed Wren.

"I believe him," said Findle.

"Me, too," said Darbin. "'Finding it' is how I get all my best stuff."

"It's true," said Hebbet. "One night, Myna and I climbed into an abandoned flat. It's dangerous for us to stay outside after dark."

A fair point, thought Norda. She couldn't understand how humans let their own kind, especially the children, fend for themselves on the streets. No dwarven community would allow that. If their parents had died, someone would have adopted them. "And you just happened to find a box in this flat?"

"Well, I did search the place. I hoped whoever had lived there hid some money or maybe something I could sell for food."

"So why didn't you sell it?"

"I tried, but the shop owners took one look and threw me out. Pretty soon I heard that someone else was looking for it. Somebody told them I had it, and we heard they were looking for me."

"Let me guess, a red-haired woman and a couple of big bruisers?"

Hebbet nodded "The only way I could get away was to climb down the sewer grate. The men were too big to come through the grate. I thought the woman would chase me, but she didn't. I figured I'd run as far through the sewers as I could go before coming up through another grate. When I came to a dead-end, I went down when I should have gone up. Pretty soon, the rat-people caught me. I think they were going to eat me!"

"Probably," agreed Darbin.

"Stop scaring him!" said Wren.

"You don't think they were going to eat me?" said Hebbet.

"Oh, of course they were. But he didn't need to say so."

"What's in the box?" said Norda.

"I didn't find a key," said Hebbet.

"There isn't even a lock," said Findle. He tried twisting gems and pressing the box's sides. His eyes widened in delight as he managed to shift a panel a few hairs' breadth.

"Let me try," said Darbin.

Findle elbowed him away. "Quit it! Look, this stone moves, now."

Together they made a little progress before their squabbling over who should hold the box set them back three or four steps. Norda suppressed an urge to snatch it out of their hands and figure it out herself.

Thistle trilled a warning and flew upward. Just as she reached the top of the second story, a fine mist formed between the roofs and solidified into a sheet of white threads. Thistle's trill turned into a sound of panic as her wings stuck in the sticky webs.

The orog's deep, wet chuckle rang down the lane. Norda looked back to see the brute hefting his studded club. Behind her, Darbin let go of the box, and both he and Findle produced their knives from under their waistcoats. Another leaf scroll in hand, Wren stood beside Hebbet, ready to cast a spell in either direction.

Norda turned to see the drothmal blocking the other end of the alley, weaponless but rubbing his knuckles in anticipation. Beside him strolled Haley, looking no taller than a child beside the barbarian. She had one arm curled around her spear, the other on the wand from whose tip trailed a wisp of gossamer.

"How did they find us so fast?" said Darbin.

"Now, now, little 'uns," Haley's voice came from down the lane, her drawl simultaneously seductive and threatening. "Didn't I warn you not to open that box? The second you touched it, my employers could tell just where you were. Besides, we already had a pretty good idea. They've had eyes on you all day."

Norda and the others looked around for a spy but saw no one else in the lane. Haley glanced upward. The weird-eyed spider crawled along the webs toward the trapped fairy. Once the size of Haley's hand, it had already grown bigger than a terrier. With every creeping step, it grew larger. Thistle's struggles grew more frantic.

The last of the spying locals slammed their shutters closed.

"I'd like to say we can do this the easy way," said Haley with a winsome smile. "But who'm I kidding? The whole reason I pay my boys is because they do things the hard way."

Norda wasn't distracted by Haley's banter. The second she heard the orog begin to charge, she whistled twice: the signal to fight. She reached out a hand to Findle and called, "Give me that!" He tossed her the box as his brother and he ran at the orog, crossing back and forth like the children chasing each other that morning.

Norda caught the box in one hand. Beside her, Wren was already casting a spell. The street in front of Haley and the drothmal cracked and yawned open.

"Nice try, cutie," said Haley. To the drothmal she said, "Go right over it. It's an illusion."

The tall barbarian strode forward, ignoring the chasm beneath him and tapping his fists together like a pair of quart milk jugs. Wren began casting another spell.

Behind her, Norda heard the stabbing sounds of the Wiseacre's daggers and the startled screams of the orog. She could almost picture the boys running up those tree-trunk legs and leaving red "tracks" in their paths, but she focused on the task at hand. There was one thing she knew Haley didn't want, and she hoped it would give them an edge.

"Hey, now. What do you think you're doing?" cried the woman as she saw Norda pressing panels and twisting stones on the box's surface.

Norda found another hidden panel that slid to the side while she depressed the second gem. She felt some mechanism beneath the lid move free. With her thumb, she lifted the lid up a hair's breadth.

"Something tells me you're afraid of what comes out when I open this box," said Norda. "Call off your boys and that ugly, ugly spider!"

"Wait a second!" cried Haley. "Don't anybody make any sudden—"

The orog roared. The drothmal hesitated. Haley's eyes went wide as she looked up. Norda followed the direction of her gaze and saw the hound-sized spider leaping down, eight hairy legs open wide to embrace her.

She fell back, mind reeling in fear at the sight of the dripping fangs between the spider's bristling palps. She raised the box in a feeble gesture to fend off the attack. She felt the mouth of the box open. She heard the screams of two men, a woman, and *something else*. The weight of the box doubled, doubled again, and slammed into her chest heavier than four bricks of gold.

The impact slammed the box shut once more. The spider was gone.

"No!" shouted Haley. "Now none of us will get paid, you little fool. You'd better hand that over right this inst—"

In an instant, the closed box felt the same weight it had before it swallowed the spider. Norda held it on the ground and raised her bladeless axe. "I don't suppose you'll ever get paid if I smash the box with the spider in it."

"Don't you hurt my critter!" Haley took a step back. When the drothmal beside her took a step forward, she rapped him on the shoulder with her spear and shook her head.

The Wiseacres ran ragged over the orog once more before dashing back to Norda's side. The brute roared and smashed cobblestones for half a minute before Haley's voice soothed him. "Come on, big fellow. We're going to get you patched up."

Norda noticed Hebbet cowering beside her, which she decided was the best place for him. She began to ask Wren whether she could free Thistle, but the sprite had already cast her spell. As the webs melted into nothingness, the fairy fluttered down, eyes bright with indignation.

"Here's what we're going to do," said Norda. "Take your boys back to where we met you. Tomorrow morning, if I'm in the mood, I'll come by to hear your new offer for retrieving this box."

"Same price?" said Haley.

Norda shook her head. "It was a big job."

The red-head nodded as if she'd expected that. "Say, double?"

"The problem with you," said Norda, "is you think too small."

"How much?"

"Sleep on it," said Norda. "But if these big lummoxes don't strain themselves carrying the gold, I don't think we'll have a deal."

Haley sighed. She opened her mouth to speak, but Norda cut her off. "Run along, now. You've got a lot of hauling to do before tomorrow morning."

They watched as Haley and her drothmal led the bleeding orog out of the lane. Thistle flew up to spy on them, ensuring they went back the way they'd come. When she signed the all-clear, Norda led them in the opposite direction.

"Where are we going?" Hebbet asked.

"First, we're going to find your sister," said Norda. "Then, while that spider-loving weirdo is gathering her cash, we make ourselves scarce."

"What about the money?" said Wren. "My tummy's rumbling."

Norda glanced back at the Wiseacres, who pretended not to

notice she was looking at them while suppressing smiles. They knew what she was about to say.

"First, we'll see what two silver can buy us," she said. She sighed. "Then we may need to bend a few rules."

A DEEPER DARKNESS

DAVID FARLAND

RAININ STRODE FROM THE INN INTO THE VILLAGE STREET to find a crowd of people gawking at his dragon. Immediately, he tightened its girth strap. The dragon's green scales glistened in the sun, but the beast felt hot, warmed by an inner fire. Its huge chest swelled as it breathed.

Rainin climbed on, adjusting the heavy crossbow that hung on the saddle behind him. As he looked out over the growing crowd, he did his best to conceal his shiver over the dark information he'd received inside.

The foul vapors from the vial the Elf queen's regent had shown him—what was it? It was neither vapor nor oil, but something between, and it had marvelous powers. It had given life to a piece of crockery, turned it into a monstrous creature that somehow moved without bone or sinew. The Elf regent had called the vial's contents "corruption," and Rainin would have thought it marvelous, perhaps even life-giving, but the regent had said that it had wiped out entire villages.

All the rules of nature were now called into question. Ice rippled down Rainin's spine.

He knew one thing for certain: the Elf Princess Mellienane was in trouble, and only he could save her.

More villagers emptied out of the tavern and crowded around the dragon, eager to see it ascend.

"Get back!" Standing next to his mount, Bolgrum stomped his feet, gave a dwarf's glare that would have soured cream, and shouted, "Back, damn you! Give the lizard some room!"

The crowd responded slowly. Everyone wanted to be in the front row for the spectacle.

Rainin sat in his saddle, tried to stop his head from spinning. After ten days of saving villages from orcs, he felt exhausted. The world needed more dragonriders.

When the crowd had backed off enough, Bolgrum turned back to him. "Sure you don't want me to come? You could use a little backup."

Had the Dwarf actually made a joke about his size? That seemed unlikely.

Rainin shook his head. "Shofarun can't carry a pair of riders for long. I'll need room for the princess."

Bolgrum gave him an appraising look. "I mistrust this," he said. "Whatever you're going to face in that damned prison, you're not ready for it."

"Don't worry." Rainin shrugged. "Dragonriders are immortal."

"So I've heard," Bolgrum said sourly. "That's why one hasn't walked the earth in two thousand years, and now they're all eating dirt and breathing worms."

"I'll get by." Rainin tried to sound positive.

"You're no hero yet, boy," Bolgrum grumbled. "Don't put that immortality theory of yours to the test. Sure, you might rise from the dead once or twice, but no one knows for sure how many chances you get."

"I'll be careful."

"In battle," Bolgrum said, "being careful isn't always advisable." The dwarf was a full-blown Selenthean Knight, and now he talked like a drill sergeant. "Sometimes caution is warranted, but more often you must be bold. You'll need to be *perfect*, boy. You don't get a second chance if a blow is clumsy, or if you let your guard fall. Remember, a small Orc will come in low, try to disembowel you or take off a leg. What good would being immortal do you if you've got no more than stumps for legs?"

Rainin was no swordsman yet. He hadn't even begun training when the orcs had swarmed over Corwell. Two weeks ago, he'd been a farmer. He wasn't the hero everyone imagined him to be.

Rainin gave a nod. "Thank you, my friend," he said, then spurred his dragon to launch with a bump of his heels. "Up, dragon!" he called, snapping the reins.

The lizard just sat, its neck drooping like a wilted flower.

A couple of peasants smirked, and a maiden tittered.

Rainin spurred harder, shook the reigns angrily, but nothing happened. "Come on, Shofarun!"

One young lad, no more than six, asked, "Do you even know how to ride that thing?"

A dozen people guffawed.

"It's not as easy as it looks," Rainin apologized.

Finally the dragon's head wheeled, slowly, to look at Rainin. One golden eye, with its long, black slit of an iris, peered at him.

Rainin wondered why the beast wouldn't take off. He glanced at the sky, clear and full of golden sun. The wind wasn't contrary. Nothing else flew nearby that might frighten the beast.

Like Rainin, perhaps the dragon was just exhausted.

Rainin decided to try to coax the big lizard. "I'm sorry,

Shofarun," Rainin apologized. "We're both worn to the bone. Let's go save this princess, and when we're done I'll let you eat a nice, fat peasant—maybe that mouthy kid."

The mouthy peasant boy backed into the crowd, eyes wide.

The dragon peered hard at Rainin, as if it understood him. It glanced at the peasant boy, and a long, purple tongue flicked out, tasting the air. The boy turned and ran.

Ancient tales said dragonriders learned to speak dragon over time. Others suggested that the minds of the dragon and the rider formed some sort of bond. Surely Shofarun understood the gist of what Rainin wanted.

The ground suddenly trembled, an aftershock from the quakes that had struck ten days before.

That seemed to frighten the beast. Shofarun spread his wings, ran three steps, flapped hard twice, and vaulted over the thatched roof of the nearest cottage. From there the serpent lugged Rainin into the sky like a fat bumblebee carrying too much pollen.

SHOFARUN ROSE SLOWLY, WITH LANGUID WING-BEATS, as they climbed above a patchwork of fields, then headed toward the red mountains. The river valleys here were lush, and the mountains beyond held oaks and ash, maple and pine.

The afternoon sun created thermals rising up from the hills, and Shofarun rode them, gliding over the land. A warm wind buffeted Rainin's face, parching his lips and making his hair stream out behind him.

The view was grand. The land below became a tumble of foothills building up to the forested mountains, with a lonely caravan track winding through a canyon. But off to his right, Rainin spotted signs of recent destruction.

A fault had opened in the earth, a crack that zigzagged about fifty miles in both directions. A chasm had formed, perhaps a mile across. Its depth was not guessable.

Water had rushed in from the sea, more than four hundred miles to the southeast, and filled the chasm. Steam still rose from it in many places, where thermal vents heated the seawater.

Rainin flew above the chasm and spotted a group of dwarven miners below, searching for ore in the newly exposed rock.

New mines, he thought. *They could be a boon for our people. And having the sea here, someday you'll be able to fish in this chasm.*

To the north, he could see a second smaller chasm. There were several criss-crossing the area now.

The Atlans said that "Change brings opportunity," but Rainin could not see much of an upside to this tragedy. The chaos that had resulted might require decades to bring to a semblance of order.

He wondered again at the dark storms sweeping the land, at the vial of inky air/not-air from that storm the Elf regent had opened.

These two things are related, a voice in the back of his mind seemed to warn. *The massive quakes, the dark storm. This is an attack, one like no other.*

And I'm going to meet the attacker, Rainin thought. He could sense dark spirits around him, feel the creeping chill, a foreboding of death. *What chance do I stand?*

Perhaps none.

Rainin had gotten a good look at the Enaros that had raised him from the dead. He was tall and handsome, dark of hair with sea-green eyes, but frankly seemed bored, as if hoping Rainin might provide some amusement. Or maybe Rainin had a purpose to fulfill. Perhaps that was why the dragonriders had all died. They'd fulfilled all their quests, met all their goals.

He could imagine his Enaros yawning as he said, "Congratulations on a job well done. Rest in peace."

Perhaps that was Rainin's goal in life, to do a job well, to earn an eternal rest.

"Now is as good a day as ever," he told himself.

A peak reared up ahead, old gray rock stretching above the tree line. He banked Shofarun to the left, so the dragon could fly around it rather than labor to go over.

Thinking about rewards reminded Rainin that the Elf regent had not mentioned what reward he might receive for saving the Princess Mellienane. In the old tales, if a man saved a princess, he got to marry her.

That was out of the question here, of course. Rainin wouldn't dare beg for so much as a kiss.

A sword, he decided. *I'll want a sword with a name, like the ones from legend.* Thrallguld had been a great sword, sharp enough to slice through a hill giant's armor. The Dwarf Farodum the Greedy had forged the blade, tempering it in the blood of Orcs and Goblins, so that it would learn to love the taste. Runic spells had been engraved along the blade by seven wizards, to bless the wielder's aim, strengthen his arm, sharpen his wits, speed his blows. The Elves had woven its scabbard from ghostly green fire and maiden's hair, bound with the will of Mad Queen Taelenas. Any blade kept within that sheath would burst into emerald flames when drawn.

Such a sword would be handy for defending atlan lands. Of course, Rainin knew he wasn't worthy of a sword with a name. A sword like that belonged in the hands of a master, not some hopeful boy.

After a long flight, Shoforun lugged them up over one final ridge. Beyond lay a vista of rolling farmland, with an ancient river twining lazily across it.

The orc prison was easy to spot in the distance; its bulky towers sprawling as it drifted over an old lake. It was like a spider, gray and many-legged, floating atop the surface of a still pool.

Like something from the Deeplands brought to the surface. A cold dread took Rainin, that thrill that crept up the spine. Something terrible lurked there.

Its daylight, he thought. *Let's hope the orcs are still deep asleep.*

As if in answer to his hopes, a war horn sounded from the prison, a bellow of challenge.

THE WAR HORN SOUNDED, LONG AND LOW, REVERBERATING through the dark prison like the bellow of a lonely lagoran calling out over a misty lake.

The Orc Lord Ummash Gasht sprang from the floor, instantly awake, and drew his battle-axe, gripping it in a right hand so strong it would have crushed a wooden haft, but his was made of iron. He balanced on the balls of his feet, squinting into the darkness, sniffing for danger.

At his side hung his left hand, unfeeling, a thing half tree-branch. During the night, it had sprouted new leaves.

Around him, other orcs lay in snoring heaps.

"Up, you dog vomit!" Ummash Gasht growled. He kicked the nearest one hard enough to crack a rib.

"Just a drill," the orc groaned, rolling over to sleep.

Ummash Gasht grabbed the small, spotted orc by his top-knot, lifted him in the air and asked, "How can a true Orc sleep with even the *hope* of battle?" He hurled the other man away as if he were food for the wargs.

Probably *was* just a drill. Their prison, Tortured Souls, floated free as a cloud above the lake ever since that damned storm last week. The roiling wall of oily vapors had come, with macabre purple lightning flashing all around, and when it hit the prison, high upon its mountain perch, the prison had broken free.

Now Ummash Gasht was as much a prisoner as his inmates. The only way off this rock was a very long drop into very deep, cold water.

He squinted at the other Orcs. Overhead, bats squeaked in the shadows. A bit of guano splattered on the steel of his epaulets. Ummash Gasht tried to wipe it off, but it just spread like snot.

The door to the sleeping quarters slammed open, and Warlord Gososs bellowed, "Up, up! We're under attack!"

Ah, how Ummash Gasht longed for a good battle! But what could attack them up here?

"Wyverns?" he asked. "Harpies?"

"A dragonrider," Gososs shouted. "To your posts! The orc who brings me his head will win breeding rights. Three litters you shall sire!"

The now wide-awake orcs all roared in excitement, grabbed their weapons and shields.

Ummash Gasht did not need time to prepare. He always slept in his armor, weapon in hand. He charged from the room, sprinting through the halls of the dungeon, his iron shoes ringing on cold stone. The place smelled of torture—of seared flesh and sweat and fiery tongs. The scent made him drool. As he passed one chamber, he heard the sweet sobbing of a child.

The war horn sounded again and again, insistent, goading.

He raced to his post at the Elven woman's door, peeked in through a grilled window to see the Princess Mellienane, a thin waif, asleep on the stone floor.

He leered at her naked form. He was not attracted to Elves, but he loved tormenting them. They were so smug.

He squatted into a battle stance, waiting. With his "wounded" left hand, he could no longer hold a shield. During the storm, he'd been touched by the vapors, some of which still roamed the prison, as alive as any animal. His entire arm had turned as stiff as a log and grown a strange green, papery bark. Each day it sprouted new leaves, and he picked them off, as if pulling big, nasty hairs.

He felt self-conscious, but several other orcs carried similar wounds. He had not yet been relieved of his post due to his arm, and for that he was proud.

His post was an honored position. Being an orc prison guard was lucrative. There was good money in kidnapping, especially atlans. Each orc "owned" a prisoner or two. They could be sold to other beings from the Deeplands, either as slaves or for food. Wealthy merchants, lords, dignitaries— none were safe. There were dozens of ways to make money off the atlans.

But this Elven princess wasn't Ummash Gasht's captive—not exactly. More than a week ago, a *creature* had brought her into the prison, a being without name, a mere shadow.

It had carried her through the prison, floating past stunned Orc guards so terrified they'd soiled themselves. As it reached a portcullis, the barred gate silently raised. When it came to a door, it swung inward.

The creature had no form, but wore a hooded cape of black over ornate armor, enameled in a shade darker than night.

It had laid the sleeping princess in this cell, let the door swing closed, and then turned to Ummash Gasht.

"Keep her well," a deep voice had warned in his mind, *"and great shall be your reward."*

At that point, the creature had simply disappeared, its cape and armor clattering to the stone floor.

Its robes and armor still lay in a corner. Ummash Gasht had used his toe to shove them into a pile by the door. The thought of picking through the precious armor to salvage it unnerved him.

Why? Because somehow the owner was still here. There was a coldness in the air, a constant chill hovering over Tortured Souls. It was as if the creature were circling in the air, waiting. Just thinking about it made a shiver creep down Ummash Gasht's broad back.

Warlord Gososs had immediately put him in charge of the new prisoner, claiming it was a great honor. The big orc wasn't fooled, however—if anything happened to the elf princess, Gososs would offer him as a scapegoat to the shadowthing in a heartbeat.

Ummash Gasht shook off his shivers. Far away, Orcs snarled as they lumbered to their posts. Their warlord's orders were lost in dim echoes.

In the distance, outside, the war horn continued to bellow.

He began reciting the Warrior's Creed under his breath, an ancient war chant:

"War is beauty, and beauty is war!
"With the ax, weak Orcs are hacked down.
"With the hammer, clumsy Orc are pounded into dust.
"With the spear, the fools among us are purged.
"Thus the best survive, and least are culled.
"Long may we live at war!
"For in war is beauty, and beauty is war."

A battle rage washed through him, sounds fading as a blood-red haze settled over the world like a fog. Ummash Gasht smiled, and as his lips drew back, his yellow tusks protruded.

He was a true orc, and until a few days ago had been flawless, a full twenty stone of brutality, not a frail, spotted orc. At his birth, the Glory Hag of the Kargoss Zur Clan had inspected all eight orcs in his litter. The runt, of course, had been summarily hurled into the fire, as was the custom. Sometimes Ummash Gasht could still hear its death cries. That was the price that came with imperfection.

He'd been scrutinized as well: fingers and toes counted, budding tusks checked, testicles examined. He'd been examined for every weakness. He'd had none. Until this *wound.* For the thousandth time, he cursed his curiosity. He'd merely touched the vapors, probing them.

Could have been worse, he thought. One orc had been enveloped by the vapors, and had turned into…a creature covered with 113 eyes that could not blink, only stare. The staring eyes could not see or water. They grew red and dry, itching, driving the poor orc mad until he sat and pulled each one out.

In the shadows of the cell, the Elven princess stirred. She roused, lifted her pale face, and peered at Ummash Gasht.

"Gar-gurzick ky!" *Flee this place,* she urged in a whisper. She spoke Orc in an archaic form, her Elven voice lending the words a musical tone that made them hard to understand. "A winged fury comes, a dragonrider who shall bring death to you all. I dreamt it. I dreamt of your head rolling across the floor."

"Shut your hole," Ummash Gasht growled. "You Elves all *want* us dead."

"Some do. Most call you unredeemable," Mellienane agreed. "I don't. I know you were once made from good beings."

She had spoken gently to him since she'd awakened, only yesterday, when he allowed her to speak at all.

She urged, "My father showed me in a dream: a dragonrider comes. Give him what he wants, and he'll depart in peace. I'll beg him to spare you. You know what he wants…."

For one second, Ummash Gasht froze.

"Spare me?" Ummash Gasht asked. "Why would you want to spare me? I have shown you no kindness."

"I cannot control how others act, but I can control how I act toward them. I can be a force for good, even in the face of hatred."

Ummash Gasht thought about that. It was an intriguing concept.

She continued, "I have studied orcs my whole life. I have learned a great deal about your people. Your...wound will make you a pariah among them. But among mine you could become a friend. You could have a home, a family."

Ummush Gasht laughed. She had intrigued him, but he wasn't going to fall for her schemes. "Clever woman. You can't escape. You can't kill us. So you hope to cripple us with doubt and fear, and let your friend finish us off."

By the way his heart pounded, Ummash Gasht knew her plan was working. A frightened orc is a hesitant orc, and a hesitant orc will wind up dead.

But he was faster and stronger than any human or elf would imagine.

"I do not want you to be afraid," she countered. "I want you to live. All life is precious, including an orc's." She spoke insistently, as if she really meant it. "You were quoting Gothmarl, an ancient Orc philosopher, just now. Three thousand years ago, he dreamt of creating a new breed of Orcs, a better race. He wanted your people to become clever and strong, so he sent them to war: men, women, children. His plan worked. The weak were culled. Now, you Orcs *are* all clever and strong. The need for wars has ceased. The time has come for you to return to the Enari races, to reconcile with the Dwarves, from whom you were corrupted."

Ummash Gasht glared at her. She held her right hand to cover her breasts, and she had retreated to the farthest shadows of her cell, but her face was full of...something he had not seen before. Longing, compassion, admiration.

She peered at him the way his mother had, full of pride.

He'd heard talk like this before, from the reviled and feared orc priests of the Purple Moon Clan. They also spouted this nonsense about peace and brotherhood and Orcs returning to the Enari races. Ummash Gasht—along with most other orcs—thought of them as a mad cult. Didn't they see? Peace would only bring weakness, a slow slide into cultural decay.

The princess just stared at him now. Ummash Gasht turned his back.

"Please, don't turn your back on me," she begged.

"I have my orders," Ummash Gasht said. He would not listen to a prisoner.

"But who gave you those orders, and why?" she asked. "I have fostered friends among the orcs my entire life. The ones you and the rest of your people hate and have cast out, because they dare to look forward instead of back. I have sent delegates to all of the tribes. If I die in an orc prison, who stands to gain from it?"

Ummash Gasht wondered at that. Why had the shadow brought her here? Was it to win some concession, to hold her hostage, or to pour fuel on the fires of war?

The truth was, he didn't know.

She took a different tact, her tone urgent. "There is no escape from this prison for you," she said. "Even if you win this fight, you'll starve here."

"Not so long as there are prisoners to eat," Ummash Gasht growled. He was hungry. The prisoner they'd roasted last night had been…tough and stringy.

When the prisoners were gone, he'd have to begin eating other orcs. Already he had started making a list.

Outside the prison, the war horn bellowed, and an orc roared a challenge.

BOLGRUM HAD TOLD RAININ TALES OF ORC PRISONS.

Tortured Souls, Rainin realized as his dragon neared, was not your typical orc prison. The soaring architecture of the place, and its faded looks, suggested that it might have been a mountain fortress once, built by the men of Valnor. It had probably been abandoned some three hundred years ago, to become a forgotten ruin until some cunning orcs had turned it to their vile purposes.

As he neared, he felt his innards go cold. Ever since his death and encounters on the spirit plane, Rainin had become more sensitive to the presence of unseen forces. The prison was gray, its recesses shadowed, but it concealed an even deeper darkness within.

Orcs raced to their ballistae, rushing to their guard posts, like cockroaches disturbed from their hiding places, scurrying into the light.

Loaded crossbow in hand, Rainin circled the prison, staying out of bowshot, and searched for a place to land Shofarun. There's wasn't any easy access, just a broken section of the castle's old Great Hall, with its stone walls and massive planks for flooring.

Rainin wheeled Shofarun, putting his back to the sun, then began his descent. A fiery ballista bolt roared past as some poor, sun-blinded orc wasted a bolt.

As the dragon neared the castle, Rainin heard the *thunk* of a crossbow. He ducked just in time to have the bolt slam into his helm and ricochet off.

A sitting target is an easy target.

As Shofarun approached the ground, two more crossbow bolts zipped past him. Rainin leapt from his dragon's back while still twenty feet in the air.

A drop of twenty feet doesn't look like much, but a commoner would have shattered his legs. Yet ever since his resurrection, Rainin found his body could absorb a lot of damage. The landing sent a jolt of pain through his calves and back, but it was a pain he could deal with.

He spotted an opening into a sunlit court through the old castle gates ahead, and raced toward it.

An orc charged from a doorway across the court, fumbling with his crossbow. It was a tusker, a green-gray beast with four tusks instead of two. The overlarge tusks looked like those of a warthog.

Just such an orc had taken his head in the grim battle at Corwell. It was just such orcs that had wiped out his city, hacked his sister to pieces, lopped off his mother's arms and left her to bleed out.

Rainin swung his crossbow up, fired. A stream of bright flames raced out, trailing clouds of black smoke as the bolt struck the orc square in the chest. The tusker exploded. Ragged bits of meat rained everywhere.

Rainin thundered past the corpse, his feet slipping in the gore. *Shouldn't have wasted a flame bolt on one inept tusker,* he realized. *Not when there's darker things ahead.*

He raced for the shadowed doorway ahead. Surely it would lead into the depths of the prison…

"YOU CAN'T WIN," MELLIENANE WARNED UMMASH GASHT. He still stood with his back to her.

At eighteen, she was nearly full-grown for an elf, and was gaining some ability with magic. She'd have cast a spell to take control of his mind, but she was imprisoned by more than iron bars. The very thought of casting a spell somehow sapped her energy, as did thoughts of escape.

"Ummash Gasht," she urged, hoping that he would be swayed by the sound of his own name. "Come with us, and *live.*"

He wheeled around at her, his tusks bared. His eyes had gone red with a battle rage.

A fiery blast shook the prison. Her rescuer was approaching…

RAININ CHARGED THROUGH A SMALL DOORWAY INTO the prison, and dodged left, placing a stone wall behind him. He squinted into the darkness ahead, seeing nothing more than a shadowy hall, and waited for his eyes to adjust. He grabbed another crossbow bolt, loaded it into his bow by touch.

His heart hammered. He could feel a shadow over this prison, something cold and slimy. Not orcs. Something far worse. It sensed him now, and began to draw near.

But a man could not see such creatures with his physical eyes, and Rainin was no spiritual master. He knew the enemy was at hand, but could only sense its presence.

Orc prisons were deathtraps, he knew, rife with kill-holes orcs could shoot from or thrust spears through. He wasn't sure he if should try to creep about or just charge through the place.

He recalled Bolgrum's warning: Sometimes being too careful is what could get you killed.

Speed, daring, he decided. *I'm a dragonrider now. Let* them *fear* me.

It was a ludicrous attitude for someone so inept at battle. In a moment of clarity, Rainin realized, *I'm going to get my head chopped off—again!*

He crouched low, caught his breath, and found his vision had cleared a bit. The orcs used no lights in this prison. Only the thinnest rays of daylight filtering through the windows in the cell doors lit his way.

Rainin sprinted down the hall, glimpsed suspicious holes in the wall. Almost immediately he heard a bow twang behind him and an arrow snick the stone wall to his right, a clean miss.

He stutter-stepped, and another bow fired just ahead. Rainin ran to a closed door and hit it with his shoulder. It was a stout door, and two weeks ago he would have broken bones. Instead, the door shattered.

Just beyond it stood a portcullis, a wooden gate bound with iron that had been lowered from the ceiling. Beyond the portcullis were shadowy orcs, a band of them.

"Let's light this place up!" Rainin shouted, raising his crossbow and firing into the dark. The flames that leapt from it flared, and he saw the shocked and terrified faces of half a dozen orcs.

One was a monster with three goat-like heads.

Of course, Rainin realized. *The corrupting fog touched this place. It's surprising that any of them survived.*

His bolt blasted into the gate, obliterating it, and pieces of wood and huge iron bolts exploded into the orcs, killing some, wounding others. The flaming debris lit the hall nicely.

Rainin drew his ax and leapt in among the orcs.

One tusker lurched into battle, a huge hammer in hand, but the speed and brutality of Rainin's attack had left it stunned. The creature roared, and the odor of its breath was astonishing, a mixture of sewers, rotten teeth, and death.

Rainin swung quickly, relieving the creature of its head. "There you are," he shouted, "a permanent cure for foul breath!"

A well-aimed spear was thrust at him, and Rainin leaned away, swung in the "Wall of Steel" style, and hacked off the wielder's arm. He had no time to marvel at how well his resurrected body fought, as more enraged orcs stampeded toward him.

Two more orcs lunged at him, and Rainin fell into the red haze of battle, swinging his ax with cold precision and insane speed.

Soon, the knot of orcs were struggling to escape his deadly reach, clutching bloody stumps or coughing up blood as they tried to flee.

Rainin swung again and again raining death-blows upon every orc within reach. He took one head from the goat-monster.

This is only the beginning, some part of his consciousness realized.

The outer guards are always riffraff. The real danger still lurks below...

Rainin cleared a trail through the Orcs, seized a burning brand of wood, and lunged forward.

Past the guardroom, the passageway split. He took the path to the right and reached a huge door, barred from the outside. He lifted the bar, shoved the door open. Warm air, stale and fetid, gushed out.

The enormous chamber was filled with implements of torture: bloody tables fitted with manacles, racks, a firepit, a drowning pool. One entire wall was hung with saws, cleavers, tongs, and knives.

The place felt quiet as a tomb, and smelled of putrefaction. It had been abandoned. His little light could not reach all the way across, it seemed, for the far corners seemed unnaturally dark.

Then, in the far left corner of the room, the shadows moved.

No, it's not that my torch can't pierce the darkness, he realized. Something is *living* here!

An oily vapor crawled over the floor like a fog. It lurched forward, then slithered to the side.

Nothing natural moved like that.

Thrusting his torch forward, Rainin began backing away slowly, as one would when facing a bear. He wanted to get away quietly. But the oily fog slithered toward him.

He knew not to touch it, but could not move quickly enough. The vapors roiled together and lunged at him.

Rainin lurched backward, but the fog wrapped about him like a boa constrictor, entangling his legs, wrapping his torso, tightening around his muscular arms, coiling up his neck.

He beat at it with his torch, but the flame did not faze the creature.

It began to strangle him. He opened his mouth to gasp, and the darkness forced itself into his mouth, its coldness a thick, blunt object piercing his throat.

"No!" he tried to cry, but gagged on the word. He did not want to be corrupted.

Then the darkness slid inside him, filling him with an iciness colder than any tomb…

"THE DRAGONRIDER WHO COMES," MELLIENANE URGED Ummash Gasht, "you know what kind of man he will be. In ancient times, the Enaros bestowed this gift only upon the bravest of the brave, the strongest of the strong, the wisest of the wise…"

There was only the dimmest glimmer of interest in her guard's eyes. He hadn't known this, and did not care.

"He will be blessed with tremendous strength and speed, like warriors only in legend."

Undaunted, Ummash Gasht grinned at the thought of facing such a challenge.

She continued. "The dragonrider will most likely be one of my mother's personal guard. You are stronger than any Elf, this I grant. You may even be stronger than him. But your people hardly live much longer than a bull. You've trained for battle for six or seven years, perhaps. In our realms, an Elf cannot become a queen's guard until he has trained for *one hundred* years. You have strength on your side, but your nemesis will have skills that you cannot comprehend."

The orc turned to her. He was a massive thing. "My ax will split him like kindling. And when I am done with him, I will have sow orcs to ride, and litters to spawn. As I do, I will suck the marrow from his bones, and drink from the hollow of his skull."

What Mellienane saw in his flat gaze terrified her. He was indeed the largest orc she had ever seen, and he could slip into a berserker's frenzy as easily as she could don a cape. There was no mercy or compassion in those eyes.

When the philosopher Gothmarl had spouted his plan to purify the orc race, she thought, *had he ever imagined he would create something so feral? All empathy was gone from this creature, all reason.*

The Prophetess Tintarriel, an Elven mage great in age and insight, had said it best: *"Over the past two thousand years the Orcs have become great warriors, strong and fierce, but with tiny souls. Weep for them. They have gained the form of giants, but with the understanding of infants. They* might still *become our equals one day. But Gothmarl has made vicious, bloodthirsty monsters of them all."*

And here, now, Mellienane finally grasped the true meaning of the Elven mage's words.

A second explosion rocked the prison, much closer this time. The boom echoed through the stone walls, and bits of plaster fell from the ceiling.

Mellienane crept forward to the grilled window, and pleaded, "Ummash Gasht, you are a superb orc. You could be great. I do not wish for your death."

The monster whirled, striking faster than a serpent. She'd never imagined that this Orc, that *any* creature could move so quickly. He leapt, his blurred fist rushing through the iron bars at her face.

Lights exploded behind her eyes, and the only sound was a dull roar…

FOR WHAT SEEMED AN ETERNITY, RAININ CHOKED ON THE darkness. He felt ice crystals forming in his lungs, reaching into his innards, quenching his inner fires, until everything grew cold.

Fear took him, fear of what he might become. A monster with three goat-heads? A dead thing with yellow eyes and rot upon his skin? A dream, an ash?

He grunted, and expelled his air with a gasp, coughing out the darkness. To his surprise, it seemed to leave. The shadow floated out of his mouth, slithering across the room, half-liquid, half-vapor.

Rainin looked down. His hands and body were unchanged, and for that he felt relieved, yet the coldness inside him lingered.

He felt *wrong*.

It has taken my soul, he feared. *Or altered it*.

He stood for a moment, then backed out the door, and barred the room from the outside. He hoped the coldness he felt was just a lingering thing. That in time it would recede.

Rainin stalked down the hallway, into a corridor lined with cells. He raced forward boldly, spotted a guard around a corner, and dispatched the creature. Further ahead, another tusker guarded the door.

Rainin raced to each orc, dispatching one after another as he cleared out the dungeon, but he felt empty. No joy, no fear, no thrill of battle.

Yet something *had* changed. Deep inside there was a stirring. The vague fear that had been troubling him, the sense that he was being watched and dissected from afar, had become keener than ever. He could almost close his eyes and point toward the heart of darkness. It was somewhere ahead, and equally somewhere inside.

Did I defeat the creature of chaos? he wondered, *Or have I become it?*

MELLIENANE FOUND HERSELF ON THE FLOOR, STRUGGLING to rouse herself. The room spun, and blood poured from her nose and mouth. She gagged on it, coughed out red. Her face felt numb, yet stung at the same time.

She climbed to her hands and knees, squinting as she tried to see anything at all.

At the end of the hallway, a door swung open, and a muscular altan stood, holding a bit of burning debris in his left hand to light his way, gripping a bloody ax in his right.

UMMASH GASHT PEERED AT THE YOUNG DRAGONRIDER, and instantly he felt afraid. The altan had just come from the old torture room, the forbidden room, where the vapors lingered. More than that, a darkness wreathed the dragonrider, coiled about him, and there was a crazed gleam in his eyes.

He has become a monster, Ummash Gasht realized, *like the rest of us.*

Maybe the Elf woman is right, Ummash Gasht considered. *Maybe I should make a deal.*

The dragonrider gave him a fey smile and said something in his rough altan tongue. He raced forward, his ax held in one hand.

Ummash Gasht leapt in the air, whirled, and swung for the dragonrider's torso.

His ax met only empty air as the altan leapt high. Suddenly the dragonrider was swinging downward.

Ummash Gasht raised his accursed left arm overhead, and the ax bit into it with a solid thunk. Bits of bark and wood flew up, and Ummash Gasht felt the blow as if cold teeth had bitten into him.

He screamed, rammed his head forward, and butted the man, hurling him backward. The blow would have killed any normal being, but the dragonrider merely slammed backward into the stone wall.

The little creature laughed grimly. He'd managed to hold onto his ax.

"Ummash Gasht, stop this madness!" the princess begged.

For just an instant, Ummash Gasht considered. He had never been a philosopher. He was a warrior, and as such he left his thinking for those higher up.

But what had that gotten him?

What was the price for blind obedience?

Deep in his heart, he knew the answer: *It makes you the tool of another.*

Ummash Gasht did not want to be the tool of some Elven princess, nor did he want to be the tool of Warlord Gososs.

For just an instant, he stood poised between the two, and his heart cried out, *I shall do what* I *want to do.*

In that moment, he was free.

Before he could act on the impulse, the dragonrider leapt and swung with furious speed.

UMMASH GASHT'S HEAD ROLLED ACROSS THE FLOOR AND thumped against the door of Mellienane's cell. The orc's body sagged to the floor.

The altan dragonrider swung his ax down on the lock to her cell, breaking it. He wrenched the door open and bowed deeply, thus averting his eyes from her nude form. "A gift, milady. One less orc to trouble you."

With one hand, the dragonrider unclasped his red cape, doffed it from his shoulders, and tossed it to her. He turned away as she wrapped the oversized garment around her shoulders.

"He was no trouble," she said in his tongue. "I believe that my gentle words went to his heart at the end." She felt saddened, defeated in a way that she had not imagined, even though she had regained her freedom.

The warrior bowed deeper, as if in apology. "Your Highness, your dragon awaits. May I suggest that we leave before more Orcs come?"

Very lightly, freed from the confines of the cell, she stepped over Ummash Gasht's corpse.

But before she could move another step, an icy wind swept

through the dungeon. She sensed a malevolent presence, just as she had on the night she was captured.

In a nearby corner, a pile of armor suddenly pieced itself together and rose. A black robe wrapped over the armor, and its hood filled only with a deeper shadow.

Mellienane tried to sound brave as she called out, "What do you want?"

The shadow creature raised a gloved hand, and pointed at Rainin.

"SO WE MEET," A DEEP VOICE WHISPERED IN RAININ'S MIND. It shook him to the bones. *"I felt your presence from the Undercity of Norentor."*

Rainin felt the vapor creature inside, still writhing. It was as if a worm inhabited him, and it was turning, turning, struggling to take control.

Yes, the dark creature was in front of him, and inside him.

"I feel you, too, stranger," Rainin answered, "and it isn't a good feeling at all."

"Then you shall know me, and die," the creature said. It pointed its gloved fist and squeezed.

Rainin felt something coiling inside, tightening around his heart, and he gasped in pain.

In that moment he saw the inside of the creature's mind. For eons it had lived in the deepest darkness, far beyond the world of Aetaltis, in the abyss between the stars. Forever it had wanted to come to a world like this, but had been denied by greater powers.

Then something had breached Aetaltis's defenses, and this creature had broken into the world.

Rainin gripped the handle of his ax as he sank, and with all of his might he willed himself forward. But his legs would not carry him. His heart would not beat. He tried to gasp for air.

The creature was afraid of light, and Rainin had only one feeble light. The makeshift torch sputtered, hardly more than a candle's worth of flame, but he snatched it from the princess and hurled it at the shadow.

The makeshift torch flew a few feet, then guttered out as a gale arose from nowhere. Rainin dropped to the ground, struggling for air.

As he approached death, his vision shifted, and he could see into the spirit realm, the blackness that was the shadow, the complexity of his own spirit.

"Dragonrider!" Mellienane called, but he could not answer. He could not save her. He turned to look at her.

In that instant, she strode forward and threw open his cape to stand naked before him. Then she did something that he had only heard of in rumor. She uncloaked fully, took down the shield that hid her spirit from view.

Blinding lights blazed in the darkness, as bright as any star. There were whites as pure as the sun upon snow, and blues fiercer than summer skies. There were reds like a furnace, and greens that put grass to shame.

She was drawing upon the powers that her mother had possessed in life, becoming a queen.

"*NO!*" the shadow cried, and in that instant it was stunned. The glory veiled by Mellienane's flesh struck it like a mighty fist, and the creature reeled from the blow. It did not just stagger.

It fell back, receding with a speed that the mortal mind could not quite fathom. It raced away, as fast as light, and Rainin could feel the creature receding, not just from the room, but from within him.

The snake that coiled around his heart burned away, and in that instant Rainin was freed. Fire seemed to rage through him, as warm and as comforting as a hearth in midwinter.

He peered up from the floor at Mellienane, seeing only her spirit. For one moment she peered down at him, and he felt more than saw her smile.

"Well met, Rainin of Corwell," she whispered. "You have a good spirit, and strong."

Her own spirit was glorious, much like his, and he sensed how difficult it was for her to show herself this way, to stand naked before him in body and soul.

She did not know his past. She had not seen how he'd died at Corwell, defending his family and his town, when all other defenders had fled. But she seemed to sense it, and approved.

He had come with only one purpose in mind. He needed to save someone. He yearned for it, the way that a heart yearns to beat, the way a dying man craves air.

"You saved me," Mellienane whispered. And with those words, she saved him, too.

MINUTES LATER, BEFORE THE SUN COULD SET OVER THE ruddy hills, Rainin and Mellienane climbed upon the back of Shofarun, and the dragon soared across the land, bearing them homeward.

NEVER A MOON SO BRIGHT

ELAINE CUNNINGHAM

MANY A SHOPKEEPER IN SELENTHEA HARBORS A CAT OR two. Here at Oxamia's Outfitters, I have eleven, and every one of the furry little bastards dived under the counter when the elf walked in.

He arched one golden eyebrow, and his pretty face took on that pinched look people get when they're in need of stewed prunes. "One day, Oxamia, you will tell me how you trained them to do that."

I poured two shots of Numos Nectar into glass thumbkins and pushed one across the counter. "Some mysteries lie beyond your reach, Ellisar. Might as well accept it."

We tapped glasses and drank. He tapped a mite harder than necessary, as if to let me know that Ellisar Divanthian, Lord High Warden of the Silver Tower, was not on board with *that* notion.

By now, you're probably thinking I have no good opinion of Ellisar. Fact is, I do. For what it's worth, I like most elves. Didn't much used to, but then one day it occurred to me that they weren't all that different from cats. Try picturing elves with fur and a tail, and they'll start making a whole lot more sense to you.

Of course, there are a few important dissimilarities. Cats, as a rule, are smart enough to avoid the sort of magic Ellisar came here seeking.

Not being one for small talk, the elf put down his glass and went straight for the table where my latest purchases were laid out for his inspection.

Like most outfitters, I carry all the supplies adventurers need to get them where they aim to go and to kill whatever might need killing along the way. I'm one of the few outfitters—the only one in Selenthea, last I checked—who will also buy and sell damn near everything adventurers bring back to the city. My specialty is weapons, both magical and mundane, but I generally stock a good assortment of trifles and treasures as well.

Ellisar walked right past the new pretties—a handful of ancient coins, a broken gold torc, and a kilt brooch studded with amber and jade. His gaze skimmed over a collection of small flasks, some of them still filled with potions or poisons or maybe just a nip of firemead. Not finding anything of interest there, he moved on to the weapons.

He reached for the crossbow, as I knew he would. Some of the weapons in this lot held more magic, but the crossbow's aura was the only one with oily streaks of Dark running through it. Ellisar is an aura-reader, you see, and he's nearly as good as he thinks he is. It's his job to find dangerous magical items and dispose of them.

To my surprise, he started chanting over the crossbow right then and there. His usual custom was to pay for Dark-infested treasure and haul it off to the Tower, where he could put a few locked doors between his business and mine. Magic is as common as bread and wine in Selenthea, but enchanters tend to be a secretive lot.

For damn good reason, I might add.

Didn't matter. The elf had nothing to fear from me. I've no interest in his sort of magic. His aura already told me more than I wanted to know about *that*.

There are risks to the work Ellisar does, needful though it might be. The Dark has a way of bleeding into whatever it touches, whether it comes from the magic you cast or the books you read or the people you pass time with. That's not to say everyone who fights evil falls to it, but given time, it'll leave a mark. The Essence surrounding Ellisar was gathering Dark like a waning moon.

You'd think he'd know that, being a Tower mage and all, but that's not how it works. There's no mirror that can show you the state of your own soul—unless you count my cats, which apparently Ellisar did not.

When he'd finished scrubbing the Dark off the crossbow, he handed me a small leather bag, heavy with coin. The Tower pays well, I'll say that for them. Shame about the crossbow, though. Shutting a perfectly good weapon away in some tower cupboard is a waste of good magic and hard currency. I knew a few people who would pay a stack of silver for a magically silenced crossbow.

"I'll take your coin any day," I told him, "but seeing as how I'm an honest woman, I'm honor-bound to tell you that weapon doesn't match your pretty robe. You go walking around like that, the other magi will talk. I've got a nice silver tiara, if you'd like to make a trade."

Ellisar sent me an exasperated look and picked up a dagger worth more than any ten pieces in the shop. "This looks as if it might hold an edge," he said in a tone suited to praising a middling sort of cheese. "Would you consider an even trade for the crossbow?"

My response was a two-fisted gesture I'd picked up during my smuggling days, one rude enough to start a dockside brawl.

Ellisar nodded as if expecting that. "What exorbitant price did you have in mind for your opening gambit?"

We fell to haggling. The shop bell jangled before we'd settled on a price, and Ellisar broke off to cast a quick cloaking spell. That was part of our deal: I gave him first refusal on new items, he didn't scare off my other customers. I had a good name among all sorts of people, including plenty of folk who had reason to avoid a Tower mage. Of course, I could still see him—a fact I've been careful to keep to myself—but his Essence was strong enough to shield him from most people, not to mention six or seven of my cats.

In walked a cheebat lad, half-hidden behind a pile of folded cloaks. Stolen, of course. The gray one on top had a faint shimmer of magic about it. That was impressive—stealing from magi required light fingers and solid brass baubles. My estimation of the thief went up a notch or two, but I saw no reason why the purchase price had to keep pace.

I picked up a corner of the magic-holding robe and sniffed it. "Lime and bluefern. Very nice. The bathhouses near the Tower favor that scent. It tends to linger in the clothes people hang in the changing rooms."

The cheebat took a step back, his eyes wary. "They told me you don't ask questions."

"Listen carefully, boy: '*This cloak smells of bath salts.*' That's an observation. '*Do I look like one of the Tower's watchdogs?*' That's a question. See the difference?"

His face relaxed into a grin. "Fair point," he allowed, "and you paint a true likeness of the guard, too. Seems to me, though, they'rc more *dog* than *watch*. If those hounds aren't sleeping on the porch, they're humping in the alleys."

He wasn't half wrong. I won't say there isn't law in Selenthea, but it ebbs and flows in no other pattern than whether the magi have more interesting things to do.

Ellisar was already looking bored, so I shot a glare in his general direction to remind him that upholding law and order was not part of our arrangement. Mind you, I picked a spot five or six paces from where he actually stood, and I took care not to meet his gaze. You don't keep several lifetimes' worth of secrets without picking up a trick or two.

Ellisar—who is generally the very picture of inscrutable calm—actually rolled his eyes. He raised both hands, palms up, and shook his head a little as if to say, *Me, interfere? My good woman, you've obviously mistaken me for someone who cares.*

Well, now, that was interesting. Amazing, what you can learn about people when they think you can't see them.

I turned my attention back to the business at hand. Magic and bath salts weren't the only scents clinging to the cheebat's stolen cloaks. At least one smelled strongly of fish, and predictably enough, out came the cats. The look of panic on the cheebat's face as they swarmed around his ankles was worth three, maybe four silver to me. He'd shave that much off his asking price just to get the deal done.

Here's the why of that: In many a hearthtale, cats trail after rogues like seabirds follow a fishing boat. Since plenty of folk take this for truth, most rogues see cats as bad luck. Me, I like them just fine. They're good company, and they put the sort of people who aim to cheat me off their stride.

I bought the cloaks fast and cheap, and after the cheebat ran off, I stowed them under the counter until I had time to give them a good airing. Since I'm one to give credit where due, I hollered for Jennet in the back room to dish out some chowder for the cats.

Cats aren't much for conversation, but "chowder" is a word they know and love. The last striped tail was whisking around the corner when the bell jangled a second time.

With an impatient huff, Ellisar started walking for the door, no doubt intending to slip past the newcomer and get on with his day.

Unfortunately for him, Jennet chose that moment to come charging into the shop like she was shot from a ballista, brandishing her clerical symbol and chant-singing in a voice four sizes too big for any halfling. Fifty pounds of red-haired righteousness slammed smack into the invisible elf, and down they went in a tangle of limbs and a chorus of curses.

The door swung open, and an invisible wave of Dark flooded the shop, too much for any living being to hold.

My hand automatically went for Soulsplitter, one of the swords I keep under the counter. Thanks to the magic she holds, Splitter can cut down undead like a warm knife through cheese. A second glance, though, told me the newcomer was alive.

Barely.

He stumbled at the threshold and would have gone down, had he not caught himself with the staff of black wood he carried.

For a moment, I forgot how to breathe. There was nothing in the world for me but a black staff, carved with runes and crammed with magic and crowned with an elaborate basket-weave orb fashioned from blackened vines and, as I had reason to know, sinew of unspeakable origins.

I'd taken three steps toward it before my mind knew my feet were moving.

"Don't touch that staff!"

Ellisar must have put a little something extra into that command, because I stopped like I'd just run into a wall. And a good thing he did, too, because the magic in that staff was hauling me in like a net-full of fish.

He strode to my side, visible now to all who cared to look. "That's a mage's staff. Very powerful. Elf-crafted, obviously."

He took a deep breath, held it until he worked himself up to telling me the next part: "The aura's signature is unmistakably that of a Bloodborn necromancer." None of this was news to me, but Ellisar couldn't know that. I pointed toward the courier, who was clinging to the staff with both hands and swaying like a tent in a strong breeze.

"What's to be done for the poor sod holding it?"

The man saved Ellisar the trouble of answering by crashing to the floor. He lay where he fell, eyes wide and staring in a face the color of cold ash.

Jennet darted forward and knelt at the man's side, a potion bottle in hand. Why, I couldn't tell you. I have never been a cleric—not that I can remember, at least—but you didn't need to be on speaking terms with the Enaros to know when a man was deader than pickled herring.

Ellisar began to pace. "I'm required to take the staff to the Silver Tower. *Protocol*," he muttered in a tone that left no doubt about his thoughts on that subject. "But of course I cannot."

"You're damned right you can't. The staff's not yours to take."

That stopped him in mid-stride. "Surely you don't intend to sell it."

I didn't much like his tone, so I lifted my chin and put some ice in my gaze. "My intentions are no concern of yours," I said, haughty as a duchess.

It was a good performance, but Ellisar didn't look impressed. "As Lord High Warden of the Silver Tower, any Dark-tainted item is very much my concern."

"Then I'm sure you're aware, *my lord*, that during in the three years we've done business, the only Dark that leaves this shop goes with you."

"Comes in with him, too," muttered Jennet.

I glanced down at the cleric. She'd come to stand beside me, shoulder to shoulder. Well, more like shoulder to hip, but there she stood.

"I don't pay you to insult my customers," I reminded her.

"Too bad," she said. "You'd get your money's worth when *that* one comes in."

"Perhaps we could return to the matter at hand?" Ellisar prompted.

That sounded like a fine idea to me. "Let's start with this: What did you mean when you said you couldn't take the staff to the Tower? Putting aside, for the moment, the fact that I wouldn't let you."

His lips thinned into a straight line. "You have no idea what such a staff can do."

For a moment, I was tempted to tell the know-it-all elf just how wrong he was. I settled for prodding the dead man with the toe of one dainty slipper. "He was a mage, I'm guessing. The damned stick drained him dry, just like it's draining the Essence from my stock." The lamp between my ears suddenly lit up. "Ah, I see. No mage could carry the staff for long."

"Indeed. It is a conundrum."

"So what's to be done?" Jennet demanded.

It was time to take matters in hand, so I did exactly that. Hooking a toe under the staff, I flicked it into the air and caught it just under the crown.

A familiar presence filled my mind like wind howling through castle ruins.

"Elliyan Wilds," I whispered. "He's there. He's close. He's *waiting*."

The color drained from Ellisar's face so fast that for a moment I thought I'd have to haul out two corpses. That wouldn't be my worst day of shopkeeping, but it wasn't what I'd call a good one, either.

It took everything I had to peel my fingers free of the black wood, to let the staff drop and roll and not lunge after it.

"I'm going to the Wild," I told the elf, "and I'm taking the staff. Might as well get your head around that."

Ellisar nodded gravely. "I understand," he said. "Numos rises full tonight. You couldn't possibly prevail against a Bloodborn, so how could you resist?"

We stood for a long moment, gazes locked. No doubt Ellisar was thinking deep and serious thoughts, but I was mostly just standing there, trying not to look as foolish as I felt.

Of course Ellisar would realize there was more to me than my face and form, fine though both might be. He saw the auras of everything, living or not. Since I've been both more times than I care to contemplate, my aura is probably as striped as a sock someone knitted to use up odds and ends of yarn.

Still, he didn't know the whole of it. It's true that people who are called back from death feel the call of Numos, but that doesn't mean I was shopping for a quick way to die.

"You can't possibly prevail against a Bloodborn," he repeated. "But I could."

I shook off my dismay and made a show of thinking that over. But when a powerful mage offers to tag along, there's really only one answer. "Get your gear."

The elf bowed to me—and let me tell you, that was a first—and left the shop without another word.

Jennet jabbed at the laces of my stomacher with a stubby finger. "Have you gone completely moonswoggled?"

"Probably. Grab a foot."

The halfling huffed and muttered, but she picked up one of the dead man's boots and I took the other, and we started dragging him toward the back door. We'd practiced this routine so often I wouldn't hesitate to perform it for royalty. Still, it takes time to drag a big man any sort of distance—far too long, I expected, for Jennet to go without expressing an opinion or two.

Sure enough, we'd only gone about halfway before her face got that look clerics get when they're about to launch into a sermon. "That's dangerous ground the elf's treading, for you and him both."

"I know."

She dropped the foot and drew herself up to her full height, such as it was. "Do you? What he's suggesting is near akin to human sacrifice. And you're on the altar!"

"*I know*. Less talking, more dragging."

Jennet clearly had more to say, but she grabbed the foot she'd dropped and we got back to hauling.

We left the dead man in the usual place and I ran up the flag that signaled the corpse carter. He comes by pretty regular, but my customers don't seem to mind. Jennet's past is nearly as interesting as mine, and while folks hereabouts don't know the particulars, they know she gets unwelcome visitors from time to time.

I turned back toward the shop, but Jennet scooted over and planted herself in my path, fists propped on her hips. "Do you know why I came running into the shop when I did?"

"One of your wards triggered, I suppose."

"Two of them," she said grimly. "Wards against Dark, both of them. The first went off when the elf came in."

A chill raced down my spine. This was worrisome news. I knew Ellisar's Essence was edging toward twilight, but to my eyes, his aura was still a long way from full Dark. Granted, there's no clear line between day and night, but why was my magic saying one thing and Jennet's another?

"You don't trust the elf, either," Jennet said.

Fact is, I did. That was worrisome, too, since I'm not inclined to trust anyone. Shopkeepers learn to tally, and when I added this new insight to my faulty reading of Ellisar's aura and threw in being stupid enough to think he couldn't read mine, it summed up to this: The rat bastard had put me under an enchantment.

But none of that mattered at the moment. The only important thing was finding and killing the Bloodborn, and I'd take help from an amorous *orog* if that's what it took.

So I gave Jennet a little shrug and a smaller smile. "You surprised me, that's all. As for the ward, maybe it's seeing what Ellisar does, not what he is. When you wrestle a pig out of a mud hole, you get dirty. Doesn't make you a pig, though."

Jennet thought this over. "That might be. I hope you're right."

So did I.

"We'll leave within the hour. Say some words over this poor bastard, then get your gear."

Jennet nodded and began to sing a weird little tune, fun of sharp angles and unexpected turns. I left the cleric to her lifework and went back to the shop to attend to mine.

There's a flask of clingfire under the counter, hidden among my cache of personal weapons. I found it and eased out the cork, careful as a thief removing a bracelet from the claw of a snoring dragon, and took it over to the staff. I wasn't surprised to see it standing upright and leaning on the counter. Waiting for me.

My fingers skimmed over the smooth wood, feeling the familiar runes, the familiar sense of life and joy and hope draining away.

"You sure about this, Oxamia?"

I tore my hand free of Nimanthior's staff and turned to face my cleric. "Make sure you bring your prayer beads, Jennet. It's time for you to earn your retainer."

"DOWN!" HOWLED JENNET.

I went headfirst into the brush like I was diving into a lake. When a halfling thinks it's a good idea to get low, I like to take a close look at the dirt.

From the corner of my eye I saw a burst of flame flash down toward the forest path, not more than arm's length from where we'd been standing. I got back on my feet in time to see a tiny dragon, no bigger than a seabird, flapping away.

A huge bird's nest, charred and smoking, plopped down onto the path ahead. Before I could wonder aloud what sort of creature the dragon just tried to fry, *the nest itself* rose up on six long, twiggy legs and skittered away.

We stood for a moment staring after it.

"That's something new," Jennet admitted.

I picked my way back to the path, brushing off my skirts as I went. Ellisar watched with disapproval. Unlike me, he was properly dressed for a trek through a magically twisted forest. He'd traded the fussy silver and crimson robes of the Selenthean magi for plain travel leathers, dyed in practical shades of dappled green and brown. Jennet was kitted out about the same. She'd braided back her mop of red hair and covered it with a broad-brimmed hat. A fist-sized wooden medallion representing Modren's hammer hung from the plain leather thong tied around her neck, proclaiming that here walked a cleric with serious purpose and bad fashion sense.

In contrast, I wore my usual sort of garb: A skirt short enough to show off my boots, which were fashioned to show off my legs. A stomacher laced to accent the deep curves of my waist and provide a shelf for the curves above. My black hair was long and loose, my face was painted. The only concession to practicality was a chemise in a flattering shade of deep green, and even that was pulled low to bare my shoulders. Except for the sword on my belt and the daggers tucked into my boots, I could have been the girl Nimanthior had found in a high-class brothel some ten years back.

Of course, I didn't remember her, but I was betting *he* did.

Just in case his memory needed jogging, I bent forward from the waist and ran my fingers through my hair a few times to tousle it up, then I gave my shoulders a little shimmy and tugged my stomacher laces a mite tighter to fluff up The Girls.

Ellisar grimaced. "Is that necessary?"

"You don't seem to grasp the tactical value of a distraction."

"Well, don't look to me," Jennet said. "I'm not undressing for any elf's benefit."

"Never a night so dark but there isn't a glimmer of light," murmured Ellisar.

"More walking, less sarcasm," I suggested.

We set back down the path. Jennet forged on ahead, and the elf fell into step beside me. "I have a question for you, Oxamia."

"You're wondering why Jennet's with us," I said. "I'm surprised you waited so long to ask. Truth be told, I expected you to throw a fuss back at the shop."

He sniffed. "Don't insult my intelligence. You want to ensure that you are given the Last Rites so your spirit can't be recalled. Why else would you take a cleric everywhere you go? And what other cleric would have nothing better to do?"

"Hey!" Jennet protested. "I've had offers."

"My question pertains to something you said in the shop. You observed that the staff had started draining Essence from your stock."

My heart leaped and sang out *You stupid cow!* before thudding painfully back into place. "I said that, did I?"

"Indeed. It was an accurate assessment. How did you know?"

I shrugged, which gave The Girls something to do. Ellisar, predictably enough, was not distracted. "It's not a simple thing to explain."

"Use small words," he suggested. "I'll do my best to follow along."

We walked a while in silence while I decided how much to tell him—and wondered how much he already knew.

Finally, I gave a mental shrug and began. "You've heard of Gilliandra Ravenwood?"

"Of course. She was one of the most powerful aura readers of her generation. Her death was a great loss."

"You're not alone in that opinion. Someone decided to drag her spirit back and stuff it into a lovely young courtesan, recently and conveniently deceased."

Ellisar's gaze sharpened. "You."

I fluttered my eyelashes at him by way of confirmation. "I don't remember that girl, not even her name. But one day we were visiting some rich patron or other and I picked up an oud and began to play. Gilliandra had never learned a string instrument of any sort, but the first owner of this body was apparently quite skilled."

"That's impossible."

"And why is that?" I shot back. "A body is more than empty vessel, to be filled with this spirit or that. Muscles have memories. Skills and habits are carved into the brain as well as the hands. Even if your head was a library to store knowledge and memory, even if all those things went with the spirit—and I'm not convinced that they do—the structure and shelves you built during a lifetime remain. A new spirit needs time to find its way around, just as surely as it needs to adjust to how a different body moves. But something remains. Exactly what, no one really knows."

Ellisar nodded, slow and thoughtful. "Do you have any of her memories? Any at all?"

Something in the way he asked, the way his gaze slid away from mine, made me suspect he'd known Gilliandra Ravenwood by more than reputation.

"No. That was several lifetimes ago," I said, putting as much finality into the words as I could scrape together. I could accept treachery from Ellisar, but sentiment was right out of the question.

"Several lifetimes," he repeated, as if this was all news to him.

"That's right. After my performance with the oud, the necromancer decided to experiment with something he called 'mind-body duality.' He drained this body dry, then pulled in a different spirit to see how much would remain of the old. He did it again and again, with various types of spirits. It got to be a game with him, I think."

"It's a marvel you're still sane," said Jennet. "Mostly."

"Yes, Nimanthior thought much the same. He experimented with that, too. Wanted to see how much I could take in before I broke apart. He finally settled on a plan that would have done the trick. I escaped first, but that's not a tale I intend to tell."

The elf stopped and seized my arm. "Did you say Nimanthior?"

Oh, it was a fine performance. Yesterday, I would have stood up and applauded.

"Heard of him, have you?" I shook him loose and kept walking. "You recognized his staff, which just happened to come to Oxamia, who just happened to be some necromancer's patchwork plaything. It's a marvel you didn't manage to put the pieces together. Why, it's almost as if some troll-begotten mage had slapped you upside the head with a spell of stupidity."

He had the grace to look ashamed. "Oxamia, you know what I do. My work is of vital importance to the safety of Selenthea. I know about the questions you've been asking, the adventurers you've funded. It was only a matter of time before you found Nimanthior, or he found you. And yes, I used that. Finding and destroying a Bloodborn necromancer is a task that must be accomplished, whatever the cost."

Since that was my thinking as well, it was hard to fault him.

"So, since you've been planning this for a while, let's hear what you've got."

"Nimanthior will be focused on you, and on his staff. As you so aptly observed, you will provide the tactical distraction."

"A sneak attack," Jennet said approvingly. "I could help with that."

"*You'll* hang back, out of sight," I told the halfling. "Last Rites take time. Chant, pray, do whatever you do to crank up that particular crossbow. I want you ready to pull the trigger when the time comes."

"*If* the time comes," Jennet said staunchly.

"And I want you to make use of this." I handed Ellisar an empty glass flask.

His eyes widened. "Is this what I think it is?"

"Clingfire," I confirmed, and gave the staff a little waggle. "This damn stick is doused in it. Soon as Nimanthior takes it in hand, I want you to light him up."

He stared at me in silence.

"What's the matter? Don't know a firestart spell?"

"Of course I do. That's entirely beside the point."

I assume he would have gotten around to the point, whatever it might be, but just then Jennet yelped. She shook one foot, trying to dislodge the vine wrapped around her ankle. A vine that ended in a grasping skeletal hand. Seems like the necromancer had found us first.

One of the locked doors in my head cracked open, and in the sudden flood of light Jennet stood taller than Nimanthior. She was a friend, the best I could remember, and I'd brought her into this mess without giving one thought to how she'd get herself out after I was dead.

Pulling the dagger from my boot, I leaped at the vine. Quick as liquor, it whipped back, dragging Jennet some twenty paces along the ground and then up into the air. She hung there, swinging back and forth from the balcony of a monstrous tower.

The plants in the Elliyan Wilds tended to be a bit complicated. Some of them were more elf than plant, which was what made this tower so terrible. It was like a giant beehive wicker-woven from living skeletons whose bones had been spun out into vines. Here and there, you could make out the shape of a skull, and tendrils reached toward us like hands, some curved into grasping claws, others palms-up and beseeching. I wasn't sure which ones chilled me more.

Nimanthior strode out of the tower. He'd changed since my escape. His hair was white as bone now. He stood taller, and was nearly as thin as the forest vines that were probably his distant kin. I wouldn't have known him but for the wooden crown he wore—the same open, wicker-woven design that crowned the top of his staff. But judging from the gleam in his crimson eyes, he recognized me right away.

I took a deep breath and started sashaying toward him, hoping I could keep his attention long enough for Ellisar to crank up a killing spell. The necromancer's gaze didn't so much as flicker. It took me a moment to notice that he was looking right past me.

"Hello, Father," Ellisar said. "I believe you sent me this?"

And then the secretive rat bastard elf took the staff from my hand and held it out to his Bloodborn sire.

Nimanthior thrust his hand into the woven cage atop it and got a good grip on the shaft. Not being one for small talk, he began chanting straight away. Ellisar kept his grip on the other end and started a casting of his own.

Essence flowed down the staff from both ends, slammed together, and bounded back to form a line of pale blue fire. The captured lightning of Essense sizzled and glowed as the elves went at it like two arm-wrestling drunks.

Not the distraction I'd expected, but I figured I could work with it.

I pulled Soulsplitter from her sheath, hauled the sword back with both hands as I ran at my former master, and swung it at his neck with every bit of strength I could summon.

Next thing I knew, I was sitting on my arse some ten paces away. Both elves were smoking now, but neither of the stubborn bastards would let go of the staff. At this point, I wasn't sure either of them could.

Suddenly, I realized Ellisar didn't intend to. Didn't *want* to.

Turns out there was a mirror that could show Ellisar the state of his soul, and warn him what he might become. With his face and hair agleam with blue light, his features twisted with agony and frozen with determination, he even looked like Nimanthior. Maybe he always had, and his enchantment kept me from seeing it.

Didn't matter. Just when I'd decided to live for Jennet's sake, Ellisar had got it in his head that he needed to die for mine. I wasn't sure which choice I liked less.

Jennet trotted over and hauled me to my feet. "Looks painful, that. If you want this over and done, I might could summon Fire Seeds."

"Fire," said Ellisar from between gritted teeth.

"It'll take you both," she warned him.

"*Fire.*"

Jennet looked to me. I gave a single grim nod. "On my signal."

I pulled a dagger, strode into the storm of Essence, and sliced open Ellisar's arm. His blood washed over the staff in a shining crimson wave as it flowed toward the Bloodborn wizard.

The flare of power in Nimanthior's Essence damn near blinded me. Half-drunk with it, he let out a howl of triumph and yanked the staff from Ellisar's grasp. His son fell, and I leaped over the heap of his body as I threw myself at the winner.

We went down, and as I'd expected, Nimanthior's first thought was to keep his grip on that staff. Before he had time to work up another spell of protection, I drove my dagger into the wooden cage and through his wrist. Then I gave it a good hard twist to lock the hilt into the weave.

I rolled free and shouted for Jennet to let fly. A handful of tiny lights sizzled past me. They passed over Nimanthior, too, and I had a bad moment or two before the clingfire caught flame.

Being an elf, Ellisar was easier to drag than I was used to. Jennet ran to help me pull him away from the screaming, cursing bonfire. That done, we stood in silence and watched the Bloodborn and his staff burn to ash.

"Might be I was wrong about that elf of yours," Jennet said. "Seeing how he went out, seems like he might've made good, given time. In fact, some might say he already did." She cocked her head. "That started out being the sort of thing people say graveside, but you know, I felt the truth of it as I spoke the words."

I agreed with Jennet on every particular but one. "He's still alive, I think."

The halfling dropped to her knees beside him and placed her head on his chest. "So he is. Not by much, though. I could heal him. Maybe."

"Give it a go."

Jennet went through her prayers and spells and what not. When she was done, Ellisar still lay insensible, but he breathed a little deeper and his color was better, from what I could tell in the near-darkness.

"That'll do," Jennet said. "Should be ready to travel come morning, if the forest doesn't kill us all before then."

"You need to work on your aim."

She snorted. "Sure. I'll practice flinging Fire Seeds around the shop, and we'll see how long that lasts."

"Maybe we should get out more often. We have all the equipment right at hand."

"That we do." Jennet tipped her head toward the pines, where Numos rose bright and full. "Sounds to me like you're reconciled to the notion of drawing breath a while longer."

For a long moment, I gazed into the limpid moonlight. The sweet, sharp longing of my exiled souls was almost more than I could bear. The spirit of the dwarf maid I'd last been, the echoes of the spirits that had come before, all struggled to break free of the body they'd shared. I could almost see them rising from me, yearning toward Numos like fingers of a ghostly hand.

But I'd been a bard some three or four lives past, and part of me remembered the power in metaphor. I envisioned myself clenching those souls into a single fist.

Nimanthior was dead, but there were more like him who needed a good hard punch to the throat.

"Smugglers tend to lay low when Numos shines full," I mused. "But come moondark, I can get us passage to anywhere we decide to go."

Jennet looked downright pleased at the prospect, and I'll admit the idea of getting out from behind the shop counter more held a certain appeal. As for Ellisar, it would do him good to get away from the Tower. Maybe if he stopped scrubbing the Dark off every passing sword and spellbook for a while, the taint would fade from his Essense.

And yes, I definitely planned to invite Ellisar to come adventuring with us.

After all, the way I saw it, the sneaky little bastard had it coming.

THE WAILING TEMPLE

MEL ODOM

– CHAPTER 1 –

CUTLASS IN HAND, CRIGHTIN STOOD IN *THE GILDED EEL'S* stern and watched the canoes approach through the falling rain with trepidation. At the ship's stern, the clouded sun dipped into the sea, its last weak rays casting the *Eel's* shadow over the murky water in front of him. A thousand yards distant, the craggy, tree-covered coastline stood tall behind the small vessels aimed like arrows for the caravel. The things sculling their short oars only occasionally lifted from the gray shadows. All of them stared at the *Eel* with yellow-eyed avarice.

"They're orcs." Crightin blinked rain from his eyes and looked over to Mos'as, his second-in-command, who stood at his side with a spyglass aimed at the boats.

Slender and barely out of his teens, Mos'as stood almost a head shorter than Crightin, who was seven years older and a handful of inches over six feet. Beardless and fair of face and hair, the younger man was a sharp counterpoint to Crightin's dark complexion and broad build. Both of them were soaked to the skin, and both wore cutlasses and knives in leather combat harnesses.

"Orcs, aye, but there are a *lot* of them." Mos'as put the spyglass into the navigator's desk beside the large ship's wheel. The breeze from the coastline held the scent of fragrant blossoms and fecund swamps. The young man's blond hair flipped in the wind in wet strands as the caravel rocked restlessly on her tether to the anchor.

Crightin couldn't argue that. The *Eel's* crew was outnumbered, but he'd put his sailors up against any crew on the Amethyst Sea.

"We could weigh anchor and depart before they reach us, Captain," Mos'as said.

"You're suggesting we run from the likes of those *creatures*?" The idea rankled Crightin. According to tales and news he'd heard in Selenthea while they'd laid on supplies, the local orcs supplied their raiding with shipbreaking, drawing in unwary captains so their vessels smashed against the hidden reefs. All of the *endrori* hated the civilized people in the Amethyst Sea. Before the Cataclysm, they'd stayed in the Donarzheis Mountains and other out-of-the-way places. Now they were spreading across the region, claiming empires through their sheer numbers and ferocity.

Whatever their intent, the orcs were bad luck, and he'd experienced a lot of that lately. Frankly, he was sick of ill fortune, and wanted to take a stand against it.

"Consider it a strategic retreat," Mos'as countered.

Crightin cursed. "Putting a pretty name to it doesn't make it any more appealing. I claimed this ship with the strength and skill of my sword arm. I'll hold it the same way until my dying breath."

"I understand, but if we stay here, we're going to get bloody. We don't need to risk our crew or this ship for the channeler's fables."

"If you run," an elegant and cultured voice warned before

Crightin could respond, "I'll not pay you another copper gate."

Frowning, Crightin turned to face the speaker. The accusation struck him deeply; he was no coward. His breath plumed gray as frost in the chill air.

"More than that," she went on, "I'll demand that you return the money I've already given you."

Slim and beautiful, dark-haired and lavender-eyed, her face a marblework of dusky grace, Tavesi faced Crightin with her arms crossed and her chin held high. Her russet woolen coat covered her from throat to ankles, but didn't hide the slim, hard body underneath. She clasped a white ash staff in one hand that bore a golden scroll head.

Steeling himself, Crightin took a breath and told himself he would not berate the woman. She was half his size, but commanded magical forces he didn't understand. He cursed himself once more for agreeing to take on her cause.

But ships ate gold the way a starving hound gulped down a meal, and he had no way to repay her advance against his vessel's and crew's services, even if he was of a mind to.

Crightin smiled at Tavesi, then bellowed, "*Archers!*"

– CHAPTER 2 –

JOINING HIS CREWMEN AT THE SHIP'S RAILING BEHIND THE hanging shields, Crightin accepted the oilskin roll offered by his quartermaster. Near ancient, as judged by his gray hair and beard, Elmgar was still a stout man who routinely thumped men half his age and could drink and womanize all night. Faded tattoos covered only some of the scars on his arms.

Setting the roll upright, Crightin withdrew the powerful horn and layered wood composite bow from within. Trapping one end between his feet, he bent the weapon and strung it in one smooth move. One of the crewmen dashed down the line, handing out quivers of goose-fletched arrows.

Elmgar squinted and hefted his short-hafted hewing ax. Testing the broad blade with a callused thumb, he drew blood that he wiped on the ax head. "May Droth's trials be fair for all of us."

"Better to add prayer that our crew hits their marks." Crightin nocked an arrow to his string, held four others in his hand gripping the bow, and waited. "In this rain, the strings are going to wet and quickly become useless."

"Aye, Captain, but our lads are versed in hand-to-hand fighting." Elmgar smiled. "They'll do right by you."

Looking down the line, Crightin knew that. They were good men, but they stood nervously, awaiting the coming battle. Anxiousness thrilled through them like hounds with the scent of a fox in their nostrils. Once the combat started, they'd relax.

"Luck be with you, Elmgar."

"Aye, Captain. And you."

Returning his attention to the orcs, Crightin looked down the shaft already dripping water. The broadhead tip held steady on the one he'd chosen as his first target. He'd already marked the next five in his head.

"Ready, archers!" Mos'as called from the tall stern castle, where he'd watch over the battle. He gripped the railing with one hand and rested his cutlass over his shoulder with the other.

Tavesi stood beside him, her russet coat clinging to her body in the wind. Gods, she was beautiful. If only she wasn't such a pig-headed—

"Loose!" Mos'as roared.

Bowstrings hummed around Crightin as he released his arrow.

The shaft sped true, covering a hundred paces in an eyeblink and splitting the heart of the orc he'd chosen. Even as it slumped over, he already had a second arrow nocked and shifted to another target.

Flying silently in the falling rain, the arrows pierced the orcs without mercy. Some fell dead in the canoes. Others toppled into the dark waters of the cove.

Crightin killed without hesitation, as fast as he could draw and release his arrows. But even though a third of their number lay dead or gravely wounded by his estimation, the orcs kept coming. He nocked another arrow, feeling the string stretching and going dead as it soaked up the rain.

"They should have turned," he said to Elmgar.

"Aye, but they haven't."

"Why?" Crightin released and drew again.

"Mayhap they're desperate."

Or they're protecting something. Crightin thought again of the channeler's mission. She hadn't been forthcoming with everything, but she'd had gold from the High Temple's treasury, enough to get the *Eel* chasing the wind out of the Free Kingdoms ahead of the guards tasked with ending smuggling.

"Prepare to repel boarders!" Mos'as marched along the sterncastle railing, his cutlass reflecting the light of the lanterns hanging on the ship.

Crightin unstrung his bow and shoved it back into the oilskin, then kicked it out of harm's way. He put a lot of store in the custom-made weapon. He filled his hands with his cutlass and one of the trident daggers he carried in his calf-high boots. When he tripped the smaller weapon's release, two extra blades sprang out from the main steel like arms set at angles, looking like the bones of a high lady's fan.

The canoes massed along the ship's hull and at the anchor line, which crewmen would cut only if necessary. In the uncertain light spilling over the *Eel's* railing, the orcs looked monstrous. As big as a man and as powerful as a dwarf, covered in green-gray skin, they glared fiercely through sickly yellow eyes beneath tufts of wiry black hair. They wore all manner of crude dress and armor, and wielded captured weapons with brute force and some mean skill.

In one of the canoes, amid a cluster that looked more like a logjam, a dark figure stood and threw back its cloak. Even in the lantern light, the figure remained in shadow, indistinct and featureless except for two eyes that burned like two hot coals. An ululating wail pierced the drumming rain, quieting the harsh curses the sailors hurled at the orcs.

The hair along the back of Crightin's neck lifted in preternatural warning. Essence users who channeled the power spread throughout the land always instilled fear in him.

Opening its cloak wide, the shadow-thing screamed a challenge in a language Crightin couldn't understand. Jagged shadows no bigger than an open hand leaped from the folds of the material and took flight, streaking for the *Eel.*

– CHAPTER 3 –

"SHIELDS!" MOS'AS GRABBED ONE AS HE SHOUTED THE ORDER. "*Shields! Look to the sky!*"

Crightin stepped behind Elmgar as the big man lifted one of the broad circular shields made of leather and thick hardwood. "I'm at your back, Elmgar."

"Just stay there, Captain." The older man set himself. "Whatever's coming, it'll have to go through me, and that won't happen as long as I'm still standing."

Cursing the foul things winging at them, Crightin cursed the channeler too, because whatever had brought them here was dangerous. Even so, the threat they faced just made him more curious. He liked to be in control, but he liked challenge as well, and those two were ofttimes mutually exclusive.

The jagged shadows flapped like bats, but much more quickly, and struck the shields like blows from dwarven war hammers, battering the crewmen back. In some cases, the shields shattered, the broken pieces held together by leather strips. Sailors struck by the shadow-creatures fell, bleeding from deep cuts.

Some of the jagged shadows sprouted crooked, segmented legs that made them look like spiders, and dropped on the fallen men. Once latched onto their victims, the creatures sucked at their blood with long proboscises.

"Clear the decks! Clear the decks!" Mos'as slashed at the nearby creatures with his cutlass. Thankfully, the things died easily enough, bursting apart in bright explosions.

Standing her ground behind him, staff planted solidly on the deck, Tavesi ignored the jagged shadows that blew up only inches before touching her. A barely visible shimmering wave, like quicksilver, washed endlessly around her body.

After the first wave of jagged shadows beat against Elmgar's shield, dying in a series of explosions, Crightin stepped from behind his quartermaster and cleaved through the skull of an orc clambering over the ship's side. Warm blood spattered his chest, but he ignored it and put a boot on the center of another orc's chest and shoved, launching the *endrori* back into the dark waters of the cove.

"Repel boarders!" Crightin shouted as he trapped a barbed spear head with the trident dagger and swept his cutlass through his attacker's neck. Stepping forward, he planted his shoulder in the dying orc's face and knocked him off the rail.

The rising moonlight and glow of the lanterns glinted off the sharp edges of the blades in the crewmen's hands as they hacked at the orcs. Most of the sailors held their positions, but every now and again the jagged shadows created gaps as they overcame a lone man. Other sailors hurried around the deck, quickly slaying the jagged shadows and spider-things that crawled over their fellows.

Elmgar struck an orc with his ax, splitting the creature from his crown to his chin. The old warrior roared in savage celebration as he yanked his weapon free and kicked his dead opponent over the side.

Even with their considerable training, Crightin feared his crew would fall in the end. There were too many of the jagged shadows, and more kept coming from the shadow-thing that released them.

A sudden *BOOM!* thundered over the ship, vibrating through Crightin's bones. Drawn by the noise, he glanced at the channeler.

Tavesi stood with her shimmering staff held horizontally in front of her, then lunged forward. A coiling mass of twisting snake-gleamings raced from it, sped across the water, and slammed into the shadow-creature spawning the winged attackers.

Staggered, the shadow-thing fell back a step as it tried to right itself. Before it could, embers ignited in its center and in the folds of its cloak, fanning to flames that burned it to glowing green ash that whipped away on the wind.

At the same time, the jagged shadows and spider-things all burst into flames, charred into nothing in a heartbeat.

Crightin and Mos'as shouted orders that Elmgar and other veterans among the crew underscored with vicious oaths as they redoubled their defense of the ship. In a few short, bloody moments, the orcs retreated.

Chest heaving, covered in blood not his own, Crightin watched the remaining *endrori* pull away in their canoes. Then he sheathed his weapons and went to help the wounded.

– CHAPTER 4 –

"WE LOST THREE." MOS'AS STOOD ON THE STERNCASTLE with Tavesi as Crightin climbed up to join them. "Nine others are too wounded to serve for a few days." Fatigue made the young man's pale features even more pallid, but his gray eyes still roved the dark coastline.

All told, the casualties were better than what Crightin had expected. Still, anger and leftover fear swirled inside him. Hands resting on his weapon hilts, he focused on the channeler. "What was that thing?"

She eyed him coolly, not shrinking before his fury, although she did keep her staff between them. "That was a *wraethdari*. Have you never encountered one before?"

"Phensral grant me smooth waves." Crightin blew out a breath. "If I knew what it was, would I ask?"

"Your lack of knowledge is not my responsibility," Tavesi stated.

For a moment, Crightin considered simply heaving the exasperating woman over the side and sailing away. They'd already earned her gold in the blood of his men.

"If I may," Mos'as said quickly, "perhaps I can clear this up."

Crightin shrugged. Before becoming a smuggler, Mos'as had studied at highborn schools in New Erinor. Crightin's tutelage came from the alleys and seaways.

"A *wraethdari* is of elven lineage, but they are bound to pure Dark essence. They gave up their flesh and blood and became shadows, and they lead the Dark Hordes."

The mention of Dark Hordes chilled Crightin's blood, cooling his temper. "You're saying there's a Dark Horde waiting in those woods?" Drawing his sword, he pointed at the coastline.

Since the Cataclysm, since the World Gates had closed, and since the *endrori* had escaped their barriers, Dark Hordes of orcs, goblins, trolls, skaah, and other predatory creatures had formed. They constituted a threat to civilized areas already challenged by a shortage of resources.

"I don't know what waits in the woods," she replied. "We're not going into the woods. We're going *under* them."

"What if another Dark Horde—"

"Perhaps it would be best if you didn't alarm the men." Tavesi frowned. "Having them lose their heads now would not serve anyone."

Below, crewmen swarmed the abandoned canoes, looking for salvage and putting an end to any survivors. The sailors dumped the bodies into the cove and used axes to sink the primitive boats.

Crightin pointed a forefinger at her and felt *something* push back against his hand in warning. "*You* brought us here. This is on you."

The channeler paused a moment. "The stakes are high, Captain. Higher than anything you might have fought for in the past."

"If that's so, then I've been vastly underpaid."

Her black eyes narrowed. "There is treasure at the end of this journey. Would that interest you?"

Almost immediately, the chill left Crightin's blood. As a boy, he'd left the stinking alleys of Port Vale a step ahead of the slave block, and taken to the sea. He'd sailed and fought and bled and schemed, and finally taken a ship of his own from the pirates who'd killed his captain. These days, he made his living carrying cargoes, many of them smuggled goods. Even then, making ends meet was difficult.

A treasure definitely interested him. He tried to mask his attentiveness, but it was too late, and he had the feeling the thrice-cursed woman could see through him anyway.

She smiled, but there was a hint of disdain on her sweetly curved lips. The scroll at the end of her staff glowed with a little golden light, wiping her smile away.

"You must decide, Captain," she told him. "The time is upon us."

"*Now*? Right after this battle?"

"A battle that you and your men won." She returned his gaze in full measure, her own mixed with challenge and derision. "The decision to go is yours, but the time to go is now. Prove to me that I have chosen the wrong man for the job, or that you are not as greedy as I thought."

Unwilling to show a hint of weakness, Crightin turned and glared at the dark waters and the dead orc bodies floating nearby. He tried not to think of the empty cargo hold, the nearly empty larder, or his nearly depleted purse.

In the end, there was no other choice.

And the thought of treasure for the taking made that lack sting a little less.

– CHAPTER 5 –

WITH THE EXPEDITION ALREADY PLANNED, CRIGHTIN clambered down into a longboat less than two hours later, slowed only by the burial at sea of the three lost crewmen, sent to the bottom with shrouds he'd sewn himself. Mos'as saw to the reassignment of able-bodied crew, all under Elmgar's command till their return.

Two other boats accompanied Crightin's. Each held seven men, as his did, and carried provisions for three days, even though they hoped to return to the ship by dawn or shortly thereafter. If they didn't return by noon, Elmgar was to sail the ship farther out to sea and wait there for two more days before leaving.

The channeler had made no mention of the *wraethdari* on the contract they'd signed, so Crightin guessed there might be other surprises she'd chosen to hide as well.

The boat pilots hung glowing lanterns on the prows and sterns, the golden nimbuses pushing back the endless darkness. Fireflies flitted through the dark foliage along the coastline several hundred yards away. The distance provided a long time of vulnerability if pursued by more orcs, which didn't rest easily in Crightin's mind, but there was no other way to avoid the hidden reefs and rocks dotting the cove.

At least the rain was now only a humid gray mist coiled above the dark water. Crightin tried ignoring the cold in the air, but it was no use. He shivered under his heavy cloak.

"Did you kill the *wraethdari*?" he asked Tavesi. Thoughts of the shadow-creature still lurking somewhere in the night gave him pause.

The channeler sat in the boat's prow, her eyes always moving, always searching. "The *wraethdari* cannot be killed," she told him. "They can only be banished for a time. When they gather enough of the Dark essence, they return."

"That's not going to be any time soon, is it?"

She turned to him, malignant mischief twinkling in those lavender eyes. "Not soon, no."

"As long as we're out of here by then, I'll be happy." Crightin pulled on his oar in time with his crewmen. The boats slid quietly through the water, bobbing only slightly. "There's one other thing I'll have you know, witch."

If she took affront at the name, she didn't show it.

"I don't care that you serve one of the Enaros. If you're hiding any secrets that get my men killed, I'll choke the life from you myself."

"Your approach doesn't inspire much confidence in your clients."

"Mayhap not, but it simplifies matters." Crightin pulled again, watching the dark coast come closer.

"And don't be too sure you'd be capable of that task, either." She turned back to scan the black landscape ahead of them.

A FEW FEET FROM THE COASTLINE, WHERE THE WATER GREW so shallow the longboat's bottom dragged, Crightin stepped over the side, plunging into the cold water with the other crewmen. Gripping the gunnel, he helped tug it to dry land beneath towering oak trees mixed with firs. The dense forest made seeing any real distance impossible.

The nearby night creatures had quieted, but every now and again one chirped or growled or snuffled in the darkness. Crightin only knew the cries and voices of a few of them. He hoped the lantern light would keep predators at bay, but knew it was just as likely the glow would mark them for anything thinking it was big enough or fast enough to attack.

Once they'd beached the boats, Crightin ordered the sailors to divvy up the provisions. Some they hid in nearby caches, digging pits in the damp soil, and others they placed in packs.

Crightin also brought out a few bottles of Malaorian busthead that dwarven blacksmiths swore by and passed them around.

"*What* are you doing?" Tavesi's nostrils flared. "Do you truly think drunken sailors stumbling around out here are a good idea?"

Crightin took a pull on his bottle, then passed it to a waiting crewman. "There's not enough in those bottles to get the men drunk, but there is enough to help take the chill from a sailor who got half-drowned and nearly killed by Dark Hordesmen getting you here. If you want my advice—"

"I don't."

"—you'll chase down one of them and knock back a draught yourself." Crightin spun on his heel and went to organize his men.

Mos'as joined him, shifting the straps on his own pack while handing another off to Crightin. "You do realize you can get more flies with honey than with vinegar, right, Captain?"

"Aye, but it's a moldering corpse that draws flies most of all." Crightin clapped his second-in-command on the shoulder. "And it draws carrion beetles that make a home of your body till they gnaw you down to the bone. It's something you need to keep in mind. That woman's not telling us everything."

"But you think the part about the treasure is true?" Mos'as wasn't greedy. He lived like a monk, and didn't share the dream of the extravagant lifestyle Crightin longed for. But he handled the ship's ledgers, and knew all too well the cost of operating the *Eel*.

"If it's not, I've half a mind to leave that woman here for the Dark Horde, and Endroren take the other half of this commission."

Mos'as grimaced. "Perhaps mentioning the Dark Lord's name in this place and during a night so dark tempts the fates too much."

"Too late." Crightin shook his head and reached for the nearest bottle of busthead, finding it sorrowfully depleted. "Just being here tempts the fates."

– CHAPTER 6 –

"WHAT IS SHE DOING?" CRIGHTIN WHISPERED.

A few yards ahead, Tavesi stood with her staff lifted. The golden scroll nearly disappeared in the low-hanging branches, but it burned brightly, now pulsing like a beating heart.

"Doing what the followers of Toletren always do," Mos'as whispered back. "Finding her way."

"Doesn't she already know her way?" That possibility left Crightin even more unsettled.

His first mate rolled his eyes. "Of course she knows the way. She's found her way to here. Now she's just got to find the place she's looking for."

Pulling his cloak more tightly around him, his right hand never leaving the hilt of the Maladorian-forged long dagger that would allow him to fight most effectively in the brush, Crightin longed for another bottle of busthead. In fact, he longed for his cabin, his warm bed, and Tiriny. Unfortunately, the spy was off gods knew where, and would return only when she was finished with her tasks and wanted his company again.

Most of all, though, in spite of the harsh words he'd spoken to Mos'as, he wished to know if Tavesi had spoken the truth about the treasure. Loot from a forgotten vault, even a small one, would go a long way to getting the repairs the *Eel* needed.

As long as the tale wasn't just a carrot to get him moving.

A moment later, the golden scroll glowed again, holding steady this time. The channeler lowered her staff and turned to them.

"This way," she said, and headed into the thick forest without checking to see if they followed, her glowing staff lighting the way.

Crightin couldn't make up his mind whether she was knowledgeable or deluded. Gripping his dagger's hilt and holding a lantern high, he trailed in the woman's wake.

– CHAPTER 7 –

"HERE?" CRIGHTIN STARED ANGRILY AT THE COLLECTION of broken pillars at the bottom of a shallow depression within a circle of low hills.

Shattered rubble lay exposed in some places, semi-buried in others by trees and creeping brush growing on the hillsides. A statue's arm, the hand broken off at the wrist, thrust from a tree trunk a few yards away. Over the years, the tree's growth had encompassed the statue, absorbing it. When Crightin moved his lantern slightly, the light fell on a stone face not quite covered by bark.

Farther out, more wreckage marked the perimeter of a small walled town. Crightin couldn't tell how big the place had been, maybe no more than a way stop or a village, but there was no denying its existence. Or that it was very, very old.

He raked his mind, searching for stories of a town here, but nothing surfaced. The location was good. The town had probably benefited from sea trade, and the surrounding forest provided resources for structures and larders. The people who had lived here so long ago had probably done so comfortably.

"Here," Tavesi stated, walking to the center of the depression.

"There's nothing *here*." Crightin stamped after her, his boots sinking into the muddy ground and squelching as he pulled them free. "If there *ever* once was a treasure here, it was taken by the people who abandoned this place—"

"Rykusa was not abandoned." Tavesi squatted down and held her hand above the ground, duck-walking in search of whatever she sought.

"Then the treasure was taken by whoever sacked this place." Crightin kept an eye on the hilltops. Any approaching enemies, human or beast, would stand out against the sky, which was now lighter than the darkness in the bowl.

"The treasure was not taken. It still remains."

"Here." Crightin snorted in disbelief.

"This was the town's cistern." Tavesi stood and looked at a patch of ground, then stepped back two paces. "They kept drinking water stored below ground."

"Likely mud's filled it in now." Crightin kicked at a clod and sent it skittering across the lumpy, wet land.

Shimmering power coiled around Tavesi's outstretched hand, sliding like twisting snakes from her fingertips to her elbow. Closing her fist, she pulled slowly, her hand and arm trembling with effort.

A chunk of muddy earth the size of a filled fishing trawler's net lifted from the ground. Waving, Tavesi deposited the large pile of mud several yards away. Drawing a breath, she reached back into the hole, this time revealing the stone surface beneath.

SEVERAL MINUTES LATER, WHILE THE SAILORS STOOD IN frozen silence, amazed at the power the young woman wielded, the top of the mud-streaked cistern stood cleared for all to see. Yard-wide blocks made up the buried structure, all of them well made and mortared in place.

Tavesi turned to Crightin. Despite the cool night, sweat covered the channeler's pallid face, and she leaned heavily on her staff.

"Are you all right?" he asked.

"I'm fine," she snapped. "Get into the cistern. Dawn is coming."

Crightin set his lantern to one side. "If you ask me, having the sun up would help."

"If you try to get inside there during daylight hours, that will be the last dawn you'll ever see."

Cursing beneath his breath, wishing he wasn't so needy—or

greedy, Crightin took a sledge from the equipment they'd brought. He set himself, feet spread apart, and swung the hammer, letting the weighted head do the work.

Steel struck stone, and sparks shot out. A hollow *BOOM* thundered below, letting him know a void lay beneath the stone. He lifted the hammer again and brought it down, wondering how long it would take to break through—and what awaited them on the other side.

– CHAPTER 8 –

LONG MINUTES LATER, CRIGHTIN BREATHED HARD AND watched as Mos'as swung the sledge. The impacts rang in his ears. Most of the mortar was broken loose around the stone block now, and it had sunk a half-inch or so. At least, that's what Crightin thought. Other times, he felt certain the block hadn't moved a whit.

He was on the brink of asking Tavesi why she didn't simply channel Essence to remove the block. She looked like she'd recovered well enough. He'd hesitated because he was sure the question would foster an argument, and he didn't want that. However, he was also tired of waiting to see if anything but mud waited below. And the morning was growing nearer.

Before he could say anything, though, Mos'as swung the sledge one last time, and the grumbling of rock sliding against rock filled the hollow. Crightin pushed himself to his feet, grabbed his lantern, and hurried to the black hole left in the cistern's roof.

He turned up the flame, no longer trying to conserve oil, and held it over the waiting darkness. Mos'as and the sailors struggled to peer into the depths around the opening.

The lantern's golden glow reflected off the dark water at the bottom and the squared-off alabaster columns that stretched at least twelve feet tall. He could only guess at how much of the columns were below the water.

Sticking his head farther into the opening, with Mos'as holding his belt firmly, Crightin held the lantern by his fingertips to get a better estimate of the subterranean room. The light didn't reach the ends of the vault, so the space was large. From what he could see, the room only contained water and the columns. More alabaster rock made up the walls he could see nearby. The trapped air smelled like it came from a grave.

Crightin pushed himself back up, aided by Mos'as. "The drop's not so bad," the first mate said, sitting back on his haunches.

"I'd like to know if we're to swim for it, though." Crightin dug a sounding line from his pack. The lead plummet attached to the thin rope weighed a half-pound, and was triangle-shaped so it would drop through the water cleanly. Moving with practiced ease, he cast it into the cistern and heard the weight splash into the water.

He listened for anything moving below. Even though they'd had to break in, that didn't mean there wasn't an underwater entrance that would allow alligators or squids or corpse-eating creepers access. Too many things on or near the Amethyst Sea lived only to kill.

Once the line bottomed out, Crightin pulled it back up and checked it. The rope was wet up to only two and a half feet.

"Like I said, that's not so bad," Mos'as commented.

"Means we're gonna get wet again," one of the sailors complained.

"Phrensral's beard," another sailor swore, "I haven't gotten dry from wadin' ashore with the boat."

Crightin looked up at the nearest man. "Get me a line into that vault."

"Aye, Captain." The sailor trotted toward the waiting packs.

Crightin turned his attention to Tavesi. "Do you want to tell us about any nastiness we're likely to bump up against in there?"

She smirked at him. "Are you afraid, Captain? I'll happily be the first to climb down."

With iron will, Crightin held back a stinging retort, but he knew the woman was still holding something back. He saw the secrets in her, and he thought he could glimpse fear there as well.

Think of the treasure.

– CHAPTER 9 –

AFTER THE SAILOR ANCHORED THE LINE AND TESTED THE knots, Crightin clambered down into the cistern while Mos'as lowered a lantern from another line, pushing back the cloistered shadows. He was determined that the channeler wouldn't be the first to descend, simply because he didn't trust her.

His feet rested on the submerged, scum-slick cistern floor, and he was again soaked almost to his waist, but this water was foul, and he hated the thought of it permeating his skin. Releasing the rope, he drew the Maladorian dagger from its sheath with a hiss. Lantern light glinted from the polished blade as he slowly turned to look around the room. The illumination didn't reach the cistern's far perimeter. He had no idea how large the chamber was.

"Come on down," he called up as he put his back to one of the columns.

Mos'as joined him first, descending the rope with the ease of a monkey. Standing in the water, he drew his knife and accepted a lantern delivered down another line. Reflections of both lights flickered against the rippling surface, and glowed against the ceiling.

Like Crightin, Mos'as put his back to one of the three-foot-wide stone columns, but faced the other way so they could watch both halves of the large chambers. They remained within sight of each other, moving slowly so they could watch the gently undulating water.

"No one's been here in a long time," Mos'as said.

"Aye." Crightin still kept his blade ready. "Makes me wonder how the channeler learned of this place."

"Forgotten secrets lie throughout Aetaltis, Captain. We've chased a few ourselves, and most were just twice-told lies."

Grudgingly, Crightin knew that was true. Every now and again, he'd given in to wanderlust, greed, or had to leave the main shipping lanes for a time, and had sailed in pursuit of an old tale or two. In some cases, they'd found those disremembered spots, but they had been empty, looted long ago, with only a handful of coppers and the occasional silver for their trouble. Treasure hunting was not for a ship's captain who had to work to keep his ship and crew intact. At least, chasing such things didn't happen on a regular basis.

"Channelers keep their own secrets," Mos'as added. "Likely this one found a mention of this place in an old book, or heard the tale from someone who'd heard it passed down for generations." He nodded at the brackish water. "Since everything has been undisturbed for so long, mayhap we'll get lucky this time, and actually find something worth our efforts."

Crightin hoped so. This trip had already cost them plenty.

With more agility than he would have expected, Tavesi clambered down next, not hesitating about dropping into the foul water. She took one of the lanterns and slid her staff out of the sling she'd rigged around her shoulders. She stood it in the water and whispered to it as more sailors descended into the chamber.

Weapons drawn, the crewmen waded through the stagnant water to take up a loose circle around their captain. Their splashes echoed off the walls, the noise indicating the chamber was even larger than Crightin had first thought. Six men stood guard at the cistern's opening to keep an escape route open.

Cautiously, Crightin ventured forward, keeping his balance set so he could still pull back in case he misstepped or encountered an aquatic predator, a likelihood that stayed constantly in his mind. He held his lantern to one side so it didn't shine into his eyes and rob him of his vision.

One of the sailors swore as he splashed face-forward into the water. He disappeared for a moment, then pushed himself back up just as quickly. "I tripped on something." He reached down into the water and brought up an object.

The hollow eyes of a skull held the darkness in cracked sockets as it stared back at them. Crightin's mouth went dry at the sight, and the hackles on the back of his neck stood up.

Three other sailors reached into the water and hauled up a leg bone, a broken ribcage, and another skull, this one child-sized and stove in at the crown.

"The town didn't do that," Tavesi said into the foreboding quiet that followed. "Their enemies poisoned the water supply with the townspeople's bodies."

"We're walking through a graveyard," a sailor said.

"This place be cursed," another sailor whispered, his frightened voice carrying over the water. "That witch is likely to git us all killed."

"Belay that, Ustine," Crightin ordered, wheeling on the man and making him retreat a step. "We have numbers, good steel, and a channeler. We're safe enough. I'm not turning tail just because we found a few moldering bones. A place like this, you're going to find bones. People die everywhere."

Silence fell over the group, but Crightin knew their fear hadn't gone away. It didn't leave him either, but he concentrated on the idea of the treasure somewhere ahead. The hostile and doubtful stares directed at his back felt like hammer blows as he turned back around and continued after the woman, already a good twenty feet farther on. Crightin lengthened his stride to catch up to her, their lantern flames painting garish, darting shadows on the pillars he passed.

Although her lantern and glowing staff barely pushed the surrounding darkness back, Tavesi didn't hesitate on her course. A short distance farther, however, the water steadily rose past her hips and nearly to her elbows. She only held the lantern higher and continued heading forward.

Crightin cursed beneath his breath, wondering if the water would grow too deep, or if his crewmen would abandon them first. He guessed it would be a close match.

Finally, as the water rose to the Tavesi's armpits, the light from her lantern reflected against the water and finally—thankfully—illuminated a wall ahead of them. Undaunted, she held the staff and lantern in one hand and began searching the pitted stone surface with the other.

"What are you looking for?" Crightin stood beside her, adding his light to hers.

"There's a passageway here."

Crightin snorted. "Did your god tell you that?"

"I wouldn't expect a sailor to make light of the Enaros, not with all the weather and monsters he faces on the ocean." Her words stung as sharply as fingernails in his flesh.

"I never disparage Phrensral." Crightin touched the old silver coin on his necklace and offered a silent prayer to the god of the seas. His grandfather, who swore it held a bit of magic and luck, had given it to him as a child.

"See to it you don't offer insult to my god either, Captain. Toletren can be just as vindictive as the Sea Father, and he's far wiser."

She stepped back from the wall. "As to your question, Toletren pulled me in this direction. I simply heeded his call, and it tells me there is a door here."

Looking up to where she was pointing, Crightin spotted a trail of thin gray smoke drifting through a small crack between a row of stones as big as his chest. "Likely that's just where the mortar has fallen away."

"It hasn't fallen away anywhere else." Tavesi passed her lantern along the wall to prove her claim. "Empty space lies beyond this wall."

"Probably just a void left over from the construction."

"Let's see if you're as skilled a builder as you are a sailor." Tavesi leaned her staff against the wall, hung the lantern from it, and drew a long knife from her boot. Sliding her knife into the crack, she ran it along the stone's surface. Withdrawing the blade, she looked at him. "There's no mortar."

"Ustine," Crightin called. "Hand me that pry bar."

"Aye, Cap'n."

With the iron tool in hand, Crightin sheathed his knife and attacked the wall. Mos'as stood at his side, ready to step in and defend his captain if necessary.

– CHAPTER 10 –

WHEN THE FIRST STONE WAS SUFFICIENTLY LOOSENED FROM the mortar, Crightin shoved the hooked end of the pry bar into the darkness, caught the edge of the stone, and pulled it forward. As the block sank at his feet, water rushed around him, sucking him toward the hole in the wall and telling him the water level in the void wasn't the same as that in the cistern.

The foul smell of rot filled his nostrils and made him sneeze. The persistent current pulled him forward, toward the space beyond the wall. He cursed, his voice echoing within the emptiness. Whatever lay on the other side was larger than he'd anticipated.

Steeling himself, he shoved a lantern through the opening and told himself nothing would attack his hand before he could pull it back.

Thirty feet away, gray and brown spiders as wide across as his outspread hand scurried and jumped across gossamer webbing several layers deep hanging from stalactites twenty feet overhead. Several of the arachnids scattered from the lantern light.

"Out of the way." With surprising strength, Tavesi grabbed his shoulder and hauled him back. "I need to see."

"Wait." Crightin stood his ground, but it wasn't easy with the buoyancy coming from the water that still pulled him toward the other chamber. The water there was two feet below the lip of the opening, but it rose steadily as the cistern's contents spilled into it. Silt must have filled up the other cracks in the old doorway. "You don't know what's in there."

"It is what I came here to find. Either go through or move aside so I may enter." At the end of her staff, the golden scroll head now glowed a faint emerald and pulsed slowly.

Resisting the urge to curse, Crightin instead turned his attention to the next stone down and began chipping at the mortar.

"Why don't you go in?" Tavesi asked. "There is enough room for you to get through."

"Aye," Crightin answered as he pulled at the stone, feeling it loosen. "I can get through the opening if I work at it, but if we come back this way in a hurry, I'd rather have an exit I can run through. You can go on, if you wish." He didn't think she would, not with all that unknown darkness waiting, but if she tried, he was prepared to block her.

Frowning, she looked at him with a trace of contempt. The stiff lines of her shoulders and back told Crightin she was tempted to go on, both to prove to him that she was brave enough, and because she was impatient. Then she forced her breath out and stepped back a pace.

Crightin dug into the old mortar, finding the going easier now that he knew the true shape of the stone. He chipped at it steadily, and the block came free. Together, he and Mos'as pulled it from its place.

Water from the cistern poured more quickly into the void, raising that level while lowering the one around Crightin just enough to notice. The empty space beyond wasn't as large as the cistern. The captain took back the lantern, still keeping the iron bar, and stepped through the opening.

On the other side of the wall, his footing gave way to a steep, uneven decline. Within three steps, Crightin was no longer walking, but floating, only occasionally touching the floor. Controlling the apprehension vibrating within him like a tuning fork, he swam on his side, holding the lantern out of the water.

"Mos'as, find out how deep this space is." Crightin didn't like thinking what might lay in waiting in the depths.

"Aye, Captain."

A moment later, the lead plummet splashed into the water behind Crightin as he swam to the craggy wall on the other side of the cave. Gradually, the bottom came up under him again and he set his feet on it.

"I mark the depth midway at seventeen feet," Mos'as said.

Plenty of room for a multitude of things to hide. The spiders had to feed on something, after all. They seemed intent enough on him when he got close enough, but he drove them back with the light and smashed a few that got too brave. None of them even came close to Tavesi, and he suspected her power had something to do with that.

Crightin clung to a jagged outcropping on the stone wall and gazed around the cavern. The arachnids jerked and skittered along the wall above him. Webbing clung to his gripping hand and he resisted the urge to pull away from the crawling things for fear of stepping into a hole or a drop-off.

Ripples pushed against Crightin from behind. He turned to see Tavesi swimming across to him. She held her staff in one hand, the top glowing under the dark water.

"What are you doing?" He held the lantern up to better see her face.

"This is the way." She stopped beside him and held onto the outcropping as well. She was shorter than him by just enough so her feet didn't touch the bottom.

"You know this because Toletren told you?" Crightin couldn't hide all of his mocking tone.

She grimaced, then pointedly ignored him. Lifting the staff from the water, she indicated the far end of the cavern to their left. "Because *that* told me."

Squinting, lifting his lantern, Crightin stared into the darkness. "I don't see anything."

Tavesi's staff head grew brighter for a moment. On the far wall, a design glowed molten orange and quickly took fuller shape, spreading into an intricate geometric pattern that made no sense to Crightin. As the design reached its full shape, a dark dot ignited in its middle—like a bad spot on a piece of fruit—and quickly spread to blot out the image.

Tavesi's staff dimmed slightly too, and she shivered. Crightin didn't think the reaction was just from the chilly water.

Crightin shook his head. "That's not a stone wall we can take apart."

"Maybe we don't have to." Tavesi swam toward the wall.

Cursing the woman's stubbornness, but still holding out hope for the treasure she'd spoken of, Crightin let go of the rock, brushing off a couple spiders, and swam after her. He held the lantern above the ripples left in the channeler's wake and watched her, thinking that if something that lived in the water went for her, he'd at least have warning.

Unless there were multiple things.

He reached the wall shortly after she did. The rasp of their breathing echoed against the rock barrier. Tavesi hung her lantern on a small outcropping and took a deep breath. Before Crightin could ask what she was doing, she vanished beneath the surface of the dark water.

– CHAPTER 11 –

"WHERE IS SHE?" MOS'AS CLUNG TO THE WALL AND PEERED down into the water.

Crightin shook his head. "As long as she's been under, drowned most likely."

"Or somethin' et her," Ustine volunteered. He shrugged when the captain glared at him.

Taking a deep breath, Crightin sank into the water and searched for the bottom. He took the lantern with him, watching water squirt through small fissures made to allow air into the device. He hoped the light would stay lit long enough to serve him. The yellow glow barely lifted the rocky dark gray wall out of the submerged shadows, but he could still see to a degree.

Ten feet down and three feet to his left, he spotted a dark shadow five feet across. He swam toward it and discovered a tunnel mouth. He stared hard ahead, seeking the glow of Tavesi's staff, but saw nothing—only blackness.

Then the lantern drowned and he lost the light. Grimly, he dropped the useless thing into the depths. He swam to the surface, spluttering and swearing as he caught his breath.

"What is it?" Mos'as asked.

"There's a tunnel below. The channeler must have known it was there, or she found it."

"Where does it go?"

"Could be somethin' lives in there," Ustine said sourly, "an' it et her for disturbin' it."

Uncertain looks flickered across the other men.

"Want to go first, Ustine?" Crightin demanded.

The gray-haired man shook his big head. "Not me, Cap'n. I'd as soon as return to the *Eel*."

"Well, that's not going to happen, so stay sharp, and if you keep trying to stir up cowardice among my crew, you'll go into that tunnel first."

Ustine dropped his gaze.

Crightin looked at Mos'as. "You still have the plummet and line?"

His first mate nodded.

Crightin took the lead weight and tied it to his sword belt. "Pay out the line. If it stops moving for longer than two breaths, pull me back."

"Aye, Captain."

Inhaling deeply, knowing there was no way the channeler could hold her breath longer than him, Crightin sank into the water again. He hoped he wasn't just swimming after her corpse. Or to her corpse. For a moment, the thought of her cold, dead arms wrapping around him rose in his mind. He forced it away.

There's treasure, he told himself. *There has to be treasure.*

Pressure swelled in his ears, and his heartbeat echoed inside his skull. Trying not to think of Ustine's grim prediction, Crightin found the tunnel by memory and feel, hooked his fingers around its cracked edges,, and hauled himself inside. He drew his Maladorian blade and clenched it in his teeth as he swam, kicking steadily.

A slight current eddied through the tunnel. He figured that meant the rising water pouring in from the cistern was flowing somewhere else, too. That gave him a little hope. Still, he didn't know for sure the channeler had even come this way.

Crightin's lungs grew tight from lack of air as he swam deeper into the tunnel, which had widened only a little. He tamped down his rising panic that he would drown, and told himself he would only swim a few more strokes before turning back, even though part of his mind insisted he'd gone too far in already.

Ahead, a green spark gleamed in the darkness. For a moment he thought he was imagining things, then it moved, swinging from side to side. Green streamers of light radiated through the water.

Emboldened, Crightin swam toward it. When he got to within a few yards of it, the green spark created an emerald oval above him, and he thought he saw an air pocket overhead. He swam through it, his head breaking the water's surface, and he automatically took a deep breath to replenish his starved lungs.

Tavesi stood a short distance away, bathed in the staff's illumination.

"What kept you?" she demanded, her voice echoing in the small chamber. "I thought I was going to have to swim back for you."

"I didn't even know you were going anywhere," Crightin argued after he'd removed his dagger from his mouth. "You're lucky I'm here at all. For all I knew, something had eaten you." He wouldn't voice that thought around Ustine.

He forced himself out of the water and up a small, narrow flight of steps to the landing where Tavesi stood. Water dripped from his clothing and the Maladorian blade in his fist.

Something was *wrong* here. That *wrongness* vibrated through his chest and down his limbs. He barely kept himself from leaping back into the water in full retreat.

Tavesi gestured to a pile of rocks she'd gathered. A shimmering force burst from her hand to strike them, making the stones glow bright red. The pile gave off enough heat to provide a welcome warmth, and enough light to burn a hole in the surrounding darkness and show two stone walls and the low ceiling.

Pale statues of coiled sea serpents nuzzled the hand of an imposing, bearded figure with a bold, challenging smile. Together, the figure and serpents rose from a cresting wave. He wore a kelp robe, beautifully rendered in the stone, and a crown of shells wound through the statue's mane of wild, flowing hair.

"*Phensral*," Crightin whispered, dropping to one knee and touching the silver coin at his breast automatically. The disc was warm against his fingers, in spite of the chill that clung to the rest of him.

"It's a statue," Tavesi said irritably.

"I know it is," Crightin replied just as irritably, "and do you know how many times Phensral has taken over statues in his likeness to walk among people?" He didn't know if that had ever really happened, but he was certain he'd heard that particular tale at least once, so it could have been the truth.

"This statue hasn't moved since I've been here."

"That doesn't mean the Sea Father isn't watching."

The channeler snorted. "Since Toletren sent me on this quest, I believe it's more likely that the Lord of Knowledge oversees us."

The line at Crightin's waist suddenly jerked, reminding him that the agreed-upon time had passed. Crightin yanked back three times in quick succession, letting Mos'as know he was well.

"Have you men that will follow you here?" The red glow from

the superheated stones played over Tavesi's face, and again Crightin thought he saw a hint of fear there.

"Some," he told her. "Not all of them swim strongly enough to get through that tunnel. I'll not sacrifice them needlessly."

"Get them and return. They—and you—will be needed."

"Needed for what? What is it your god has sent you to do?"

"I'll tell you upon your return."

For a moment, Crightin considered arguing. He had the upper hand for the first time since she'd rented the *Eel.* He enjoyed the feeling of being captain of his own ship again.

Before he could say a word, however, she waved him off. "Go!" she ordered. "Or you'll never reach that treasure you seek."

Crightin smiled. "Whatever the treasure is, it's obviously lain here for some time. Mayhap it can wait a while longer."

"Can it?" Tavesi scuffed a boot through the water. "Already this room has filled a few inches. Mayhap there's enough water in the cistern to fill this place, and you won't be able to hold your breath to get to the next cavern above the surrounding water levels."

Looking around, Crightin realized she was right. The chamber was filling, and he knew it wasn't a large space. The fact it was filling told him it was lower than the outer cavern and the cistern. He stifled a curse.

"When I get back—the *instant* I get back," Crightin told her, "I'll have the story of why we're here, and what we're to do."

She tapped her staff, and the emerald glow at the end grew stronger, warring against the red light from the stones. She turned to examine the chamber, no longer dealing with him.

After tying the sounding line to a jagged section of wall, Crightin dove back into the water, silently cursing her insufferable arrogance the whole way back.

– CHAPTER 12 –

"YOU HAVE GIVEN THOUGHT TO THE POSSIBILITY THAT THE chamber where you left the channeler will fill with water before we can claim the treasure and return?" Mos'as asked. "*If* there's even a treasure to be had."

"Of course I have." Along with his oaths against the channeler, that likelihood had also rattled around inside Crightin's head during his swim back to the outer cavern, and it still bothering him now.

It would have been smarter to forego the risk of going after the channeler, but he had bills to pay, repairs to make on the *Eel* that weren't going to make themselves, and a crew to feed. Gods above, after this debacle he probably also owed them a keg or two of rum, too.

"If the channeler dies without paying us the rest of the agreed-upon sum, we'll be hard-pressed at best." Crightin blinked water from his eyes and clasped Mos'as' shoulder. "This is the best course before us at this point." He smiled. "Besides, would you leave a woman to whatever waits on the other end of this swim?"

Mos'as scowled. "No, and you know I would not."

"So we've a plan, then?"

"Aye." Mos'as nodded reluctantly. "Leaving the six crew guarding the cistern entrance, and swapping out those among them who can swim, we've got only twelve that can make the underwater distance that lies ahead. And that is counting the two of us."

Crightin put on a confident smile. "Plenty to carry treasure back with them. Phensral willing, there will be an abundance of gold, and enough time to make a second or third trip for it."

TRAILING A HAND ALONG THE SOUNDING LINE, CRIGHTIN

swam more quickly through the tunnel, followed by Mos'as and the ten sailors who followed capably enough. This time he had breath to spare when he reached the chamber where he'd left Tavesi. The red stones had died down to a dim glow barely an arm's reach across.

Maladorian dagger in his fist, Crightin strode up from the water. Immediately he noticed the level was at least a couple inches higher than on his previous trip. Time was quickly running out.

Mos'as ordered the sailors to break the lanterns out of their waterproof oilskins. In short order, their light filled the cavern.

"Where is she?" Mos'as stepped forward, lantern held high, chasing the darkness back. He held his naked cutlass in his fist.

Wheeling around with his own lantern, Crightin quickly searched the cavern. The channeler was gone. Four solid rock walls framed the chamber. "She couldn't just disappear."

Yet, he was certain his sailors were thinking the woman could do exactly that.

Or that something disappeared her.

An uncomfortable itch wriggled down Crightin's spine. For a moment, he thought about ordering everyone back into the water and to the cistern. As bad off as the *Eel* was, it was better to be a live captain of a wounded ship than a dead captain with no ship at all.

"Look." Mos'as crouched and shone the lantern on the rocky floor near one of the walls.

Joining him, Crightin spotted dark red splashes on the stones. He knelt, dabbed a forefinger in one, and licked it. The salty taste was unmistakable.

He spat. "Blood. Still warm."

"It has to be hers," Mos'as said, "if no one else was in here."

"Someone else had to be in here." Crightin stood and glared at the wall. "There's no reason for her to do this to herself."

The rising water slowly pooled across the stone floor around

Phensral's statue, a silent threat that grew more deadly with each passing heartbeat. Crightin couldn't help but think the Sea Father was reclaiming his lost territory.

"Then someone took her." Mos'as held his lantern close to the wall's base and searched carefully.

"Can you imagine someone living down here in—" Crightin looked around, "—*this*?"

"No, but perhaps there's a way past this wall."

"If there is a way through, doubtless whatever treasure might have been down here is long gone. Anyone who passed this way before us would have made off with it." Crightin felt miserable at the prospect, and not at all guilty for wanting to simply return to his ship.

Except that he couldn't, of course. Not without knowing what had happened to the woman, and not simply because he had signed on to care for her well-being. He was an honorable man—to a degree—who just happened to be a smuggler.

"Curse me for a fool for actually caring about her." Shaking his head, Crightin knelt and searched the base of the wall as well.

"Not quite as much of the pirate and smuggler as you'd like to be, eh Captain?" Mos'as asked with a knowing grin.

Crightin glared up at his friend. "Don't be cheeky."

"Wouldn't think of it." Mos'as shrugged. "Okay, maybe a little. But I'm proud that you're not as cold-hearted as you profess to be."

"We'd all live longer, and with fatter purses, if I were." Crightin knocked on the wall with the haft of his Maladorian dagger, checking for hollow spaces beyond the rock.

A gaseous, yellow-green cloud spewed from an invisible crack in the wall. Crightin scrambled backwards, somehow keeping his feet under him. Hooking Mos'as by the elbow, he propelled him backward as well.

Curses burst from the throats of the sailors behind him,

underscored by the rasp of weapons pulled free of wet leather.

In the space of a tensely drawn breath, the small cloud formed into the head and shoulders of a bald, emaciated old man who looked just short of Aelos' gates. The Keeper of Mysteries guided spirits to their rest in Lensae's halls. This man surely had both feet firmly lodged there.

The old man's eyes looked like deep pits of coal. His cheekbones appeared on the verge of slicing through whatever passed for flesh in his current state. His lips were thin and dry-looking, like those of a fish left too long in the sun.

Crightin held the lantern between him and the spirit, for he was certain the cloud could be nothing else. "Back, foul thing, back before I burn what's left of you!" He didn't know if fire could burn ghosts, but he knew from personal experience that many dark things feared fire.

"*Heeellpppp*," it whispered in a voice that seemed robbed from the grave. "*Shhheee saaiiiddd youuuu woooullldd heeellpppp.*"

"No one said that," Crightin replied.

"Ttthhhee ccchhaaannnnnneeellleeerrr tttooollldd meee tttthhiiiissss."

In spite of himself, Crightin asked, "Where is she?"

An arm lifted from the gaseous thing's side, only then coming into view. The spirit pointed at a nearby place. "*Heeerrrreeee. Iiiiffff yyyoooouuuu wwwouullllddd hhhaaavvveee hhheeerr llliiivvvveee.*"

Mos'as stepped forward and shone his lantern on the wall. "There's a keyhole. Hold my light."

Uneasily, Crightin put his lantern on the ground, then took Mos'as' lantern and held it close to the nearly invisible keyhole.

Reaching into his boot, Mos'as drew out a leather kit that contained lock picks. Like all the men on the *Eel*, smuggling hadn't been the first criminal career the younger man had taken on.

Mos'as set to work. The picks raked and rasped quietly against metal, not stone. A true craftsman had fashioned the lock so that it blended into the rock.

"Who are you?" Crightin asked the spirit.

More of the thing had materialized now, still seeping from the crack in the wall. The old man was short, thin, and stooped with age. His knuckles looked like blades on the back of his hands.

"*I am Guirr, once a priest of Toletren in Warkin.*" The spirit's voice had grown stronger, but was still thin and faint.

"Warkin was the town up top? I thought that was Rykusa."

"*No.*" The spirit shook his head slowly. "*I know nothing of anything above. Warkin was a city before the Cataclysm shattered the world. The land around the town swallowed us.*"

The spirit's words chilled Crightin as he realized what the old man was saying, that he'd been down here since the Cataclysm. "You've been down here for *hundreds* of years?"

"*Yes. Since Arche strove to hold our city together against the onslaught that plunged Warkin into the earth beneath it. We heard the awful hum that filled the world, and we saw the blue glow that bled from the great Gate that once stood near us. Then... we fell into this place, this* grave, *where we have been ever since.*"

Water sluiced around Crightin's boots, growing steadily deeper. "You were trapped here?"

The spirit shook his head. "*No. We* died *here, and we have lain here for hundreds of years, unable to pass on to the Halls of Lensae. Arche has kept us here, fueling the spell that allows his family and him to live in this place. He embraced Endroren's shadow, and became a part of the Darkness. We are his prisoners.*"

"'To live?' You mean, Arche and his family live as flesh and blood after all this time?"

"*Yes. But that time has not been good to them. His family and his men have been driven mad by hundreds of years of living in the shattered palace Arche claimed with his power, or perhaps from the spell itself, and I am not certain that Arche himself does not harbor seeds of insanity."*

Crightin's mind spun as he tried to grasp everything the spirit told him.

Mos'as stood and stepped back. His fingers caught a hidden edge of the wall, and he slowly pulled the disguised door open to reveal another tunnel. Water began running freely into the room, but Crightin's attention was drawn to a patch of blood on the wall.

"Where is Tavesi?" Crightin asked.

"Arche has her. His shadowmen captured her, and took her to the palace."

A chill chased down Crightin's spine. *Shadowmen*. He'd heard of them, but hadn't ever encountered one. Yet. Creatures of the Darkness, silent as the grave, they existed as dim memories of their former selves, but evil drew them to killing and feasting on the flesh of sentient races. Nothing good ever remained of those who succumbed to Endroren's wiles.

"Good steel can kill them," Mos'as stated quietly. "I have seen shadowmen slain."

Crightin took comfort in that, but not much. "How many of those things does Arche have?"

"*Seventeen.*" The spirit stared at Crightin. "*Please. You must come. Arche drains essence from us, only to let it replenish so he can drain us again and again and again. Our spirits are worn, and soon I fear nothing will be left of us.*" The old man's chin trembled, and his anthracite eyes glinted wetly. "*My people are in agony. A few of our people were allowed to live, to breed and serve as livestock for the Shadowmen. We spirits deserve our rest, and our living descendants deserve their freedom. Toletren told me he would send champions to help us, but it has taken so very long.*"

"We're not champions, old man. Merely men."

"You seek your companion. If you do not find a way to defeat Arche, she will surely die."

Taking a fresh grip on his dagger, Crightin considered what lay ahead of them. There was no promise they'd fare any better than the channeler. He couldn't just go after the woman. That couldn't be the only reason for risking his life. His men would see that as a sign of weakness. He couldn't choose to risk their lives for hers—she who was not even one of them.

He looked directly at the spirit. "Is there treasure?"

"There is. All a man might wish, and more."

Crightin turned to his men, who stood against the far wall, listening to every word. Fear showed in their stances, but greed gleamed in their eyes.

"All right, you dogs!" Crightin roared. "You heard there's treasure! Let's go see what we can make off with!" He followed the lantern light down the narrow tunnel as the flowing water gurgled around his boots.

– CHAPTER 13 –

OUT OF YEARS OF HABIT INSTILLED BY A KEEN DESIRE TO live through any and all dangerous circumstances, Crightin counted steps as he went and noted how the tunnel slanted down. Due to the steeper incline, the water thinned to a stream as it gathered speed and rushed toward whatever lay at the other end.

If anyone guarded the end of the passageway, they surely had noticed the stream by now. Those people—or *things*—would be prepared, might even be on their way to intercept them in the dark, narrow tunnel.

Crightin held his naked cutlass beside him, the lantern light playing over the blade's keen edge. The spirit hovered at the captain's side, mostly formed now, though his legs weren't visible.

"Who is Arche?" Crightin asked.

"*Our captor,*" the spirit said. *"I thought that was clear."*

"He wasn't always your captor."

"*No...*" The spirit looked frightened. Crightin couldn't get over the incongruity of that: a dead man who could still fear...something. "*Before he became our captor, Arche was a priest of Elendra, the Muse.*"

"The patron of bards and protector of true love?" Crightin tried to make sense of why a follower of Elendra would do what the spirit claimed. He glanced at Mos'as, who only shrugged. "How could someone who served Elendra turn to Endroren?"

"A woman broke Arche's heart, and turned him bitter. He believes the goddess deserted him, would not grant him the love he desired, so he found another to worship."

"A jilted lover doesn't bury a town in the bowels of the earth."

"*When Arche served Elendra, he was strong in the ways of magic. After he turned to Endroren, he became stronger still. They say those who oblige the Lord of Darkness without reservation are the strongest of all those who serve the gods. Endroren is pure evil, and no other god is so clear in scope. Arche is very powerful.*"

"If Arche buried the place to protect it from the Cataclysm," Mos'as said, "why hasn't he released everyone? Why still hold them captive?"

"*He did not bury Warkin so it would live. He entombed us so that he might imprison his queen. He will not allow Dyneme to escape him again.*" The spirit's lips thinned into a distasteful frown. "*When Arche served Elendra, he was tasked by Lord Stetin to marry the lord's daughter to Captain Temos, the firstborn of General Bluz, who was the lord's strong right hand.*"

Shadows danced in the tunnel ahead, making Crightin almost fall into an attack stance, and he only just pulled himself up short.

"When the Cataclysm took place, when so much power was loosed upon the world, Arche claimed a portion of it as his own, and made a pact

with Endroren. As the world crumbled around us, Arche strode through the streets with shadowmen at his heels, killing whoever got in his way and feeding them to his dark creatures. He slew the general, the captain, and our lord in the palace where he lives now. And he claimed his bride as she wept over the bodies of those she'd lost."

"She still lives?" Mos'as asked quietly.

"Yes. If you would call that living. Dyneme is only a shell these days. She breathes and talks when Arche wishes for her to, but he refuses to let go of her, though it is obvious her mind has shattered under his abuses. He chooses not to see the empty vessel he holds."

The more Crightin heard, the more certain he was that they should find Tavesi, grab whatever gold they could, and head back for the *Eel.* The last thing he wanted to do was confront a priest of Endroren.

Ahead, around a corner the lanterns' glow barely brought out of the shadows, green light dawned. At first he thought the light was from Tavesi's staff, but it quickly grew too large, much stronger than he thought the channeler's power would allow, alerting him to the tunnel's mouth.

"Douse the lanterns," Crightin ordered, and lifted his own to blow out the flame.

The sailors did the same, grumbling nervously as the oppressive darkness fell around them.

Hearing the rasp of his own breathing, Crightin slowly crept forward. The spirit hovered at his side, a mere shimmer, barely visible in the darkness. He knew Mos'as walked beside and slightly behind him because they had worked together so much.

At the tunnel's mouth, Crightin stepped to one side and Mos'as took the other. Outside the passageway, a large, pale green star hung near the top of the huge cavern. Stalactites splintered the globe and its radiance like fangs, and Crightin couldn't help feeling they were stepping into the maw of a monstrous beast.

The green light also revealed a crooked, snakelike path where the water continued down the incline.

Under the artificial star sat a huge, ornate, domed palace that long ago had been a beautiful building, at least sixty feet tall and nearly ten times that distance across. Twenty-foot walls surrounded the palace and once had offered intimidating defense, but now they stood cracked and uneven. Gaps shot through the wall, some only inches wide, while others were large enough for wagons to rumble through two and three abreast.

A tattered cloth hung limply from tall ramparts. Along the broad walkway spanning the intact sections of the wall, a few shadows carrying swords and spears paced restively.

"Shadowmen," Mos'as said quietly, confirming what Crightin had already guessed. "Though I have never seen so many."

"So many?" Crightin echoed.

"Shadowmen like dwelling among people," Mos'as said, "but they do so only for nefarious purposes. They infiltrate groups and create chaos and mistrust among assemblies or towns, so that other *endrori* who serve Darkness might more easily kill those who stand against Endroren. Usually they work individually, or in a small group."

"*These serve Arche,*" the spirit said. "*He binds them together to protect him and control those who still live. Once they were men, greedy men who sought power as Arche did, and he took them as his own, remolding them in Darkness.*"

"Where is the channeler?" Crightin asked.

"*In the palace.*"

"Of course she is." Crightin stared at the dome atop the palace. In the weak green gleam, spotting the round black disk anointing the top of the dome proved difficult, but it was there. The sign was known in every port Crightin had sailed to as belonging to Endroren.

"It's not truly a palace any more, is it?" he asked.

"*No,*" the spirit replied. "*Arche has made the building into a temple for Endroren.*"

"So, we're not just invading the stronghold of an undead madman," Crightin said, "we're stealing into a temple dedicated to the Lord of Darkness."

"*Yes.*"

For a long, silent moment, Crightin stared at the scene before him and weighed the odds. He didn't care for them, and he knew his men cared for them even less.

Then a woman's scream split the stillness.

– CHAPTER 14 –

SINKING BACK INTO THE SHADOWS, CRIGHTIN CURSED AND gripped his cutlass more tightly, wishing he was back aboard the *Eel.*

"*That was not the channeler,*" the spirit said in hushed tones, again making Crightin wonder what could possibly exist that could scare someone already dead. "*That was Dyneme.*"

The scream repeated, and the shadows atop the ramparts shifted, turning back to the dome, as if attracted by the screech of hopeless grief.

"What is Arche doing to her?" Mos'as asked.

"*Mayhap nothing.*" The spirit folded his hands over his chest, his face furrowing in sorrow. "*On occasion, Dyneme remembers what it was like to be human and whole, and she also becomes aware of what she is now. She mourns her loss.*"

Another scream echoed throughout the cavern, followed by another and another that came from different throats.

"*Then others take up her cries,*" Guirr said. "*Both the imprisoned living and the trapped dead.*"

Several more cries rang out, the tortured chorus gradually dying away, leaving only silence once more.

"*She never remembers for long.*" Gleaming tears tracked down the spirit's face. "*Will you aid us, Captain Crightin?*"

Chilled by the horror that had echoed all around him, Crightin shook his head. "I am only a man, Guirr. My crew are but flesh and blood. You need more help than we can provide."

"*We do.*" Guirr nodded. "*That is why Toletren sent the channeler to us. She can triumph over Arche, but she needs your help to survive long enough to fight that battle. Toletren saw fit to send you and your crew as well.*"

Before Crightin could say no, which he fully intended to do, a startled oath burst from the throat of one of his crewmen. Crightin turned, intending to knock the man's head for making the noise, and saw yellow eyes gleaming in the black passageway behind the sailors. A quick look assured him there were a dozen or more pairs beyond the first that he glimpsed.

"H-how did they get *behind* us?" one of the crew stammered as the sailors shrank back from the orcs choking the tunnel.

Crightin suspected the orcs had watched the expedition debark from the *Eel* and had followed, waiting for their chance to attack. He also suspected that the six crewmen guarding the cistern opening no longer lived. Or perhaps, if they'd had warning enough, they'd scattered to the woods.

In the end, it didn't matter. The orcs blocked their return through the passageway, and there was no way of knowing how many stood between them and the *Eel*, or even if Elmgar still held the ship. Or if it still lay anchored off the coast.

Going back was not an option. Crightin cursed himself for a fool, then committed to a skeletal plan for survival.

"This way!" he roared, striking the stone wall with the flat of his cutlass. "This way if you want to live, you dogs!"

Responding instinctively to the command in his voice, trained by dozens of battles on the Amethyst Sea and even more throughout bars in as many port cities, the sailors hurried past him.

Crightin grabbed Quatas, the most senior among them, a man he knew could follow orders—especially if his life depended on it.

"Quatas!" Crightin yelled so the man could hear him over the curses and fearful cries of the other sailors. The orcs also snarled and growled, screaming death threats both in their harsh native tongue and in the common language. All in all, the angry, panicked babble of voices all around him was nearly deafening.

"Cap'n?" Slender and wiry, Quatas tried to slip out of Crightin's grip, but couldn't manage the feat. His shock of red hair spilled like dark blood cross his powerful shoulders.

"Mos'as and I will slow the orcs as long as we can. Follow the spirit. Go where he tells you and do what he says. If you don't, may Phensral take your eyes for pearls, or I'll kill you myself when I find you—and I *will* find you."

"Aye, Cap'n." Quatas stumbled away, then bellowed for the crew to follow him as he trailed after Guirr, who floated quickly down the incline. The mob sprinted after the mate and the spirit.

Thinking the killing was going to be easy, the orcs broke into a run, screaming and raising their axes and swords in gleeful anticipation.

Glancing at Mos'as, knowing they'd fought together in enough desperate situations that each could place his life into the hands of the other, Crightin set himself. He knocked the lead orc's ax blow aside with the flat of his cutlass, then rammed his shoulder into the creature's broad chest and face with enough force to shatter its jaw, snapping off one of the two jutting lower tusks.

With a surge of strength, Crightin hurled his opponent back among its fellows, knocking a handful of them down in a flailing tumble on the ground. He swung his cutlass, the keen blade reflecting the pale green of the artificial star, and splintering the light as it clove through another orc's skull.

Yanking his blade free, Crightin staggered as a new opponent rushed at him from the side. This orc's knotty fist wielded a dagger made of a long, curved tooth tied to a wooden handle. It tried to grab Crightin around the throat with its muscular arm and swing the makeshift blade at the same time. The captain blocked the blow with a forearm, then spun and cracked his other elbow into the orc's face hard enough to shatter bone and turn his bulbous nose into a shapeless, wet smear on his face.

Mewling, the injured orc fell away, right in the path of the next wave. They showed no mercy as they lunged forward, stomped over it, breaking its feebly flailing limbs and stepping on its bleating head.

"Mos'as! Look out!" Giving ground, Crightin plucked a ring from his vest and slid free a small weapon consisting of three iron balls twice the size of his thumbs, all held together by thin, razor-sharp wires.

Mos'as stepped back, dragging an orc with him while pulling his cutlass free of another's hacked ribcage.

Crightin swung the *swokalack* over his head, the balls spinning out along each wire strand, swinging farther and farther out. Originally designed by people who had journeyed into Aetaltis from one of the Gate-worlds, Crightin had persuaded a dwarven artisan he knew to build more of the weapons for him. They were costly, but worth their weight in gold during situations against multiple foes.

As the *swokalack* spun, the wires continued feeding from the weight of the balls, running out to six feet. The wires cut the air in a hissing scream. When he had the wires to their full length and the speed up, Crightin let fly at the orcs as they raced at him.

The *swokalack* sailed through the air and wrapped around the cluster of lead orcs, catching arms, legs, and torsos within its lethal embrace. Immediately, the weighted ends whipped around appendages wherever they found purchase. As the encumbered orcs pulled against each other to be free or to maintain balance, they yanked the razor wire deep into their own flesh, as well as that of their fellows.

In the space of a breath, a half-dozen of the creatures came to a dead stop, some tripping and falling, all bleeding copiously from long cuts that ran down to the bone. Yowling in pain and terror, the stricken orcs sawed at the wires, but they were made of good steel, and held against knives, teeth, and swords. The knot of wounded orcs held—for a moment—against the others raging behind them.

But they wouldn't hold for long. Already the line staggered as the ones behind shoved and punched at those in front, triggering shrill screams of protest.

Crightin strode toward Mos'as, who was holding off three orcs with his notched cutlass and his Maladorian dagger, blocking, stabbing, and slashing in gleaming arcs of steel. Stepping behind one of the orcs, Crightin stomped the side of the creature's leg, shattering the knee with an explosive crack of bone and toppling it with a shriek. He split a second orc's skull with his cutlass as Mos'as blocked his third attacker's spear thrust with his cutlass and shoved the fighting dagger into the orc's throat.

"Break away!" Crightin said, only then noticing a half-dozen slices along his arms. Any deeper and they would have disabled him. Pain also wracked his right side, where he'd taken a glancing blow from an orc cudgel. The skin was bruised and tender, but still whole.

Mos'as was likewise bloodied on his arms and his face. Crimson all but obscured his left eye before he wiped it clear with the back of his hand.

Turning from the dead and dying orcs, Crightin looked down the incline to where the sailors had reached the halfway point to the cracked palace walls.

Together, he and Mos'as ran for their lives. Spears clattered around them as the orcs launched their missiles. The atlans' longer strides gave them a moment's respite, but the rest of the orcs charged after them in, bloodthirsty, howling pursuit.

There was only one place to run to—the corrupted palace ahead, and within its walls a madman lay waiting.

– CHAPTER 15 –

THE LEAD CRIGHTIN AND MOS'AS HAD GIVEN THE SAILORS allowed them to reach the palace walls without incident, but the shadowmen now poured down from the ramparts, all moving in eerie silence.

Blood pounding in his head, slightly winded from the run at full speed to overtake the sailors, certain now that at least a couple of ribs were cracked, Crightin joined his crew at the palace wall near a gap wide enough to allow a person entrance. Breathing deeply, steadying himself, he eased through the eight-foot thick barrier, the jagged edges of the crack scraping his leather armor.

Two shadowmen sprinted easily toward him across the scattered rubble inside the wall. Both looked vaguely manlike—atlans once upon a time, by the look of them—with a bruised grey pallor, dark, sunken eyes, and yellow teeth bared in expectant hunger. They carried swords and shields and wore mail armor, and though the armor should have been ringing with every step, it was as silent as a still pond.

Crightin's hackles stood at fearful attention. Taking a fresh grip on his cutlass, he turned to Mos'as, who stood firm at his side. "You're certain these things can be killed?"

"I've killed them myself, Captain," Mos'as answered. "It was a hard thing to do, because they can take a lot of injury, but it can be done."

Stepping out from the gap, Crightin waited under the pale glow of the green star, cutlass in one hand, Maladorian dagger in the other. "Come on then, you vile things! Come on and die!"

The shadowmen split, the lead one attacking Crightin, while the other went for Mos'as.

Though the shadowman's sword looked insubstantial as he swung it, with wisps of darkness peeling off it as though ripped away by the swing, the weapon smote Crightin's cutlass like a blacksmith's hammer. The smuggler captain nearly dropped his main weapon, his hand rendered partially numb from the impact. Incredibly, the blow was also as silent as a chaste first kiss between lovers.

Surprised by the silence and the power of the strike, Crightin staggered back and resettled his grip, ignoring the fiery pain in his bruised side.

"*You've come a long way to die, atlan,*" the shadowman promised. The words were quiet and sibilant, and they seemed to leave a greasy film in the air. "*I will enjoy sucking the marrow from your bones.*"

Several clever retorts ran through Crightin's mind, but he gave voice to none of them. He couldn't speak in the face of the thing before him and be certain his fear wouldn't echo in his words. Before he could launch an attack, the shadowman strode toward him and swung his blade again.

This time Crightin parried the blade with the dagger through sheer instinctive reflex, turning the black sword aside, and followed with a blow to his opponent's left shoulder that grated pain through his injured side. The shadowman took the cutlass on his shield and laughed before beginning a blurred flurry of several blows that drove Crightin back and back again.

Whoever the shadowman had been in life, he'd had a swordsman's skills, and they were better now because of his magical nature. Crightin sustained three stinging cuts, each of them the result of only just saving his life, and all weeping blood under his armor. The one at his neck throbbed in time to his heartbeat, burning as though covered in fire. For a moment the notion of poison crossed his mind, then he dismissed it. It was too late to take back the wound. His breath roared as he struggled to keep up with his opponent's attacks, the air burning his throat as sweat flicked into his eyes.

After a fierce exchange, Crightin double-feinted, catching the shadowman off guard for less than a second. He managed to sink his dagger to the hilt under the creature's chainmail at the bottom of it's stomach. His opponent stepped back with a hiss of pain as yellow ichor flowed from the wound, but seemed none the worse as he attacked again, driving Crightin back another step, to within arm's reach of the wall.

He was so focused on the battle that Crightin saw no one else around him. It wasn't until a spear point burst through the shadowman's chest and armor that he discovered someone else had taken a hand in the combat.

In disbelief, the shadowman looked down at the spear skewering his chest, and the yellow gore sluicing down his chain mail. The baleful dark eyes dimmed and he slumped, falling at Crightin's feet. Black, thready wisps danced up from the corpse, and Crightin wondered if the thing would just dissolve away right in front of him.

He yanked his attention back up to the sailor holding the spear. Quatas eyed the unholy corpse, looking both triumphant and fearful, as if thinking the shadowman might simply rise again.

"Well done, Quatas," Crightin gasped, shifting to attempt to ease his battered ribs.

"Aye, Cap'n. Wasn't gonna let you die alone, if it come to that." The sailor drew himself up, but kept a respectful distance from the corpse.

A short distance away, Mos'as slashed the second shadowman's throat as the creature writhed on the ground, impaled by two spears wielded by a pair of sailors.

At their feet, Taihin, one of the younger crewmembers, lay with his neck severed near in twain. His dead eyes gazed sightlessly up at the green star. Irkal, his seamed face gray as ash, sat on some rubble with his arm wrapped around his guts. Blood seeped from below his wound.

"Can you walk?" Crightin asked the wounded sailor, hating to ask because he doubted the man would survive for long, but staying here wasn't an option.

Irkal nodded, his long hair hanging in his face. "Aye, Cap'n, if I've someone to lean on an' we don't go too fast."

"I've got him, Cap'n," Emold volunteered. As Crightin remembered, the two were cousins, or related by blood in some other way.

"See that you keep up. We've got orcs behind us, and more shadowmen and a crazed priest ahead. They'll show no mercy." Flicking yellow ichor from his cutlass, Crightin headed toward the palace.

The pursuing orcs were clustered on the other side of the gap, howling in impotent fury as they beat against an invisible barrier.

"*Arche banned the orcs from the palace grounds*," Guirr said as he hovered into place beside Crightin. "*He doesn't trust them among the human cattle he keeps.*"

That made sense; if the orcs stayed hungry along the coastline, they would put up a better defense out there. At least that cut down on the fronts he and his crew would have to fight on.

By Guirr's count, though, at least fifteen shadowmen and gods only knew what else yet remained ahead of them.

Around them, Dyneme wailed again, and dozens of other voices added to her tortured screams, the cacophony rising until it filled the cavern.

– CHAPTER 16 –

"DON'T FACE THE SHADOWMEN ONE-ON-ONE!" MOS'AS roared when they came upon a group of four on the broad stone steps leading up to the palace. He carried a spear now, which he'd taken from the rubble littering the grounds. "We still outnumber them! Use those numbers!"

The bones of many victims lay across those grounds as well, thrown away after the shadowmen had finished feasting on them. One of the creatures they faced held the bloody arm of some hapless atlan in one hand, like a snack it had brought to munch on after whatever threat to its master was settled.

Crightin squared off against the shadowman that lunged at him and attacked with a rapid combination of blows. Past experience told him he was more than a match for all but the best warriors, and even then it would be close to a draw, and only the warrior with luck would remain standing at the finish.

Yet the shadowman's strength and speed saved it again and again, until Hisop got behind it and brained the creature with a war hammer to the skull. Head smashed, yellow ichor leaking through broken bone, the shadowman fell and rolled down the steps.

Sucking in a breath, with new agony flaring from his ribs, Crightin took stock of his men. Irkal lay dead, his guts spilling out due to either physical effort or another injury—Crightin wasn't sure—and Emold lay beside him, his face a bloody ruin, and an ichor-drenched blade still clenched in his fist.

Quatas killed another shadowman with a spear twixt wind and water as it turned to chop at a sailor behind it. Mos'as hamstrung a third with a quick slash, and Shyar spiked it through the head with his *haladie*. Like Crightin's *swokalack*, the double-bladed knife had come through the Gates, and been handed down through Shyar's family for generations. The fourth shadowman fell to two more spear-wielding sailors even as Crightin headed toward it.

The wailing continued around them, and Crightin felt certain it was in part caused by the knowledge of the battle raging around the palace. Here and there, men, women, and children, fearing for their lives, darted among the tumble-down outer buildings, running like mindless forest creatures fleeing a fire. He couldn't imagine what it must be like to live as they had lived, only to eventually become food for the monsters keeping them prisoner.

"*Hurry!*" Guirr called from farther up the steps. "*Arche gathers his forces against the channeler!*"

Trying not to think that he was only rushing to his death, and that the thoughts of his men weren't wandering in that direction either, Crightin pressed an arm to his ribs as he ran up the broad stairway after the floating spirit.

The steps ended at the first floor, leading to a wide veranda holding the bases of a dozen statues, while the shattered statues of warriors and robed men and a few women lay nearby. Someone had deliberately destroyed the sculptures, and Crightin guessed they represented the dead lord, or maybe his ancestors.

Torches lit with pale topaz flames revealed the arched doorway ahead. Guirr sped through it and into the passageway beyond, with Crightin relying on the spirit to watch out for them as he followed, with what was left of his crew at his heels. At the same time, he kept a careful watch on the shadows. The spirit wasn't infallible, and didn't have as much to lose as a living man.

The tortured wailing echoed more loudly here, until it seemed Crightin would never again hear anything else. As the passageway branched out, turning into a maze of identical corridors, he pulled out one of the finger-length chalk sticks he carried in his kit for situations such as this. At every cross-junction or T-intersection, he marked an arrow on the wall where he turned, skipping across an intersection if they went straight.

In a few moments, they reached a public room, entering a veranda at the edge of a long flight of steps that led down into the center of the large chamber. Crightin brushed sweat-damp hair from his face and gasped for breath as he stared down at the scene before him.

Six shadowmen, all nearly twice the size of great apes he'd seen in the Zhamayen Jungle, surrounded Tavesi, striking at the channeler again and again. Gripping her staff overhead, its scroll piece glowing bright green, the channeler stood unmoving within a shimmering globe that was barely visible except when struck. Blows from swords, axes, and fists caused showers of green sparks to arc out every time a black weapon or fist hit the magical barrier.

Around the shimmering globe, three shadowmen lay, threads of darkness pulling away from their corpses. Crightin grinned mirthlessly, knowing the channeler had found a way to kill them, too.

However, his good cheer deserted him when he realized the cumulative damage from the woman's attackers was steadily shrinking the protective globe. Even now, it wavered, bending and giving way under the offensive force.

In front of the tall lord's seat, shaped as a falcon with its wings spread, their feathers formed of jade spears, stood a tall, handsome man who Crightin took to be Arche. He wore black silk robes and held an obsidian staff in his right hand. His handsomeness was surprising. He looked like a waif in tapestries of the goddess Alantra, the Great Mother.

At Arche's feet, a beautiful young woman crouched, her hands bound in black iron chains. Her dark hair falling around her olive-complexioned face as she wailed in sorrow and loss.

Arche drew his staff back and swept it forward, screaming something Crightin couldn't hear over the incessant keening. A roiling mass of sable flames exploded from the end of the staff and sped toward Tavesi. When the flames struck the globe, the shimmering barrier rocked back and disappeared for a moment before flickering back into existence, just in time to absorb a new flurry of blows from the shadowmen around it. Amid the siege, Crightin glimpsed Tavisi's face set in determination, her teeth gritted as she withstood an overwhelming assault that would have killed any one else by now.

"*Captain Crightin!*" Guirr shouted. "*You must strike now!*"

Steeling himself against the throbbing pain in his ribs, Crightin glanced at Mos'as and saw the younger man bloodied but ready. The captain turned to his surviving men, hoping they had enough fight left in them to carry the day.

"C'mon, you war hounds! Loot and fame are here for the taking for any heart brave enough to seize them!"

Cutlass brandished overhead, roaring like one of those great apes of the jungle, Crightin led the way as he plunged down the steps.

– CHAPTER 17 –

CRIGHTIN HOPED THE SAILORS WERE FOLLOWING HIM, BUT

didn't turn to look because he was quickly sizing up the situation before him. Mos'as ran at his side, a coiled, focused dervish of destruction awaiting release. No one ever guessed how efficiently Crightin's second-in-command could kill until they had seen him in combat.

Before they reached the battle, Arche loosed another ball of black flame that sent Tavesi's globe spinning across the floor, with her twirling within it. She fell to her knees as the magical barrier flickered around her, like an ember trying to catch under a pile of tinder.

A shadowmen reached her, thrust an arm through, and grabbed her torso with a gigantic hand. Howling in bloodthirsty triumph, it yanked her up from the debris-strewn stone floor.

Pain shot across Tavesi's face, but her features revealed no fear. She brought a hand up and shoved it into the shadowman's face. Immediately, the creature flung her away and screamed in agony, its cries piercing the awful wailing that filled the palace for a moment.

When the shadowman reared back, Crightin spotted smoking burns covering its features, like someone had poured acid on it. Crumpling to his knees, shadowman clutched his face in his hands and strove to regain control of himself.

The five other shadowmen seized the opportunity to close in on their prey.

"You are weak, channeler!" Arche yelled. "Toletren fears Endroren! As all living things do, and the gods must!" He thrust his staff forward again, and a smaller mass of black flames leaped from it.

Forcing herself back to her feet, Tavesi held her staff out before her. The black fireball smashed against it and shattered. The flames ricocheted into the wounded shadowman, and one other that had lunged at her. The four others were almost upon her, and Crightin had no doubt that the young channeler would soon fall under their blades.

He threw himself forward, slamming the Maladorian dagger into the closest shadowman's shoulder, and used it as leverage to pull himself up onto its back. The monster whirled to address this new threat, but even as it tried to stab him, Crightin slit its throat with his sword, sending yellow ichor fountaining over its chest.

As the dying thing fell, Crightin leaped forward again, landing in a crouch next to Tavesi. He rose, dripping weapons at the ready, to face her remaining assailants.

She swayed on her feet, eyes not quite focused and blood dripping from three parallel lacerations on her cheek. Her red face looked near- blistered, and her hair was singed on one side, and smelled like it had been burned. Evidently her defenses hadn't quite held off all of Arche's attacks.

"I thought you'd gone back to your ship," she said to Crightin with only a little rancor.

"I thought you knew better than to let yourself get captured," he replied. One of the shadowmen reached for the channeler and he blocked its attempt, drawing blood with four different cuts from his blades.

"Shadowmen are hard to see in the dark." Tavesi parried a sword with her staff, shoving the creature back hard. As she did, Mos'as' head appeared over the thing's shoulder. Pulling himself higher on its broad back, he shoved his dagger into the shadowman's ear to the hilt. It slumped and fell, and Mos'as rolled free to stand on Tavesi's other side. Together, the two swordsmen held back the remaining shadowmen as Tavesi lifted her staff again.

Another black fireball streaked at them. Before Crightin could fight his way clear of the shadowman he was battling, the channeler hurled a green fireball that met the other magical projectile several feet in front of them.

A blinding flash erupted when the two forces collided, throwing heat and flames in all directions. The explosion set one of the shadowmen on fire and bowled over two sailors that tried to take cover. Smoke rose from the three smoldering bodies. Crightin wasn't sure who among his men had gone down, but Mos'as was still with him, and they still faced two healthy opponents along with the wounded one.

Around them, the wailing continued, now superseded with a grinding, cracking roar that shook the palace. As Crightin prepared to attack the shadowman in front of him, a long, jagged crack opened in the floor, splitting like chain lightning into smaller fissures across the parquet. Sections of the shattered dome rained down to smash into the floor. The debris sent up massive dust clouds that choked Crightin enough to throw an arm up over his mouth and nose to breathe. His eyes stung and watered, trying to keep the grit out. His ribs burned has he labored to draw in air.

He whirled to the channeler. "Is this your doing?"

"No." Worry tightened her eyes, and she had thrown an arm over her mouth and nose as well. She coughed, tears running down her dusty cheeks.

"*It's Dyneme,*" Guirr said.

Crightin had forgotten about the spirit, but Guirr floated only a few paces from him. "Dyneme?"

"*She has lived as Arche's* thing *for so long, shaped by his dark power for so many generations, that she has absorbed some of it.*" Guirr stared up at the fissures now spreading across the remains of the dome. "*She has chosen to strike now, in this time of his distraction and weakness, to destroy this place.*"

"No!" Tavesi shouted. "Not before the essence of those bound to Arche can be freed! She must be stopped!"

"*There's no stopping her,*" Guirr said. "*Her mind is shattered. There is no reasoning with her now.*"

In front of the lord's high seat, Arche staggered as the ground shook harder, staring around fearfully as everything he'd built and held in his iron grasp for so long now began to come apart on him.

Even amid all the destruction, Crightin remembered the treasure he'd been promised, and didn't feel guilty about that after everything he and his crew had been through, the lives lost, and the repairs the *Eel* required. They needed something from this. No, they *deserved* it. They had *earned* it.

"The treasure!" Crightin faced the spirit, ignoring the fresh pain shooting through his side. "You promised us treasure! Where is it?"

"Are you mad? Is treasure all you can think about at a time like this?" Tavesi shouted. "There are souls to be rescued and redeemed! I am bound by Toletren, and through him, to Aelos to rescue the imprisoned essences here!"

Crightin ignored her. She had her beliefs and goals, he had his. The dead were dead, and as long as he lived, he needed his ship and crew. The channeler would never understand that. He stared at the spirit. "Tell me where I can find the treasure."

The palace shook again, more of it breaking loose and thudding onto the floor, only to slide into the widening cracks that opened deep into the earth.

"*The treasure room lies behind the lord's seat,*" Guirr said.

Crightin stared at the falcon-winged seat, and Arche standing before it. He smiled at Tavesi. "It seems that for once your desires and mine match."

"Not in this."

He pointed with his cutlass. "We both have the same foe standing in our way."

The cavern shook once more, and this time water welled up from the cracks in the floor, the roiling brine rising above the toes of Crightin's boots.

He cursed. "And we're sinking!"

– CHAPTER 18 –

THE REFLEXIVE ASSESSMENT WAS WRONG, THOUGH, AND Crightin knew it the moment he'd said it. By its very nature, a cave couldn't be sunk. It could only be filled with water, and from the cold temperature and the salty stink of what poured in around him, the fissures had let in the sea.

He looked at Tavesi and Mos'as. "Are you ready?"

Mos'as nodded.

Tavesi sprinted past him, neatly avoiding a shadowman's hand as she splashed through the swirling water.

Swearing, Crightin threw himself after her, vaulting onto the back of the shadowman as it turned to grab her. Pain burned through his ribs, but he pushed it away. Plunging his Maladorian dagger into the shadowman's eye before it could defend itself, he leaped down and raced after the woman. Mos'as pounded after him, both men calling to their surviving crew.

Within only a few steps, Crightin dropped into a fissure and sank over his head before realizing that the channeler was somehow running *on top* of the water, easily outdistancing him.

Waves coursed across the surface of the small lake forming in the public room, gathering force as they grew, almost strong enough to knock Crightin down as he ran. When he fell into the gaping holes and submerged, he kept his wits about him and quickly shot out of the water and found solid footing again. The light of the topaz torches became a haze across the rising seawater.

Somehow, the steps at the bottom of the tall seat remained intact while everything around them shattered and fell. Dyneme still sat there, wailing. Other humans poured out of rooms arrayed around the lord's seat and tried to join her, swarming past Arche. The priest blasted them with his dark powers, then lashed at them with his staff, killing one after another mercilessly.

Tavesi paused long enough to set herself and hold her staff out again. When she pushed forward, a shimmering bolt shot out and knocked Arche off his feet. He sailed back and slammed into the high seat, but immediately rose to his feet and threw another fireball at her.

Tavesi tried to block the magical assault, but this time the flames only separated and curled around her. She dropped into the water and disappeared.

Steeling himself, Crightin reached the steps, followed an instant later by Mos'as. Soaking wet, pained by several wounds, they pushed through the crazed survivors of the entombed city. Neither one went gently, thumping heads and breaking bones as they struggled to reach Arche.

Grinning madly as more of the cavern tumbled down around him, the Endroren priest turned to meet them. He raised a hand, and an incredible force knocked Crightin off his feet. The impact felt like a sledgehammer against his ribs, the pain almost causing him to black out. Landing in the water a few yards away, the breath knocked from him, the captain strugged to regain his footing. Crouched, dripping seawater, trapped in agony, he reached to his armor, pulled his remaining *swokalack* free, and whirled it overhead as Mos'as took cover behind a shield he'd seized somewhere along the way.

Arche knocked Mos'as back with another bolt of pure arcane power. Before he could turn to face Crightin again, the captain let fly with the *swokalack.*

The razor-sharp strands followed the weighted balls and wrapped tightly around Arche. Screaming in pain and rage and madness, the priest struggled to free himself, making the strands cut deep into his flesh, and his blood to pour freely.

Crightin ran toward the man, drawing his dagger as Mos'as

regained his footing and charged as well.

Incredibly, Arche broke the razor strands with his bare hands, ignoring the damage they inflicted upon him. Three of his fingers and one thumb dangled from strips of flesh, the joints sliced through. But black shimmers began running across him, and his wounds started to heal.

"That's it," Arche gloated. "Come to me, so I can kill you up close!"

Knowing he would only be inviting death if he turned away, Crightin ran forward, hoping the priest was making empty threats. Arche gestured again, and Crightin slammed into an invisible wall. Dazed by the impact, his pummeled ribs feeling like jagged spears in his side, Crightin dropped to his knees in water that was now up to his armpits and steadily rising higher. He struggled to regain his befuddled senses splintered by pain he could no longer push away, managing—in spite of everything—to hold onto his weapons.

Arche strode to him, a maniacal look on that too-handsome face. "You will rue the day you decided to come here, fool!" He stretched forth a hand, and an invisible pressure suddenly gripped Crightin's head, squeezing so tightly he was sure his skull would burst like rotted fruit at any second.

Mos'as lunged forward, cutlass raised high, but Arache caught him with a gesture and froze him in place, dropping him to his knees as well.

Darkness flickered in Crightin's vision, dimming the topaz lights. The pain was immense, beginning to crush his skull, blocking everything else out. He couldn't breathe, and his heart pounded.

From the corner of his eye, he saw Tavesi rise from the water only a few yards away.

"Die, vile one!" the channeler roared. She thrust her staff forward, and a shimmering wave leaped from it to fly past the dark priest.

The grip on Crightin's head ebbed and his vision cleared a little as Arche turned to Tavesi and laughed. "I told you, Endroren is more powerful than any—"

But Tavesi was casting again—this time directly at Arche. With a look of surprise, he flew off the ground and backward. At the same time, the falcon seat jerked into motion, turning its wings under so the razor-sharp feather-spears jutted out.

Arche hit them and the points ripped through his flesh, piercing his chest and puncturing his heart. He struggled for a moment, shimmering as he used his power in an attempt to recover or strike back, but then the Darkness left his eyes, and his head lolled limply as blood dripped from his wounds.

Panting, taking shallow breaths to help lessen the pain in his side, Crightin stared at the carnage around him, barely believing they had survived. Tavesi staggered, and would have fallen had Mos'as not caught her and offered support.

Slowly, the wailing ceased as the water passed the top of Dyneme's head. Crightin stepped toward her, intending to save her from drowning.

"*No,*" Guirr said at Crightin's side. "*There's no saving her now.*" He waved a hand toward the other people who stood unmoving on the steps, slowly being engulfed by the water. "*There's no saving any of them. They were all lost long ago. This will be a mercy for them.*"

Remaining still, unable to watch those deaths, Crightin turned to the spirit. "The treasure."

Guirr pointed at the wall behind the falcon seat, where Arche's body still dangled. A fissure had split it wide enough for a man to walk through. Inside, the topaz torchlight glinted against gold and silver and precious stones.

The sight of it all took Crightin's breath away, again.

"*That* is what all of this has been about for you?" Tavesi accused, her face spotted with blood and blisters, short burned hair clinging to the side of her head.

"At first, it was the gold you promised," Crightin admitted, "but after I found out about this, I wanted my share of it." In spite of his pain, he grinned at her. "Don't tell me you won't carry out what you can take."

"I'll take what I can," Tavesi said. "Toletren's temples can always use donations. But *this* is my true treasure." She placed a hand on Crightin's shoulder.

His vision blurred, and when he blinked, he suddenly saw what looked like shimmering crystals floating up toward the cavern's ceiling. A calm feeling came over him, despite the cold seawater rising around him, and his restlessness to get the treasure and find a way out eased. "What...what are those?"

"Those are the essences of the people Arche imprisoned here for so long." Tavesi smiled. "They're free now, on their way to Numos and Aelos, so that she might guide them to the Golden Halls of Lensae."

Crightin stepped away from her, no longer able to ignore the rising death around them. "Unless we find a way out of here, we may well be joining them." It galled him; the treasure was right there, so close he could almost touch it, and him with no way to carry it away.

Or to survive the flood.

"I wouldn't think it like you to give up so quickly, Captain."

"Captain," Mos'as called from inside the treasure vault. "You'll want to see this."

Wading through the hip-deep water, Crightin ducked through the gap and into the vault. The room was eighty feet across, he didn't know how deep, and filled with piles of treasures.

Mos'as and the five surviving sailors filled their purses as well as packs and pouches they'd found along the way. Quatas and Shyar piled more loot on top of a shield.

Crightin grabbed a gold urn and filled it with gems and gold coins, wincing as he ignored the silver, knowing full well he couldn't take all of it. "We need to find a way out of here, Mos'as."

"We already have one, Captain." Mos'as pointed up.

Looking above him, Crightin spotted bright pink light painting the edges of a fissure at least three hundred feet up.

"That's the dawn," Mos'as said. "That opening runs clear through to the surface."

"That's also close to three hundred feet," Crightin snarled, "and it'd be a long climb even if we *weren't* so weighted down."

"We don't have to climb," Mos'as explained. "The water's rising. All we need to do is rise with it, let the incoming sea do the work. The town was below the current sea level, and I'm betting the surface is up there, too."

"How do you propose we rise with this treasure? If we try to carry it while swimming, we'll drown." Despite the situation, Crightin did see a slim ray of hope.

"You're the captain, Captain. That's your course to set." Mos'as scooped up another fistful of gold coins to top off the urn he held. "But you need to think of something quickly, or we're going to have to give up most of this."

The water level was already starting to fill the vault, rising over most of the treasure. Then the whole room shook, and rock tumbled from overhead. The fissure closed a little around them and the water level rose dramatically.

Casting his gaze around, Crightin peered through the lightening gloom as more of the dawn's light invaded the vault. The far wall now stood revealed a hundred and more feet away, honeycombed with niches. Guessing what those openings held, he swam to them, hoping that a woodlands town would work in timber, not stone, even for its most important family.

Reaching the wall, he peered within one of the niches and saw a sarcophagus nestled inside. He rapped the surface with his knuckles and heard the hollow thump of wood, not stone. Setting himself, he grabbed one end of the sarcophagus and heaved it out.

The sarcophagus plopped into the water, promptly sank, along with Crightin's dreams of escaping with his riches, then bobbed back to the surface a moment later. The buoyancy raised Crightin's hopes.

Restraining a shout of victory out of respect for the dead and because the wrath of gods had visited the entombed town far too much to risk such casual disregard, Crightin shouted for Mos'as and his men as he pushed off the sarcophagus' lid. He had a brief impression of a handsome woman carved on it, then it was gone, floating away on the rising water.

"*What* are you doing?" Tavesi demanded as she joined him.

"Salvaging what we can." Crightin scooped out the rags and bones that remained of the woman once interred there, dropping it all into the water.

"You can't do this."

"Trust me, channeler, the people inside these boxes are done with them, as done as those whose essences you freed from Arche." When he had the sarcophagus empty and floating high in the water, he pushed it to Mos'as, who filled it with treasure.

Under Crightin's direction, the work went quickly. By the time the water covered the treasure room completely, five sarcophagi floated toward the fissure, now glowing with early morning light.

The cavern quaked again and again, and falling rocks sent them all dodging aside, but gradually they guided the sarcophagi up on the rising water like small watercraft until they reached a valley. The water level gave them access to dry land before carving a new creek in the broken landscape.

Not trusting the vagaries of fate, which smacked too much of the gods' handiwork to suit him, Crightin ordered his men to pull the makeshift treasure chests to high ground. They all struggled to accomplish the task, but the mud helped, removing some of the friction.

As they pulled the last sarcophagus clear, the land quivered and rumbled, and the fissure leading down to the entombed city shut tight and uneven, like a poorly-stitched wound.

"All that gold down there," Quatas lamented.

Mos'as clapped the man on the shoulder. "Be glad we got this, and that your head is still on your shoulders, where it should be. This cost enough lives as it is."

Wondering where they were, all sense of direction lost during the night's exploration and battles and strangeness, Crightin climbed the rise, feeling all the bruises and hurts across his body growl at him. His ribs felt like a mass of searing coals had been embedded within them, and he shuddered when he thought about peeking at it under his shirt. With the sun to his back, he looked to the west-southwest, where he thought *The Gilded Eel* should sit at anchor. At first he couldn't see her through the thick trees, then he spotted her tall masts with sails furled as she rocked in the harbor.

His heart swelled with gladness.

Smiling, he turned to his crew. "The *Eel* awaits us in the bay, you dogs. Mos'as, send two men to tell Elmgar we need assistance. I'll stand everybody to the first round in the first port we make."

"Aye, Captain." Mos'as chose quickly, and Quatas and Shyar loped off to fetch help.

"Keep a sharp lookout," Crightin reminded the others. "Orcs still lurk about." He watched them for a time, and they made the distance to the coastline unimpeded. Then he turned to the channeler.

Tavesi sat cross-legged in prayer, gripping her staff in both hands. As Crightin watched, her wounds slowly healed. Feeling itchy himself, he gazed down at his cuts and scrapes and burns, noticing that they no longer plagued him. Slowly, they too healed, and the fiery pain in his ribs faded to a dull ache.

The channeler's lavender eyes opened and she looked up at him, perhaps not with favor, but with no intended malice.

"And what of you, channeler?" Crightin asked. "Will you let me stand you to a drink? After all this, you deserve one. Unless that goes against your beliefs."

"I'll allow it," she told him.

"In spite of the things I did against your orders?"

She hesitated for a moment before speaking. "Those trapped essences are now free, thanks to your efforts as much as my own. Toletren exists in all times, never trapped by a single moment, so I must believe that he knew how this voyage would turn out. His hand must have guided me when I chose you." She paused and smiled a little. "We yet live, which is surprising, and would not have happened were we not favored by our gods."

Although he wouldn"t tell the channeler, Crightin had already promised himself—and Phensral—that he would gladly tithe from his share of the treasure at the next temple dedicated to the Sea Father that he found. So he didn't disagree with her pronouncement.

"You buy the first round, Captain," Tavesi said, "and I'll gladly purchase the second."

ACKNOWLEDGEMENTS

Thank you to the true
CHAMPIONS OF AETALTIS!

A. C. Massung • Aaron & Peggy Allred • Aaron "Itchy" Tranes
Aaron Bevard • Aaron Markworth • Aaron Richter Winston
Adam S • AJ Hare • Alexander Murray-Watters • Alysia Murphy
Amanda and Jason Fuesting • Amanda Johnson • Amelia Smith
Andre Velez • Andreas Gustafsson • Andrew Beirne • Andrew Carrick
Andrew Crocker • Andrew J Clark IV • Andrew Kilburn
Andrew Piseck • Andrew Taylor • Andy Hoffman • Angie Batgirl
Angnomander • Ann Evelyn Morris • Ann McFall
Anna Victoria Garrison • Ansel Chin • Anthony R. Cardno
Arne Radtke • Ashli Tingle • Austin Barth • B.J. Haun • Bill Duwe
Blake Berryhill • Bo Sprotte Kofod • Bob Farnsworth • Bradley Russo
Brady Kleinhans • Brandon Carangi • Brandon X Luke
Brannigan Cheney • Brendan Ihmig • Brett Daniel
Brian E. Johnson • Brian Galloway • Brian Slater • Bryan R Stahl
Bryan Young • C. Corbin Talley • C.A. Suleiman
Callum Stoner • Cassidy Singleton • Catherine T.H. Ford
Cathi Falconwing • Chachi • Chad Bowden • Chad Kelble
Chap Godbey, CDR, USN • Charles S. Anchors

Charlotte Allen • Chris Bekofske • Chris Jameson
Chris Leon and Tater the Shih Tzu • Chris Matosky
Christina Crosby • Christopher Shaikh • Clint Okerstrom
D. Lynn Smith • D. Thomas Feddon • Dale Mazzola
Dale Strickland • Dan Brewer • Dan Neely
Daniel C. Calhoun • Darth Cibeous • Dave Hermann
David "bluesguy" Tannen • David A. Nolan • David Birt
Dean F. Sutherland • Demian • Diane Bekel
Donald J. Bingle • Doug Eckhoff • Douglas Northcote
Douglas Park • Douglas Reid • Dreamch2 • Dreaming Isis
D-Rock • Dwayne Hauser • Dylan Birtolo • E. Myers
Eddie Patton • Edea Baldwin • Elizabeth Chatsworth
Elizabeth Kite • Eric Allsop • Eric Brace • Eric Burtch
Eric Slaney • Erik Scott de Bie • Erik Yocum • Evan Ladouceur
Evaristo Ramos, Jr. • Faith Clendenen • Falk Flottrong
Felicia Fredlund • Fen & Mitch Eatough • Fr. Cory Sticha
Francis • Fred W Johnson • G Huguelet • Gabe Zuehlsdorf
Gary "archermoo" Denney • Gary Phillips • Gary Vandegrift
Gavran • Geoffrey S. Tillman Jr. • H Lynnea Johnson
Harold V. Campbell • Harrison Paul • Heather Parra
Heidi A. Wilde • Henri LEVANTAL • Henry Lopez • Hexeter
Howard J. Bampton • Ian A MacKinnon • J D Stockwell
J.A. Dalley • J.R. Murdock • Jackie Myers • Jacob Bentley
Jake Chipps • Jakub Narebski • James Jandebeur
James L. Wright Jr. • James Morphew • Jamo Hanlan
Janito Vaqueiro Ferreira Filho • Jarrod Fredericks • JartStar
Jason & Jennifer Demeter • Jason DeLong • Jason Gardiner
Jason Tryon • Jasyn Jones • Jenn Whitworth • Jeremy Kear
Jeremy Reppy • Jeremy Yoder • Jery Schober
Jessica "busdjur" Rickardsson • Jim & Joellen Foster
Jinnapat Treejareonwiwat • JKLM Eggleston

Joe Hollowell • Joe Maron • Joel Nagy • John Desmarais
John Grigni • John Hall • John Idlor • John Livingston
John Sturkie • John T. Overath • John Van Stry • Jon Nials
Jon Shelky • Jonathan Dinger • Joseph M. Canero
Joseph S. Fleischman • Josh T Lamber • Jouni Miettunen
Juan Peredo • Justin (Nameless) Burr • Justin Wong • JW
Karen Lytle Sumpter • Karl Gallagher • Katie R. • Keith Hall
Keith Thomson • Keith West • Kelli & John Kochan
Kelly M. Wood • Kelly Swails • Kenny Soward
Kenta Washington • Kevin Minor • Kevin Riegle
Kyle Mack and Laura Taylor • Kyleigh Thompson
Lance D. Gallop • Lance425 • Larry J Couch • Leah Webber
Lee DeBoer • Lennhoff Family • Leo Huang
Leshia-Aimée Doucet • Liz • LJ Heydorn
Lori & Maurice Forrester • Lou Anders • Luc Ricciardi
Luke Dore • Luke Taggart • Manoshi Quayes • Marc Margelli
Marc Nicol • Marc's good friend Uvoyshea
Margaret St. John • Marijn van Zanten • Mark "Moose" LaGuardia
Mark Cromwell • Mark Ping • Martin Blake • Matt Cowan
Matt Vartabedian • Matthew Eberle • Matthew Morris
Matthew Tanous • Max Pfeffer • Megan Redlawsk
Mel Grindol • Michael A. Atkinson • Michael Connell
Michael Fedrowitz • Michael Frost • Michael Horgan
Michael J. Maier • Michael Jarvis • Michael Leaich
Michael Shehan • Michael Skolnik • Michael Stim
Michael Workman • Mike Basinger • Mike Fry • Mike Hampton
Mike Staton • Missy Gunnels Katano • Molly Findley
Mysterious Reader X • Nataya Castillo • Nathan Seabolt
Neil Crampin • Nick Sharps • Nick Watkins • Nicola Moretto
Nihonjoe • Nimrod Daniel • Odin Shafer • Osye E. Pritchett III
Parker S. • Pat Cdr • Patrick M. Holland • Patrick Stahl

Paul Albrecht • Paul Partida • Paul Sheppard • Pearce and Sean Haley
Pepita Hogg-Sonnenberg • Pete Griffith • Peter Hansen
Peter Hutchinson • Peter Niblett • Peter O'Meara • Proof482
R. Daniel Paddock • R. L. "Rat" King • R.K. Modena
R.T. Bryson • Rachel Ransom • Rafael Braido
Ragnarok Publications • Randall Lemon • Randi Misterka
Revek • Rhiannon Rippke-Koch • Rich and Lissa Hailey
Rich Howard • Richard C. White • Richard Eyres • Richard Pulfer
Rick Underwood • RJ • Rob Karp • Robby Thrasher
Robert D. Matthews • Robert Early • Robert F Towell
Robert K Stewart • Robin Bayless • Roger Donald Martin
Roman • Roy Romasanta • Russell Ventimeglia • Ruth Ellison
Sam Novosad • Santiago Hoyos • Scott Fitzgerald Gray
Scott Iekel-Johnson • Scott Maynard • Sean Louvel • Sean Miller
Shane Harsch • Shawn T. King • Shiro • Sidney Ortiz • Simon Dick
Sir Jamie Howe • Spencer Luster • Stefan Gore • Stefan Leonhardt
Steffen Vulpius • Stephanie K Piegzik • Stephen Ballentine
Stephen Meyer • Stephen 'Skuldren' Howard • Steve Drew
Steve Grigson • Steve Hamaker • Steven Carroll • Steven M Irwin
Storium.com • SuperTekCop • Svend Andersen • T. E. Gregory
The Campbell-Kibler-Mortman Famliy • The Ogre Meg
The Stubby Shillelaghs • Thomas G Cook • Thomas S. Darragh
Tierce Vraie • Tijon Lené • Tim Dougherty • Timothy Cobb
Timothy Fitzgerald • Timothy H. Ott Sr. & Family
Timothy Murphy • Timothy Walker • Tomas Burgos-Caez
Tomas E. Diaz • Tommy Foster • Tommy Lewis • Tony A. Thompson
Tor André Wigmostad • Tracie Kneeland • Vincent E. Hoffman
W. H. Horner • W. Jake Bono • Walter Bryan • Walter F. Croft
Walter J. Hayes, Jr. • Warren P Nelson • Wayne Ligon • Will Donovan
William Kirtley • William Robertson • Wrinkles • Y. K. Lee
Yankton Robins • Yasemin Baran • Yurii "Saodhar" Furtat